THESE EVIL THINGS WE DO

A Novel & Four Novellas

Written and Directed by

Mick Garris

Encyclopocalypse Publications
www.encyclopocalypse.com

TABLE OF CONTENTS

INTRODUCTION
BY MICK GARRIS

The great author and screenwriter Richard Matheson once told me something as profound as it is obvious.

"Books are internal," he said. "Film is external."

It's why people so often say, "the book was so much better than the movie."

Well, they *are* different languages. Film is a composite art form, incorporating the arts and crafts of writing, acting, music, editing, cinematography, architecture and production design, costume design... just about any art you can imagine comes into play in filmmaking.

Making a movie is also a very communal art form. It takes a very large village, indeed, to shoot a film. It's hugely social; you're surrounded by maybe a hundred cast and crew members, and that's just during production. Multiply that number manifold if you want to count all that takes place in pre- and postproduction.

Writing books and screenplays, on the other hand, is a very solitary-- some would say onanistic- endeavor. You're on your own as you face the keyboard day after day, weaving something that's meant to be read by its audience, when the page itself is the final product. You're in your head, but you're also in the heads of the characters whom you've created. Their interior worlds—their thoughts, their dreams, their mental conundrums—are allowed to be on full display.

Books and movies are two very different disciplines. I love them both.

I didn't anticipate, at the age of twelve, when I seriously began writing short stories, that I would ever become a professional filmmaker. Before twelve, I imagined a future as a cartoonist and animator. My father had studied as an artist and was quite good at it. He created a couple of remarkable comic strips and books, but he never was able to crack that business. His work went unpublished, and all that art school and talent and passion ended up being for naught. He had a wife and four kids to feed, which didn't allow him such frivolous pursuits, so he ended up working nine-to-five, and never fulfilling his artistic dreams.

So, art was my first love, and I took to copying comic book caricatures of Woody Woodpecker, Fred Flintstone, Bugs and Daffy, and just knew that would be the path to my dreams.

But at that magic, *Stand By Me* age of twelve, my artistic passions switched gears. I got an 8mm movie camera for graduation from junior high and took a typing class in summer school. It's only recently that I realized these things both happened in the same year, and they had a simultaneous and equal effect. I began feverishly writing O. Henry-meets-Poe horror stories, devouring *Famous Monsters of Filmland*, and mainlining horror movies and television.

But I also picked up that movie camera and started learning the tricks that it could do: you could make people and things disappear at will, or move them around in ways that were impossible if you just posed them one frame at a time. I remember getting a "Sneaky Pete's Magic Kit" when I was maybe nine, but *this!* The movie camera was *true* magic! I didn't know what a director was., I had never heard of cinematography. But I was teaching myself ways to put pieces of film together to tell a story, and it thrilled me.

And it still does.

I love the process of writing, sitting in my office and just granting my fingers free rein to express themselves however they like. I love words and I love stories. It's not work for me; it's total pleasure... except, of course, for those times when you're writing for a studio or network, and they have very specific notes that they want addressed in very specific ways, and not always in the service of making the best movie possible.

Making movies is hard work with very long hours. That's not a complaint. You're surrounded by creative people all joining forces to make something special, and a film set is an incredibly exciting place to be. It's worth the hours and the struggles to push that boat up a mountain. There's a huge sense of accomplishment to completing a film or television show, especially if it connects with an audience and becomes something that the world around you embraces and loves. If you're very lucky, that'll happen to you.

I love the process. I love film. I love discovering new ways to tell stories. It's exciting and fulfilling.

And exhausting.

Most of the fiction I write takes place in the down times after I've finished shooting something. When you're writing—or making—a movie, you have to deal with budgetary issues, casting, egos (not only actors', but from every dog who wants to lift its leg and leave its yellow stain on the movie), stunts, locations, daylight hours, rules and regulations, and just the nature of a hundred people making your film.

The writing process has none of those concerns. The

characters are who you imagine them to be, not the actors available and affordable at the time you need them. You can imagine huge sets and locations, and don't need a single penny to build them. Your stories can be set in a character's mind or in the most remote and magical locations, and it won't cost a thing to go there.

I love writing and making movies, and I love writing fiction. They're very different media and require totally different approaches. I cherish the explosion of creativity that happens on a set filled with imaginative, gifted people. I equally adore the quiet opportunity of existential peace in creating work meant only for the page. Screenwriting is the creation of the blueprint from which dozens of people will work. Fiction is its own beast, and the words really matter. It can be a deep dive into the psyche. Or not. Your choice.

The stories you will find in this volume represent those times between setups, where I was writing just for the page, just for the words and stories and characters laid bare before you here. Not all the people within them are wonderful, and some of them are downright awful.

If these were movies, that would be a problem. No one would greenlight movies about awful people. But in a book... well, the book is an entirely different animal, as you're about to discover.

Awful People

Four Novellas

FREE

ONE

Revelation woke me like a punch in the face when I realized I was spending more time thinking about the end of my life than on how to live it.

It wasn't that I had a death wish; but my life was lived so numbly, in such somnambulism, that I needed a wakeup call. And that fateful phone rang when we took a Christmas trip to see Alfredo's folks in the Coyoacán neighborhood in Mexico City. They were still piqued that I had not learned their language, even though the twins were fluent and made fun of me because I couldn't tell when they were cursing in Spanish. There weren't fights or shouting matches or anything, but I could practically taste their resentment. Their boy had married a blue-eyed blonde of Scandinavian heritage, an atheist island in a sea of Catholicism, ever the outsider. I guess I should have learned Spanish, but it just seemed like so much work. I wish I'd done it when I was young, when my brain was more pliable.

So I found myself daydreaming on United flight 293 to Los Angeles, glad to be going home, but my mind miles and miles away. The twins were in zombie silence, thumbs fluttering wildly over their gaming tablets in the row in front of us, Alfredo snoring like a bull in the aisle seat, crumbs of tortilla chips and drying spots of chunky salsa nestled on the expanding girth of his waistline, one arm flung over my armrest, leaving no room for me. All I had was the window, which looked out into a wash of grey inertia. I could make out grids of pastures and farmlands below, through the pregnant clouds that held us in their womb.

But my thoughts were not of geography, or even of my family. As I gazed out over the faint curvature of the earth below, I thought about what it might be like for the plane to lose power and plummet into the ground, smashing into the patchwork grids below like the winning "X" in a game of tic-tac-toe.

It didn't scare me, nor did it cause me anguish or anxiety. Rather, the thought of exploding into the earth was kind of pleasant; restful, even. Everything would just stop; and that would be pretty nice, wouldn't it?

Like I said, it's not that I was eager to die or anything, but that morning, on that plane, in that sky, my mind turned, as it had so often recently, to resignation, to surrender, to the Grim Reaper. My life, free of highs and lows, could end for me, and it wouldn't really feel tragic. It would just end... and the thought of that didn't bother me in the slightest.

It's how I'd been thinking lately, without even realizing it. Like I was done. Like I had nothing to look forward to. And it was not just Flight 293; this had been going on for some time. I remember watching a movie where a killer was using a bolt gun on his victims, and I thought that looked like a nice, quick, clean and easy way to go. Bam! A perfectly round quarter-sized hole in the forehead and immediate peace. I wouldn't mind going that way: fast, unexpected, over. It seemed more creative than just a gun, although a bullet in the head had its own appeal, even if it would certainly create more of a mess, what with the exit wound and all.

I imagined death in many colors: but only my own, not others'. Obviously, I didn't want my husband and children to die with me in a fiery plane crash; hell, I didn't really want to die myself that way. But death didn't scare me. In fact, it didn't scare me nearly as much as the grey nonexistence of my life.

As I'd lay in bed, trying to read my way to sleep against the crashing tide of Alfredo's snoring, earplugs a constant aggravation-- though not as bad as hearing his bovine trumpeting-- I would set down the iPad for the night, close my eyes, and fall into the circling abyss of near sleep, wondering if it would all go to black that night forever. Not waking up wouldn't be something I wanted, but it wasn't something I dreaded, either.

Typing "the end" to my life just didn't intimidate me. I felt like the highs had been had, and had been ironed into flat submission. I found it difficult to be eager or joyful anymore; there was no *great*, there was no *spectacular*, there was no *thrill*, there was no *wonder*, and there was no *adventure*.

Could it be that, at the age of thirty-nine, the rest of my life, with luck, would be to remain at this even keel, to coast blindly toward greying hair, an expanding waistline, sagging breasts, middle age, and an empty nest with a big TV playing "Real Housewives" in every room? It certainly seemed that way, felt that way, rolled over me that way like an unforgiving planet.

How the hell did I get here? How did I lay down my paintbrushes, roll up the canvases, trundle the easels off to the attic, and trade my paints for Cheerios, Strawberry Rollups, and Adventure Time Walkie Talkies?

I know I'm a terrible mother. No, worse: I'm a terrible human being. I didn't want to have a child yet, let alone twins. Maybe ever. But it happened, and the Big Bang produced mirror- image infants who screamed incessantly.

"It's not your fault," the pediatrician told me. "If it's not a milk allergy or nuts or a twisted intestine or a blocked colon, then it might just be the luck of the draw. Some babies just cry more than others."

A lot of good that did me.

I loved them. They were beautiful; how could I not? Babies of any species are adorable, right? And these angels, with huge, round green eyes, a blend of Alfredo's chocolate brown and my own sky blue, were soulful, with long lashes that fluttered adorably. Their skin was warm, like milk with a touch of cocoa, smooth and precious. As babies they were helpless, and I was the help. Alfredo was peacock-proud of his progeny on the weekends when he took them to the park. They needed me, and I needed them, as well. I was there to provide for them. I did not even realize that everything I was began to evaporate so that I could tend to them.

Three o'clock in the morning is the most horrible time of day. And it's the time that the boys chose to exercise their newly discovered lungs, with shrieks that bored through my brain like a diamond drill. Their screams were inhuman, pitiful, horrendous, filled with pain and anger and fear. I would pick them up--both of them--and rock them as Alfredo snored like Ferdinand, oblivious, an immovable object not even aware of the irresistible force.

I bounced them, I sang to them, I kissed them. Sometimes it calmed them, but as often as not, it had no effect. On the lucky pre-dawn playtimes they would go to sleep after an hour of attention; more often they would vomit on my sensible cotton nightie and scream some more.

And now they are five years old, always sick and angry despite no diagnosable illness, puking and crying and fighting with one another. The only time they are quiet is when they grab my phone or my iPad and take it over to play stupid, repetitive, brain-numbing games with cartoon birds or zombies eating bloody flesh. They don't want to hear stories, they don't want to play in the park across the street, they don't even want to be in each other's presence. They just want their eyes glued to a capacitive screen with animated images nothing like the real life that surrounds them. They don't eat food unless it's of an exclamatory color not found in nature; they only want to drink juice or soda. And they certainly don't want anything to do with me.

I didn't realize all of this, of course, until that Socratic fist to the face that clobbered me on flight 293. It was a revelation, humiliating and flesh-creepingly guilt-inducing—but undeniably true—that, though I surely loved my children, I didn't really *like* them.

And I liked myself even less.

I told you I was a horrible mother. A horrible person.

But I was also dead.

Yes, blood pumped through my veins and I breathed in and out. I had conversations of unspeakable inanity with five-year-olds about hitting the umpteenth level of Fortnite that carried over to dinner time, when Alfredo would grunt into his chair, exhausted from whatever it was that he did for a living that involved going to an office in the morning and returning in the evening, enervated and depleted and in no mood to talk unless it was to try to convince me to fuck him.

In the beginning, before babies and belly fat and reality TV, when I wore touches of makeup, sneaked soft dabs of sexy scents behind my ears and under my breasts, when I couldn't wait to surprise my no-holds-barred, experimental, insatiable Latin lover with a questing mouth and a new silicone toy from the Love Shack—and his mouth watered like Pavlov's hound at the sound of my voice and my moans and sighs—we delighted in pleasing one another... over and over and over. And over.

I loved the taste of him as much as he did of me. When did that stop?

Oh, yeah. When I got pregnant. It was me, at first, with morning sickness he couldn't understand. He loved it when my breasts expanded, but when my belly swelled—and it swelled double duty, filled as it was with two six-pound hellions—his interest in the goddess Eros deflated with mine. Another god, or goddess, tossed aside as two lives seemed to grind to a halt.

Before: He wrote and I painted. We were both good—really good, if I may indulge a bit in the sin of pride—and we talked of his novels having covers I would paint, that we would together create a mix of media never done before to blaze new creative trails that others would copy but never equal. We stayed up all night with fresh ideas, brilliant speculations, and afterward explode together in undreamed-of couplings that far exceeded our own sexual fantasies-- which were themselves, by the way, pretty fucking imaginative. We were in a state of constant creative and physical arousal, often not discernible from one another. Our two bodies had become one, flesh meeting and devouring flesh in a heat and hunger that could not be sated. We lived on fire.

After: time and babies doused the inferno.

Surely it doesn't happen to everyone. Surely there are couples who maintain the ferocity of their passions beyond childbirth. Surely creative combustion continues for others. I've seen them, I've watched them kiss with tenderness, their eyes burning with the happy secret passions that will light like tinder when they get home and the kids are in bed. I know it's there, and I envy them.

But they are not us.

It's not that I feel unfulfilled; it's much more passive

than that. I'm tired. I don't laugh much. I don't want to do anything but sleep. And I'm getting fat. Alfredo abandoned his authorship, unable to kindle his own imagination after sitting at a keyboard in an office all day from nine to six—or so he tells me—and he never ever picks up the Martin guitar that sits warping by the fireplace we never light.

I'm too tired to be sad. I'm too leaden to try to fix it. I look at Alfredo watching the World Cup while the boys are fighting over whatever the hell it is that they're fighting over this time, and I realize that I'm dead.

And I don't want to be dead. But I am.

I'm also angry. That came as a surprise to me, too, but I find myself constantly on edge: moody, irritable. I honk the horn when the idiot in front of me doesn't move when the light turns green. I huff and grumble when the old woman in front of me in line at Trader Joe's counts out her pennies to pay for her vegetables. And if the kids won't eat the dinner I make for them, which is always, I yell at them and send them to their room for the night.

I'm a bitch. It's like I'm having my period 24/7, but without the blood. When did this happen?

People loved me, loved to spend time with me, to share in the glow that I carried everywhere with me. I was never at a loss for friends or lovers, had deep and delicate relationships on every level. Women shared their secrets with me, and men shared anything they could with me. I wasn't Class President popular, I was *Real World* popular, always being invited to lunches, dinners, movies, parties, social gatherings of every stripe.

That's not something I wanted to keep up forever, of course. Getting married changed some of that—and in a good way. I loved just being home and cuddling and watching a movie and feeling like a couple. It was cozy and sexy and romantic. And after an impromptu sexual tussle on the couch, I would grab my sketchpad and draw Alfredo at his very most vulnerable, naked and spent, with eyes that opened deep into the love he couldn't hide from my pencil. And then he'd write me a poem, an ode with such open emotion and romance that it bordered on the mawkish. But it warmed me from within. I loved feeling him come inside me; it was warm and strong and an injection of our romance, physicalizing what we felt in our hearts, sharing our bodies and making the two of us one.

But then, the two of us made two more.

There was a scare at first: Edgar's heart didn't seem to want to work when he first emerged from me. It beat in fits and starts, and though they tried not to let me know through my stupor that they were concerned for my baby's mortality, their faces couldn't hide their fear... which only amplified my own. This was my first birth, after all, and I went into it with a grand sense of fear and paranoia from the very beginning.

But Edgar pulled through—it was all up to that crucial first couple of hours—and he and Allan are mirror images in all ways physical. Predictably, Edgar became the sensitive one, quiet when alone, and the one who tended to draw on the iPad as much as play mind-numbing shooting games. Allan, though probably only evident to me, had a harder edge, was pushier, more prone to bullying his way from me or Edgar or Alfredo. And when he didn't get what he wanted, was the most eager to scream for his supper.

I thought it would just be a couple of years of my career that I'd set aside to rear my progeny: that it would be a brief time-out before I was able to dive headfirst into my work again; that motherhood would fill me with reservoirs of emotional depth and visions to convey as my art and craft deepened until I was able to explode with brave new images of experience and imagination leavened by my complex new life.

Rather, it turned off the tap.

My studio became the nursery. Toys littered the hallways, and the piles and piles of laundry—mostly shitty diapers that after a while no longer repulsed me—never shrank, even though the washer and dryer were running twenty-four hours a day. The easel couldn't fit into the overstuffed closets, and had been shamed into the garage, cobwebbed and forgotten.

Okay, enough. I'm whining, aren't I? Millions of mothers go through a lot more shit than I have. And it's what I've been telling myself for the last five years. I've been dutiful and committed and forgotten entirely the career path I had chosen and abandoned. I never pondered such abstractions as my own happiness. It seemed selfish and churlish to do so, right? I became a wife and a mother, full time, full stop. Just like all the other wives and mothers with overloaded lives who are filled with joy and cheer and happiness. Just like those women who brighten every time they see a child—their own or anyone else's—and smile and want to touch them and share in their warmth. Just like I used to be when I'd see somebody with a dog.

And then. And then.

I didn't live, I breathed. I served.

Last night, Alfredo came home an hour or so late. The boys were fighting me, refusing their baths, hitting each other with a selfie stick and a plastic light saber. There was beer on Alfredo's breath, which was no big deal, but his eyes were heavy-lidded and unconcerned. The boys, naked, were chasing each other and whacking each other, screaming and actually bleeding, and Alfredo had the gall to scream at me, "Would you shut those fucking kids up?"

Then he went into the bedroom and slammed the door

behind him.

I exploded. I was sorry immediately after it happened, but I grabbed both the boys, roughly—more violently than I'd ever grabbed them before—and, one neck in each hand, slammed them hard against the wall, so hard that Allan's head made a dent in the plaster.

"Stop it!" I screeched. "Do you hear me? If you don't shut the fuck up this minute, I'll kill you!"

Two wide-eyed, naked, latte-skinned boys jolted into silence, never having had such an experience. They bled from cuts they'd made on each other with their whipping toys, but that hard hit against the wall and the grip around their necks that practically stopped them from breathing shocked them into submission as never before. They gawped at me in horror, never having been manhandled in this way. I told myself it was the only way I could get their attention, fully realizing that's the excuse abusers always give when they terrorize their own offspring.

I let go of them, and they tumbled to the floor, like marionettes with their strings clipped.

In funereal silence, the boys lifted themselves off the ground, coughing, avoiding my eyes, and marched silently into the bathroom and started running the bath.

I looked up to see Alfredo staring at me, not blinking, not speaking, from the bedroom door, seeing me as he'd never seen me before. I don't have any idea what way that was, but I had never seen that expression—or *lack* of expression—on his face before.

This had to stop.

What kind of monster had I become? And what was next?

I stood panting for breath, my heart lurching in my chest, my brain throbbing to process its sudden awakening.

I could not stay here.

I was going mad. And I worried about what I was capable of.

* * *

Home.

It was quiet and still when I suddenly jolted awake from suffocating claustrophobia, panting and gasping and covered in sweat. I surely screamed, catapulted into heart-pounding consciousness as the rest of the house was buried in slumber, but it was a cry into an empty volcano. Fredo, oblivious, was breathing through the wind tunnel of his mouth against my face. No matter how often he brushed, the faint, fetid stench of tooth decay assaulted me. I turned away from him, and felt the warm, moist breeze on the back of my neck. What could I do but resent him? I've begged him to see the dentist, but I'm not going to nag.

The curtains were open, and a full moon peeked through at me, draping me in an ice-blue slice of light. The room whirled around my bed, and the sound of my own heartbeat pounded deep in my ears. I could not shut it out. My pulse slowed as the carousel of the bed lost momentum and slowly came to a gentle halt. The night was pure. The night held secrets, a promise. And it held a full moon.

Something was happening to me. I was changing. I was becoming aware. I'm not sure awareness is such a good thing, though. Perhaps life is better lived swaddled in ignorance, or at least obliviousness. I blame it on the moon. I blame it on lycanthropy. It was a metamorphosis every bit as compelling as growing fur, fangs, and teeth, even if that transformation was only happening inside my head.

La luna llena called me to the window, and I could not

resist its summons. I rose from the bed, wearing only a baggy, old, sexless-mommy T-shirt with a faded picture of an eyeless Donald Duck casting disapproval on me. I felt tired, old, androgynous. In monochromatic blue moonlight, I surely looked like the animated corpse I felt I had become. Pulled by lunar magnetism, I stepped quietly to the window. The moon wore a mocking face, and I knew it was laughing at me. Under Donald's empty smile, my body sagged like a bag of mashed potatoes. I lifted the shirt over my head, and stood naked in the chill light, and felt myself firm up. Aroused by the gentle waft of cool night air, my skin prickled into gooseflesh, my nipples alert. I turned from the moon to Alfredo, who still slept soundly, his hefty breath rhythmic and annoying. His oblivion to my nakedness in his sleep was no less complete than in our waking hours.

I stood in front of the mirror and dared look—truly look—at myself: face, body, aura.

The moonlight washed away the weight of motherhood, the southbound aim of my nursed-brown nipples, of wifehood, of servitude, and for the first time in some years I saw the woman who hid underneath. Yes, there was softness around the middle, but it could not hide the womanhood, the individual, the singular creature who once had been me that lay underneath. I could see *me,* and my heart pounded. I'd been in hiding so long I didn't think I'd ever come out to play again.

Despite the cool air, I felt heat begin to surge through my body. Even in this light, I could see color come to my face, sanguine, brilliant as the furious flaxen garden of my unruly hair. I could see my pulse throbbing in the artery in my neck. My skin was smooth and warm, and I felt my face relax, realizing it had been taut with tension for a good five years. My forehead relaxed as if injected with psychic Botox.

Frown lines eased and grew faint. Unbelievably, my heart was beating again!

The bedroom door was ajar, and my first thought was that one of the boys might see me standing there naked, and I covered myself in shame. Then I realized what a stupid thought that was. They were five-year-olds. They'd seen me naked before, had nursed these breasts into pendulousness. What difference did it make? There was something Biblical about the rush of shame I felt about my body, especially after I had just glimpsed its beauty again.

I walked into the hallway, which was still and silent, and stood there, waiting, not knowing for what. Grace, perhaps.

Stepping down the corridor, I approached the glow of the nightlight that peeked out from the boys' room. Blissfully asleep, they appeared almost angelic, in opposition to the devilishness of their waking hours. They had both climbed into the same bed and were hugging one another, an act of sweetness rarely displayed in the full light of day. They were beautiful children. But they were also vampires. Perhaps they did not feast upon the blood that pounded through my body, but they sucked me dry of everything else. I took them in, saw the reality of them, their sleeping little bodies void of impishness, anger, pain, and whatever else animated them with shrieks; and, okay, I'll say it: *evil.*

Pretty babies. I would miss them.

I went to the kitchen. The microwave clock showed that it was 3:30 in the morning. The neighborhood was as still as the house. It felt downright post-apocalyptic. I crossed to the refrigerator and drank pomegranate juice directly from the bottle, something I'd chided both Alfredo and the boys for, but growing a *fuck-it* attitude from this night onward.

I couldn't stand wearing the T-shirt anymore, and pulled it off, feeling free and revealed and reborn all in that simple move. I moved through the house like a stranger, stepping over the detritus of family life and into a brave new world of... *something else.*

I moved back down the hall to our bedroom and stood in the doorway. Alfredo had not budged from where I had left him, and his breath still whooshed in and out in gales. *Sleep, baby*, I thought. *Never wake up.*

I stepped toward the walk-in closet ready to rewrite my life.

The house slept around me, and, seemingly, so did the planet. I used to be the somnambulist, but suddenly I felt wide awake. New.

Dangerous.

I went deep into the closet, lit only by a shaft of icy moonlight, past the piles of T-shirts and sweats and mommy gear, quietly revealing the clothes that hung on actual hangers: dresses, skirts, blouses. The clothing of a woman, not of a dowager mother. Most of them were years old, but some of them still fit and flattered me. Perhaps I still cleaned up pretty good.

I peeked out past the closet door and Fredo continued to snore softly, still deep in narcotic slumber. His indifference emboldened me. My favorite dress, raw silk and as red as my heart, beckoned me, as if with the promise of a kiss. I slipped it over my bare skin, and though it was a little tight against my otherwise bare body, I thought of it as a hug. I slid into a thong that did not betray a trace of VPL, braless and unfettered, and felt something I had not felt since before the babies.

Excited.

I stepped into a pair of heels and grew three inches and twenty pounds of confidence.

Alfredo turned over, reached for me in his sleep, but,

not finding me, settled back into deep, rank breathing.

I slipped past him, out of the bedroom and into the hallway, regenerated, feeling a little pretty, even. I tiptoed into the bathroom down the hall, closed the door, and dared to turn on the light. Someone I barely knew stared back at me from the medicine cabinet with wide azure eyes. I liked her. She lived just this side of beautiful. Behind the mirror, behind the clutter of medicines and suppositories and ointments and creams and emollients lay archeological evidence of an abandoned culture: mascara; liner; lipstick in a bold and sassy red. For the first time in months that may have leaked into years, I took them into my artist's hands and gingerly applied them. Soon, the face that looked so deeply into mine transformed from washed out and blandly pleasant—at best—and took on a glow of femininity; that face that had swollen and weathered stepped into a time machine and came out the other end flushed with youth.

I knew this woman, once upon a time: she was an artist, she was bold, she was playful, even a bit coquettish. And though every bit a woman, she was also part girl.

And this Woman, this Part Girl turned off the bathroom light and stepped out into a sleeping family household, beheld the silence and felt her stomach rumble in fear, anticipation, and excitement.

She—I—stepped into the kitchen, opened the pantry and the fake Wondra box and withdrew the rubber-banded roll of $2,000 in cash that was kept there in case of earthquakes or other emergencies, shoved it in my purse, slipped the keyring from the hook by the door, and stepped out into a black sky that was purpling at the edges.

The garage door opened with a rusty creak like a tree falling in an empty forest, so I guess it didn't make a sound to anyone but me. I looked briefly at the Lexus SUV and the Z4 roadster, and never stopped to think about it. I never wanted to drive that giant utilitarian monster machine again. Let Alfredo ferry the kids to school and soccer in it. It was time for me, at long last, to drive the racy little speedster.

I started the car, and its engine thrummed through me. I was horrible. I was selfish. I was a bitch.

But I was alive. I was free.

TWO

The night sky was so blue it was purple. My heart pounded visibly beneath the crimson silk as I pulled off of Wonderland and onto Laurel Canyon. The Valley was bright and clear and deserted at 4:11 a.m., and the stars above profuse and profound. L.A. is never deserted, and the traffic is a constant. But this early, on this morning, I had the Boulevard to myself, and I drove as if I owned it. I opened the windows and let this brave new world breathe on me with chilly breath, guiding me into a hidden promise.

I didn't have a clue where I was going. I was going *away,* and that was enough for now.

Hitting green lights all the way, I navigated north until I hit the 101, which was just giving birth to a new litter of cars.

East or West? I asked myself.

To the East lay desert; to the left, the sea. Given such a simple choice, I roared up the ramp onto the Ventura Freeway, westbound, my hands quaking in a palsy of excitement, my heart still a sledgehammer in my chest. When I reached full velocity, the wind through both open windows whipped hair across my face, but I was oblivious. All I could see was the road ahead, beckoning. It was as if all that was behind me didn't even exist.

The road was smooth and flawless, and the Z4 zipped atop it in a whisper. I was startled when I looked down and saw that I was doing eighty miles an hour. It felt good, savory, a tiny personal rebellion. I stepped a little harder on the gas and smiled as my speed crept up near ninety.

I rocketed through the San Fernando Valley as it slept without acknowledging my presence, burning through Sherman Oaks, Encino, Woodland Hills, Agoura, drawn to the sea by some kind of primal, lizard brain.

Doubt and guilt tried to tug me back into consciousness, to humanity, but I beat it back with Neanderthal force. Every turnoff begged me to go back where I belonged, to wifehood and motherhood, to Stepford, to invisibility. Reason was the angel on my right shoulder, Freedom the devil on my left. But Freedom socked Reason in the eye and gave her a shiner, and though I slowed when I saw a CHP cruiser over the rise ahead, my direction did not falter. I took deep breaths of the purple sky that was yet to turn fetid with rush hour pollution, and continued West, as the freeway wound through the ever-expanding girth of Los Angeles development, still clueless as to my destination, but headed there nonetheless.

Pacific Coast Highway offered me another choice, but it was an easy one: North or South. A hundred and thirty miles south was Mexico, which was spelled *A-l-f-r-e-d-o*. To the north was infinity and beyond: the vast California coastline, a roll of the dice and hidden jackpots everywhere you look. I made my wager and turned right, as the southbound lanes to my left were starting to fill with robots on wheels, heading to work before the inevitable tide of traffic overwhelmed their only route.

Darkness held tight to me, and with every mile further

away from home, I felt another pound lighter.

I told you I was a horrible person. It just took me until now to realize just how completely wretched I was.

Lights were coming on in the cheek-by-jowl multimillion-dollar homes that were smaller than our canyon cottage, crowding Malibu's bend of PCH with their Hollywood hierarchy, but it did not leaven the darkness of the night.

Braless and sheathed in red with lips to match, I felt like a femme fatale in my little roadster, and the morning chill whistling through the car made me break out in a blizzard of gooseflesh. My heart had slowed—just a bit—though I still breathed deeply, filling my lungs with release.

Not that I was no longer nervous. It's just that I pushed back with muscles I didn't know I had. I felt like the Z4 humanized: sleek, fast, and with a newfound direction... but not a destination. It felt so good to be free-flying on PCH I didn't even remember that I'd had an origin.

Los Angeles and its County lay behind me now, and the little Beemer growled as it wrestled effortlessly up the climb to Summerland, quaint and dark, barely a speck with its lights extinguished, invisible and charmless without the sun to paint its many colors. California needed its vaunted sunlight to be California. It was sleepy at night, an early-to-bed state that kept grandmotherly hours which contradicted its worldwide reputation.

I felt like a spider scampering up the leg of a pretty, sleeping woman, alone on the narrowing freeway as I sped past Montecito and the new Miramar hotel that had taken history and pushed its face in the sand with a huge, new, modern, charmless, bullying facelift. Nobody was really *from* California, so no one had a sense of history about it, had no qualms whatsoever about knocking down an icon and shoving a glorified mini-mall in its place. Fires and floods had done their best to turn back the tide of unfettered development, but Nature was no match for commerce.

The state belonged to *me,* Goddamn it. I was born in Santa Monica, my mother in Van Nuys, my father in Long Beach. Interlopers and squatters from Idaho, Utah, New Jersey, and England made fun of us and moved here by the millions, stealing all that was unique and lovely and private and turning it into a vast Disneyland of apartments that no one could afford, took our history and shat upon it, ate it up and regurgitated it in bland mauve tones, indistinguishable from one another. They knocked down the oaks, bulldozed the black walnuts, and disguised cell towers as palm trees.

I wanted my California back.

I knew that was never going to happen, but I was feeling brazen, even breathing in a hint of control. Literally and figuratively, I was in the driver's seat, and the engine purred beneath my feet.

My eyelids began to gain weight, and it was clear that I'd been up all night. The enervation of sleeplessness began to grow leaden in a surprising suddenness that felt dangerous. Drive-time was over. It was time—at least for the moment—to stop.

I hadn't been in this part of the state for at least a decade, certainly not since well before the twins were born, and suddenly this seaside town reached out its hands to hold me and rock me to sleep.

There was still California here, and as I was afraid I'd fall asleep at any moment, I took the beach exit off the highway into Santa Barbara. Rows of proud palms danced a gentle hula in the predawn breeze that wafted in off the ocean. Whitewashed Spanish architecture with terra- cotta roofs still stood proud, in perfect repair, though they dated from the 1930s. And although its borders expanded like blood into gauze with ticky-tacky franchises and faceless condos and towering apartment buildings, Santa Barbara had tightly regulated the city center, and it even smelled of history: the flowers were perennial, sweet and fragrant, enticing, and beckoned me.

But I wasn't looking for the city; I was looking for *escape*.

* * *

Just off the highway, the car slowed to a crawl, as did Santa Barbara. I rounded the little cove spiked with cattails, and a family of ducks came to life, mommy duck guiding the ducklings into their hiding place as my headlights swept across them. The car eased around the curve as I watched them hop into the water in a flutter of white wings and webbed little feet.

I remember when I used to come up here as a girl calling their ancestors Foot Ducks, because they would dip their bills into the water and pop up snorting a "*pfft*" sound. Like "*foot*".

Foot ducks.

Rolling toward the old Fess Parker Hotel (now a Doubletree by Hilton, naturally) on the right, a dramatic view of the Santa Barbara shore lapped at me on the left, its quiet waters rippling gently, reflecting the azure glow of a three-quarter moon.

The purple sky began to pink at its edge. It was 5:40 a.m., but night still held sway. I needed it to still be dark, as I felt the need to hide: from Santa Barbara, from my family, from myself.

Yawning like a cartoon cop, I easily found a parking spot right on Cabrillo on the beach. Dawn had yet to rise, though it threatened to soon, and I had the beach entirely to myself. Even the lights on Stearns Wharf were dark. Soon enough it would be jammed with tourists in board shorts and Crocs and the aromas of cotton candy, waffle cones and popcorn would overtake the salty scent of the sea, but for now, I owned the ocean, and all that I could survey.

Popping the trunk, I pulled out a purple fleece blanket belted in nylon that we carried around for just-in-case.

Just-in-case never happened until now.

I kicked off my heels and locked them in the car, stepping into a pair of flip-flops, outfitted and made up as I was for a night on the town that was not to be, and carried the blanket across the strip of green lawn and onto the spit of sand. I unrolled it and it flapped in the wind that kicked up suddenly, slapping me in the face. Holding it down against the sand, weighting down one end with my purse, I felt grit in my eyes, and it washed away in tears.

I sat on the blanket as the breezes calmed and allowed the water to hypnotize me, the reflected moon melting into the sea. When was the last time life had been so calm and quiet? Was there truly such peace on the planet? It had avoided me somehow.

My heart suddenly started to pound in an arrhythmic marching band percussion section.

My hands started to shake and I broke into a shiver that had nothing to do with the night temperature. Hot anxiety washed through my veins like bleach. I could feel it burn and throw my heart into overdrive, fighting against the peace that drifted about me. The sense of melting into my environment was batted away by my conscience, and I was certain that I'd never sleep again.

But then, like slipping a needle into a big, fat vein, the last traces of night entered me and spread through my body, slowing the roller coaster of my heart and pulling the curtain.

Without warning, peace now held me in a caress, and I melted into slumber, just as the edge of the new sun was pinking the horizon.

I slept dreamlessly, adrift in a deprivation tank of my own creation, falling deep into its dark abyss, a sleep deeper and more silent than I'd ever known. The inky, insensate blackness of my slumber closed like a bank vault.

* * *

That descent into nothingness shattered like a bad-luck mirror when I burst awake to the vibrating chant of my iPhone screaming from my purse. My eyes snapped open and my heart pounded from the shock. Disoriented to find myself laid out in the sand and dressed for a night of clubbing, my sense of time and place slowly seeped into my cottoned brain. Dizzy from the drunkenness of escape and two hours of sleep, I groggily reached into my purse with sleeping fingers and fumbled for the phone. By the time I withdrew it, it had stopped.

Bleary-eyed, it took time to focus onto the notifications on the lock-screen: the call was from Alfredo, as was a long string of text messages that preceded it.

As I held it, it burst into another shivering shout of a ring in my hand. Alfredo again.

I picked up the phone and threw it with all my might into the rising tide that was reaching for me, where it dropped into the water with a satisfying *splurp!*

An old man walking a matching pair of glossy black Italian greyhounds down the beach stood still, watching me with curiosity. The dogs were trying to pull him forward, nipping and snarling playfully at one another, but he just stared at me from under a wide-brimmed straw hat and aviator sunglasses, standing atop scrawny but baggy legs, judging me. His face hung in a perpetual scowl, ready to shout "Get off my beach!"

And now he was coming toward me.

I turned to the sky, ignoring him, feeling the full radiation of the rising sun as its beams devoured me. Everything was too bright through my bleary, surely bloodshot eyes. I don't know if it was sand or veins swollen with sleep deprivation that scraped painfully every time I blinked, but there was crust in the corners of my eyes.

The lanky little dogs were almost upon me now, fighting their leashes to get at me, and I cowered. The old man tried to rein them in but was unsuccessful.

"Whiskey!" he shouted. "Barnaby! Down!"

But the hounds broke free, and soon were on me, covering me in lapping canine kisses. "I'm sorry, I'm so sorry! They just love making new friends!"

The dogs were so frantic for love that they burrowed into me, licking my face and doing a high-speed hula against me. I couldn't help but love them back.

"It's okay," I said as I stroked their lean, eager bodies. "Are *you*?" the man asked, concerned.

"I think so," I said. "Rough night?"

I thought about that, not knowing exactly how I felt. It had been a momentous night, but rough? No, not rough. Not yet.

"No. Short night."

"Well then. Okay."

He wasn't grumpy at all. It wasn't his fault that the years and gravity loosened his skin into a perpetual frown. He smiled, and the corners of his mouth lifted that sagging flesh into a smile radiant with crystal-white dentures that gleamed in the new sun.

"Just wanted to make sure you were all right. You know, the phone and all." Yeah, the phone. Sunk like a stone.

"I'm fine, thanks," I said, brushing sand from my dress as I stood, feeling as old as he was. "I didn't need that anymore."

"Morning, then," he said, intuiting my desire for privacy. "Come on, boys!"

The fickle little dogs had had enough love, I guess, and when he gave their bejeweled leashes a tug, they climbed off of me and scampered joyously across the beach toward the pier, and he did his best to keep up.

I wobbled a little on my feet as I watched them go. Life was starting to gather now that the sun was up, creeping from the town onto the beach. The sunlight felt harsh after such a momentous night, and I felt a bit rudderless, not running on the hamster-wheel of motherhood and matrimony. I wondered what Alfredo was doing under the onslaught of cranky twins and breakfast time.

I looked out at the sea, then up to the hills that crowned Santa Barbara. I looked at the car, still parked on Cabrillo, roiling in second thoughts.

I'd better go back now, I thought. *I can't really do this. Do what?*

Run away!

I was suddenly overwhelmed by nausea and dropped to my knees. I lurched over my cramping stomach and vomited guilt into the sand. My mouth stung with the taste of bile, and my brain reeled from mixed emotions and the lack of sleep.

I needed to shed my mouth of the bitter flush of sin that poisoned it. So, I stood up, brushed the sand from the wrinkled silk of my dress, whipped the grit off the purple blanket, and rolled it up. Cars whisked past in both directions on Cabrillo now, and I knew that my solitude was fleeting. Lives intersected here, and though I felt like a single red ant in an army of black ones, I was also increasingly aware of the lack of walls around me.

I checked to see that I could leave my car here for a while, as California cops are notorious for ticketing and towing the moment your time is up, but I was clear for several hours. So, sheathed in silk and shod in flip-flops, I popped the blanket back in the trunk, locked the car, and walked along the shore to State Street.

I'd fallen asleep alone and awakened a part of a thriving, surging population. Santa Barbara was smiling in her perpetual sun, palm trees proud and proprietary, the temperature always seeming to hover at seventy-two degrees. This, I realized, was as perfect as California gets anymore. I had grown inured to the constant development of Los Angeles, just accepted it when an English cottage from the 1930s across the street from my house was knocked down and replaced with a three-story monstrosity that bulged all the way to the edge of the property line, followed by the one next door, and then the one on the opposite side. Charming neighborhoods of proud, struggling artists were overtaken by the Mongol hordes of faceless corporate franchises and condos, pushing the struggling creative types further and further from town.

But Santa Barbara seems to revere and protect its history, and thereby the history of California and the West. Even though it was filled with cars and pedestrians, the mood was peaceful here, and despite the irritation of my raw, bloodshot eyes and the pounding headache of my sleep deficit, I felt a calm I didn't even realize I had been missing.

When I reached State Street, I saw it all at once, as if through a 200mm lens-- a compression of people, places and things. The shade trees protected a long thoroughfare, and the town was alive... and I felt like its beating heart. I liked this low-rise, bustling downtown, loved that it all seemed to match, unlike my crazy-quilt, ever temporary L.A. After years of high-speed life tending to a home and children and a husband, it felt... a little *scary*, to be honest. But a good kind of scary, the kind you'd pay for, like a great horror movie, or maybe, even more appropriately, a roller coaster ride. I didn't know yet if my car was climbing or hovering at the peak, waiting to rocket downhill at a hundred miles an hour.

I walked up State, feeling oddly hollow, as life reverberated around me. Everybody on the bustling sidewalk seemed to be smiling, engaged, and none of them seemed to be in a hurry. It wasn't much after 8:00 a.m., but it felt like I'd stepped into the middle of someone else's day. There was an invisible forcefield around me, separating me from all who passed me by. I wanted in.

My own personal fog was slowly lifting, and the cottoned sound that penetrated my cocoon was brightening with each step I took up Santa Barbara's central artery. Every direction I looked charmed me, whether it was the pierced and tatted 20-year-olds making out like... well, 20-year-olds, proudly embroidered in a Public Display of Affection, or twin bodybuilders jogging in place with their matching Afghans, long, golden hair taking to the wind in their wake. Everyone was making the most of their young day, even the bleary-eyed old woman who was taking what were the last vestiges of tobacco from a couple dozen butts she'd collected, and rolling it into papers and lighting up for a deep, satisfying drag before hacking up a big, green load of phlegm and launching it into the gutter.

Then she started to laugh, loud and bellicose, to no one in particular. Or perhaps to someone only she could see. Laughing and shouting: "Oh, you don't think that's funny? Well, what the fuck is funny to you? I think it's pretty fuckin' funny!" And then her laugh turned to screams. "Just keep your fucking hands off of me! I'll call a cop! You hear me? My brother's a cop and he'll break your fuckin' face open!"

And then, the laughter again. I kept walking, keeping my

distance. Nobody else seemed to pay any attention to her, and she soon evaporated into an anonymous background player, her taunts to invisible tormenters echoing off into the side streets.

But mostly the people who swarmed the street were pretty, athletic, smiling, mobile. And now I was one of them, among them, a newborn soul cast adrift in their midst.

As I strode amongst the growing throngs of people, a new sensation started to fester. I didn't know what it was at first, but it slowly came into focus. Although I was *among* them, I was not *of* them. No one I passed ever seemed to look at me. Certainly, no one smiled at me, or even acknowledged me. I was draped in a cloak of invisibility, and it kind of stung. For years, I rarely was by myself in public, other than shopping at Trader Joe's in sweat pants, or at doctor appointments, always a wife or mother.

Pre matrimony, pre motherhood, *I* was pretty. I *am* pretty. And most men called me beautiful. But now, even dressed as I was—and that was, I thought, nicely womanly; at least, that was my intent—I was ignored. Men passed me by without a glance. I garnered no sideways looks, no flirtatious smiles, and I was surprised to feel that it *bothered* me.

I broke out in a panicked sweat of anxiety. Maybe I didn't belong here. I had made a horrible mistake. I *knew* I had made a horrible mistake even as I was making it. It was time to turn around, go back to the Z4, join the thickening rush hour dash for Los Angeles and pick the kids up at preschool before anyone knew the difference. I froze in place as the blind public swarmed around me, and I could feel sweat dampening the silk beneath my armpits. I wanted to cry. But I wouldn't, God damn it. I wouldn't.

And then, I imagined life at home. The screaming. The fighting. The bottomless pit of my missing soul. The pot belly as it swung loosely over me as Alfredo went through the motions on our weekly Friday fuckfest. The dried-up tubes of paint, the canvases gathering dust in the attic. The missing me. In my imagination, shivering in flop-sweat in the middle of State Street, choking on the taste of guilt-bile, I picked up a double-barrel shotgun, jammed both barrels between my teeth, tasted steel and oil, pulled back the triggers, and launched my brains out of my skull and onto the wall.

I had three choices: a) to go home with my tail between my legs and submit to Family Life; b) Lights Out; or c) taking a taste of greener grass. I was sure a) would lead to b). There was no choice to be made. I opened my eyes, smelled the jasmine around me, the breeze of the New World crooking a beckoning finger to me, the languid gentility of the stucco-and-Spanish-tile Old California and its promise of a better life, watched a sidewalk artist sketch in chalk on the sidewalk, his young face already leathered by the constant exposure to a hypnotic sun, and made my choice.

The scent of roasting coffee called to me, and my stomach rumbled as I walked past the Paseo Nuevo. The choice was life or death, if not my own, then almost certainly of my children. If I didn't blow my own brains out, I might be driven to something more drastic.

The choice, for the moment, at least, was made.

I crossed the street and stepped through the doors of a charming half-indoor, half-outdoor little cafe called Mourning Coughee. It was already humming with a very young clientele hunched over their MacBooks, thumb-typing their every thought on their phones, earbuds whispering tinny playlists, noisy young bearded guys laughing and shoving each other. I was a good decade older than most of them, and not one of them took notice of me. But the place was lively, inviting, and the scent of roasting coffee beans was exhilarating. It was a scruffy little independent cafe, cluttered with unmatched, overstuffed sofas and easy chairs, tables with fading Ouija and chess boards laminated onto their surfaces, towers of tattered board games and well- thumbed books stacked haphazardly on rustic wooden crates.

Though misleadingly pierced and tatted with carny-worker metal and outré artwork, the barista was unexpectedly sweet, attentive, and ever smiling. "Hi, Beautiful," she said. "What can I get you?"

My stomach chose that moment to let out the roar of an awakening black bear, and she broke into peals of contagious laughter, and I couldn't help but join in.

"A large Americano and the cranberry oat bran muffin."

"Great. The muffins just came out of the oven." She poured my coffee into a giant mug shaped like the head of Frankenstein's monster, and grabbed the steaming muffin with a pair of tongs, placing it on an old blue-and-white Miramar Hotel saucer. Nothing matched here, and I kinda loved that.

"That'll be nine-eighty," she said.

"Smells good," I said back, as I dug around my purse to pay. "Hang on."

The purse wasn't that big, but I fished through its contents, not finding the roll of cash I'd brought with me. I started to panic as an impatient line was forming behind me, and fumbled through it more frantically. Finally, I dumped its contents onto the counter and sifted through, but there was no point.

The money was gone. Someone had stolen it from my purse as I lay sleeping on the beach.

THREE

What the fuck?

The morning was raw, and so was I. The nightly double dose of Ambien CR didn't even get the chance to wear off on its own. The twins were screaming and fighting—their default morning greeting—and jolted me awake like an icepick through the brain. I burrowed my head into the pillow like an ostrich, but it didn't do much good.

"Mom! Mom! Where's Mom?"

I didn't even have time to consider the question when the bedroom door came crashing open, and the twins charged onto the bed.

"Dad!" Edgar screeched. "Allan peed on me!"

"Well, don't bring it into the bed!" I screeched back. "Go tell your mom." I tried to cover my head with the pillow.

"Mom's gone!"

I sat up. "What do you mean, 'mom's gone.'

Where is she?"

"I don't know," Edgar or Allan said. The wet one.

"Go wash up and get ready for school." I stood up, pharmaceuticals still lingering in my woozy skull.

"But I've got pee on me!"

"Alright. Come on, goddamn it."

I trudged into the bathroom, pulling them behind me as they followed, shoving each other, resenting them for ending my sleep.

"I didn't do it on purpose!" Allan yelled at his brother.

"I was asleep!"

"Doesn't matter! You peed on me! I got your pee on me!"

"Enough!" I threw the door open to the kids' bathroom and

started to run the bath. They were still pushing one another, and Edgar's head hit the tile with a dramatic thunk. Naturally, he started to scream and cry. Nothing happens here without drama.

"It's not my fault!" Allan cried.

"Stop it! Both of you!" I grabbed Edgar and tried to calm him, though I really wanted to strangle him. "Now get undressed and into that tub!"

"Mr. Bubble!" Edgar shouted. Never speech, only screech.

"The water's flat and icky!"

I dumped in the Mr. Bubble and they tiptoed into the foam.

"Ouch! Too hot! Too hot!"

"All right!" I turned up the cold water and swirled it with my hand.

Where was Dina? This was her job, not mine. In fact, that's all she had to do: get these kids off to school and do whatever the fuck it was that she did all day.

Must be nice.

I lifted the boys into the tub and left them alone to fight in there while I searched for their mother.

"Dina?"

I wandered through the house in my boxers and V-neck. I felt old, heavy, my head still throbbing. There wasn't much house to wander through, and certainly no place to hide. I knew from experience.

The kitchen was empty, save for the spilled Cocoa Puffs and puddles of almond milk (Allan was allergic to dairy). The living room was a nuclear explosion of abandoned toys and games and coloring books, all to the accompaniment of the furious five- year-old scream cantata duet streaming from the tub.

"Dina!"

No Dina. I looked in the garage, and the Beemer was gone.

Why did she take *my* car?

I was confused. Something must have happened. She never left the house before she got the boys off to school.

What the fuck?

As the boys tried to drown each other in

the bath, I called her mobile, but there was no answer. I tried again. Nothing. I texted her.

"If you kids don't settle down in there, there's gonna be hell to pay!"

I was so fucking tired. I really didn't want to deal with this. I just wanted to take a shower and get to work.

The ruckus did not settle, so I charged back to the bathroom with threats.

Wham! I slammed the door open and it cracked against the wall.

"Enough!"

They could see anger in my eyes, could tell that I was about to lose it, and they stopped cold, eyes wide, wondering what I was capable of.

And so was I.

I dreaded coming home from work these days.

Dina was always angry, it seemed, sedentary and obstinate.

The house felt funereal every time I entered it, filled with tension and unruly childhood and displeasure. Resentment and anger radiated off of her, and I didn't know why. But I know that it didn't help my mood any. I walked on eggshells all the time, knowing that any wrong word would launch her fury. She was unhappy, I get that. But she didn't have to fuck up my life, too, much less the kids'.

I toweled off the boys and sent them to

their room to get dressed.

"I guess Dad's going to take you to school today."

"Yay!"

Somehow that made them happy.

I could feel the fireball of my anger surging inside my chest and sent Dina another text. I tried to consider where she might have gone—and why—but came up empty… and pissed off. No note, no warning, nothing. I could not imagine any reason for her not to be here.

I texted her again, and it disappeared into the ether. No

"Delivered". No "Read".

I realized that her dark moods were contagious. I found that I was always pissed off, too, when I was in this house. Ever cautious of setting off another shitstorm, I rarely spoke. It was easier that way. Maybe it would have been better if we'd never had the kids. Or would there just have been other reasons for her to go explosive? Perhaps it was her nature, and it was getting to be my own. But it seemed entire days went by where we did not speak to one another. I became The Quiet One.

Eggshells.

I hated that I had to go to an office job, to a time clock and a station in a sea of desks filling pharmaceutical orders online, staring at a screen all day long, never having a conversation, only typing and clicking and refreshing screens. I had grown to hate monitors and keyboards, and felt my eyes were probably melting.

I had abandoned my passion for telling stories, and not only because of the failing eyes and carpal tunnel. I was depleted. I had no more stories to tell. The sight of a monitor and a keyboard came to represent prison, my own highjacked soul, whatever that was worth, and it no longer beckoned me to create in the middle of the night. I was on the treadmill of making my rent and dehydrating my creative juices. Before the twins were born, I could dive into my writing as soon as I got home—perhaps after a very heated hour or so of spontaneous combustion in bed with Dina—and give birth to page after page of characters and ideas and the joy of authorship.

I don't know whose idea it was to have kids, but it was a bad one, a terrible one, the worst idea in the world. But it is done, and we live with it, and I work my ass off in a job that— if I allowed myself to think about it—I despised, to feed them and clothe them and send them to school, while Dina marinates in her misery. I mean, what does she do when they're in kindergarten? She could paint, she could get part-time work and help out a little bit, she could even go back to illustration.

But she doesn't, and I can't say a thing about it without launching her into another orbit of anger. She thinks she's doing me a great favor when she fucks me once a week, if she's not feeling premenstrual or tired or crampy.

So, I was going to be late because she decided to take off somewhere without telling anyone, and I had to take the little monsters to school.

What the fuck had become of my life?

FOUR

I stood there in a panic, knowing I couldn't use a credit card if I meant for this escape to be successful. I could-- and would-- be tracked, and for a ten-dollar breakfast? The barista's sweet smile was expectant, but I could see it was wearing thin as the line surged behind me with eager coffee consumers.

I was about to just tell her I was going to be back after a trip to an ATM when a hand reached from behind and slapped a fifty-dollar bill on the counter in front of me.

"I'll take care of that," came a low, almost guttural voice that came with the hand. "And give me a large Ethiopian with a double shot and an onion bagel."

"Got it," said the barista, and turned to get his order.

I turned to face the angel coming to my rescue, and told him, "You don't have to do that."

"I know I don't," he said. "But I want to."

His eyes played hide-and-seek in the crinkled squint under a prominent brow. Laugh lines were deep and exaggerated by a ruddy suntan into a pale, creased laugh-line roadmap of a life thoroughly lived. He'd been leathered by the sun, and he wore an open short-sleeved button-up shirt over a tight, well-defined torso and slender but subtly muscled arms. His skin, adorned with soft, golden hair, was a bit loose over his musculature-- whether from age or the sun's radiation was anybody's guess. His greying hair fell in disheveled coils almost to his shoulders, and there was a light crust of sand on his forehead and shoulders and sandaled feet. His eyes were pale, but I could see a trace of cataract before I broke my gaze and blushed and thanked him. They were just the least bit bloodshot, as well. Years in the sun made it difficult to discern his age: he could be in his thirties or his fifties, it was hard for me to tell. His smile was kind of devastating and, well, *beachy*, if you know what I mean.

"I would say I'm happy to help a damsel in distress," he said, "but I know what year this is. So I offer my full respect."

It was a nice backhanded attempt at acknowledging my womanhood, but still felt old- fashioned and sexist.

"Respect accepted... as well as the breakfast." I told him. "Do you have a business card? I'll pay you back."

That made him laugh. "Look at me. Do I look like I have a business card?" He had a point.

"I'm Ethan," he said, extending a rough, callused hand. I took it and shook it, and it overwhelmed my own.

"Dina. Nice to meet you. And thank you."

"And you, Dina."

The line was getting eager and anxious behind us, and the barista handed the beach bum his coffee and bagel, then leaned around us to take the next order.

I scouted through the crowding coffeehouse and spotted a couple of *Día de los Muertos*- tattooed hipsters getting up to leave, opening the only spot to be found in the place. I speedily sharked my way to it, settling into the creaking leather rocking chair and brushing away the crumbs and detritus of their muffins with the side of my hand. I looked up and Ethan stood in the middle of the shop, making a show of looking around for an empty seat before he came wandering my way.

"Do you mind?" he asked. I shook my head and he took a seat opposite me.

"Of course not." I did, really. I just wanted to be alone for a bit, as much as I was beginning to enjoy the novelty of being out and about in an outside world filled with life.

Ethan was fit and handsome in a rugged way that was not really my style. And right now I felt off-center just being one-on-one with another man, a stranger, a tanned, sculpted, confident bubbling stew of testosterone. I had always been drawn to the sensitive-artist type.

He pulled his chair close and put his rough-hewn hands on the table. It was too close, too intimate, and I'm sure I pulled back a bit. He took the hint and eased himself back in a casual, natural way.

"If you'd rather have some privacy, I can take it out and be on my way. I'm usually a to- go kind of guy, anyway."

"No, no, that's fine, stay," I said, though I did feel otherwise. I appreciated his attempt not to make me uncomfortable, but I also knew that he was saying it to endear himself to me, that he knew I wouldn't send him away like a disobedient puppy. I fell for it and I knew it, and I felt like an idiot. But worse, I had forgotten how to converse with strangers on my own.

Especially a stranger who kept looking directly into my eyes without ever losing his smile. A stranger most women would likely find handsome, but not me. Not now, not here, not on the first morning of my new life. Even so, I couldn't help but notice there was no wedding ring on his finger, nor a pale strip of flesh where one might be found.

He could sense my discomfort, I could tell, and he did his

best to put me at ease. "Another day in paradise," he said. I nodded. Hard to disagree.

"What's your sport?"

"I'm sorry?"

"You're obviously an athlete. What's your sport?"

I looked at him for a long silent moment, befuddled, before I broke out in laughter. "Does that one really work for you?"

It was kind of cute when he blushed before joining my laughter.

"It has in the past," he said. "Maybe I should have tried 'what's your instrument?' But I didn't want to risk the double entendre."

"Nice."

Seeing him squirm girded me a bit. I could feel the tension loosen, just a little. I never imagined that I would be laughing again so soon.

"Look," I told him, "I really appreciate you picking up the tab, and you're a very nice, handsome guy, but I'm not looking for that right now."

"Looking for what?" He was playing the innocent, *who me?* card now. I pinned him in a mock glare. "You know what I'm talking about."

He put up his hands in surrender. "Okay. Uncle."

"Okay. We've got that out of the way now, right?"

"Right."

I grabbed my coffee, surprised to find that my hands were shaking. I could only hope that he didn't notice, even though a bit of my Americano spilled over the side of Frankenstein's head. The first sip was scalding.

"So," he said. "What *is* your instrument?"

I mock-glared him again. "Don't try it, mister."

He smiled. "But you *do* play an instrument, don't you?"

"Did," I said. "The viola. But I gave it up when I was a freshman in high school."

"I knew it."

Well, there was going to either be conversation or awkward silence, so I gave in. "And you?" I asked.

"Guess."

"Hmmm..." I narrowed my eyes. "Lead guitar. And you were in a band, but never made a living at it."

"Bingo!" He looked genuinely surprised. "Shot in the dark."

"No, seriously. I still play once in a while at a little bar on Ortega. The Press Room. You know it?"

I shook my head. "No. I'm not from here."

"It's a nice place. Kinda tiny, unpretentious. Pretty much anyone can play there, if they're halfway decent and can bring in a handful of friends willing to pay for a drink or two."

Hint, hint.

"I can't remember the last time I've been out to hear live music," I told him. "No shit?"

"No shit."

That really seemed to surprise him.

"Then what do you do to fill that hole in your heart?"

I faltered. A little knife had discovered that hole, which had been kept a secret, even from me.

He could see that he'd hit bone and leaned back into his chair, giving me space, attenuating his smile. He didn't apologize; he didn't acknowledge the truthful wound he had poured salt into: but, neither did I. He just leaned back and looked down into his coffee and took a long sip. I did the same.

"So..." he said. "What replaced the viola?"

"Sorry?"

"I can tell you're creative. When I was a kid, I used to make up stories, but that kind of went away when I got into college. I started playing guitar and never had any desire to go back. You just look like someone who didn't give up the viola without replacing it, right?"

The Perceptive Beach Bum. I'd never met one of those before. I considered him for a beat before I spoke.

"I'm an artist. I paint." I didn't tell him the "used to" part.

"I knew it!" He was so proud of himself. "I could *smell* it on you!"

"Careful, Cowboy," I said, on the verge of taking it personally, feeling ripe from my night on the beach.

"No offense intended," he said. "Almost none taken."

He smiled, and so did I. But I kept up my wall. I felt raw, unprotected. I hid behind another sip of my coffee.

"So..." he began, and left it hanging there. "Yes?"

"What do you think of busting that Live Music cherry tonight?"

"Excuse me?"

He blushed, kind of adorably.

"I didn't mean it the way it sounded. I was just extending an invitation to come hear my band tonight." I liked how I was able to jar his insouciant confidence. I felt a little bold making him squirm a bit. "I mean, if you're not busy. No cover or anything. And it's just a couple blocks away."

He could see that my resistance was strong but teetering.

"I mean, *band* might be overstating the case, but I get together with a group of guys and play kinda semi-regularly."

"I like the sense of commitment," I said.

"You can bring a friend, if you like. Or several." I saw what he was doing there, making it look so casual, and that I could bring a date, even though he knew I wouldn't.

"We'll see," I told him, immediately regretting spouting a motherly bromide. "Busy schedule?"

"I don't know yet." I was taking control of the conversation, and it felt good.

"Well, should you get the urge, the Press Room is on Ortega, just off State. And if you think we suck, they've got a great jukebox with lots of seventies and eighties English music. We start at about eight, or whenever at least ten people show up."

I blushed when I suddenly felt that I was smiling.

"Okay, thanks." I almost said *we'll see* again, but caught myself just in time. He nodded and flashed a grin that glared between creased dimples.

"Cool. Nice to meet you, Dina."

"Nice to meet you, Ethan. And thanks for, you know, picking up the tab."

"My pleasure," he said, and stood before anything could go wrong, knowing exactly when to make his exit. "Maybe see you later."

"Maybe."

He walked away, sipping his coffee, and I watched him walk all the way out until he was devoured by State Street, never looking back.

I took a long drink of my cooling coffee, and, once he disappeared from view, my recalcitrant brain suddenly switched gears.

What the fuck was I going to do without a penny to my name?

FIVE

I decided I had to take a chance. I'd been away for less than a dozen hours, so I doubted that the National Guard was searching for me yet. I would leave Santa Barbara soon—I'd *have* to—before I could be tracked by my transactions. So, I wandered State Street, brushing oatmeal crumbs from my scarlet silk bodice, in search of an ATM. I didn't have to walk far; there was a Chase Bank just a couple blocks up the street, and I entered my PIN number and pecked the buttons to withdraw the maximum: four hundred dollars. I was going to have to make this last.

Not so fast.

The screen went dark for a moment, then illuminated with a scolding: "Insufficient Funds.".

What the fuck? There should be at least three thousand dollars in our checking account! I tried again, only to prove the adage: insanity is defined by doing the same thing over and over expecting different results. The results never differed. I was going to have to access the savings account.

I girded my loins and entered the bank. My heart was pounding as I approached the teenage teller who waited for me with acne and an eager smile.

"I'd like to make a withdrawal from my savings account," I told her.

"Sure, I can help you with that," she said. I put in my ATM card and entered two thousand dollars.

My hands were shaking. I felt like a criminal on the lam. "Can I see an ID please?"

I reached into my purse and withdrew my driver's license and offered it up to her, but my hand was so palsied that I flung it past her and onto the floor behind her.

"Sorry!"

"No worries, ma'am."

Ma'am? Nobody had ever called me "ma'am" before.

I tried to laugh it off, clearing my throat as she tapped keys on her computer and opened the cash drawer.

"Twenties okay?" she asked.

"Twenties are fine," I said, and folded them into my purse as furtive as a bank robber, then scurried out as quickly as I could.

What the fuck was I so paranoid about? Sure, they could track my withdrawal, but I'd be miles away by then, and no one would be the wiser. It wasn't like I was going to move here or anything. Calm down, I told myself as I put my back against the wall of the bank's exterior, my heart pummeling its way out of my chest.

You're free, remember? Oh yeah. Free.

It was time to get back to my car and hit the road again, to fly that freedom flag high, to take to the road and flex my wings before they were clipped again.

I took deep breaths, and my heart began to find its cadence again. I was rebooting. I had nothing to worry about. I had some money, I was reclaiming my life, and I'd been reenergized by a glimpse of what California once was and would always be, had been ratified by the generous kindness and flirtations of a handsome beach rat, and it was time for me to continue my adventure. That's what freedom was all about, wasn't it?

Breathing normally, my heart's cadence returning to a California rhythm, I started walking back to the beach and my car.

The breeze was gentle and warm, a baby Santa Ana, and I was regaining that chunk of confidence I had bitten off that had allowed me to leave home in the first place. My first stop had taken me to this beautiful town, reminded me of what beauty there was out in the world outside Mommy and Me, preschool, McDonald's, Dora the Explorer, and really rotten, quiet, weekly sex.

Every step I took back toward Cabrillo Street and the little Z4 was liberating and filled me with regret that I could not stay here. The sun was golden, the sky as blue as the sea, the palms swaying in a seductive rhumba. I will miss you, Santa Barbara. Our affair was brief but lasting. I will not forget you. The closer I got to the ocean, the greater my regret that I had to leave. I turned the corner onto Cabrillo as recumbent bicycles whizzed past with little flags whipping in the wind, the seashell sounds of the gentle waves lapping at the beach soothing and inviting me, as I headed to where I had left my car...

And found a silver Mercedes SUV in its place. My car had been towed.

Six

Fuck this!

Enough! *Enough!*

SEVEN

I was truly and horribly fucked. And terrified.

No car, almost no money, no future. Not even a present. On the shoreline of freedom, I felt caged, a wolf in a trap about to chew off its foot. My heart began to race again. If this were a movie, the camera would be whirling around me, laughing voices coming from all the surround speakers, and I would collapse and the screen would go to black before cutting to the next scene. But I was living this movie, and no deft turns of the screenwriter, no time-passing cuts of a nimble editor could thrust me into the next scene. I stood reeling on the curb of Cabrillo, across a busy avenue from a beach that was waving goodbye to me, and had no idea what I was going to do next.

How far was two thousand dollars going to take me? How much was it going to cost to free my car from the impound lot? I would be lucky if any of my cards were working by now, and if they were tracking me, they might already have honed in on my bank withdrawal. Not so difficult to do, I would guess. I had to be smart about this; either that, or go home.

Home. Is that what it was? What did that make me? A homemaker? A Mad Housewife?

Was my attempt at escape an act of sanity or its absolute inverse?

All I knew was that it was getting increasingly difficult to breathe. I felt as if a potbellied pig were sitting on my chest. My pulse was erratic and so strong that I could hear it pounding in my ears. I stared out into the choppy sea, my flesh aflame but doused by cold sweat, causing me to shiver. I tried to think, tried to consider the options, tried to figure this out, but my brain yanked its blackout curtain shut with a slam, and my synapses were dying of inertia.

The ocean called to me, literally roaring my name in oceanspeak: *Dina...*

I knew it was my saboteur brain, but it was calling me, regardless. The ocean wanted me, and I answered its siren call.

I crossed the street, not even looking as cars whipped past me and honked in anger. I had cast caution aside, because... why not? If a Porsche SUV had plowed me down, there would be no Butterfly Effect rippling from my death. The earth would continue to turn obliviously as they scraped me off the pavement and shuffled me into an anonymous cardboard box.

But I was not hit; I was, after all, invisible, a ghost in a skin suit, and I reached the other side of the road in the wake of leaden ennui, screeching tires and angry epithets. I slipped off my sandals and walked to the water's edge, stepping ankle-deep into the shockingly cold ocean, igniting gooseflesh that crawled all over my skin like a marauding army of ice ants. I dragged my feet through the water and sludgy sand along the shore toward the pier, eager to lose myself in the gathering crowd.

Would that I could.

I stepped into my shoes and onto the rough, wooden

pier, my forearms across my purse, now draped around my neck, as if making a delivery to Fort Knox. I was not about to lose this bundle of cash, the lifeline to my future... if I had one.

I walked out to the edge of the wooden pier, a dark silhouette moving amongst the bright and cheery, a shadow hidden from the sun. Popcorn popped, ice cream melted, parents and partners selfied themselves into significance as I glided between them unseen. At the end of the pier it was quieter, past all the bars and fish shacks and gift shops. I rested my hands on the wood and stared out into the sea.

It was another perfect day, for everyone but me.

The sea rippled gently. Gulls begged for popcorn. A toddler dropped his father's iPhone into the water. A teenager sneaked a smoke behind the ice machine. A woman nursed her baby behind the snow-cone cart, a pink flannel Winnie the Pooh blankie draped over the child and the breast, shaming nature.

A sailboat glided across the Pacific, its mast pointing like a finger directly at the sun.

And I stood there, turning to stone, my eyes unblinking, and the ruffled sea turned to glass. The wind died and the gulls disappeared. I stared, unaware of the burning glare of the sun. I looked down into the water far below, the still, silent water, no longer lapping, just motionless as a pond as somebody watching the world pushed the pause button.

Way down below me, reflected in the mirror of the motionless ocean, a woman stared back at me, a woman nearing forty, her face evacuated of expression. A youngish woman whose time was up. She beckoned to me, called me to join her in the sea.

Jump, she whispered.

I was back on that plane from Mexico City, staring down at a planet that wanted me deep within its center.

Jump, whispered my reflection.

Jump, whispered the Planet Earth.

It became a chorus, rhythmic as the waves that resumed lapping at the wooden ankles of the pier.

Jump. Jump. Jump.

The swells grew in size and tore apart the woman who called to me like a siren. Her image was swallowed by the foamy water, and my somnambulism snapped.

Fuck this! I shot back.

I was not going to burst into tears and go all girly because my fucking car got towed. It had taken all the courage I could muster to break free from the yoke of sleeping sickness from which I had awoken, and I was not going to let something as simple as an entire planet stand in my way. I had made the great escape, and by god, I was not going to be hooked and reeled in by circumstances over which I actually wielded some control. Reclaiming the course of my life, I broke loose of the chains of fatalist mesmerism, bought a snow-cone—every flavor and color, rainbowed with promise—and turned my back on the dead end of the ocean once and for all.

EIGHT

I flagged down a traffic cop as he was gliding on a Segway from car to car, issuing parking tickets as if they were invitations to the annual gala. I hated him at first sight—that too- white California cop smile, the cop shaved head, the reflective cop sunglasses, that perfect- grammar cop talk—but pushed down my gorge and asked him what happened to my car. He was more than happy to give me the business card for Smitty's Towing Service, where I would probably find the little Beemer, all locked up safe and sound.

"Thanks," I grumbled, mostly to myself.

"Have a good day!" he chirped before gliding off into the sparkling Santa Barbara sun.

I didn't even have a phone to call them. So, I headed up the main drag to find a cellular shop to pick up a burner.

For forty dollars I was able to buy a cheap LG TracPhone with a Pittsburgh phone number, four hundred minutes, and even some data I would likely never use. I unboxed it as I sat in front of a very active surf shop, tossing the detritus into the trash and activating the very disposable unit. Simple and quick, it felt clandestine, bordering on the criminal. The lit screen glared at me, dared me to make a call. I pulled out the Smitty's card, and, both hands shaking, tapped in the number.

The woman who answered was very polite, in that we've-got-you-over-a-barrel-and-   what-are-you-going-to-do-about-it kind of way. I told her the year and model and license plate of my car, approximately when it must have been towed, and asked her what it would cost. The total was five hundred twenty dollars. Let me repeat that: *five hundred twenty dollars!* And I had two thousand to my name. More than a quarter of my funds just to get my car out of hock, just hours after it had been yanked off the street. I simmered. I boiled. I steamed.

"Hang on a minute," she told me, oh so sweetly.

Seething, paranoia struck deep. Why had she asked me to hold? Had there been a police bulletin put out on the car already? Was this a trap? *Already?*

Oh, shit. *Oh shit oh shit oh shit!*

Should I wait on the line? Could they track this phone? Was the net closing in?

I felt like I was living in a Raymond Chandler novel, but with too much sunlight to call it *noir.*

I could hear loud clanging and voices speaking Spanish echoing in the distance, and I waited. And waited. It seemed like an hour, but was probably closer to ten minutes. I was so close to hanging up, fearing that every move I made would lead to my being found and apprehended, for something or other that had to be illegal. The perspiratory bath of guilt was drenching me.

Then, finally, Lady Sweetness and Light was back on the line with her voice of honey. "I'm sorry I kept you on the line. Thanks for holding, Ms..." She waited for me to fill in the blank, but I was resolute not to. After waiting an awkward beat, she continued.

"It looks like we don't have a car by that description, ma'am."

"Wait," I fumfered. "*What?*"

"We don't have your car here."

"I don't understand. If it was towed by the Santa Barbara Police down on Cabrillo at the beach, could it be anywhere else?"

"We are the only tow lot contracted by the city to service all shoreline tows." I was way too friendly with Panic by now.

"Where else could it be?" I asked, trying to keep a grip. "Well. It's possible that it was stolen."

Oh, fuck. I hadn't thought of that. This was getting worse by the moment. "Stolen?"

"Maybe, ma'am. I wouldn't know. But if it's not in our lot, there's a strong likelihood that somebody took it."

I looked at the phone in my hand as if it were her face. I resisted the temptation to throw it to the ground and stomp on it. I ended the call without a *thank you* or *goodbye*.

Fuck. This was not going the way I'd hoped. I mean, I didn't have anything resembling a plan beyond my escape. But this sucked.

State Street was long, especially on foot. And the search for a room for the night was exhaustive and exhausting. It was high season here—if there is a season that is *not* high in Santa Barbara, I have never seen it—and rooms were at a premium. *No Vacancy* signs predominated my journey along the length of the city's main drag. The Motel 6 was booked up, and so was the Rose Garden Inn and the Sunset Motel and the Quality Inn and the Agave Inn and the Sandpiper Lodge and the Best Western Pepper Tree...

You get the picture.

The afternoon was waning, and so was I. Maybe I would

end up sleeping in the park in front of the Mission, or on the lawn in front of City Hall, with all the other homeless. I could think of worse places.

But by now, hunger was overwhelming my search for shelter. I knew I could sleep anywhere, even on the beach again, if I had to (though if I did, I would stick my bankroll between my legs). I felt grimy and hungry and thirsty and subhuman, set adrift with two grand, my purse, and the clothes on my back. This was not a good start to my brand new life.

So I left State Street, needing to pinch pennies and still fill my begging stomach. So I made my way to Milpas Street, and eventually to La Super-Rica Taqueria, where I could fill up for next to nothing, splurge on an icy Mexican beer, and scrub my face and armpits in their restroom.

Somewhat sated, lightly buzzed by the rare beer, and feeling a bit more human after washing up and brushing my teeth, I emerged from the world's greatest taco stand and into the day's curtain call. The sky had gently darkened as my mood was beginning to brighten... just a little bit.

It was one of those fabled California sunsets. Puffy scuds of cloud smiled in a ring around the sun, weighing it down into the sea. Twilights are fleeting on the West Coast, but though this was brief, the slowly descending color-wheel curtain of sky went from eggshell blue to orange to pink to purple. The tacos and beer were the panacea I had sought, and my breathing was calm and rhythmic again.

I still had no idea what the fuck I was going to do next, but it wasn't crushing me now. The clickety-clack mechanics of my brain had been oiled, and I walked back out into the balmy evening that caressed me with its gentle fingertips.

Little white lights erupted in the trees that lined State Street, giving it a very Main Street, Disneyland USA feel. It wasn't real. It was as far-removed from our Little House in the Valley as it could be. I walked on the cloud of my dream of freedom, fortified, prepared to do battle with all that stood in my way.

And there would be plenty, of that there was little doubt.

As the sun sank and my spirits rose, I checked the map on my new plastic phone. Ortega Street was just a couple of blocks from where I stood, and it was nice to have someplace to go.

* * *

You had to be looking for The Press Room to find it. The signage was microscopic, but the door was open and the gentle scent of decades of beer wafted out and crooked its finger at me. Hesitant to enter, I peeked inside. There were only half-a-dozen patrons within, and a football game played silently on the three giant screen TVs on the walls. The members of the band were tuning up in the dark on the tiny little stage in the corner, and even though he was facing away from me, huddling over his guitar, I recognized Ethan's silhouette immediately. He was wearing a white wife-beater and loose, well-broken-in, low-slung jeans with busted out knees.

Feeling stealthy, I slid quietly and anonymously onto a red leather barstool and ordered a beer, my second today. Probably my second in five or six months, now that I thought about it. It was good to be sitting down.

The band finished tuning, and somebody turned on the red and amber stage lights, and the music began. Ethan stepped up to the mike, and without any opening words, started singing J.J. Cale's "Crazy Mama". His voice was rough, conversational, and not particularly accurate, but it kind of worked for the song. And he looked good bathed in red light. The band played it slow and lazy, comfortable and comforting, if bordering on sloppy. It sounded good, especially after a beer. Another dozen or so people came into the club as the band played on.

Though I quietly kept to the shadows, when the song ended, Ethan pegged me with his seen-everything, ocean blue eyes, and his serious, starving-artist face broke into an open, genuine, vulnerable smile. The stage lights deepened the creases in his face, and he was just seething, coiled testosterone behind his Stratocaster.

"Hey, Dina," he said into the open mic. "Thanks for coming."

I blushed, feeling a little like a groupie, and the handful of people in the bar all turned to look at me. I just tossed him a simple salute, and the band started playing something I didn't recognize that probably came from the seventies.

Alfredo played the guitar, too—well, he *had* played guitar, before consigning it to the same locked-up chamber in which his writing had been sequestered for the last few years—but he played an acoustic, Mexican folksongs and flamenco strummed and thrummed on nylon strings. It was passionate, romantic, filled with Latin fire half the time, and mournful tears the other. When he played, way back when, the music was soulful and expressive, and it always made me want to fuck him.

Ethan, frankly, was not a very good musician. He could handle the chord changes well enough, but his solos, when they weren't directly mimicking the records they came from, were simple and a little clumsy, sort of like Neil Young, but without the sense of commitment. The classic rock the band played dated from before my time, and just felt kind of bushy and grey, but the band was having fun, and that in itself was infectious. That and the two glasses of white wine helped me forget that I didn't have a place to stay that night.

* * *

After a half-dozen songs or so, the bar was more crowded, and the band took a break. Ethan cradled his guitar on the stage and passed through a crowd of well-wishers, ignoring them, and slid onto the barstool next to mine, kissing me on the cheek.

"I'm glad you're here," he said.

"Well," I said, "I didn't have anything else to do."

"I didn't think you'd come."

"Bullshit."

"Okay, then, I *hoped* you'd come."

I wasn't about to step into the double entendre. "You look good," he said.

"Thanks," I said, resisting the urge to add *so do you*.

"No," he said as he took my hand, and his pale ocean eyes twinkled. "You *really* look good."

"Yeah?"

"Yeah."

I appraised him, aiming at inscrutable.

"You're not going to fuck me tonight, you know."

He didn't even flinch. "Perish the thought," he said.

NINE

Oh, sweet Jesus!

My legs were wrapped around his head as he nursed between my thighs, the wet heat of his tongue coursing through me in burning waves.

Jesus! Oh Jesus!

I ignored the detritus around us—our puddle of clothes, the dead-soldier beer and wine bottles, the surfboard against the wall, the bicycle next to the headboard—and was abandoned to sensation. I had surrendered to it and the alcohol key that unlocked my inhibitions and my own morality. I knew I shouldn't be doing this, I didn't *want* to be doing this, how the *fuck* was I doing this... but *Jesus fuck* it felt good.

I was an idiot, I was a fool, I was a monster. But it wasn't me, really, it wasn't me, I wouldn't be here if it weren't for the fucking wine. Which made it, and me, even worse.

I pulled his face tight against me; I didn't know if I was going to come or not—it had been ages—but it was driving me insane. I hadn't felt this in so long, so long, so long. We rutted madly on the floor of his little clapboard house—more of a shed than a house, really—and I had never felt this naked, this raw, this cannibalistically ravenous for flesh. I needed—truly *needed*— to be penetrated.

The bed was a mattress on the floor, surrounded by apple crates of ragged old LPs, a couple of elderly guitars and stacks of surf magazines.

I was panting, starving, and he lifted his head to breathe, staring directly at me with hungry eyes, his chin gleaming with lady juice. His breath wafted hot and hard against my most sensitive areas. I needed to be kissed, even tasting myself on his lips. So I pulled his face to mine and devoured him. I sucked on his tongue and breathed his breath like a cat.

"I really need to you fuck me," I said, my voice a hoarse whisper.

He stood up, fully aroused, and reached into a drawer on the little end table, fumbling for something. He came back to the mattress and dropped to his knees, tearing open the wrapper and sliding out a condom with thick, nervous man-hands. I hadn't seen one of those in years, as Fredo had had a vasectomy after the twins were born.

As he wrestled with it, the heat seemed to wash from me, and I fully saw what I was doing.

How did I get *here*?

"Fuck!" he burst, fumbling with the rubber, trying to unroll it onto his manhood, which was quickly losing its state of arousal.

I was gasping, still body-hungry, aroused to the point of explosion, though I felt it slipping away.

"God damn it!" He was getting *angry*. "What's the matter?" I asked. "Nothing! Just a minute!"

He was using his hand to make himself hard again, wrestling with the condom, trying to do both things at once.

"It's okay..." I said. But it wasn't. It really wasn't. "I said just a minute!"

I lay back, watching him, going cold as the moon as I watched him struggle.

He finally got the prophylactic on, but he was only half-hard. He dropped to his hands over me and pushed it against me, but it wouldn't go in. It slid all around my entrance, squishy like a fish, and shrank as it tried repeatedly to gain entry.

"Fuck!" he said each time he tried to push into me. "Fuck! Fuck!" But no. No fuck.

Nothing he did with his hands could help the situation, which only pissed him off more.

He leapt to his feet and slammed a fist against the wall, which shook the entire little shack.

"It's okay, Ethan," I said. "We're not in any hurry." His glare into my eyes was frightening.

"It's *not* okay! Just a fucking minute!"

I cowered as he kept wrestling with his manhood. I cautiously tossed out a question. "Do you have any of those pills—"

"I took a fucking Viagra! *Two* of them!" he spat at me. "I said just a minute!"

The more he manhandled his cock, the softer it got. The condom dropped onto the floor with a wet splat.

He hit the wall again. "Fuck!" And again.

And with a "This is bullshit!", he picked up the lamp on the nightstand and slammed it against the wall, shattering it and putting a crack in the plaster. This was scaring the shit out of me.

I scrambled over to my dress on the floor and grabbed it. "What the fuck are you doing?"

"Look, this isn't working. I think it's time for me to go."

"The fuck it is! I said just a minute, okay?"

He was completely limp by now. It was going to be a lot

more than a minute. Those ocean eyes just looked a little crazy now.

"You're scaring me," I said.

He stopped, as if suddenly cured of blindness. "I'm not going to hurt you," he said.

"I'm not sure that's true," I whispered.

I grabbed my dress from the floor and slid it over me as he just watched in silence. I did it slowly, never taking my eyes off of him. He went quite quiet and still, looking as foolish as most men—even good-looking and fit men—do when standing naked and vulnerable and impotent when all they want is to inseminate the world.

He stood there, blue as a marble statue in the shaft of moonlight that reached through the tattered curtains partly opened over the single window. He stared at me, his mouth thin and tight, his eyes unblinking.

I eased the dress over me, and a sudden sensation chilled me. Froze me.

I felt as if I were being watched. Not by Ethan, but by someone, something, greater than that, greater than either of us right now. Something from above.

No, nothing spiritual, no higher power, nothing ecumenical or anything like that.

Watched. By eyes, not conscience.

I looked around the room. We were quite alone. There was nowhere anyone else could hide in this little box. I felt shame, I felt tawdry, I felt cheap, drunk as fuck, self-abused, self- destructive. But I also felt watched.

I stood as I stepped into my underwear, weaving, almost losing my balance, taking my time, cautious, never moving my eyes off of him, and he remained still, his eyes likewise not leaving me.

There was a breath against my ear, and I jerked my head.

"*What?*"

There was nothing there. "What," Ethan said.

I shook my head. Then I stepped into my sandals and picked up my purse, never, ever taking my eyes off of him. He looked like a hand grenade with its pin already pulled. He could explode at any minute.

"I'm going to leave now," I said, not knowing what was going on behind those inscrutable eyes and that tight face. "Okay?"

He nodded slowly, still fully naked in the moonlight, and I kept my distance as I moved a step at a time to the door.

And then the voice. "Mom?"

I froze.

It was light and airy, barely there. More sensed than heard, but it was a voice and that was the word.

Ethan did not seem to hear it, but it locked me into stillness.

"*Mom,*" it had said, so faintly it could have been a heartbeat. But it wasn't. And I knew that voice. It was one of the twins, without a doubt. Too wispy to be able to tell which one, but it belonged to one of my sons.

I kept listening, trying hard to get it back, and Ethan cocked his head as he stared at me.

It didn't repeat. The feeling of being watched did not abate, but the whisper did not repeat. Perhaps it was guilt, after all. And Jesus, did I have a lot to feel guilty for.

I stepped past Ethan, as dressed as I could be in contrast to his Neanderthal nakedness, and put my hand on the rusted old doorknob.

"I'm sorry," he said.

"Me too," I said as I dashed through the door and stole back out into the night. I was almost out of earshot when I heard another crash inside his little jungle hut off the alley.

And then... gone.

* * *

I walked and walked and walked and walked. There was no way I was going to sleep on sand or lawn; I needed a bed and I needed it tonight. The neighborhood was seedy, especially by Santa Barbara standards, and not one I was familiar with. It was late and it was dark, and we were far removed from the tourist havens of State Street and the beach.

I emerged from the funky little working class neighborhood of narrow crisscross streets onto the relative life of Milpas. Night had gone murky, and virtually everything was closed, even the gas station. Still, I walked at an accelerated pace, grateful to still be in possession of my life, even though its value at present seemed questionable. A car passed only every couple of minutes or so, each cast of headlights a threat, something to fear. My eyes were blurred with unspilled tears, and I fought back every urge to sob.

Before long, a lighted sign reached into the blackened sky behind a copse of rangy pepper trees. *MOTEL*, it read in fluttering neon. Or actually *M TEL*, as the "O" had burned out long ago, and the *L* was flickering. No name, apparently, just *MOTEL,* which, at this point, was good enough for me.

It was old and wood-framed, set back from the street and almost hidden. It was draped in ancient brown pepper fronds coating the wood-shingled roof. It hadn't been painted in decades; it was weathered and charmless, and just right for tonight. The door was unlocked, so I stepped into the seedy little office, expecting Norman Bates and taxidermied birds on the walls, but it was dark and empty, with a cracked linoleum counter. The place seemed frozen in the 1950s, except for an ancient computer sitting dark and disused next to the little desk lamp, the only source of illumination in the room. An anachronistic glass ashtray sat overflowing with Winston butts.

"Hello," I called out to the back room, if there were, indeed, a back room.

There was no answer, of course, so I swatted the old-school counter bell with my palm a few times, but the *dings* just rang out and died. As my pupils got accustomed to the dim light, I noticed a grimy plastic button on the wall, with a hand-written sign in felt marker over it that read "*Press bell after midnite.*" I pressed it long and hard, but didn't hear anything. I wasn't sure if it was in working order; from the looks of the place, it shouldn't be. So, I gave it a minute or so, then pressed it again.

I pressed it a third time, and the door behind the counter opened, and a massively obese woman of indeterminate age squeezed through it, fanning her hand in front of her face as if she smelled something horrible. Her clotted grey eyes were magnified into saucers by her inch-thick glasses.

"All right, all right," she grumped, struggling against her bulk to the counter. "Keep your shirt on, girlie, I got the bat signal, okay?"

She was covered by a faded-but-once-wildly-colorful tropical print muumuu, worn through as thin as tissue paper. It was obvious she wasn't wearing anything underneath, as the dark areolas smearing her pendulous breasts were more than apparent through the thin cotton sheath. Her face was like a bleached tomato, colorless but for the purple lips of a cardiac patient, the scraggles of her pepper hair pulled back in a tight ponytail. She was missing most of the top row of her teeth, but her horrendous underbite more than made up for it. She put her hand over her mouth to hide a belch, but it reeked of garlic nonetheless.

"I'd like a room for the night," I said, and she rolled her eyes.

"I didn't think you were here to play tiddlywinks," she said, pulling out a credit card machine: the old analog kind that you had to slide over the card to make multiple copies. "Forty- five plus taxes makes it fifty-two fifty."

"Cash okay?"

She sighed, pulling out a grey steel lockbox, pulled the key on a chain that was hiding between her pendulous breasts, and opened it up.

"Fifty-five plus taxes makes it sixty-three ten."

She took the four twenties from me, counted out my change with her face almost flush with the countertop, despite the Coke-bottle thickness of her glasses. She locked it up again and turned to the wall of keys. None of them were missing, and why was that a surprise?

"Best one I've got is number eight in the back. You won't hear the freeway back there."

I took the key gratefully, headed back through the overgrown courtyard, and unlocked my palace for the night.

The door was flimsy and the bed a lumpy single that hid under a thin, stained blanket and a bedspread that I threw to the floor right away. I wouldn't have wanted a black light in that room.

She was wrong about the freeway; though traffic was light this late into the night, long- haul trucks trumpeted like elephants as they fought their way up the grade to leave town. Now and then a glow of amber headlights or the blood-red fire of receding taillights would seep through the blinds and wash momentarily across the walls, but soon I wasn't going to notice.

I stepped into the tiny cubicle of bathroom, a graveyard of stained and cracked porcelain fixtures and a tiny tub with clawed feet and a mildewed shower curtain.

What had my life become? And in not much over twenty-four hours, for God's sake. I hovered over the toilet seat, unwilling to make contact, and peed and peed and peed.

Exhausted and conquered, I flushed and stepped back into the room and fell onto the bed and into a coma.

* * *

My slumber was subterranean.

I could feel the slashes of light as they roamed my face, but my eyes would not, could not, open. I felt as if I'd dropped into a cave with no floor, plummeting into a darkness so overwhelming that I'd never emerge. Never had I slept so deep. So deep. So deep. Dragged underwater, tied to a bag of stones.

And then…

The weight shifted.

I sensed, rather than saw, the cold light that tickled my face.

I was back on top of that horrible, lumpy, grimy motel bed, consciousness little more than a breath in my ear. I was drooling; I could feel the puddle on my cheek.

I felt the corner of the bed next to my feet sink down with weight and a rusty creak from the sprung springs.

Someone was sitting on the edge of the bed.

I came quickly awake, though my head swirled in the alcoholic fog that filled it, and the room about me swayed and whirlpooled. Using all of my strength to pull myself from the depths of slumber, I grunted and rolled onto my side.

My eyelids were stuck together as if by glue, and I palmed the sleep away and struggled to open them. My vision was blurred, and the room was cast in total darkness, but I could see it.

Someone-- small and silhouetted by the glimpse of moonlight between the blinds-- was sitting on the corner of the bed, watching me.

I gasped and rubbed my eyes, trying to focus, willing my irises to open. My overacting heart was pounding visibly in my chest. The figure was immobile and inscrutable, shrouded by the absence of light, and was fixed on me. The blur was dissipating now, the image sharpening, but the darkness was not going to recede.

I tried to speak, but words became mangled and locked in my throat.

The prehistoric rumble of a semi roared up the highway outside, its headlights combing through the cracks in the window to cast just enough light to make out the features of the shadow that sat so still on the corner of my bed.

"Mom," it said, the word light and drifting to me like a dark breeze. "Why did you go?" It was Edgar, my little boy. The sensitive one.

And he was covered in blood.

TEN

My boy. My baby. "Edgar!" I gasped.

He just looked at me, his eyes unblinking, the whites now crimson with burst blood vessels. I was immobilized by the horror of it, my baby drenched in blood, his face pale and ghastly, his unlined little-boy features evacuated of childhood and joy. Pink tears ran down his face as one hand held onto the side of his head.

"Mama?"

He lifted his hand from his temple to reveal a ragged hole that ran blood. He lifted his hand forward to me, as if to show me something, and I could not help but look at what he offered me. His cupped little hand was filled with blood and what looked like clots of brain.

I screamed and forced myself to sit up, reaching to snap on the light and wrap my arms around him in a single move.

But in the sudden burst of light, my baby was gone.

Stunned, I looked around the room, now empty except for me. Crazy Mama. Crazy, fucked up Mama, on her own and on the road.

What the fuck? I mean, really, what the fuck?

The room reeled, and another diesel brontosaurus thundered past, but the night was otherwise silent. No crickets, no night birds, no bloody little boy. Just me and my guilt, alone in the shittiest motel room in the shittiest motel in Santa Barbara. My only-partially-surfaced mind tried to focus around it, still weighted down by the heft of my sleep. I reached out and touched the edge of the bed where my son had sat, and it felt warm to me. And then I noticed, between the wrinkles, two perfect little red dots on the sheet.

Blood. Still wet.

This couldn't be a dream, surely not a nightmare. And it couldn't be a hallucination.

Right? I mean, *right*? Could you lose your sanity in less than two days?

Or had my mental decline begun long before?

And then the lamp went out. The bulb's ancient filament reached the end of its life, and I was returned to the dark. Except for me, the room remained empty. The shadows did not return my son to me.

"Edgar?" I whispered. "Baby, are you here?"

I don't know which would have been worse: if he *had* answered, or if he *hadn't*. Well, he didn't.

Still, I got up and tottered dizzily to the little bathroom, lightheaded and queasy. I flipped on the fluorescent light, and it stuttered into service. The overhead lighting exaggerated the cruel creases and luggage beneath my eyes, but did not reveal Edgar. The only living thing here besides me was the black moss at the bottom of the shower curtain.

I don't dream. I never dream, at least not so I remember. I've never been wakened by a nightmare before, but I was sure that a nightmare wouldn't linger so corporally into wakefulness. A weight settled on me, a heaviness that was leavened by uneasy fear. I was unsettled, and the sour fright that curdled my stomach made it lurch, and I vomited the tacos and beer and wine into an unlovely, uncontrollable eruption of puke into the toilet, spattering the seat. Its horrible reek made me throw up the rest of it until I was dry-heaving and covered in sweat.

I flushed, but it kept timidly swirling in the toilet bowl, which played with its food as the water rose up, threatening to overflow. It died just below the rim, and I pulled myself back into the room, and sat where my boy had been sitting moments ago, but taking care not to sit on the blood, which remained, spiting me.

Gravity pulled me down onto the bed and the pillow sucked my head deep into its acrylic stuffing, and I couldn't do a thing about it.

* * *

When I woke the following morning, my body fought a revolution against me. It ached everywhere; my head pounded like a foundry, each heartbeat the slam of a ten-ton machine smashing the rock of my brain into pebbles. My eyes were gritty, and my stomach had been overtaken by a furious lion, roaring its disapproval.

I was drenched in perspiration; mascara and foundation were puddled all around my head on the thin, grey pillowcase. The waking was sudden—none of this "where am I?" nonsense of a cheap thriller. I knew exactly where I was. I only *hoped* I had been dreaming.

But no, the reality of my presence in this pit, this melodramatic halfway house between life and death, was all too real.

Hung over by alcohol and despair, still haunted by the visions of the night before, I sat up, pain throbbing throughout my entire being. The room seemed even smaller as the daylight crept through the film noir blinds that couldn't shut it out if they wanted to. Though it wasn't even 7:00 a.m., the eager sun fought its way into the room and filled it. I saw clearly now the water-stained ceiling, the peeling wallpaper (who the hell used wallpaper in the last fifty years, anyway?), the missing chips of paint.

I looked down on the sheet next to me, and there they were: two drops of blood. Who knows? They might have been mine... though I was at least a week away from my period, and had always been pretty clock-like in my cycle. Or, disgustingly, it could have been old... though it was still a nearly fresh crimson, not an aged brown. Surely the sheets had been laundered before the bed had been made up for the next customer. Right? Surely.

Or, it could have been Edgar's.

My bleeding son, whom I had seen so clearly, so absolutely before I fell into a deep, drunken slumber, could have given me a nocturnal visit to blame me for his death.

Which door would you choose?

What would have been the most likely?

I didn't believe in ghosts. I *don't* believe in ghosts. But it all seemed so real.

My purse was on the floor next to the bed, its contents spilled sloppily across the floor. The mirrored face of my new phone, the cheap little burner, reflected a branch of sunlight onto my face, blinding me.

Calling me.

I stared at it, unable to get the image of my bleeding child out of my head. I still felt anchored by chains to the bed, sitting there and unable to stand, feeling I weighed 400 pounds. The glare of sunlight hurt my eyes, the irises wide open and unable to adjust, and I scrunched them tight.

When I opened them again, nothing changed. I was still alone in the empty, grim little room, two dots of blood staring at me like judgmental, bloodshot eyes.

The phone. The phone.

I should call home, just to make sure the kids are okay, I thought.

Really? After barely more than twenty-four hours away? It had taken everything I had to finally make my move to break away, to be free, and already I was second-guessing myself.

But my son! I saw him covered in blood with a hole in his head! Something might be wrong!

The phone lay there, silent but somehow malignant, knowing it had all the answers: the ones I wanted to know as well as those I didn't.

And then, as my cobwebbed brain battled itself in silence, the nasty little burner *rang*, making me jump.

Unknown Caller, the screen told me, and continued to ring.

It couldn't be for me. I just bought the damned thing yesterday, and even *I* didn't know the number.

Still, it continued to ring. And ring. And ring... many more times than any phone should ring before it gives up. But, finally, it stopped, and I was relieved.

Relief was short-lived, however, as it started to ring again, louder this time. More insistent. Dizzy, I reached for it, held it, felling it vibrate in my hand a dozen times before I poked the *talk* button. I didn't even dare say "hello".

There was that dead silence that comes before a robocall begins its spiel, that sense of no connection whatsoever, and then a quick burst of digital static. I was just about to disconnect when, in the depths of that static, I could just barely make out a voice. A distant voice. A *child's* voice.

Edgar's.

I could barely make out the words in the fuzz and buzz. "Mama," it said. "Come home."

And then it went dead.

I was frozen. I stared at the phone, but it was done with me. The voice, and the bed of static that carried it, was gone.

Come home, Edgar had said. My son needed me. Something was terribly wrong. Girding myself, I pecked out our home landline number, hesitant to finally hit the *call* button, but only for a moment. *Click.*

It connected and rang, but voicemail picked it up after the sixth ring. I tried it again with the same result.

Again. And again.

My stomach curdled as I thought about what to do next. I knew what it had to be. I dialed Alfredo's mobile. It rang fifteen or twenty times before going to voicemail. I didn't know what my new phone number was, so I didn't bother leaving him a message. I tried his office, but there was no answer there, either.

Well of course not. It wasn't even 8:00 a.m. yet. Nobody was ever in the office before 9:00.

I tried his mobile again, and once again, there was no answer.

I made the decision then and there: if I couldn't reach anyone in the next hour, I would suck it up and go back home. I had to see if everything was okay.

I was terrified.

ELEVEN

I left the motel before Santa Barbara woke. All was still and quiet, and the sky overhead was darkening as I scurried across the center of Milpas, without a car in sight with the potential to plow me down. I was confused by the silence of the city before I realized it had to be Saturday. The week had ganged up on me in a matter of forty-eight hours or so, and now it was pulling back. I headed across the town, newly met and quickly left, eager to get out, to find out what was happening.

A fat drop of water struck me in the eye, startling and momentarily blinding me. Another one hit my scalp like a shot from a kid's BB gun. And then the pelting began in earnest. Rain was breaking out, suddenly and forcefully, battering at me with the kind of instant storm you find in Southern California, where it rains or it doesn't, with little in between. The rain is increasingly rare in recent years, but when it does break loose, it pummels relentlessly.

I picked up the pace, jogging through the quiet neighborhood streets, heading north toward State Street, rarely passing a soul. The street names were mostly in Spanish here, and none of them were familiar. All of them had pretty little gardens with happy flowers that mocked me as my mind reeled with images of my baby boy covered in blood. Beaten by the rain, I tried calling home and Fredo's cell, but neither of them answered. Of course.

Thunder rumbled in the distance, and the wind started to kick up, too. Every footstep threw up a splash in its wake as I dodged the deepest of the instant puddles that were filling to trap me. The weight of the rain pushed low, dead fronds from the palm trees that lined the road, causing them to fall into my path and trip me.

Nature, it seemed, was trying to stop me. But I was determined to be the irresistible force that would overcome her immovability.

I was soaked to the bone by the time I got to State Street, and found myself standing under the awnings of Mourning Coughee, which seemed to be the only place on the boulevard that was open for business. The rain pattered against the dark green canvas above me, and water flowed off of me in rivers. I squeegeed myself with my hands as much as I could before I rushed through the deserted patio and into the café, wrung gushes of water from my red silk dress.

I entered and rushed straight into the restroom, passing through the otherwise empty coffeehouse like my own storm. Once inside, I attacked the paper towels and blotted my hair dry as well as I could, pressing rough, dry paper against my body to soak up as much of the water that logged me as possible. Then I saw the hot-air hand dryer and triggered it, over and over, standing against its raging dragon breath as it warmed and dried me and my ruined dress, a patch at a time. I wouldn't want to pay their electric bill after this.

Only damp now, I exited the bathroom, as dry as I was going to get, my hair a tangled mess, my face scrubbed free of makeup and mascara, practically fresh out of a new womb, though I still couldn't stop shivering. The intimate little shop was filled with the warm scent of baking and a dense curtain of coffee and cinnamon. It was completely different from when I had been there the day before (Jesus, was that only *yesterday?*): empty of customers, the sky dark through the picture windows that faced the street. The lamplight was warm and spotted in pools around the room, the sun having taken a hike for the day.

I suddenly noticed how hungry I was and went to the counter to find my old friend from the day before doing duty, a vision in tattoo ink tigers and angel wings, her piercings glinting a welcome to me.

"You okay?" she asked with genuine concern. "Um…" I said.

"I know, stupid question. Sorry. What can I get you?"

I was queasy and ravenous at the same time, my stomach empty, but sick at the thought of eating.

"Just a muffin and a black coffee. Please."

She knew better than to ask why I was in such a state. She was young, but had the wisdom of a bartender. At least this time I had the cash to pay for it, though I had to peel the bills from a soggy roll that sat in a puddle in the bottom of my purse. The barista just laughed.

"At least it's water," she said. I conjured a smile that couldn't work itself into a laugh.

Taking my steaming coffee and warm muffin to huddle in a corner table at the window, I watched the storm outside taunt me, rage at me, stand in my way and keep me from moving. I could hardly breathe, still unable to flush my mind of the vision of Edgar drenched in blood with a hole in his head. My brain hated me, and so did I.

I gulped my coffee and felt it burn the pit of my stomach.

I deserved it.

I pulled out the phone and saw that I only had a 9% charge; I would have to make this last. I plugged it into the wall before noticing that there had been a couple of calls I hadn't heard, both of them received after I left the motel: one from Unknown Caller... and another from home.

Fumbling the phone, I dropped it to the floor, where its face cracked. Horrified, I picked it up and dialed home. The cheap plastic face now was shattered, but the phone itself still worked. The number rang. And rang. And yes, rang. The voicemail answered this time, with Alfredo asking me politely to leave a message. I disconnected without accommodating him.

Then I noticed that my friend, Unknown Caller, had left a message of his or her own. I tapped through the cracks to get to it, but it was just noise: hissing and a couple of bursts of crackles, but no voices. I hung up and stood and stared out the window at the deluge outside. It was Biblical. A bolt of lightning lit the sky, and the boom of thunder followed immediately. It was close.

This was just what I didn't need.

I unplugged and stood at the door, hesitant to leave. The barista was watching me; both of us were trying to figure out my next move.

"Hang on a sec," she said, then disappeared into the back room. She emerged a moment later, an umbrella in her hands.

"This has been in lost and found for weeks. Take it."

"Thank you," I said.

The umbrella was a big, heavy one, with a wooden handle and a bright red crown that gave me more protection than I could have hoped for, though my sandaled feet and everything from my knees down were soaked.

I charged down State Street toward the ocean, more swimming than walking, my mind filled with blood and fear. I was washed in guilt, and felt anything but free.

It took me about fifteen minutes to make my way through the curtain of rain to the Amtrak station next to the beach. My timing was good; there was a train to Union Station leaving at 9:27, with a stop in Van Nuys a couple hours later. With luck and a good Uber ride, I could be home before noon. I had about half an hour to wait, so I plugged in and tried calling Fredo's mobile again. No luck. I tried work again, but only got the voicemail before I realized that nobody was going to answer today. It's Saturday, remember?

Another call home, but still no answer.

Then the metallic scream of the braking train arriving at the station snapped me to attention; I grabbed my purse and umbrella, dashed through the canopy of rain, and climbed on board.

Unsurprisingly, the train was nearly empty. The storm had robbed the California tourists of their fabled golden sunshine, so they stayed inside and watched television. I had virtually the run of the train. I settled into the window seat halfway down the center car on the ocean side, and stared out as the train began to crawl out of the station, sneaking behind the Biltmore, then revealing a breathtaking view of the cliffs and the crashing sea that you could never get from the freeway.

Rivulets of rain gouted down the windows like clear blood, warping my view of the virulent Pacific as it raged against the shore. This was so unlike California, mocking every fantasy every Midwesterner ever had about the Golden State. But it is a state of extremes; when it's dry, it's too dry, combustible and malicious. When it storms, its floods overwhelm towns, render roads impassible, and shut down life for millions.

The day was so dark, so fierce, so relentless.

My phone was down to 6%, so I plugged it in and stared at it, daring it to ring again. It just lay there silently, passively, drinking electricity.

I was heading south, running in reverse to where I began, erasing my departure, abandoning hope, giving up. I felt twelve years old, punished, being sent to detention. I had no car, no clothes, no nothing, not even the freedom I had won by abandoning everything. The train was in no hurry, and rumbled down its tracks mercilessly. I could see bolts of lightning flashing between black, heavy clouds over the sea, and the subsequent booming explosions rumbled angrily, scolding.

Then I noticed that I was not alone in the car: a man with long, thinning grey hair sat on the aisle in the very back row. When I turned, he quickly whipped his head back behind his newspaper.

He'd been watching me.

I slunk lower into my seat as the train wrestled up the hill toward Summerland. Before long, I heard the rattling of his newspaper. I slowly peeked between the seatbacks behind me, and saw his paper moving in his hands.

I think he was masturbating.

Sickened, I unplugged the phone, got up and headed into the furthest car from him that I could find.

I settled into my new seat in a completely empty car, plugged back in, and watched the beach towns drift past, the wheels of the train ratcheting rhythmically, hypnotically, reminding my brain of all the sleep I had missed. I was lulled, in that place where characters beckoned you from an upcoming dream, begging you to leave your wakefulness and join them in something impossible.

The character welcoming me into sleep, though, was young and tiny, covered in blood, and had a hole in his head.

That thrust me back into awake, a place I no longer wanted to live.

* * *

The deluge lightened the further south we traveled, but the sky remained belligerent and opaque. Exhausted, hung over, and defeated, the rumble of the train soothed me somewhat.

There were still long stretches of undeveloped land in Southern California, but it wouldn't be long before all of that agricultural acreage would give way to mondo condos and mini-malls, car dealerships and thousand-home "planned communities". It would all be woven into fabric of greed and commerce.

But for now, it calmed me to pass the furrows of orange trees, avocado, and strawberries soaking up the storm.

I'm not going back, I told myself. *I'm just going to check on the kids. Once I know they're okay, then I'm back on the road. I'm going to be smart about the money and credit cards while I'm home, rent a car, and then back to my journey.*

It's only a dream, a nightmare.

Don't let your fear create a roadblock to your freedom, I told myself. *Your journey has only begun.*

I felt stronger as the train gained speed on its southward trek. By the time we passed through Ventura, I was raising my own personal feminist flag in my head again, letting anger overtake the fear that had taken root in the crevices of my brain. By the time the train pulled in to pick up three passengers in Moorpark, the rain had stopped completely. At Warner Center, the clouds actually began to clear, and as the blue sky revealed itself between cauliflower clouds, my mind brightened as well.

Bad dreams are bad dreams, perhaps Freudian warnings, but not openings into the world of the supernatural. My dream mind was acting out, chiding me in Victorian warnings for daring to leave my family. I would see that Edgar and Allen were okay and be on my way. Again.

Van Nuys station is barely a station at all, merely a rail stop with an awning and automatic ticket machines and a parking lot. On this cool Saturday morning, the station was deserted. I was the only passenger to disembark there, and no one else came onboard. The San Fernando Valley felt evacuated, weirdly post-apocalyptic, reflecting itself in the puddles of rainfall that remained in the wake of the storm. I downloaded the Uber app, signed in, and within three or four minutes, a black Prius with a dented driver's side door pulled up, and the silent, middle-aged Korean driver waited for me to let myself in. I climbed in, buckled up, and waited to go, but nothing happened.

I gave him my address in Studio City, and he nodded over and over. I looked into the rearview mirror, and saw that his eyes were locked on me. He didn't look away when our eyes met; he just sat and waited.

"Um," I said. "Can we go now?"

He started up with a jerk that threw me back in my seat, and weaved his way through little Valley street squares, avoiding the freeway, despite its emptiness.

He said something, but his accent was so thick that I had to ask him to repeat himself. I wished I hadn't.

He spoke more slowly and emphatically. "Do you know your lord and savior, Jesus Christ?"

I couldn't believe I was getting this from an Uber driver.

"Please," I said. "Not now."

"If not now, when? Maybe later too late!"

"I'd really rather not talk right now."

He shut up, but he kept looking at me in the mirror with hard, judgmental eyes, all the way down Burbank Blvd., up Laurel Canyon, and ultimately to the scene of the crime. I had already composed the one-star review I would post in my head. I was pissed.

The Jesus Prius disgorged me in front of the house, and sunlight was glinting off of the beads of rain that still clung to the trees. Shimmering in post-storm beauty, the neighborhood was silent, but I couldn't decide if it was peace or foreboding that cast the greater hush. The stillness first calmed, then unnerved me. The Lexus was in the driveway, not in the garage, which I found to be a bit odd. Alfredo was casual about most everything else, but was anal retentive about the cars. To have left the SUV out in the rain wasn't like him.

The house seemed to hold secrets. Why was it so quiet at 11:45 on a Saturday morning?

I girded my courage and went up the stone path to the front door. It wasn't locked, so I walked right in.

There were no lights on inside, and the curtains were shut, so the house was dark. Still.

Not what a Saturday morning should feel like in a house with five-year-old twin boys.

Everything was wrong.

I stepped into the middle of the living room, and the only sound was my breathing.

I walked up to the foot of the stairs. Aside from the usual arsenal of boys' toys strewn here and there, nothing seemed to be out of place.

But that fucking *silence* made me break out in gooseflesh. My motherly spidey-sense knew that there was only something awful lying in wait for me.

The first step on the stairs groaned with pain. Or maybe it was me. But it was a sorrowful, portentous sound. Pausing briefly to see if the sound triggered anything from the silence upstairs—and it didn't—I continued to go up.

At the top of the stairs, it was smell, not sound, that arrested me. Metallic smoke, and a rusty tang gave my nose a slight burn.

The door to the boys' bedroom was slightly ajar; I could see the color-wheel shadows of their nightlight making patterns against the wall inside. Our bedroom door was shut tight. The second floor was much darker than the first.

I walked slowly to the boys' room, stood at the entrance, and the door slowly eased open with a sigh.

On its own.

It was worse than I ever could have imagined. Two boys lay on their twin beds, one in Star Wars PJs and the other in a striped T-shirt and underpants, both of them soaked in blood, which spattered the wall in Jackson Pollock patterns. Edgar's eyes were still open, though clouded. Blood pooled at the base of his little concave chest and clotted and hardened at the hole in his temple. Allan would have looked like he was asleep, his eyes angelically closed and peaceful, save for the hole in his belly. His little T-shirt had ridden up to his chest; the gunshot or gunshots had pretty much disemboweled him, as his little pink tummy had been rent asunder.

I froze in shock, unbelieving, not sure how to register this. It couldn't be real; it couldn't be true. It didn't happen, it *couldn't* happen, not here, not in my home, not to my boys, not in Studio City, not here, not now, not *ever*!

It was a nightmare, I was still on the train, I'd fallen asleep, just like when I saw Edgar in the motel room the night before. Right? *Right?*

Wrong.

I started shaking, frozen on my feet in front of my children, who lay still in death, bathed in their own blood, beautiful children who laughed and cried and could be angels or devils, who could be more than I could handle, yes, but were *children, babies*, and now they were dead. And they were dead because I had not been here to protect them. Tears ran down my face as I crumpled to my knees. I couldn't breathe. I couldn't speak. All I could do was vomit all over the floor and cry.

I held my head in my hands, sobbing, shrouded in the reek of coppery rust and the evacuation of my stomach, realizing that what lay before me was true and real. Death was no longer a secret behind the curtain, an abstract fear, but rather two decimated little boys, twinned, only the hair parted on opposite sides and the gaping, gouting bullet holes differentiating them from one another. I reached forward and touched Edgar's face, and it was horribly cold, and my fingertips left a slight dent in his cheek. Allan's skinny little wrists had always shown standout veins, but not today. They were smooth and white, almost blue. I had to touch him anyway, but wished I hadn't.

The boys were frozen in time.

The blood. The stench. The horror. The silence.

Their blood was thickening, hardening, clotting. They had died while I was seeking release from my tether to them, so this had to be my fault. There was no question. They would not be dead if I had been home to take care of them. Their blood would not be wallpaper patterns dripping down over their headboards. Their hearts would still be beating. They would be laughing or screaming or fighting or sleeping. But they would be alive.

But they weren't. They were lying still, bathed in sticky black blood, their little chests stilled forever.

I bent down and pulled Edgar's immobile corpse to my chest. Never mind the blood, never mind the death. He was my boy and he needed me. I wrapped my arms around him and rained tears into his tousled hair. I squeezed him tight, and he didn't hug me back, for the first time ever. I lay him back down and turned to Allan, who, were it not for the bloodbath, would seem wrapped in gentle sleep. My bodice red in Edgar's blood, I knelt before him and held him tight, kissing his temple, the taste of his blood in my mouth. I savored it.

I lay him back down and stood, dizzy, disoriented, wearing their blood and a cloak of overwhelming sadness, regret, and shame.

Who could have done this? And why? And where was Alfredo when all this happened?

How could he let this happen?

Where was Alfredo?

The question grew horns.

I looked out of the boys' bedroom door and back into the hushed, dark hallway. Our bedroom door at the end of the hall was closed. Before noon. Taking a last look at my lifeless children in their sanguine-soaked little twin beds, I turned and stepped out into the hall.

Daylight crept up the stairs from the first floor, but its glow was dim. My steps into the hallway were clumsy, drunken, hesitant.

Our bedroom door was never closed, especially in the daytime. Our house was never this quiet, and it felt strange, foreign to me.

I got to the door and opened it, slowly, carefully. A wedge of sun broke through the bedroom window, right onto the bed as if it were a spotlight. The honey-color beam presented my husband to me, his back against the headboard of the bed, a gun in a hand that lay palm-up next to him, his head thrown back, and a Rorschach aura of blood and bone chips and matter fanned across the wall behind him, released from the hole at the top of his head like a Roman candle.

My stomach was empty. My heart was voided. What had I married?

And who the fuck was I?

TWELVE

My memories of everything up to that point are razor sharp, but all that happened in the days that followed is a narcotized blur of sleepwalking. The call to 911, the flurry of police activity throughout the house and its conclusion of the obvious: that my loving husband had slaughtered our children in their beds then blown his fucking useless brains out while I was away at a movie. At a movie. At a movie.

Pharmaceuticals replaced thought in my evacuated brain, clouding it with cottony, nonexistent content so that there was no room for dreams of my babies, my often-naughty little handfuls who hugged me so fiercely and would kiss me on the lips when they told me they loved me. No room for all the blood, all the viscera, the pain and all the sorrow. No room for anger, for rage, for depression, for regret. No room to despise my husband--my fucking husband-- who robbed two little boys of their lives, a mother of her sons, and the world of two beautiful little babies. My brainpan was occupied by a hooded thief who evacuated me of everything in my mind and my heart so that I wouldn't hurt so much.

I barely noticed when Fredo's parents barged into the house, his mother screaming and crying, the rosary wrapped around her fist as she cursed her anguish all over me. *Blame me*, I thought. *I deserve it.* And believe me, she did. His father barely said a word, but his eyes were red and rheumy, filled with tears that never seemed to spill, and his breath was rank with tequila.

Me, I had no parents, no family, and honestly, not even any friends, not since Alfredo and I got married. After that, I was no longer an artist, no longer a woman. I became a wife and mother. So now, I couldn't even think of anyone I wanted to call, especially with my mind all boggy and foggy.

* * *

The funeral was, well, funereal.

I hated the bright sun in the cloudless blue sky that mocked the three open graves at Forest Lawn. I despised the primary-colorful sprays of flowers that laughed at my tears. I thought that those rivers had run dry, but discovered that they never would. Salty trickles would spring from the corners of my eyes, unbidden, unexpected, but rarely far away.

Despite the rawness of my heart, antidepressants wrapped it in gauze and it beat to its slow, reverent rhythm, steadily, rarely changing its cadence. I didn't speak, but there was no one there who wanted to talk to me anyway.

Alfredo's mother, father, two brothers, sister-in-law, a couple of uncles and a grandmother all wore the same hateful glare under their tears, as if I had pulled the trigger. My own tears could not possibly match the depth and quality of theirs, their scowls seemed to say. Somehow, they were suffering more than me. More than the mother of the two slaughtered children, more than the woman who put them to bed, bathed them, fed them, loved them, and yes... sometimes hated them.

How could an occasion so dire, so awful, so filled with sorrow and shame and horror be so illuminated by a fearless, joyful sun, be scored by the happy songs of California towhees flitting from branch to branch of the grand, towering oaks? How could something so bleak be so bowlderized by beauty?

The priest nattered on as if he had actually known Alfredo, which he most assuredly had not, and the tiny audience sat stonily beneath his bloviations until it was time to lower the caskets into the eager dirt mouths of Forest Lawn.

I had never been so alone.

I left the canopy of California sunshine and drove back to Studio City, up the winding roads to an empty tomb of a house. I had spent the last few days in a hotel, but as lonely as I felt, there was never a night when I was entirely alone.

I stepped inside for the first time since I had discovered the bloodbath.

The house was spotless. One of those crime scene cleanup companies had scrubbed every trace of the slaughter from view. It was sterile like a hotel room. No toys littered the floors, no Mister Bubble spilled on the bathmat, no Rick and Morty T-shirts hanging off the TV stand.

Rather, all evidence of a pair of lively little boys had been decimated in the process. I stood reeling in the living room, blinds closed, lights off, craving the dark, hiding from the cruel sun. My pupils grew as my heart shrank.

The house was an ogre that wanted to eat me. There was no solace in its quiet darkness. All I wanted to do was sleep, just sleep, and forever was a nice goal.

I stood at the throat of the stairs, but did not have the energy to go up. I just stared into the shadows that dropped off to full blackness, the belly of the beast. I wavered, dropped to my knees on the bare mahogany floor, so shiny that my devastated face was reflected back to me. I could never go up those stairs again.

I walked into the kitchen, filled a glass with water, and took another of those little yellow pills that are supposed to make you feel better.

It didn't work.

I took a blue one next, maybe two or three blue ones, lay down on the couch, and began to drift into a woozy, watery half-sleep. But as they say, there is no rest for the wicked. Just as I was falling off the cliff of slumber, my heart was arrested by distant cries. Still whirling, I sat up. I thought I had not even fallen asleep, but the crust in the corners of my eyes told another story.

That, and the fact that it was now dark outside. There were no lights on in the house, and that was the way I wanted it.

But I didn't want those cries that were calling me from upstairs. Neither could I resist them.

I knew those voices better than anyone knew them. I felt them as well as I heard them.

They were painful, mournful, operatic. I stood and almost fell, the yellow and blue tablets dancing a waltz that spun in my head. I gripped the elbow of the sofa to keep from falling, but the cries from the second floor did not cease. It was clear that they were not going to stop unless I went to them to see what was wrong.

Reeling like a drunken sailor, I grabbed the banister and took my first step up. It groaned with me. I stood still, got my balance, and continued up into the void.

The voices continued to cry, plaintive, desperate, and I followed them, girding myself, knowing full well what to expect.

Their bedroom door was partly open, and the slowly revolving colored lights inside made patterns across the ceiling that leaked out into the hall. I took hold of the doorknob, still reeling, and pulled open the door and stepped into the room. It had never looked so clean, so orderly, so utterly lacking in occupation. All the toys and books and games and clothes were neatly put away, and the room lacked any source of life whatsoever.

The cries had ceased, and the silence, other than the whisper of the light machine projecting the solar system on the ceiling, was complete.

I sat on the corner of Edgar's bed, my eyes filling yet again with tears as I patted the shallow crater that his little body had made in the mattress, and lay down on it, drifting into nowhere land, as the bed sagged next to me and two little bodies rested their weight on it against my own, and told me that they loved me. That they wanted to be with me.

They kissed me goodnight.

* * *

I woke to emptiness, my feet hanging over the end of the child-size bed, the smell of my boys still fresh in my head. Sunlight through the open window poured all over me, thick as honey.

I couldn't bear the silence, I couldn't bear this house, I couldn't bear the thought of blood and viscera and hate and death and sorrow and agony all trapped in this airtight cracker-box family home. It wrapped around me like a straitjacket, bound me in claustrophobic pressure. I couldn't breathe.

I had to be free.

I showered, but still was dirty. I brushed my teeth, but all I could taste was death.

I stood at my bedroom door, not sure I could enter, seeing the crown of blood bloom onto the wall behind the bed. But it was ghost blood I saw. The actual red stuff had been cleaned into oblivion, bleached and obliterated. Alfredo was in his grave. Surely that was not his bulk under the clean sheets on the mattress, waiting for me to turn my back.

Surely.

The Ghost Blood receded into the wall again, and the bedclothes lay slack and inert. No mound beneath.

I rushed to the dresser, and without even looking, threw random clothes into a suitcase, latched it shut, and stumbled with it down the stairs and into the garage.

Back where I had started.

The garage was as dark as the day was bright, so I sat behind the wheel for a moment, awake only in the literal sense of the word. I had lived this movie before, and the only way out that I had ever known was to run. But running is what got me to where I was now, wasn't it?

I started the car, and its throaty rumble vibrated through the seat, charged my hands on the wheel. I pushed the button and the garage door opened like Kharis's tomb. I pulled out onto the street, tailed by voices reverberating.

"Mama," cried the voices of twin five-year-old boys in my head. "Don't go!" I went.

I couldn't help but turn back. Disappearing behind me as I pulled away, two little boys drenched in their own blood stood at the edge of the driveway, watching me go, red tears running down their cheeks.

All I could do was drive, so I drove. Up the coast, past the beaches, beyond Santa Barbara, climbing California like a stepladder, rung by rung, making my way north. I put on music, but it was cloying, intrusive, annoying. I tried talk radio, but everybody was hating everybody so vociferously that it jangled my nerves. I played an audiobook, but minutes would go by where I realized I had no idea what the reader had read. My mind was an exit-only route. There was no admission from outside this rotted brain.

I wished I had two little boys fighting in the back seat over Minecraft, or whatever it was they fought over.

But I didn't. I just had me, and I was shitty company.

So, I drove. California never wants to end. Hour after hour passed; the Lexus took me through San Luis Obispo, Hearst Castle, points beyond. Day lapsed into cloudless evening, evening into the black of night. I wasn't looking for beauty, I was looking for distance, for something I should have known I could never achieve.

I should have known better than to seek freedom one more time, but all I knew how to do anymore was run.

Then, glancing into the rearview mirror, I saw my boys siting there, staring into my eyes, waiting for my gaze. It became apparent at that moment that my boys would always be with me, traveling with me, keeping me company, reminding me that I was the reason that they were dead. I would never sleep alone again.

I could run, but from what?

No one was chasing me; I could not run from what was a part of me, of my own flesh and—especially—blood. My boys were me and I was my boys, and we were inextricably bound.

Highway 1 was narrow and constantly winding as we rumbled further north, traversing cliffs of hellish heights, just a whisper away from a leap into Heaven. Big Sur was a siren calling, summoning us up the skirt of California, giant pines and redwoods tying together wilderness and civilization, thousand-dollar-a-night resorts hidden amongst them for the well- heeled nature lovers in their Teslas to feel like they were living in a real, prehistoric world, the primordial planet that was being killed off, acre by acre, condo by condo, to make room for more stuff, more bodies, more technology, more humanity.

My boys were still in the backseat, staring holes through my head. They weren't in my brain: they were *there*, with me, wordless but unblinking, in their usual seats in the back of the SUV, obediently buckled in, waiting for what was to happen next. Ready to spend that night with me, as they had every night since their slaughter, no, not in my dreams, but in my bed, wherever I was, wherever I tried to sleep. They were with me then, and would be with me every night to follow, love and accusation wrapped together like two hands making a church and steeple.

They sky was slathered with stars you couldn't see from the city, and the moon cast its glow magically, invitingly, as we passed the over Julia Pfeiffer Falls, new asphalt patching the road where it had recently been repaired after having given way—again—to relentless rains that crumpled it up and made it useless every few years.

Allan spoke first. "Stop here, Mama."

I looked at his face in the mirror. He was smiling without a trace of guile.

I pulled the Lexus over onto the crest of the road, high above the tiny beach, lapped lazily by midnight waves below. Quiet. Motionless. Finished.

Edgar spoke next. Little Edgar, the sensitive one, perhaps the one that I, if I were to allow myself total honesty, I had loved the most. The one who needed me most.

"I love you, Mana," he said simply. How could that be?

His stomach was a bloody, fleshy hole, organs torn apart, stinking, evacuated. Covered in blood, heart stopped forever, a memory of a five-year-old from now to forever. How could this stilled, slaughtered, innocent creature even conceive of a word like "love?"

His eyes were pooled with tears that began to run down his little cheeks. Like I said: the sensitive one.

"We love you, Mama," Allan said, completing the circle. And I believed him.

"I love you, too, my babies." I meant it. I'd never meant anything as much as I meant that right then. I loved these little creatures who shared my heart, my soul, my DNA, my biology. "I love you so much."

They climbed over the seat and sat next to me. Edgar took my hand and brought it to his face, wet with his tears. He kissed it, one finger at a time, then held it to his cheek.

Allan, the rowdier troublemaker, was every bit as angelic as his brother. He kissed me sweetly on the lips. Like Edgar, I began to cry. The tears launched wrenching sobs as I felt more deeply than I ever had before. My heart pounded, and I choked on my cries.

"I'm so, so sorry, babies. I love you so much..."

Their eyes were filled with tears as well. The Lexus sat idling on the ridge above the beach, breathing steam into the starlit night like a resting dragon.

"So much..."

The boys were both wide-eyed in innocence, looking for all the world like a Keane painting, so sweet and gentle and open.

I was them, and they were me. We were one, and always would be, for better or for worse.

There is no such thing as free.

"Then prove it," Allan said, taking me by surprise. Blood leaked out of the hole in his temple, and my heart skipped a handful of beats.

"What?" I said.

"You say you love us," he said. "Prove it." My mind

fumbled; I was lost in confusion. "What do you—"

"Prove it!" he shouted, angrily.

But he didn't give me the chance. He stomped his little Keds-clad foot onto mine, slamming the accelerator to the floorboard. The rear wheels of the SUV spun wildly, and the Lexus began to dance in rubber smoke. I slammed my left foot on the brake pedal, but it was too late. Its tires screaming in agony, the car launched, crashing through the concrete guardrail and into a night of unparalleled clarity.

Time slowed and seconds slept into minutes as we took flight. The moon, three-quarters full and pleased with itself, illuminated our family drama, and reflected it onto the Pacific Ocean as we went airborne over it.

My boys stared at me, and I could not separate their anger from their pain from their love.

Their blood flowed anew from their wounds as they gripped me tight in their little hands. We plunged through the cloudless sky, a meteor of life and death, en route to finality, to a different consummation of love and devotion.

I was back on Flight 293, an arrow drawn from the quiver and shot into the center square of the tic-tac-toe game. Aiming to crash and stop the ennui, the pain. Back where this story began, high in the sky and plummeting to earth. But this time, it was not just a daydream.

Eternity opened its jaws and swallowed us whole, as the stars winked in approval. "Love makes you free, Mama," Allan said before we were claimed together as one. *Free*, I thought. *Free*.

Free.

UGLY

I locked the Scagletti with a chirp and headed to the elevator before I noticed the dollop of bird shit right above the windscreen. That stuff will eat right through the lacquer given half a chance, so I poured some Fiji water on it, whipped off my jacket, and polished it away with my shirtsleeve before the chemical action had a chance to work its evil. A four-hundred-dollar Mr. Alex shirt is a small sacrifice when it comes to saving the finish on a three-hundred-grand Ferrari.

I always carried a spare set of clothes in the car, just in case I wouldn't be making it home to Point Dume on any given night. So, I stripped off the shirt, allowing the cool late morning breeze to caress me for a moment before I replaced it. As I slid the clean shirt off of its hanger, I noticed I was being watched by a dark-haired woman in a two-year-old Mercedes S550 that just pulled into the parking structure opposite me. She made no move to exit her car, just settled behind the wheel and her gold Chopard shades, watching me as if I were performing a private strip tease for her.

And perhaps I was.

I had just come from the gym, so I was freshly showered and newly pumped and tanned, and I must say I was glowing. I'd had my chest waxed on Monday, so I was feeling in my prime, and consciously ignored her as I took my time changing shirts and tucking the tails deep into my low-rise vicuna Brioni trousers. I knotted my tie anew, slid into my jacket, and sneaked a look as she finally got out of her car and headed to the elevator.

I don't know why I hadn't recognized her earlier, as she was a client: Evelyn Kilborne, nee Carleton, nee Fassenden, nee Karp, serial wife of the rich and famous.

I had restructured a botched Brazilian butt lift and done her eyes a couple Christmases ago. She looked good, too, her recently freshened breasts free-floating under a loose salmon silk chemise. Had to be forty-two, but looked no more than thirty-five. She smiled at me, and nary a crease marred her perfect visage.

She was beautiful.

The elevator dinged its arrival, and I gallantly ushered her inside first.

"Which floor?" I asked.

"Yours," she replied with a smile that would have been coquettish in a twenty- two-year-old. "I'm scheduled for a peel today."

"Of course." I looked at her creamy complexion. "Take off your glasses," I said.

She obeyed, of course. Being a doctor empowers you in ways civilians cannot imagine.

"You're early for a peel. Your skin is perfect. Don't overdo it, or you're going to lose elasticity."

"Seriously?"

"Seriously." I reached out and stroked her face, and I could swear a heard a soft moan. "You have beautiful skin. Don't abuse it."

"Thank you, Doctor." It grew even more beautiful when she blushed. I find blushes charming.

"Warren," I corrected her. "You and I are way past the 'Doctor' stage." I could practically smell her arousal and sense the clenching of her thighs. "Just ask Jessica for some Guerlain Orchidee while you're here, then make an appointment in three months or so."

"You're sure?" she asked.

"Positive," I answered.

"Well," she said, "you know best."

"Yes. I do."

Right on cue, the elevator reached the penthouse floor with a soft ding, and we both stepped past the subtle little brass *Perfected Nature Clinic* sign and into the lobby of my domain. It was filled with late morning light, Rodeo Drive and Wilshire Boulevard laid out in a golden triangle beyond us. I placed my hand against her back, bare beneath the silk blouse, and guided her to Jessica at reception, plucked my iced soy chai latte from Irena, checked the calendar, and headed back to my inner sanctum. On my way, I heard Evelyn ask Jessica for a parking validation, and shook my head. If you can't afford to pay for parking, then find another surgical aesthetician. Besides, I own the parking structure.

I entered the office and took a seat behind the teak table, buzzed through a half- dozen emails and checked my News Feed, which offered nothing of interest. I shot my usual morning office arrival pic and posted it, then flipped the MacBook closed and turned on the music as I sipped my chai. The office was at a steady sixty-eight degrees, as always, despite the swelter of the Beverly Hills summer.

Irena tapped gently on the door before she entered. She was quite lovely, if not perfect. Her natural blonde hair was a bit wind-tousled and hung down to the center of her back. Her lips were a bit on the thinnish side, but not so much that they needed plumping. Her eyes were of different colors—one green and the other blue, a remarkable example of heterochromia— but it worked quite agreeably on her. She needed just a touch of rhino-shaping that we were already discussing, and it wouldn't be long before a mini-brow lift was in order, but she was holding up pretty well for her mid-30s. The Eastern European accent was frosting on the cupcake. But in truth... she just lies there, expecting pleasure, not really offering it. Our fling was brief and eventless, and she had settled into employee servitude rather gracefully and without drama.

"I saw the board, but give me the highlights for children," I said.

She glanced up at me with a brief gaze I considered wistful, then ran down the day's work. "A mastopexy to begin with at eleven, a couple of peels after lunch, otoplasty on your actress friend at three, and then a phalloplasty to finish the day."

"Nothing like a little phalloplasty to finish the day. Enlargement?"

"Oh, God, no. Just aesthetic shaping. Eric Hardy. Vivid is sending him over."

"Right, fine. I'm a little concerned about starting the day with a mastopexy, though. I'd rather have begun the day with the peels, then work up to the surgeries."

"Of course," she said, unwilling to be chastened. "But this was last minute, you had an opening, and she is paying a premium."

Irena understands how the game is played, which is why I keep her around. She's good at this. But we will have to get that nose perfected sooner rather than later. It reflects badly for clients to see someone working here who is less than flawless. And it distracts me.

"Great, thanks, Irena."

She accepted her dismissal with a smile and left a wafting breeze of Caro's Poivre in her wake. I breathed deep of her wake, downed the dregs of my latte, and went in to scrub up for the day's first procedure.

Keep the stitches tight and tiny, that's my secret. Vitamin E is bullshit when it comes to erasing scars; just keep from keloid scarring in the first place, don't plunge into the flesh like a butcher, put the pieces together with care and precision, and you can assemble the parts with perfection. There are various emollients that will keep the skin supple and vibrant, but it's the cutting-- at an angle to overlap and layer the pieces together when it's time to suture them-- that's important. I can—and will— sell you very expensive creams that will be good for your skin, but it's the deftness of the surgeon and the creativity of his blade that makes the difference. They come out from under my knife better than any higher power could create. *He* makes them human; *I* make them *perfect*.

The first patient of the day was a case in point. Haley Weathers was 26 and had already birthed a couple of babies. Obviously, that's none of my business, but if you're going to have babies, don't expect to be perfect. Your belly will stretch and your breasts will enlarge, leaving loose skin and drooping flesh behind. I'm just saying. But she wanted a litter, and like I said, that's none of my business, though it certainly does *contribute* to my business. Being so young, the ravages of childbirth had left her in surprisingly good shape. She'd obviously been keeping up a regimen at the gym, so her tummy looked good. But the breasts were deflated and hung low on her chest. They needed a boost, and they needed it now. There's not a lot you can do about the stretch marks, but I could make them pert again. I mean, Photoshop is fine, but not if you want to do the talk show circuit. HD cameras are merciless.

They'd been nice breasts, to be honest. And size was certainly not an issue. We didn't need to enhance them, so there would be no implantation going on. But the lift itself could bring her back to the catwalk, even in the nude, with the right amount of body makeup. She had been a beautiful young woman, but with these bags on her chest, well, it was hard for me to take. It made her downright ugly.

I was able to lift and define them with very little sculpture, actually. Within about eighty minutes, they had become twenty-six-year-old breasts again, saluting at full attention, beautiful and perfect all over. I smiled as I checked out my handiwork. Some tweaking, a little gravity defiance, and in a couple of hours I'd just clocked in another $17,000. And it was just the first procedure of the day.

Fuck James Cameron; *I'm* the fucking king of the world.

It is my job to make the world more beautiful, more aesthetically pleasing, to take what nature provides and make it better; to stave off the ravages of illness, age, and gutter luck, to take a giant rock and turn it into a beautiful sculpture. Beauty is not just a matter of taste, either, no matter what the unattractive may say.

Symmetry, color, smoothness and shape are not subjective. They've done all kinds of tests that prove it. Give little babies a choice between beautiful faces and ugly ones and they'll choose the pretty ones every time. It's science.

I went into my bathroom to wash up after the surgery and looked at my own face in the mirror. Nature had been generous to me: the symmetry had been laid out as if on an artist's grid; if you held a mirror to the middle of my face—as I have done on numerous occasions—it would look the same as it does on its own. The pores on my nose had been a bit generous, but it wasn't difficult to shrink them with a simple combination of astringents. The nose itself was noble and sturdy, and I was blessed with a full head of nearly blue-black hair, as well. I let it grow long to give me the look of an artist; some might call it my "Fuck You Haircut." My eyes were an even blue, the color you would choose if you were looking for tinted lenses. When I smiled, I had dimples, but no laugh lines. My eyes might crinkle a bit in laughter, but there were no crows' feet. It would be a good few years before I would have to do anything about them. But I'd been keeping an eye on one area of concern. Two very light lines seemed to be crossing my forehead. I had to nip that in the bud, so I got the syringe and a bottle of Botox and made the injections then and there. I massaged my forehead, applied a light dusting of a custom powder I'd had made that was a perfect match to my tanned summer skin, and I was ready for the rest of my day.

I'm proud of what I do, and the world is a much better place because of it. At the middle of the day, I decided to walk a couple blocks to the Grill on the Alley for lunch. It was a noisy, active place that was filled with an older Beverly Hills crowd, Hollywood agents and their beautiful clients, and I enjoyed the energy and the buzz of the room. There would be a fair share of tourists there, as well, but Beverly Hills tourists are a slightly higher caliber than the ones in Hollywood, and they'd settle for the tables off in the hinterlands where no one would have to see them when they ate. Fortunately. Inhabitants of the fly-over states seem prone to eating with their hands.

So, I settled into my usual booth and ordered the John Dory and a vodka Arnold Palmer. I sopped up the bread in a puddle of olive oil and burned through my texts and emails on my iPad, when Randy Setwell marched right up and slid tightly into the snug booth, snagging the tablecloth with him and yanking it away as he sat down. He apologized and fumbled to put everything in its place before one of the attentive busboys took the job in hand and smoothed it all over in seconds. Randy was embarrassingly overweight, and his face was flushed and sweaty—not just now, but all the time. His chipmunk cheeks and weak chin were forested by a formless graying beard, and his thick horn-rim glasses shrank his violet eyes into beads behind them. He reached his hand out to shake mine, knocking the water glass over in the process. The busboy, who was keeping a careful eye out for just such an incident, was quick to mop it up.

I couldn't avoid shaking Randy's hand, and it was soft and moist. It was hard to keep my gorge down, but I did my best to be civil with him. Part of my future may well rest in his hands. But I did hope that he'd finish before they brought my food.

"Hey, Warren, I was hoping I'd run into you!" he exclaimed. He seemed only to speak in exclamations.

"And bingo! Wish granted!" I said. "You have two more."

"I'm keeping those a secret!" he riposted. I didn't give a shit.

"What's up, Randy? Any news?" Randy had produced our pilot, THE KNIFE, a reality show that followed me around and recorded my life.

"Bravo is close!" he, well, exclaimed. "If we can make the numbers work, I think we're home. E! wants a shot, but I don't think they can come up with the dollars."

"That is good news," I said. We'd shot it at least six months ago, and I just assumed that it had died the ignoble death that the previous four pilots centered on me had succumbed to.

"There's one thing that I think would really push it over for them," he said, leaning in closer, as if we were friends or something.

"What's that?"

"A name. If we could shoot a procedure with one of your celebrity clients, then I think we're there."

"If I shot a procedure on one of my celebrity clients, they would no longer be one of my celebrity clients." You'd think it was obvious.

"It doesn't have to be someone in their prime, you know! They like washed-up TV stars! It's even better if their lives are already humiliating! You know, get a David Hasselhoff to get pec implants or something and they'd eat that shit up! Somebody like him would piss on his own mother to get back on TV!"

"I don't know, Randy, my business is a bit more, well,

refined than that."

"It might be the difference between your own television series and no television series."

"I've driven this highway before, Randy. The clinic grossed seventeen million last year. I don't *need* a TV show."

"You get this show and you'll gross double that next year."

It gave me pause.

"Double?"

"Doctor Beverly Hills *doubled* his clinic's gross in the first year after he went to air."

"Shit."

"No shit."

He grinned. There was spinach between his teeth, which were widely gapped. Braces, Bleaching, and Bonding would get him started. "Just think about it, would you?" he said. "Suzanne Somers butt lift; Kirstie Alley lipo; Tara Reid boob job; Bridgette Nielsen facelift; Steven Seagal penile implant. That's great fucking television!" He was exclaiming again.

I was fast losing my appetite. His entire body was quaking in excitement, from his man titties-- which were doing their best to hide the huge swathes of sweat under his armpits-- all the way to his belt, which was straining against the earthquake of his belly. Spittle was collecting in his beard.

"You're putting me off my lunch," I said.

"Not all of 'em," he assured me. "But if you get just one, it's a home run. Just promise me you'll think about it, okay? They're gonna want an answer by Monday."

"Okay," I said. Anything to get him to leave the table.

"Promise? Pinky swear?"

"I promise," I promised.

He left, a shit-eating grin devouring his face. I thought about it. Then I was done thinking about it. No fucking way. Not unless they financed the whole season up front.

At that moment, Eric appeared with my John Dory. I took a big gulp of the vodka Palmer and stared at the fish and broccoli trunk. I couldn't eat it. Looking at ugly people makes me literally nauseous. Randy's grotesquerie actually pissed me off. I mean, we all have a choice about the flesh sheaths we wear. I couldn't understand how he could allow that pork rind jacket of fat to keep building up around him, squishy and sweaty and smelly, despite the antiperspirant. Unkempt hair, grotty fingernails, thick glasses. I found it hard to be around those so lacking in pride that they polluted their surroundings with their presence. Get on the fucking treadmill, lay off the breakfast burritos, get some Lasik and manscaping and you might improve your life... if not *mine*. I realized I was starting to growl, and I was not about to let this... this *producer* poison my day. I had to get the fuck out of there and breathe.

I normally keep out of the sun as much as possible, but the Southern California ball of fire beckoned so romantically that I could not spurn her call. The minions were out on Rodeo Drive, and I was happy to walk amongst the Look-At-Me darlings as they promenaded the boulevard in their slinkiest, most revealing summer togs.

Nature and nurture had proffered up some prime examples of humanity, draped and polished and primped to perfection, displayed for my appreciation, and the bad taste was rapidly wiped from my mouth. It was my duty to give them my attention, and I was glad to abide. At its best, the human form was the greatest contribution of art the world had to offer.

When it is properly attended to and presented, human flesh is magnetic, sleek, electrical. When it glows with a healthy, smooth, even sheen, I just want to rub up against it like a cat, to breathe it, to taste it. I get all tactile. Several such bodies strode past me on the Drive today, and the blend of the palate of skin colors and scents was heady. It made me smile. It was not entirely sexual, but it was difficult to remove beauty from the realm of the sensual, from the desire to touch and stroke and penetrate such loveliness. It was primal, even primordial, beyond intellect; emotion that bordered on the Jurassic.

Though I am quite comfortably heterosexual, I could also appreciate a well- turned-out member of my own gender. I didn't want to fuck it, or even touch it, but I could certainly enjoy a good-looking man with a tight, molded body in an artistic sense.

Surrounded by sterling examples of the human race as they meandered restlessly from *boîte* to jewelry salon, I grew happy, content, even delighted. The sun was high, there was a subtle breeze rustling the palm fronds overhead, and I was surrounded by prime cuts of well-pampered humanity in the balmy Beverly Hills heat. Life was good. I decided to celebrate with another latte; I'd get it ice- blended this time.

I wandered a few blocks over to Cañon and into the Namaste Tea Room, not willing to be defiled by such corporate refreshers as Starbucks or Peet's; I was in that good a mood. The place was deserted when I entered, and there was a hush barely enhanced by the gentle sounds of Tibetan bells. The lights were dim, but the place was obviously open for business. There was no one behind the counter when I entered, which was strange. There was a little brass bell on the counter, and I picked up the tiny wooden hammer and rang it.

I heard movement from the back room, then someone emerged in a shambling silhouette to the counter.

"I'm sorry," it said as it moved forward into the beam of light spotted from overhead. "I didn't hear you come in."

Her appearance froze me. It was a young woman, lumpen

in shape, with limp, unwashed, dirty blonde hair that hung listlessly over her eyes, which were heavy- lidded and hazel. But most notable was the very center of her face, a nasty proof that there is no God: it was made even more repellent by a cleft lip that had been hastily sewn up in some third-world patchwork, leaving her visage deformed and hideous. What would have been shocking in Pacoima was truly repulsive in Beverly Hills.

I could barely keep my gorge down.

I wanted to leave the store, but I was frozen in place by her unexpected appearance. We looked each other in the eye, our gazes locked, hers unblinking and seemingly thoughtless. I'm sure my own eyes were wide with shock and disgust, but she was no doubt used to that, if she were allowed to go out in public.

"What can I do for you?"

I felt my stomach rumble and my throat constrict. But I reacted slowly and by rote. I stuttered and spat out my order: "I'll take an organic masala chai with vanilla soy, ice blended, please."

She looked at me as if I were speaking a foreign language, trapping me in her sloe-eyed gaze. I repeated it, though God knows I didn't want this creature preparing anything that I might actually intend to *ingest*. "Organic masala chai with vanilla soy, ice blended."

"How do you make that?" she asked, speaking distressingly through her nose.

"I'm sorry," I said. "Do you *work* here?"

"Not usually," she snorted. "But Uncle Ryan is in the hospital, and Mom had to leave suddenly. She couldn't reach Sheila or Amy, so that leaves me."

She looked at me through the hank of hair that curtained her muddy hazelish eyes.

I started to feel a bit dizzy. Even from a distance I could feel the air as it blew from her nose like a bull, so I backed away a few steps.

"What was that again? Organic chai, right?"

"With vanilla soy, ice blended."

"I can do that."

I suddenly really didn't want that. I could see that she bit her nails to the quick.

"You know, I think I'll come back when the regular staff is here. I'm pretty particular about my lattes."

"No, please, let me do that. I can do that." She slipped on some clear plastic gloves and started rummaging through canisters of tea, cartons of soymilk, and various powders and syrups. She kept her eyes on me throughout the process, and I felt unable to escape the otherwise empty parlor. It was starting to creep me out.

"Iced?" she asked.

"Blended," I replied.

She dumped everything into the blender, then threw in a cup of ice and fired it up, watching me without blinking as the machine ground away in an annoying metallic roar. Soon the process was complete, and she set it down in front of me in a tall glass.

"I'm sorry," I said, "I meant this to go."

"Oh," she said, watching me through the eyes of a basset hound. The lower lids gaped wide and pink, like Malcolm McDowell in A CLOCKWORK ORANGE when he's forced to watch filmed sexual acts without being able to blink. "Go ahead and have a seat. What kind of music do you want?"

"No, really, just dump it in a paper cup and I'll take it with me."

"It's awfully hot out. You sure you don't want to have it here?" Totally sure. "That's okay. I'll take it with me."

She stared at me for a moment, motionless, then pulled out a paper cup and poured the concoction in and lidded it in cornstarch plastic. She handed me a paper straw and I poked it in as I paid her.

"Taste it," she said. "I want to make sure it's okay."

"I'm sure it's fine," I told her, just wanting to get the fuck away from her before I threw up.

"Just to make sure. I can make you another one if it's not perfect." Perfect. She said *perfect*. As if she had any right to even use the word. But I just wanted out, so I took a sip.

It was actually pretty good.

"Is it okay?"

"Very good, thanks."

"You sure you don't want to have it here where it's nice and cool?"

Nice and cool sounded horrible when spoken through her nostrils. I took another long sip just to not have to look at her.

"No, I'm in a bit of a hurry."

"It's hot out there."

It was. I was suddenly feeling a bit twirly, just slightly off-balance. Maybe the heat was more extreme than I had thought.

The taste of cinnamon was heady, really delicious. And the frozen blend slid down my throat like a soothing snake. I grabbed the counter for a second as my mind filled with helium. My body took a step, but my head stayed behind. She gaped at me, and her gaze felt like a slimy blanket.

I felt *hot* all of a sudden, and the only thing that might fight off the fire was the icy latte. I took another long pull and swallowed. Brain freeze. A spike of pain stabbed me between the eyes. Something was really, really wrong. I was starting to feel nauseous. I took the drink and stumbled toward the door. But I couldn't hold onto it; it slipped from my hands and spattered the floor in a wide, wet, mahogany pattern. My foot slipped in the latte, and I sprawled on the linoleum. What the fuck was going on? I wondered if I were having a stroke or something.

I pulled myself to my feet, wavering like the ancient mariner, feeling as empty as a hologram. As I reached for the door, I heard a hard, metallic *clank*. When I reached out to push it open, it was *locked*.

I turned around in slow motion, reeling, and saw the repellent creature behind the counter staring at me. Even more repulsive, she was starting to *smile*. Her teeth were horrifically staggered.

"Maybe you should stay," she said, happily.

I tried to shake my head, but it was too heavy to budge. I tried to speak, but my tongue was thick and my lips couldn't form the words. I just gulped and floundered like a goldfish dumped from its bowl onto the floor. And then this *creature* shambled out from behind the counter and crossed the room, her shadow growing as she drew closer until it devoured me. She turned off the lights, put the *Closed* sign in the window, lowered the curtains, and squatted down next to me.

"You're pretty," she told me.

I tried to tell her that she was *not*.

She stood over me on the hardwood floor, her flower-print dress ruffling in the air-conditioned breeze. It opened before me, revealing dimpled cottage cheese thighs that gathered about her knees, and I forced my head to turn so that I could look away. But it was too late to un-see what I had seen. She knelt to her naturally padded knees, staring deeply into my face. I turned, but she took my head in both her hands and forced me to look at her. It was not a pretty sight.

She just kept staring, a strange delight lighting her murky, half-mast eyes. I could barely focus on her, which was a relief.

I could feel my nostrils closing up as my face started to feel flushed. I had to breathe through my mouth. A bluish tint seem to settle over the room, and when I turned my eyes, even in the dimness, all the images seemed to have the lag of a cheap video camera.

Then she stood, and I noticed for the first time that she was wearing a nametag. This being was called *Brittany*. I couldn't move; well, I could wriggle and jerk a bit, but nothing that required any kind of control. My body was flushed with heat, and I felt a tingling running through my veins, centering in my crotch. Unbelievably, the center of my being was feeling arousal.

Brittany picked up my feet and started to drag me across the floor. The vicuna slid effortlessly across the polished oak, so it took no particular strength to move me. Her palms were hot and clammy, even through my socks, but her grip was firm, deft, committed. She pulled me to the thick leather couch in the quietest corner of the room. Once there, she gathered herculean strength and actually rolled me up onto the couch. I'm six foot three and weigh about one-ninety-five, so that was no mean feat. She had the strength of the gorilla she resembled.

She was panting with the effort, and I lay on my back into the thick, squeaking softness of the divan, helpless and hard, staring up at her. She wiped her brow with the back of her hand and looked at me, the smile dropping from her face like a lead weight. She stared, still breathing hard through her nose. A bubble inflated and deflated from her left nostril before it burst and she wiped it against her sleeve.

Then she reached out and touched my face, as if she were Zsa Zsa Gabor in QUEEN OF OUTER SPACE, where the female inhabitants of the planet have never seen a man before.

I had no idea what she had planned for me, but it was a plan that was hatched spontaneously. She could not have known I was going to come into the shop; I didn't even know myself until I was strolling down Rodeo. But here I was, drugged and at her mercy, her swampy, fetid breath gusting out of her mouth now against my face and nothing I could do about it. And with the constricting of my nasal passages, the flushing of my face, and the stiffening of the most private part of my anatomy, it became obvious to me that that narcotic latte had obviously been spiked with Viagra.

Brittany reached down and undid my tie, sliding it out from under my collar and dropping it to the floor, staring me in the eye without blinking the whole time. Then she rolled me over and slid off my jacket before returning me to my back. One by one, she carefully unfastened the buttons of my shirt, opening it and running her damp, stubby hands over my immaculately groomed chest. The horrid intimacy of her skin against mine curdled me; I felt invaded, despoiled. I tried to pull away, but had lost control of my motor system and just had to lie there and take it.

Then she took her hands away and stood over me, looking down at me. It was a relief, as if I were being released by a squid.

Finally, she spoke.

"Do you think I don't see your contempt?" she asked me, surely not expecting an answer.

"Do I repel you?" Again, it was surely a rhetorical question, as I had lost any ability to reply. "Well, what a shame. You repel me."

Ha. As if.

"I'm sick of the way you look at me. Every time you come in it's the same."

Every time? I'd never seen her before.

"You don't see me, you look away. You spoiled, arrogant, rich, pretty slimeball."

Yeah, the spoiled, arrogant, rich, pretty slimeball she wished she could have.

That *any* woman wished she could have. But I would not be had, and certainly not by the troll under the bridge, even in my worst nightmare; I would only *have*.

Unfortunately, she was in control now. To my horror, she reached down and unbuckled my belt. After pulling off my shoes, she whisked my pants down and off, and they nestled softly on the floor. My private parts rebelled against me, engorged and raging, pharmacology and primal pulse fighting the true repulsion I felt, raised in mutiny like a flag. She stripped my boxers off as well, revealing my staff as it hovered proudly an inch or two over my stomach.

She looked at it as if she had never seen anything like it before, and surely she hadn't. It *pulsed* with the pounding of my heartbeat, and she just watched it bounce. I tried to roll off of the couch, but I didn't have the control, and she wouldn't let me. All at once, she *backhanded* it, and it hurt. It did not, however, diminish its pressure, which maintained its proud stature. She watched it wave back and forth like the Queen of England in a parade.

I was terrified to think what might be coming.

"You want me, don't you?" she asked in all seriousness. Then she broke into howls of canine laughter.

"I disgust you, don't I?"

I wouldn't have answered even if I could.

She slapped me across the face—*hard!*—with the back of her hand.

"*Don't I?*"

She knew she did. And I feared what was coming.

"Good."

Then she grabbed my manhood, gripping it in both hands, so hard that it hurt. The head was so red it was almost purple as she squeezed it. Then she let it go. I was barely breathing, my eyes clenched tight. But my relief would be short-lived.

When I opened my eyes, I saw that she was stepping out of her king-sized underpants. They were flowered cotton, big, ass-covering granny pants that dropped to the wood floor with a thud.

No. Please, no.

Still dressed, other than her pantaloons, she climbed up to stand over me on the couch, the leather squeaking under her wide bare feet. I cowered from the view of her thick, matted black web of pubic hair, tried to turn away, clenched my eyes as tight as they would close. And then, to my absolute horror, she lowered herself and, using her hands, guided me into the thick, pungent entrance to her horrible, dank cavern.

Oh, God, the horror! The horror!

She stared at me the entire time as she raised and lowered herself onto me like a Thanksgiving Day parade balloon. She was expressionless, just staring, glaring, *watching* me as she rocked and I helplessly penetrated her. When I tried to look away from her she grabbed my face in both her hands and forced me to look her in the eye. Her face grew flushed and she began to grunt, but never took her eyes from mine, fixed and focused as she sped up the movement.

It was horrible. Her loose, flaming hot and perspiring flesh was slapping against me with a sharp, ghastly spanking sound, feverishly building toward her own personal detonation, and my Waterloo. Faster and faster she pounded, her eyes never leaving mine and never blinking, her breathing accelerating, blasting me with the furnace of her dragon breath. When I would try to close my eyes, she would pull them open with her blunt, nail-chewed fingertips to make me watch. I couldn't believe that my manhood would betray me like this, that it would not only remain rigid and questing, but that it would build in intensity, as if I were fucking a perfectly fashioned runway model rather than the beast from the haunted cave.

Faster and faster, and she became disgustingly more lubricated. And then, certainly without intending or even wanting to, I—or more accurately, a singular mutinous portion of my anatomy—ignited within her squishy-squashy body. She smiled a Mona Lisa grin as she started to buck, achieving her own personal nirvana. My bastard member continued to contract spastically as she trapped me tight in her clamshell grip. Her eyes closed at last as she allowed her body to be overtaken by her orgasm, and shook, quivering as it raked over her, seemingly overwhelmed by its power and magnitude.

Finally it subsided, and I could feel my head begin to clear. I lay on the couch, stuck to the leather by a layer of perspiration, as she climbed off of me and looked at the sticky, still chemically rigid pole that would not subside. She grabbed some napkins from the front counter to clean herself, then climbed back into her voluminous underpants. Then she gave me the finger, tossed a pile of napkins to me, though I was unable to do anything with them yet, and walked away.

"You can let yourself out," she said as she held up some kind of remote control, unlocking the front door.

Then she went behind the counter and into the back room, closing and locking the door behind her. I could only stare at the door, devastated, violated, sickened.

And now, at last and for the first time, impotent.

I had seen horrifying things in my profession—the flap of a face removed by a car crash, a zookeeper's midsection mauled by a chimpanzee that wanted its toy squeaky monkey, a beautiful teenager's face and chest rotted away by a flesh-eating bacterium—but watching my fluids leaking out of Jabba the Hut, seeing her turn from me with the glow of satisfaction as she tossed napkins on me to wipe away the residue of my fouling by her... it was by far the most horrific of all. The first thing that happened as my body began to return control to me, as the effects of the drugging began to fade, was to vomit painfully and repeatedly all over the floor of the teahouse. I wiped myself furiously until I was raw, but it was never enough to feel clean. When I could stand, I rushed to the door of the back room, pounding on it with everything I had. If it had not been made of steel, I'd have shattered it.

But the shop was quiet, and I stood there in my unbuttoned shirt, my member a flesh compass pointing out the guilty. I sobbed with fury, but was alone and powerless. I slid into my clothes and out of the shop, radiating hate and anger. I rushed quaking through the sunny streets of Beverly Hills, hiding from the gaze of all around me. I felt empty and foul.

I rushed right to the car park, phoned Jessica and told her to cancel the rest of the day's appointments, and tore out of the building like the proverbial bat out of Hell.

I turned left on Santa Monica and found myself trapped in the plaque of Beverly Hills' most clotted artery. I fumed and shouted and tried to weave my way around the lazy, otherwise preoccupied assholes that blocked my way home. The Scagletti squealed as I pulled it up onto the sidewalk and ripped around the sludgy traffic that taunted me, took Beverly up to Sunset, and tore ass toward the beach.

At least, that was my plan. But the traffic here was dire as well, and I just had to sit and crawl with the proletariat, inching my way towards Dead Man's Curve, cursing the gods, my stomach empty and screaming, my privates raw and prickling. They seemed to be crawling, *alive*.

There are no shortcuts heading from East to West in LA; every road is over- burdened, impossible and impassible. You just have to sit and wait, especially while they're rebuilding the 405, which is fucking *always*. I tried the radio, but could not stand music right now, and the talk was dominated by the screeching right-wing maniac harpies that made me want to kill myself when I was in a *good* mood.

So I suffered in silence under the relentless sun of a Southern California summer, filled with hate and loathing and fury and disgust. It only bloomed as the car, which was built to blur, crawled along behind fume-belching Chevys and Fords and countless other pieces of shit that didn't deserve to share the road.

By Westwood, I was filled with vehemence; by Brentwood, I wanted to smash into every car that was in my way; by the Palisades, I wanted to blow my brains out; and by Malibu, I was ready to kill. I truly felt capable of taking a life. One certain life

I pulled into the driveway as the garage door opened its maw, then drove inside and let it swallow me. I sat in the car, quaking, furious, my hair matted by the wind. Finally, I climbed out of the Ferrari, slamming the door behind me, and did the same with the door into the kitchen.

The house was still and quiet. The distant sound of the waves crashing against the cliffs below the house tried to calm me, but nothing was going to extinguish the venom that was coursing through my veins. I charged into the bedroom and tore my clothes off. Even the grandness of the setting sun outside the French doors of my bedroom could not wither the anger that festered within me. The sky turned bright orange and the scuds of clouds flamingo pink, but they left me unaffected. Once stripped, I went into the bathroom, turned the shower on as hot as it would go, and stepped in under the scalding spray, soaping and scrubbing the detritus of her attack off of my body. The bathroom was all windows, allowing me a full view of the cliffs of Point Dume as I bathed, and I watched the sun sink into the sea along with my heart. The purloining of my manhood, my success, my testosterone, my singularity and my very *being* by this beast, this creature, this curdled mutation, would not go unavenged.

I turned on the 80" OLED, but it was just colors, bright and annoying, a screeching cacophony of voices and images that just jumped all over the place, yelling at me before they ignited into headache–inducing surround sound explosions. I turned it off and switched on the stereo, but it too grated rather than soothed.

Off. Silence. Solitude.

I could see myself reflected in the glass that made up most of the exterior walls facing the ocean. It was hard to tell by looking what had happened to me, which was a good thing. I couldn't stand to see myself staring back at me so plaintively, so I turned off all the lights and sat in darkness as the Pacific Ocean swallowed and doused the fiery sun, then turned silvery as it reflected the emerging moon. I cracked open a prized bottle of special-occasion Ladybank single malt and sipped at it, but even that burned as it went down. I gave up and climbed out of my towel and into bed, where I lay awake for another hour or two before finally throwing back an Ambien tablet. After another sleepless hour, I swallowed another. In another ten minutes, I was asleep, thankfully dreamless.

The early return of the sun awakened me the next morning, and I spent a blissful three minutes of consciousness before remembering what had happened to me. So I rose, made a smoothie and ate my granola with vanilla almond milk, and jumped back into the shower, needing to be cleaner, ever cleaner. I shaved and noticed that my crotch was still prickling.

I hoped that it was because it was time for my pubic waxing, and not because I'd *caught* something from the creature called Brittany. So I shaved there, and once it was smooth, the creepy-crawlies ended. The ones inside, on the other hand, wriggled through my brain like earthworms.

Showered, shaved, and exfoliated, I dressed and wore the face and costume of the prosperous and popular Beverly Hills cosmetic surgeon that everyone knew. Into the Scagletti, out of the garage, and eventually onto Sunset, which was remarkably light on traffic.

The air at the beach was still cool, and it felt restorative as it blew through my hair. My gorge was settling as I wound my way across the West Side, racking up imaginary points as I zoomed through imaginary Brittanies all the way to Beverly Hills.

I pulled in to the parking garage and sat there in the rumbling Scagletti, filling the concrete tower with high-octane fumes. Finally, I put the top up and powered down, locked the car with a chirp and headed to the elevator. I pushed the button and waited. And waited. And waited. I pushed it again. And again. And again. I snorted through my nose, then pounded on it like a banshee, slamming the side of my fist against the button until it turned red and bruised. Fucking piece of shit! I kicked it, and kicked it again, and again; but it resisted all my persuasions and just pissed me off. I yelled at it in growls and howls, not words, then resigned myself to the stairwell, which, even in Beverly Hills, smelled like urine.

My A. Testonis clanged hollowly but musically as I made my way up the metal staircase, which was an escalating oven, hotter and hotter the higher I climbed. By the time I reached the penthouse, I had perspired all the way through my shirt and into the pits of my Caraceni, making the sweet, almost floral natural scent of its Venetian wool reek. I would not wear it again.

I was in a foul mood when I finally entered through the whispered hush of the clinic's doors. The ladies knew not to address me when I wore this mask of foul temper, so I just strode past them and into my private chamber. I sat behind the gleaming, empty table, just breathing through my nose and glaring at the Chinese Fighting Fish in the aquarium, daring them to piss me off. The sun outside mocked me with its joyful brightness, as the air conditioning chilled my sweaty flesh and the damp clothing that stuck to it. I didn't even turn on the light; the window filled the room with more than enough illumination. I lifted the remote and shut the blinds. The only light now came from the aquarium, and the Chinese fighters cast huge liquid shadows across the walls. It was only 11:00 a.m., but my head was already throbbing.

There was a barely audible tap on the door. Irena knew to exercise caution with me. I aimed the remote at the door like a laser weapon, and it opened unto her.

"Mrs. Jameson is prepped and ready for her lipo, Doctor," she practically whispered, expecting a growl in return.

Resigned, I slid silently into my white coat and went in to scrub up.

Ellen Jameson was thin as an Italian greyhound, but whenever she overindulged, she imagined pounds of pudding forming around her waist. True, when she gained ounces, they found their way to her midsection, as the rest of her was so skeletal.

Her ass was so tiny that it was one flat cheek with a hole. So she would come in to do penance for her hot fudge sundae, and I would pocket another six grand, a dirty cannula and a nearly empty fat collection jar.

We gave her a general anesthetic, because none of the upper

classes really want to be conscious when they're undergoing a procedure. Nobody wants to see the fat collection gun sucking buttery yellow sludge from under their skin and watch it splatting out into the clear glass collector. Even the sound of the process alone is like a fat man with sputtering diarrhea in a public restroom. So when I walked into surgery, Ellen was deep in twilight sleep, her face at rest, resembling nothing more than a corpse, her taut facial skin holding her lids open a bit to reveal the whites of her rolled-back eyes. Oxygen was fed through a tube in her nose, she'd been scrubbed, and her belly painted with brown antiseptic.

Just looking at this dowager pissed me off. I grabbed the suction gun as if it were an AK-47, wiped down the tip of the cannula, searched for the barely visible pockets of fat, then jammed it into her skin, pumping it in and out like a rutting weasel, jamming it, grunting without realizing it, cramming it hard and deep beneath her skin, gritting my teeth in an unconscious snarl. I looked up and held out my hand for a wipe-down and Beth's face was frozen in horror, which she tried to whisk away as quickly as possible.

"What?" I growled.

"Are you okay, Warren?" she asked, timid with trepidation.

I had to be careful. This could bite me in the ass; even with my malpractice insurance, which was sky-high (though I had never been sued), just one matron of the Hills with a hotshot lawyer husband could mean the end to my professional life as I know it.

"I'm okay, Beth." And I was, for the moment. But this day could not go on like this.

I took a deep breath and let it out, steadying myself. I had to let my sane, confident self take control. *Peace*, I thought. *Ice. Cool.* I looked down at Ellen Jameson's withered, concave stomach and the ripple of her ribs. The extraction gun rested in my hand, eager to suck, but I held it back for a moment longer, letting the cannula sit under her skin, eager to swallow. There was very little blood, and the incisions were tiny. There would be bruising, but there always is. And it would hurt a bit when she woke, but that helped the patient feel like something had truly been *done* to her. It's all part of the effect. She would know she'd had *work* done.

Even-keeled again, I had Beth wipe my brow and slowed down the maneuver, easing my way into the tiny pouches of pudge and sucking them away, finishing it up gently and carefully. And, of course, artfully. She would be as sleek as an anorexic anaconda.

The day was busy, and I had to make up for the overflow from the cancellations yesterday. I was not very chipper or conversational, but my mood did not get in the way of my work, which kept my mind off of what had happened to me the day before. But when the day was done and the lights turned off and the office door locked for the day, there was nothing to block my thoughts of the hideousness of Brittany, and how she had stolen my intimate being from me. I could feel my heartbeat accelerate and my skin flush. Now, the Monster of Cañon Drive was eating my brain. My mind was filled with the repellent images of a jellied, hare-lippped creature named Brittany climbing atop me and repeatedly lowering herself upon me, coating me with her excretions and befouling me forever. All I could see was ugly, and it was bright red.

I wasn't ready to go back to my car. I heeded the clarion call of Rodeo Drive (if you pronounced the name of the street like the cowboy carnival, all would know you were a rube: the accent was on the second syllable, of course, which rhymed with "A"), and stepped out into the brief flare of California's golden summer twilight.

Valets hopped as the beautiful and fashionably dressed denizens of the Hills climbed out of their Bimmers, Bentleys, and Benzes and into 208 Rodeo, Urasawa, and McCormick and Schmick's, but I barely took notice of them. Beauty was all around me—the people, the cars, the architecture, the sunset, the jewelry, the soft kiss of a Southern California summer breeze—but all I saw was ugly: the Chinese Crested crapping on the sidewalk in front of Il Fornaio: an ancient, rotund, apparently female *thing* with coarse, white whiskers sprouting from her chin, creeping along in a walker and dragging an elephantine leg covered with sores, dirt, and ragged bandages apparently inherited from Im-Ho-Tep; a 1979 Datsun B210 with Arizona plates filled with shouting, pimply teenagers, holding up traffic and belching clouds of choking black smoke from its tailpipe; and perhaps worst of all, an ugly couple kissing.

What had become of this neighborhood? Once a symbol of all that was special in the world, Beverly Hills was being poisoned by the zombie invasion of the ordinary, the defective, the casual, the fat-over-belt, biscuits-and-gravy-eating, *TMZ-* worshipping, gum-chewing lower classes. I thought we'd priced them out of this neighborhood decades ago, but it appears that the lives of the privileged are so revered that the *hoi polloi* will go into hock to rub up against us.

My life was devoted to beauty, yet all I saw around me was ugliness.

I had to go to the habitat of this ugly beast and yank its heart out, slay the dragon, extinguish the flames of its breath.

Having a curdled mind and an angry monkey on my back, I walked mindlessly in an increasingly tormented rage up Rodeo Drive, turned right on Brighton Way, round the corner onto Cañon, and found myself across the street from the Namaste Tea Room. Its glass windows were tinted, and I could not see inside as night was beginning to shroud the evaporating daylight. A tiny, tasteful *Open* sign was propped inside the window. I stood there and watched for several minutes before a young mommy pushed her twin babies out in a double-wide stroller, onto the street and around the corner. The shop stood still on its quiet block, no customers coming out or going in. It was after seven o'clock, and this block was winding down, the action moving closer to Wilshire. The *Open* sign sat there, begging for final customers, but there were none to be seen.

A group of three pretty young things were laughing as they came around Canon behind me, tossing their hair and acting all Californian. They were all teeth and enhanced breasts and spray-tans: quite sweet, actually. But I was not in the mood. Not now.

I was watching the shop, but could see them in my peripheral rearview vision as they spotted me and came to a stop. They whispered to one another, thinking wrongly that I could not hear them; well, I didn't hear their words, but I knew what they were talking about. The boldest of them, a frosted brunette in what had to be a tastefully revealing Chanel, approached me as she brought a slim, tapered cigarette to her lips.

"Do you have a light?" she asked me.

I'm sure I expressed even more disdain than I felt. "Do you know what cigarettes will do to your face?" I asked back, freezing her into place. She looked at me with wide, Bambi eyes, blinked twice with ultra-long lashes. "They'll put creases in your lips, turn your skin grey, suck all the moisture out of your flesh, and create a roadmap of wrinkles all around your eyes, your cheeks, your forehead, and your neck. No. I don't have a fucking light."

I think she sobbed once before she flipped me off and dragged her girlfriends away in a huff. "Faggot!" the blonde called out when they were a safe distance away. They were disposable. I had my pick of the litter when I wanted it. And I didn't want it now.

I looked up just in time to see a hand turn the little sign in the teashop window to *Closed*, and the lights inside go off. I backed into the shadow of a palm tree and waited for several minutes for the door to open. A twenty-year-old boy with dyed black hair over his eyes and tattoos of horror movie stars on his slender biceps came out first, followed by a girl with creamy mocha skin barely covered by a ribbed white wife-beater and a beautifully proportioned shaved head. It took balls for a woman to shave her head so completely, but it worked on her. She was stunning.

Her lush lower lip was pink, in stark contrast to the glowing brown of the rest of her face.

The girl pulled the door shut behind them and locked it up. The boy and she left on foot in opposite directions, and the street went quiet again. There was no sign of Ugly Brittany anywhere. Just to be sure, I waited several minutes, then gave up, walked back to the car, and managed to speed home to the Dume.

My tolerance for the unattractive and aesthetically challenged was always low, but now it grated against me, pissed me off, boiled my blood. I found myself in a constant state of anger; anything could set me off. In the days to follow, the girls at the clinic kept their distance, afraid of igniting the powder keg of my fury. All I wanted was to work, to keep my mind occupied on creation, on art, on beauty, on perfection. That kept my head straight, kept me moving forward like a shark, which would die if it were to remain motionless.

I, too, experienced a sort of death by inertia. As soon as

I was finished for the night, my brain festered all over again, and Brittany Fever would break out all over my body. I would walk down the street each evening, park under the shade of the date palm, and wait. Invariably the shop would be shuttered by the Black-Haired Boy and the Cocoa Angel, though one night it was a lone, middle-aged Latina who locked up. For nine weekdays straight I followed the same regimen, only to be foiled each time by my evasive quarry.

But then, on day ten, a Saturday, I found myself in the Golden Triangle early in the morning to pick up my iPad, which I had left in the office. The town was still recovering from a raucous Friday night, still sleeping it off when I got there. As I came off of Santa Monica Boulevard, my mind wandered as I changed the playlist on my iPhone, and I passed my turn onto Rodeo. I realized it just before I hit Cañon, with enough time to skid into a quick right turn. I turned onto Cañon just in time to see a familiarly trollish water balloon of a body coming out of Namaste and locking the door in its wake. I gasped, and my heartbeat doubled, pounding a tattoo against my ribcage. I stomped the Scagletti to a tire-shredding halt and saw her look up at me. She froze as she recognized me, taking in my snarling rictus of hatred. Neither of us could move; she dropped her large iced whatever it was and it splattered on the sidewalk against her feet. I could feel my breath turn to quick, shallow panting.

I slammed the car into gear and tore a quick U-turn, skid marks following me to the other side of the street where I squealed to a stop, threw open my door and charged out and after her.

Brittany remained rooted in place, a fat, misshapen, hideous deer in the headlights, her snaggle-toothed mouth agape and drooling, her Billy goat eyes like watery eggs. Before she could even react, I threw open the passenger-side door, hefted the punching bag of her body with a weight-lifter's grunt, threw her inside, slammed the door, and rushed back to my side, yanking my door shut and locking it tight.

Before she could resist, I grabbed the seatbelt and pulled it around her soft, pot- bellied body, and locked it in place. There was no more give in the belt, it was that tight. She was that grotesquely fat. I pulled the shirt off the hanger from behind my head, wrapping the sleeves around her mouth and the headrest and tying it tight.

She struggled like a beached sperm whale, but her never-exercised, flailing, sloshing bag of squishy bones was worthless against my pumped and primed musculature. I pulled off my tie and tied it taut around her wrists, swiftly undid the seatbelt, slid it between her arms, and locked it into place. She fought and huffed and puffed, but this time *I* backhanded *her* across the face, and though it seemed to have no effect in calming her down, it made me feel a hell of a lot better.

I glared at her, breathing hard from the struggle, just looking at her, my disgust building. How could someone let herself devolve into *this*? We are given our bodies, some of them challenging, but they are our temples, our shrines; we have the responsibility to make them into odes to the beauty of humanity, corporeal art of the highest kind, flesh sculpture to illuminate, to titillate, to provoke, to inspire.

But here sat a thing called *Brittany*, a human tenement, guilty of the Eighth Deadly Sin: being *ugly*.

I wanted to spit on her, to vomit her away as you would the stomach flu. I wanted her washed down the gutter to the sewer with the rest of the detritus that was carried out to the sea and out of our lives. I'd hired a great architect to build my home to my standards of beauty, brought in one of the area's highest paid interior designers to furnish it and my clinic. I dined in restaurants of style and elegance that served foods where presentation was as important as flavor, dressed in clothing that looked as good as it felt, that flattered me and my form. I spent a lot of time and money to surround myself with beauty and perfection; indeed, aesthetic purity was my life's work, my vocation and my avocation. And yet, lashed to the buttery leather upholstery in one of the world's finest evocations of automotive elegance, this worthless, meaningless, mindless example of physicality in its lowest form glared at me with some kind of sense of superiority.

"You are so fucking *ugly*!" I spat at her.

She choked on the sleeve of the beautifully tailored shirt that held her head strapped in place, trying to pierce me with muffled words that could never be heard, and I just backhanded her again.

"*Shut the fuck up!*" I screamed at the top of my lungs.

She stopped struggling. Her expression changed, from hatred and anger to *fear*. And it made me smile. She would regret what she had done. Perhaps she thought she was trying to teach me a lesson or something. Well, it was my turn to play professor now.

As hard as it was to look at her, it was easy to decide what to do with her.

I took one last reconnaissance of the area to see that no one was watching, then slammed the Ferrari into gear and laid down another patch of rubber in the quiet Beverly Hills morning. I could retrieve my iPad on Monday; I didn't need it now.

I drove up the long drive to the house as the gates eased silently shut behind me, then drove into the garage, which closed like the curtains at the end of a play… but this show was just beginning. She had started to struggle again on the way here, but a hard chop to the throat cut that short. She was lucky she could even breathe, and she knew it. Her breath wheezed through her wounded, possibly even ruptured trachea, tears and snot running down her face. It made me sick to look at her... but now I had to *touch* her again. I lifted her out of the car, and she lay like limp weight, her repulsive bulk shifting like a giant silicone implant. It might have been better had she struggled.

But she chose passivity, which was fine with me. It didn't ease my anger a bit.

Like many successful Southern California cosmetic surgeons, I had a small operating room built within the house. I didn't use it often, but there are celebrities who are afraid of being seen even in the *neighborhood* of a plastic surgeon, so great is their fear of the tabloid press. They are willing to go to great expense, with an emphasis on the *great*, to keep their procedures a secret. I could tell you some of the extremely rich and famous patients that benefitted from my artistry, but then I'd have to kill you.

Morning sun streamed through the door-to-ceiling windows as I pulled her through the kitchen. She bucked and tried to scream through her incapacitated throat, really giving me my morning workout. I grabbed a trash bag and wrapped it around her mouth, and that shut her up just fine. Her burlap muumuu, or whatever it was, slid her across the gleaming marble tiles like a sled, and I didn't even look at her as I pulled her out of the kitchen and onto the bare, polished ash wood hallway, through the living room, and back to the private clinic.

She was struggling more than ever now, but her protestations were weakening and she was drenched in her potent sweat as I worked up perspiration of my own trying to heft her onto the operating table. I'd lifted dead weight equal to hers before, but it didn't squirm and shift and get me wet.

With a final animalistic grunt, I plopped her onto the table and stood over her, breathing heavy, then locked her down with thick leather straps. Her eyes were wide and her breathing broken as she struggled to take in oxygen through her blocked nasal passages. I went to the cabinet, withdrew a syringe and a rubber-stoppered bottle, jammed it in without bothering to disinfect it with alcohol first, then plunged it deep into her carotid artery and ejected clear fluid into her thick red blood.

Before she could count to ten, if she could get that high, she was unconscious. Immobilized, this bulging slattern might have been even *more* repulsive. Inert, at rest, her flesh spilled off the sides of the table; expressionless, her face was drawn toward the floor by gravity. When I unwrapped the Hefty bag from around her head, her cleft lip lifted to reveal two of her most crooked yellow teeth. Her mouth opened, and breath came in and out in great, long, sleepy draughts.

I couldn't look at her any longer; I had to turn away. I stepped to the sliding glass doors that looked out onto the Ficus trees blowing in the ocean breeze overlooking the cliffs and watched grey-bellied clouds begin to roll in to obscure the face of the sun. The room darkened, and I had to turn on the lights, which were lemon-warm and relaxing. Funny how it could be a hundred degrees inland, and still be grey and cool just a few miles west at the beach.

The day was growing dark to catch up with my mood. Even though I had regained control of my own destiny, I bristled inside. Then I went to the chrome and glass casements, opened them up, and slid the array of medical instruments out in its pyramid of drawers.

The perfect, polished surgical steel gleamed under the soothing lights, and my spirits rose as I laid them out before me. Oblivious, Moby Brittany lay vulnerable before me, so I took the shining shears, fighting down my gorge, and snipped through her clothing and lay her bare. Her breasts slid down from her chest, hanging on either side. Her thighs spread out from one edge of the table to the other, and still spilled over. I hooked her up to the gas, and she began to breathe it easily, and was sure to be unconscious for at least the next few hours. My gloves firmly in place, I swabbed her down with antiseptic and stared at her, wondering where on earth to begin. With a body like this, I guess it didn't really matter.

Decisions, decisions.

I plugged in the Hercules aspirator, then hooked up the fat collection gun and the attached 12-hole harvesting cannula. I had a high-volume harvesting canister, but even at 3000ml, the largest size that was available, it would have to be emptied repeatedly. This was one big fucking girl. Unable to stand looking at this sorry, drooping excuse for a body any longer, I flipped the switch and began the chugging suck of the machinery, wiped down the cannula, and slid it beneath the skin of her belly. I worked it under her flesh, plunging the wand in and out, in and out, as it sucked and spat pink and yellow curds into the canister. Her body jerked now and then, but it didn't bother me. I just kept going. Suck and spit, suck and spit, the wand snorted and hocked repeatedly, rhythmically, efficiently, leaving loose flesh where the mounds of her fat once resided. Before long, I was in my zone, doing my job, body sculpting, and for a while I forgot whom it was that I was actually working on. Sucking the fat from this fleshy thing before me was natural, procedural, and I moved from belly to thighs to arms to back to ass, operations I would have done separately under normal circumstances. But here, no; here, I wanted it to hurt. I wanted it to be felt. It needed to be done and it needed to be done now. I don't remember how many times I emptied the jar of Brittany fat, but it collected in at least a couple of trash bags, nasty stuff that I would have to incinerate later.

I was tired and hungry now. I hadn't eaten anything all day, and my stomach was starting to rumble. I looked up to see that I'd been at work sucking the sludge from this overstuffed body for over three hours, and my vision was starting to blur. This is a procedure that should never be done alone, but I felt some pride that I had accomplished it by myself. I looked down at the evacuated results of my handiwork and smiled. I felt powerful.

And really hungry.

Making sure my patient was fully strapped to the table, I left the surgery and headed to the kitchen for a sandwich. I'd picked up some takeout salmon and eggplant at Spruzzo the previous night that I had never gotten around to, so I got out some 9-grain bread, slathered it with coarse mustard and some petals of spinach, and closed my eyes in delight as I took a big mouthful. But I hardly got the chance to savor it when the air was rent by the most horrific scream I'd ever heard. I am loath to use such a hoary hyphenated descriptor as *bloodcurdling*, but that was the only way to describe it. The cry was a high, wavering squeal, shrill and agonized and filled with terror. At first, it drew goosebumps, and I froze with a mouth full of unmasticated salmon. Obviously, her vocal cords were still intact. When the howl grew more plaintive and painful, I smiled and chewed my weekend brunch, letting the voice ring out in what was to become a song to me. It grew louder and more filled with choking sobs, so I finished my hasty meal and returned to the surgery and the source of the mournful wails.

"Good morning, Glory," I said with chipper abandon. "How are we feeling?"

We were reflected in the full-length mirror I had placed *just so*, Brittany and me, a perfect view from her perspective. She was still strapped to the operating table, naked, fish-belly white, the loose folds of her vacated flesh hanging from her like empty laundry bags. She could see it quite clearly, and she could not take her eyes from the display of her shameless, defatted body.

Her voice grew hoarse as her high-pitched screams began to fade into inarticulate croaks. Tears soaked her hair.

"What did you do to me?" she shrieked.

"People pay me a fortune for what I'm doing to you," I replied.

"You're fucking crazy!"

"Am I?"

"You're crazy and fucking disgusting!"

"Hm..." I replied, as if considering what she had to tell me.

I gave her my most charming smile before I stuffed a wad of gauze in her mouth and taped it shut.

"Mmmfff!" she said. "Mmmfff!!! *Mmmmmffff!!!*"

I sighed, not interested in continuing this conversation.

"We've done some pretty extensive lipo," I said, "leaving a *lot* of loose skin. We'll have to tighten you up a bit, don't you think?"

"Mmmfff!" she said, as I might have guessed.

I slipped into a new pair of Latex gloves and snapped them around my wrists.

I lifted the folds of loose, colorless flesh, and it felt empty and useless. Skin not wrapped warmly around a shapely body or a lovely face has no worth. I squeezed it, and it was squishy in my hand. Feeling was obviously returning to her body, as she winced and tightened and *mmmfff*ed again.

"We're going to have to get rid of some of this excess skin, aren't we?" There was a lot. The shears would be more effective to begin with than a scalpel here. I picked them up and cleaned them with antiseptic, looking at the reflection of my eyes in their hungry blades.

"Awake or asleep, Brittany?"

Her eyes were as wide as they could go without falling out of her head.

"Awake you can watch the process, which is actually quite fascinating. Almost like creating the most perfect, form-fitting clothes from an elegant designer. Of course, it will surely be painful. I mean, even with a gallon of local anesthetic, we *are* going to be cutting through a *lot* of your skin. So, you might choose to be unconscious if you're a little squeamish. Your choice."

She started to quake and violently shake her head.

"I'm sorry," I said. "I can't quite understand you."

She grunted and strangled and tried to spit words out from behind the tape but was completely incapable of communicating a simple answer.

So, I picked up the mask, put it to her face, and turned up the gas. By the time I lowered it, her eyes were already at half-mast, so I dramatically snipped the gleaming shears in her face a couple of times before she lost consciousness, then gathered up the loose flesh and began to cut.

The initial trims were, of necessity, bold and indelicate. Clipping and snipping is not so refined as the detailed sculpting that would follow with the scalpel. But even the removal of vast quantities of flesh requires some surgical care. I loved the sound of the scissors as they bit away chunks of the gelid drapery of her loose flesh; and soon, a human form began to reveal itself from underneath. It was like the first rough chunks of marble that a great sculptor would bash away before revealing the beautiful statue that lay waiting to be unveiled... just bloodier. I found myself humming Coldplay's "Yellow" to myself as I trimmed the fat that fell to the polished granite floor with a fleshy *splat*.

Snip. Plop. Staple. Snip. Plop. Staple.

The process was time-consuming and tedious, but far from laborious for me. It energized me, tested the boundaries of my talents, invigorated the artist that lived within my own flesh sculpture. I was really enjoying this.

With the bulk of the flab now trimmed away, I would soon dig into the more artistically demanding assembly of the body laid out before me. But first I had to attenuate the broad strokes, refine the scissor cuts with the brushstrokes of my scalpel. I'd had a collection of them made specifically to order by an old artisan on Pico, who crafted them not from surgical steel but from silver. They were softer than steel and could neither be used as often nor as vigorously, but their cut was finer, more delicate; more *elegant* somehow. And they cost a fucking fortune. But no one else had instruments like these.

So, I moved in closer, gently slicing and carving and molding the smooth, evacuated skin to the frame that lay beneath. The skin was still young and supple, with a resilience and elasticity that was eager to be guided into shape. Shaping the stomach was *de rigueur*, really something I'd done over and over. The thighs were also undemanding. I had one former movie star who had taken her approach to middle age poorly, and had binged for several years on cocaine, Seconal, tubs of gelato, and Mrs. Field's cookies before making a very public Weight Watchers deal, then placing herself in my hands and on this very operating table. It had taken a series of procedures over a period of months, but I made her svelte again, and her multi-media weight-loss campaign put her back on the covers of all the tabs, and she's got her own sitcom premiering in September. I'm sure I don't have to tell you who she is.

But this *Brittany*, this was a different story. She was fat, but she was also hideous. This would require far more than just trimming and slimming and sculpture. She was fucking *ugly*, a reprehensible, slovenly waste of space. She despoiled Beverly Hills; she would ruin any day just by being seen. She was a troll, a troll who thought she could use me, fuck me, pleasure herself with me.

Well, she couldn't.

I don't fuck trolls.

So, I painted with my scalpel, I stitched with style and panache and delicacy, and got lost all over again in my work. My passion. My *art*.

I don't know how long I'd been working before I noticed that fatigue was settling into my hands, which were starting to tremble a bit. The sun had long ago dropped into the sea. Brittany's breath still whooshed out of her nose in a peaceful rhythm, but I realized as I started to come out of the trance of my work that I was growing tired. I stepped back, took a deep breath, and stretched, twisting at my waist from side to side until my back let out a satisfying *crackle*. And then, I cranked the operating table into its standing position, and took in the fruits of my handiwork.

The body was almost unrecognizable as it stood before me, conjuring images of the Bride of Frankenstein. It had a shape now, rough, but human. The rows of black stitches were coarse but temporary and had been carefully aligned so that the resultant scars would hide in private places, and even when they had been refined in the smaller, more specific, beautifying procedures, would eventually not be noticeable. The breasts would need filling and shaping, as would her ass, but the groundwork had been laid, and her frame was actually a perfectly respectable one under all the hideousness that had been cut away.

I felt like Donatello. A very tired Donatello.

I cranked the table down to halfway between prone and standing position and started to clear the floor of the discarded flesh, loading up yet another couple of garbage bags before I disinfected the granite. I tied the bags tight and took them out to the kitchen. It was too much trouble—and there would be too many questions— to take this stuff into the office and send it out for incineration. I know that Hefty bags are not sterile, but if I double-wrapped them I doubted that it would create much trouble down at the city dump. It might prove to be quite the feast for the feral creatures that dined there.

The bags in hand, I cast a look over my shoulder at the trimmed and sutured body that lay exposed before me under the warm lights of the surgery. The body had a shape now, beyond the patchwork: a shape that promised, a shape that beckoned. And on top of it, a revolting, repellent head. I looked at this creature with contempt, detached from my work as an artist now, seeing it anew for what it was: a vile corruption of humanity and nature, an insult to life itself. It just pissed me off all over again.

I was tired and hungry and sweaty and covered in the scent of Brittany. I headed directly into the bathroom to strip and shower, content with the work that I had completed. There was much more ahead to do, but I was confident that it could be done. I scrubbed up all over and looked out across the ocean outside. It was a cloudy night, and there was no moon.

Night had settled in my head. I took a long, deep breath, closed my eyes for a moment to calm my heartbeat, then turned off the light and headed into the kitchen.

I tossed some baby greens and baby corn and heated a pan and was just starting to sear the graceful slab of Hanwoo beef I'd had delivered from the best place in Koreatown when I heard her. Not screams, no; she was too weak for that, I suppose. But in the distance, I could hear her sobs, long and deep and wracking. In the thick of activity and a burning hunger, I'd actually forgotten about Brittany. She could wait a few minutes; I wasn't going to fuck up a Hanwoo filet over her. So, I let it grill for about thirty seconds, flipped it over and did the same, then laid it out on the plate with the vegetables and dug in while the steak was still steaming.

It was incredibly delicious, its pinky-red center giving just enough chew to release its intense beefiness.

Sated, I stood from the table and washed the dishes. I would hate to come into the kitchen in the morning and find dirty dishes waiting for me. I carefully wiped them dry, put them away, then followed the sounds of the continuing sobs to the operating room. I was in slippers now, padding silently down the hall, so that she didn't hear me when I reached the door. I stood there for a full minute or two and watched her cry obliviously, the tears rolling down her face as she stared into the mirror. I almost felt some sorrow for her, so wracking were her sobs; but then the clouds cleared, and a shaft of blue moonlight broke through, illuminating the hideousness of her face as she looked up at me. Her sorrow was replaced by a sudden burst of crimson anger, and she tried to scream at me from beneath the tape. Even with her mouth stuffed with gauze and a strip of silver tape holding it tight, I could make out the two words she kept yelling beneath the muzzle: *Fuck you! Fuck you! Fuck you!*

It just made me mad.

"I don't fuck trolls!" I screamed back at her, then slammed the door and made my way to bed.

Sleep came easy and deep, for once without any pharmaceutical assistance.

Once my head hit the pillow of my marshmallow bed, I

was out. I didn't wake until Irena called at eleven the next morning to ask me when I'd be in. The guy on that police procedural was scheduled to get his eyes done at 12:30, and one of my regulars had scheduled a labiaplasty later in the afternoon. I looked out to see that the sun was high and vibrant, the colors outside were rich and sharply focused, and I felt fresh, newly born, even *happy*. I was really in the mood for blepharoplasty, and even the labiaplasty could be fun... on the right labia. I told her I'd be there in time, and then set about my morning *toilette*.

I felt scrubbed and pink and jolly as I went from the bathroom to the kitchen to blend up my morning smoothie. It was summer, so I was able to make it with a fresh peach, which was a treat. Frozen peaches just would not do. Clean and refreshed, I filled another glass with smoothie, popped in a straw, and went back down the hall and into the surgery.

Daylight filled the room; Brittany darkened it. She was wide awake, with circles under her gleaming red eyes. The stitchwork across her body was crimson and raw, with just the tiniest bit of pucker. I'd tend to that later. Bruising was just starting to appear on her otherwise smooth, ghost-white flesh. She looked up at me, morose, forlorn, without the energy to even generate her hatred.

"Hungry?" I asked, all chipper and shit.

She didn't even have the strength to growl. Her nearly translucent skin was shining with oil from her overactive pores. Her hair was lank and greasy, but her body... well, her body was no longer her body.

"Here," I told her as I removed the tape and gauze from her mouth and extended the smoothie. "Have some breakfast." She turned her head away.

"It's delicious. I just made it."

Her stomach gurgled in protest.

"You sure?" I pushed it up to her face again so that she could take the straw in her mouth. She looked up at me, hungry, but filling with hate.

"You'll be sorry if you don't take it now. Last chance until this evening."

I kept it in front of her revoltingly bifurcated mouth.

"One. Two. Three. Four. Five. Six..." By *seven* she had taken the straw in her mouth and started to suck. This time, I was the one who had to turn away. She slurped and swallowed disgustingly.

I interrupted her meal with a handful of painkillers. "Here," I told her. "You'd better take these." She hesitated, but knew better to refuse them, and I dumped them into her mouth so that she could swallow them. And then, she hungrily gulped some more.

Soon, the straw started to sputter, and the glass was empty.

"No more French fries and pizza for you, Brittany," I said. "The body is a temple.

Do you understand me?" My own body reared up in anger again. "A *goddamn temple!*"

I threw the glass into the corner, where it shattered theatrically. She cowered, and I took a deep breath and slowed my heartbeat back to normal. *Ice. Cool.*

"Have a nice day," I said, then closed the door in my wake, leaving her to face the mirror for the rest of the day. To *reflect*, I giggled to myself.

I enjoy the intricacy of eyelid surgery, to remove the folds of flesh and bits of fat in a way that looked natural, organic, without the wide-eyed stare and inability to completely close one's eyes that is the trademark of so many talentless technicians. Cosmetic surgery has become a business, a void that pulls the ham-fisted, money- grubbing flesh-cutters in with its promise of high pay and renown. These carpenters with a scalpel make life difficult for those of us who aspire to more, who see our work as a calling, who are divinely inspired. I'll say it again: it's the difference between art and craft. The work before me was on a face that was seen weekly on ten million televisions across the country, so it had to be subtle, beautiful, natural, yet take a dozen years off of his appearance. To take a face that is well- known, even well-*loved*, and freshen it, to christen it anew without the *tsk-tsk*ing of TMZ or a mocking three-page spread in the *Enquirer* was the balancing act I was born to perform. The actor—again someone you'd know, starring in a series titled with an abbreviation—was understandably skittish, but he, and all those who advised him, who were legion, had given me his trust... and a fistful of cash. And I would earn it.

In a matter of hours, the man had lost at least a decade; in a matter of weeks— less than the length of your average series hiatus—he could show it off.

One single-minded task led to the next. I had only about a half hour before beginning Mindy Perkins' labiaplasty, so I washed up, hydrated, and listened to a few minutes of Joyce Cooling to replenish my mood while the staff prepared the surgery. Mindy was about to shoot her first-ever nude scene, and was justifiably concerned about her rather oversized and asymmetrical vaginal lips. It was a big break from her fourth-billed role on that ensemble cable sitcom to female lead in a big David Fincher *noir* thriller, and would bring her a lot of attention. The last thing she wanted was to finally show it all with the unfortunate crotch of a seventy-year- old. I had to pretty that pussy in the event that it would be seen on a sixty-foot screen. She had a rather spectacular body in all other regards, from her tight little breasts and taut tummy to her beautifully pert and rounded little ass, but nature had been less kind between her legs. It wasn't that uncommon, really, and to tell the truth, the procedure was a joy to perform. In days, she'd be ready for her close-up, Mr. DeMille.

I was fine during the operations, which filled my conscious mind. Work invigorates me, takes up all of my thought processes. But in between, all I could think about was the work-in-progress that was strapped to the operating table at home. So when I finished work, I couldn't wait to go home... and work.

I stopped at Spruzzo again for some takeout before I got back to the house. I got the filet with rice instead of potatoes, and for my patient, the chicken piccata with steamed vegetables, but without any of the starches. She didn't need those.

She was asleep and snoring when I arrived. It was still a couple of hours before dark, and the sun cast a lemon wedge of light over her body. When I came in to inspect her, her eyes opened, staring balefully and hopelessly at me. Drool was running down her chin.

"How are you feeling?" I asked, as if I gave a shit.

"Fuck you," she said.

"Do you kiss your mother with that mouth?" I asked her. She didn't think it was funny. Not that it mattered.

"Let's see how you're coming along."

Her body lay completely undraped and exposed. I swabbed the sutured areas, which were many, but they were looking good. The post-operative swelling had already substantially subsided, and the wounds seemed to be closing up nicely. I had done excellent work. I cranked the table up into the standing position again.

"Take a look," I told her. "You're on the verge of having a lovely body."

"Fuck you!" she said again. This was getting monotonous.

"Hmm…" I said as I looked her over. "What's next, implants? Or should we just start right in on the face?"

"*What the fuck are you doing to me?*" she suddenly screamed at me. "*Let me go!*"

I walked right up to her hideous face.

"You're ugly," I told her. "I'm fixing you."

"*I don't want to be fixed!*" she shrieked. "*I don't NEED to be fixed!*"

"Well, that's not for you to say, is it?"

I cranked the operating table down against her struggles, then sprayed her with a cleansing disinfectant while she fought the sturdy leather bonds. It was a struggle she could not hope to win. I taped her mouth shut again so that I at least didn't have to hear her potty mouth any longer. It was really beginning to irritate me. Then I opened up the padded metal tour case I'd brought home from the office, and laid out an assortment of black market Eurosilicone breast implants in various sizes.

Silicone isn't legal in the United States, but who was going to know? Saline and soy oil are all right, but there's nothing like the feel of silicone if you want lifelike breasts. Dow and Mentor and Allergan are constantly trying to come up with new and "safe" replacements for silicone, but nothing they've come up with to date comes close to its naturalness. Getting them isn't all that difficult if you are as connected as I am. Not that I'm a black marketeer or anything, but when you've reached a certain level of stature in this industry, they all come to *you.*

Brittany looked like about a thirty-four under those hollowed breast carcasses lying on her chest, so I held an ample pair of glass-transparent hooters up to her.

"What do you think? D, maybe?" The giant balloons looked ridiculous, like the tits on a Las Vegas lap-dancer.

"Just kidding!" I laughed, but she cowered in horror. I swapped them out for another pair.

"I'm thinking maybe... I don't know, somewhere between B-minus and C-plus." I considered a few sizes before deciding conclusively. "B-plus. Definitely a B-plus.

Perfect for that frame." A frame that was, by now, actually petite.

She struggled again, and I thought she might start to pop a stitch or two, so I reached over, placed the mask on her face, and turned on the gas.

"'Night, Brittany," I said, and she went deep into sleep.

Her nipples were somewhat undefined, a rather large pink smear, and it was a little tricky to make the incisions so they wouldn't leave a solid line, letting the darker rose tone drift into the stark whiteness that surrounded them. But I found the right place and the right angle, and soon the bags had been popped inside and sutured up. I worked them into place, and even through the gloves, they felt rather lovely, soft and fleshy. They even fell slightly to the side as she lay prone, unlike most boob jobs you see on the beach that stand up straight no matter what the position. Even under sedation, and having just been sliced and sewn, the nipples contracted naturally as I felt them, indicating good circulation and full sensitivity. I smiled, giving way to pride.

A blepharoplasty, a labiaplasty, and a mammoplasty: that was more than enough for any surgeon's day. It certainly was for mine. Yawning, I went into the shower, scrubbed up, then went into the kitchen and put together a tray of food for her.

She was just waking up as I entered the room with her food, still groggy but aware.

"You must be hungry," I said.

She looked up at me, weak, broken, almost pitiful. She didn't even bother to hiss at me; she merely nodded. She hadn't had a meal in a long time.

Oh, fuck. I didn't realize it until now, but I was going to have to feed her by hand. I couldn't trust her enough to unbind her hands. I rolled the stainless steel tray next to the operating table and sat down next to it. I strapped on another set of latex gloves and cut the food up into little bits and fed them to her with my fingers. Her lips touched me as she sucked a big bite of chicken into her mouth, and even through the rubber it made me shiver to feel the contact of her hot, wet maw.

"Do that once more and you'll never eat again!" I shouted. She just chewed and swallowed, staring rusty daggers into me with her bloodshot, drooping eyes.

I wiped my wet fingers onto a towel, then continued to feed her. Suddenly her head popped up and she clamped her teeth onto my fingers! *Hard!*

It was a pit-bull grip, and she just dug her canines into me, shaking her head like a Jack Russell with a rat, her jagged, ragged teeth digging deep into my digits. She even snarled, growling and biting, jerking her head, her saliva flung all over me until I made a fist and slammed it into her face.

Stunned, she pulled back, her fangs parting, and I yanked my hand away from her and held it to my chest. The fucking bitch had bitten through the latex and into my flesh. *I was bleeding!*

I took her dinner plate and threw it to the floor and stormed out of the room and into the bathroom, where I washed out my fingers and treated them with disinfectant. They didn't need stitches, but bandaging them, even with a liquid bandage, would interfere with the delicacy of my touch.

I had to think it was worth it.

Even though the next day was a Saturday, I woke early,

transfixed by the wind- sailors out on the sparkling, glassy waters beyond the French doors of the bedroom. Point Dume twinkled in the California morning, and a gaggle of seagulls put on an airshow against the powder blue sky. My mood was high, the sun warm and bright, and a new day had ignited.

Showered, shaved, fed and evacuated, I made my way down the hall to the surgery. I had left the door open a crack, and quietly approached, not knowing whether Brittany was awake or in slumber. I quietly, surreptitiously peeked inside to find her wide-awake, craning her head from her prone position, staring into the full-length mirror across the little room. Her eyes were devoid of the somnambulance that was so characteristic, peering hard at the reflection of her body before her. She squirmed under her bonds, trying in vain to see more of herself, her expression curious now, even fascinated. She looked at the stranger's body that she now wore, and I could swear she was *pleased* with it.

Hm. I'm not sure this was the reaction I had sought.

"Nice, isn't it?" I asked, breaking the silence, and whipping her head around to me.

"*Mmmfff!*" she snorted. "*Mmmfff!*"

Her outrage seemed forced now, phony, a charade.

"A shame about that ugly fucking face, though, isn't it?" \

"*Mmmfff! Mmmfff!*"

Oh, hell. The day had started so well.

She struggled and grunted and tried to yell through the gag, and it was really getting to me. Enough, as they say, is enough.

I walked over to the stainless steel instrument tray, picked up the largest scalpel, and cut her fucking throat.

Now maybe we could have a little quiet.

The laceration was thin, followed the crease in her flesh exactly, and would easily be hidden when the wound had sealed itself. But with a quick couple of flicks of the blade, the vocal cords were cut, and I could get some relief from her relentless caterwauling.

I stitched it up in just a few minutes and made ready for the real work to begin.

"I warned you," I told her as I peeled the gaffer's tape from her mouth. "Now scream all you like." I ripped the tape off of her mouth to accommodate her.

She tried to howl, but the only sound she could emit was like a steam leak. I could take that.

And now, the face. The face.

This would be a challenge. Where to begin?

Her nose was prominent, with a large dromedary hump in the middle, and hung down into a big drooping hook at the end. She'd had virtually no chin before the liposuction, but there was competent chin and jawbone structure newly revealed from under the fat. Her brow was simian and her ears clumped like fists. Her eyes were hooded by lids that made her appear stupid, inattentive, dull. Perhaps she was all of those things, but she certainly didn't have to look it. Some of the dumbest people I've ever met are some of the best-looking.

But her mouth. The lip. *That lip*. That hideous, leporine split where there should be a philtrum turned her from human to beast. *This* would require patience; *this* would require persistence; *this* would require artistry.

This would come last.

The starting place presented itself clearly, since it was the very center of this oh- so-offensive face. So I gassed her, flayed open the nasal structure, picked up the hammer and the osteotome, and began the sculpture anew, chipping away at the overly generous cartilage in her proboscis to turn it from a trunk into a human nose.

The brow was at least symmetrically over-abundant, and it didn't take much more than an hour to refine it into a gentle slope that gracefully swept from the hairline to elegantly shade her eyes.

The eyes were a project in themselves. The day grew a beard as I moved on to give them shape and character, the illusion of thought and reflection. This was in some ways the most demanding, the most challenging of the procedures, and maybe even the most prone to failure. Somehow I was still energized by this operation, an operation that should have been several operations and spanned months to do properly. But properly was the only way I knew to do my work, and I would not settle for less than perfection here. My hands were deft and talented, and the work directed itself.

I unfurled the ears like blossoms opening to the sun. It didn't take a whole lot to fashion them into slender, natural shape. I'd had to cut away some of the cauliflower, but if I could do it for a Golden Gloves champion, I could do it for this valueless creature.

And then, finally, I began to tenderly, subtly craft a new upper lip to replace the repellent cleft that had been so clumsily closed in childhood. Borrowing snippets of discarded face flesh, I patched and worked and reworked to fashion a beautifully natural dip beneath nose and lip, pale and pink and seamless, the cuts minute and cautious and nearly invisible. In time, they would completely disappear. Then, the lips themselves had to be abetted, given just a slight bulge to make them distinct from the face around them, to give shape and expression to her mouth. I would never pump up the lips to give the dim-witted appearance of the fish mouth so popular on the catwalk for the last many years. Every day I would pass women on Rodeo with gawping guppy faces that looked like you could stick them to a window by the mouth. The mouth alone had to have taken a good four hours to reconstruct and beautify.

Night had fallen and a new day was in the works when finally I had completed the fine-tuning and suturing, and set about cleaning it all up. There would be refinements, of course, but the work, for now, at least, was done. The sun bellowed as it rose and covered us in its blanket of amber rejuvenation. In the warm morning light, I inspected my work, ran my fingers lightly over the fine, almost microscopic lines of stitchery, prodded the elasticity of the flesh, squeezed newly constructed breasts and gluteus, gently guided my hands across this newly created body, even stroked the redesigned face so expressionless in repose. The lips, overly swollen for now, seemed to beg for a kiss... the kiss of life.

I could not believe my own eyes, but the evidence was here before me. I could see beyond the stitches and the bruised flesh, the swelling and the abrasions. I had singlehandedly taken the worst thing in the world, the bane of my existence, a roadblock to human evolution; I had taken something horrendous, something foul, something unspeakably *ugly*... and I had made it *perfect*.

It was time to sleep.

Hell, even God rested on the seventh day.

Brittany's recovery was astonishingly quick. Though purple blossoms of bruise covered her face and stomach and thighs and ass, they faded and yellowed at a rapid rate, soon taking on a fresh, healthy, lively pink tone. Despite years of neglect and abuse, her skin was eager to take its new shape, to grow together as if none of it had been cut away, and the sewn-together patchwork between the puzzle pieces of assembly joined as if newly minted, clean and even expanses of unmarred flesh, with tiny pink lines that, in time, would completely vanish as the naturally decomposing stitches themselves had. The others came out easily and naturally.

I moved Brittany into a tiny room in the guesthouse behind the garage, and she did not protest; she *could* not protest. The cutting of her vocal cords made her quite agreeable and seemed to have domesticated her. The fight had left her, and even though she could whisper "fuck you" to me as often as she liked, she seemed to have lost the compunction to do so. She was sore, but she was healing in silence, and chose never to look at me, which didn't bother me a bit.

When at last she was able to stand, I walked her to the bathroom, lay her in the oversized Jacuzzi tub, and let her marinate for a while in the bubbling restorative Malibu waters, dumping in some bubble bath to get her cleaner than she'd surely ever been in her life. I could see the mother of her grime forming at the top of the foamy water and took the hand shower and cleaned her completely, then washed her hair for what had to have been the first time in weeks. It took three or four shampooings to get it squeaky-clean before I conditioned it.

No longer bound to the operating table, she now recovered in relative freedom. I found that bonds were unnecessary, that she was overwhelmed by passivity. I had broken her as she had tried to break me. I found that I could leave her locked in her room and her own memory foam bed without binding her hands or feet, and I could return to find everything around her intact. So I was able to continue working in Beverly Hills without worrying about what I'd return to at Point Dume. I brought her food—usually fruits and vegetables with some whole grain breads and the occasional carbs, and plenty of Vitamin C, zinc, and animal protein to help the healing process—and she slept almost all the time.

After some weeks, I'd had an arduous day at the office. There had been an accident at Sunset and Stone Canyon in Bel-Air in the early morning hours, and the cops managed to pry a certain right-wing talk-radio mogul and the morning-show TV host—both of whom were married to female spouses—out of the wreckage and into my operating room in Beverly Hills without the press finding out. No doubt one of the officers on duty would sell his phone-cam footage to the press for an astronomical amount sometime in the near future, but for now, at least, the secret would be kept.

The radio maven's scalp and one ear had been torn from his face and left dangling, while the TV celebrity had a punctured scrotum and a pierced testicle. The former's wounds would be visible no matter how good a job I performed restoring him, at least for a while; the latter's could be easily hidden from public view, and might not even affect his ability to father children, should he choose to. What they would tell their wives was up to them.

So, it was a long day, and I was tired and ready for the solace of Point Dume. The house was quiet when I entered, and I just wanted to shower and go to bed. I figured that Brittany could wait until breakfast to eat. I sat down on the couch to check my messages and emails and Facebook and LinkedIn and all, then opened the security cam link to Brittany's room. It took a while for the connection speed to catch up, and the screen was black for a while as the color wheel rotated frustratingly in the center of the screen. Much longer and I would have just given up and gone to bed.

But the screen finally resolved itself from blocky, blurry, jerky soft focus into a decent-definition overhead shot of the room. It was dark and the image grainy, but I could see that Brittany was sitting up naked on the bed. It was a very wide lens so that it could take in the entire room, and she was tiny in the picture. But she seemed very intent, and her arm seemed to be moving furiously. She was facing the full-length mirror opposite the bed. I switched to the bed cam, which was a full-body shot, facing her. She was oblivious to the hidden cameras, and her eyes were wide and fascinated as she stared directly at her reflection in the mirror, one hand cupping and squeezing a breast and pinching its nipple, and the other rubbing in furious circles between her wide-open legs. Though I could not hear her, I could see that she was huffing wildly. I could not take my eyes off of the screen; nor could I ignore the insistent erection that suddenly grew in my lap.

She was fucking *hot*.

My face was flushed and my heartbeat heightened as I rushed out of the house and across the back lawn to the guesthouse. It was a brilliant summer moon, three days from full, and there wasn't a cloud in the sky to soften its light. Even here at the beach the air was a balmy breath, warm and seductive. I crept silently to the door and lay my ear against it, just listening. I could hear her inside, panting, huffing, unable to moan. I could not fight the excitement welling within me. I pulled the keys out of my pocket and unlocked and opened the door, spreading a beam of blue-white moonlight across the bed and her naked body as if in a Weegee crime scene pop-flash photo. As I stepped into the door, my shadow wrapped her up until I slammed the door beside me. We were locked in stillness on opposite sides of the room, eyes glued to one another, unable to even blink, her hand still in place between her legs but motionless. The only sound was our breathing.

But irresistible force could not be held from immovable object for long; animal magnetism pulled me to her bed, shedding my clothing, led by the divining rod of my desire, and for the second time—which was really the *first* time—I entered her. But this time, I was entering newly constructed perfection... except for those fucking teeth. But even though kissing was not on the menu, it did not take long for the two of us, so brightly ignited, to explode together.

At first, I feared hurting the flesh I had taken such pains to construct, afraid to split her at the seams. But her healing had proceeded so completely, so perfectly, that it became apparent that there was no physical reason to hold back. We coupled violently, ferociously, acrobatically, our sex feral and unlocked, a slippery sheen of sweat between us. She became as aggressive as I, climbing atop me and taking control. I let her get away with that a couple of times before flipping her over and about and piercing her and controlling her as I was made to do.

Dawn rose to wake me, lying in a puddle of my own perspiration, draped across her now-flawless body. She was still asleep, her mouth wide, a soft snore rustling the pillowcase. Not able to bear the look of those teeth, I gently closed her mouth and took my leave. She came to as I was on my way out, but that did not slow my exit.

In the shower I scrubbed myself clean, my body bulging from the brisk aerobic workout of the night before. I looked out of the clear glass windows of the bathroom as I washed my hair and could see her tiny naked silhouette in the window of the guesthouse across the yard. Without willing it so, I became aroused all over again, and sprayed the suds off of my hairless body and down the drain.

I wrapped a towel around my waist and called in to the office to tell them that an emergency had come up, and that I had to go out of town. I wasn't sure when I'd be back. Still in the towel, I grabbed the keys, crossed the garden, and entered the guesthouse. And Brittany.

For two full weeks we explored the limits of physical sexuality, coupling creatively and constantly, her silence prompting my verbal urges, which made her even more eager and adventurous. Every orifice was explored and penetrated in all ways possible—and some that theoretically weren't—and each millimeter of human flesh was tasted and tested and put into play. We sexed until we were sore, then rested up and experimented with body parts other than our sexual organs. The one thing I could not do was kiss her and that jagged-stalagmite-stalactite mouth. She was welcome to use it in any way she liked—and she did—but just not on my mouth.

I thought that I had been a creative and experienced and indefatigable lover, and had been told so on many occasions, but this, *this* was the *nea plus ultra* of sexual experience. I had never spilled so much seed, and surely she had never attained blast-off so often as she did here. I counted a full dozen of her orgasms in a single two-hour coupling.

And then, it was time to wake up.

The day was in full bloom. Some cottony clouds had been set adrift across a cerulean sky by a gentle whisper of a breeze. Rolling waves crested in the distance with just a trace of white foam, and a lonely barge passed across the horizon. The gardener had just finished feeding and pruning the flowerbeds, and a riot of primary colors shouted for attention. The great outdoors beckoned, and it just seemed wrong to be contained within these walls.

I stood and looked down at Brittany, both of us spent, our flesh and faces aglow from the activity of the past fourteen or fifteen days. She looked up at me, her face a question mark. I had no answer; indeed, I did not even understand her query. I was finished, sore and spent and raw, and ready to take a long, deep breath. I stepped into my pants and out of the guesthouse, leaving the door open behind me.

Barefoot and shirtless, I walked through the garden to the edge of the cliff and stared down at the waves crashing against the rocks below. I had been operating on a purely intuitive level for the last couple of weeks, led by animal instinct that had wrestled intellect to the ground and beat the shit out of it. As I breathed the breath of God, I felt cleansed, replenished, even reborn. I became... *thoughtful.*

My reverie was broken by the sound of bare feet approaching through the grass. Brittany, still naked and fully revealed to the world for the first time, approached me and gently laid her hand on my shoulder. I looked up at her, and saw her fully for the first time, outside in nature, lit by the sun, her hair a soft corona, her skin flawless, a perfect body topped by a lovely, voluptuous, Hurrell portrait of a face. Perfection. I had had this perfection, tasted it, penetrated it, experienced it fully.

In fact, I had used it up.

She opened her mouth, trying to say something, perhaps something profound.

Maybe even something loving. But there would be no words; she was unable to speak, thank Christ.

So, I looked at her, saw her immobile, gorgeous, physically perfect, sexually astonishing self laid bare before me, and I felt nothing. I had been drained of all attraction to her; my fire had been doused, Eros abandoned completely. I took in my brilliant creation and realized that I had used it up.

So, with a swipe of my arm, I shoved her off the cliff and watched her flawless body tumble through the air and shatter against the jagged rocks below. She could not even scream.

What, did you think this was a fucking love story?

Life goes on. I've returned to the office to spin miracles, to make silk purses out of sows' ears, to take what nature and nurture have fucked up and set it right. My lot in life is to make the world a more beautiful place, to weave a tapestry of human glory, to make life a little more perfect.

I walk down Rodeo Drive, basking in the wonder of

Beverly Hills and its three hundred and fifty days of sunshine a year, surrounded by the finest, most prosperous, most beautiful people on the planet, and I know I'm a part of that. Of course, there is still the occasional nasty-looking specimen trudging through the lightness, something vile and ugly that casts its pall on an otherwise perfect day. But now when I see something horrific like that, I think, *I can do something about that.*

Tyler's Third Act

It had been sneaking up on me since Entertainment went online, but I guess the beginning of my end came with the Writers Guild strike in 2007. Not that I was a total Luddite; I did all my script work on an iMac, browsed my emails over hot green tea every morning, watched a couple of the funny videos that some other writer had forwarded to me. But if they were more than a couple of minutes long, I just couldn't pay attention to a little window on my monitor. It's hard for me to enjoy movies in miniature.

Why had I shelled out over ten grand for a new plasma screen, uncompressed 7.1 Dolby surround, and the whole Blu-ray thing, anyway? So I could watch a YouTube home video of some pudgy, pimpled adolescent act out his Jedi Knight fantasies, blown up to eighty inches of stuttering, cubist blocks?

No. I love movies, even if they're on television; movies have scale and scope and an emotional investment in stories and characters. I'm not going to watch LAWRENCE OF ARABIA on my iPhone, thank you very much. Movies are made for the big screen, and if it can't be an eighty-foot screen, eighty inches can still make do. Four point five just won't cut it for me.

All right, I tend to digress. I promise not to lecture a couple of generations who can't pay attention to a film if it's not in full, blazing color. If you can find joy in homegrown mobile phone movies over the craftsmanship of the best of Hollywood's greatest technicians, well, I feel sorry for you, but the planet keeps turning. If cavemen had developed camcorders before cave paintings, then there never would have been a need to write or paint to communicate; they'd have sent videos of their latest kills instead.

Bitter? Hell no, not me.

But after the strike ended in 2008, my world, if not

the state of photographed drama, changed for good, and that was bad. The great unwashed, uneducated, undead masses discovered reality TV in greater numbers than ever before and rushed like lemmings to leap from the cliff of scripted dramatic entertainment. They hibernated to their computers and PlayStations, evacuating the cinemas and home theaters, their eyes fluttering in unfixed attention-deficited fragmentation, Blackberried and text-messaged to the point of cranial vacuousness. If it required brainpower, it was abandoned for a quick barrage on a tiny, portable screen: a snack, a punchline in search of a joke.

But like I said, the world turns with or without me, spinning into oblivion, choking on its own dust. Ashes to ashes and all that shit.

When we emerged at long last from the noble fight against the studios and the producers, our Nikes worn thin as we marched obediently across the studio entrances, the viewing public had lost interest in my line of work. Life before the strike was remunerative, if repetitive, going into the second season as a staff writer on LETTING BLOOD, a medical procedural on NBC that reveled in the viscera of forensic investigation and the hot young personalities behind it. Okay, hard to make a case for art in the sea of commerce, but still... better than a YouTube video of a colonoscopy, right?

Regardless. Life as I had known it, when I was about to enter my first season as a producer on a series, was shattered by the strike. The series, like most others, was shut down and replaced by DATING DADDY, yet another reality show, this one featuring young women paired unknowingly with the oblivious fathers who had abandoned them in their youth, set up on blind dates with hidden cameras to catch them when they unwittingly engaged in daddy-daughter sex.

DATING DADDY, while dutifully scorned by the watchdog critical press, was embraced in record numbers by a drooling, knuckle- dragging populace hungry for all but the nudity and money shots, which were tastefully obscured with a digital blur. The uncensored DVDs and pirated downloads alike scored record numbers.

So LETTING BLOOD was put to a painless death, and the Nielsen families had either adopted the babies of reality or abandoned network television, never to return. While the networks, panicking to find they'd been forsaken by the brood they had so abused, tried in vain to find the lowest possible denominator to reach out to, they were as savvy to the ways of the modern world as the soon-to-be-retired idiot President from Texas, and they found their world, too, collapsing.

Scripted series were still produced, but they were broadcast to the vast darkness of outer space, perhaps to be viewed eons in the future by multi-eyed alien lifeforms with perplexed interest in life on the primitive third planet from the sun. Even the successful creators of series and their showrunners struck out repeatedly with their pitches; new series from the prophetic geniuses of seasons past crashed and burned with an industry that collapsed in an operatic prelude to the 2008 housing industry and financial markets.

Sure, basic cable had a measure of scripted successes, but their audiences, as well as their paychecks, were minuscule by comparison. Only the self-congratulatory Emmy Awards noticed them.

So when work was available at all, which was increasingly rare, it was at a greatly reduced rate. No one was making the big dollars from just a year or two before. Even the feature film business was teetering: illicit downloads and gaming took over from the box-office figures that just a year earlier had reached record levels. The only way to get your movie green-lit was to anchor it to a star... but even that was no guarantee. And the indie market that had so powerfully reawakened with LITTLE MISS SUNSHINE and JUNO and other low-cost, big-box-office Cinderella stories had collapsed in narcoleptic slumber.

So here I sat, watching the number of incoming emails decline as the ED drug spam grew in direct proportion to my depression. The house I had bought to celebrate my newly acquired status of LETTING BLOOD producer was already worth less than I owed on it, so I sold it at a loss of some three hundred grand, and moved into an apartment on a shady street overlooking the Los Angeles River in Sherman Oaks. I know that sounds cozy, but if you're not a local, you should know that the Los Angeles River is not what anyone from elsewhere could possibly define as a river: it's a concrete trench that runs through the San Fernando Valley that overflows on the six days a year when it rains in Southern California, but is otherwise a dry, baking cement gulf between nice homes and shitty little apartments. I now occupied the latter.

I went hat in hand to series I wouldn't even consider watching to get a single script assignment. Working for scale looked mighty good to me at this point. I wrote spec pilots, a couple of feature scripts, and was even halfway through a novel as my savings account stayed on a binge-and-purge anorexic diet... without the bingeing. I pitched all the broadcast networks, the Turners, the pay cablers, even the chintzy little digital channels way up at the end of the channel guide on your satellite system. I got the thumbs-down all the way down to the Fine Living Channel.

A bunch of my wretched brethren had turned to the great god of the Internet for solace, creating shows that they owned and producing them on a shoestring. Maybe one day they would find a way to make a living off of it, but I just couldn't get it up for that; that day, as sung by Ruby and the Romantics, was yet to come. I just didn't see a home for drama until true convergence had taken place, where everything from broadcast networks to YouTube came through the same pipeline to your giant screen in high definition. And that wasn't then.

Way back when, I'd had big dreams about writing movies, working my way up to directing my own original screenplays, a reflection of my own unique sensibilities. Of course, I never imagined creating blockbusters; I would be happy churning out my own: Cronenbergian-del Toronian-Aronofskian indies that would find a small but devoted following that allowed me the freedom to do Work That Mattered. It wasn't much to ask, but I was on my knees for years before the growing Pisan Tower of rejected spec scripts landed me an agent and a freelance episode of CHARMED.

So, my career history in a nutshell: a no-name, personality-free career bouncing from one television series to another, scripting for shows that *someone* watched, but no one that I knew. The chapters of my existence were brief and relatively drama-free: a Writers Room Romance or two that never went anywhere, an expanding waistline and contracting imagination, and growing cold-pizza-induced carotid blockages. My bank account grew and life was predictably comfortable. I had co-workers but no real friends, could type a blazing 50 words a minute, and sat before my home cinema alone to appreciate the Blu-ray beauty of my John Ford collection.

And now, the rug of my life tugged out from underneath my unsteady feet, I was wedged alone into a Sherman Oaks two-bedroom-two-bath, with nothing but my movie collection at rest in the second boudoir. I felt like a mime in a shrinking-room routine.

It was getting scary; the residuals were shriveling and

arriving less frequently. Most of the shows I'd worked on seldom lasted more than a year, and therefore were neither repeated nor syndicated. If I was lucky, they were bought by third-world nations, learning about shitty television as they shuffled their way haltingly toward civilization, providing me with coffee money. Movies and television were all I knew; as the debtors grew more hostile in their collection techniques, it became clear that I needed a job. My agent was useless; he had more important clients than me breathing down his neck. My skills were limited, and, at the moment, had little commercial value. Movies and television turned a shoulder to me that was so cold that it burned my fingers.

I sat in front of the 27" screen of my iMac, fingers poised as if ready to pound out a polonaise, but there was no music. Fear and creative impotence froze me in the glare of the monitor, bathed in its icy blue glow, keyboard silently awaiting keystrokes that never came, daring me to unleash an unbroken flow of genius that would take me past the world of series television, to the toppermost of the poppermost, A-listing for the rest of my life, leaving the Conelrad Agency for CAA and the heady aroma of true success.

I was not up to the challenge. My psychic dick shriveled, pulled back, retreated, went to sleep. Failure curdled my guts and I broke out into a sweat. I could not pull my eyes from the monitor, magnetized as I was to its beckon, held prisoner by its insistent presence in the otherwise darkened room. The Pioneer plasma wall screen in the living room behind me was dark; the iPhone had been silent for days; the Arclight down the street offered nothing but popcorn and projected pabulum. No, it was this glowing, one- eyed monster that held my future. I was no longer a child of cinema, not even the son of television. That night, after two acts of pleasantly dull existence, the third and final act of my life was about to begin.

I could never love this virtual world of virtual entertainment, but I would embrace it. If I fed this cyclopean monster the blood of my being, it would feed me. And I had just the idea for the first course.

It was time to create a website. There had never been a reason in the past: I was too busy to put together a MySpace or Facebook page, and even if I had, who would have been drawn to it? Well, beyond my mother, who is in a home and wouldn't even recognize me if I stood right in front of her—and she has never used a computer in her life. The exes would just want to pelt me with nasty responses to my postings... if they were even that motivated. And there certainly were not any Tyler Sparrow fans out there clamoring for news on my work.

So, I clicked on a GoDaddy ad on my Yahoo! homepage and registered TylersThirdAct.com before someone else beat me to it. Then I downloaded instructions on building a website and cobbled something together that actually was pretty attractive, filled with personal photos from my life's initial chapters, with liberal use of shots from all the series I'd worked on, as well as some candid shots from a couple of the C-list actresses I badgered into going out with me, and created the plan.

I'd discovered long ago that the most voracious Internet audience seemed to be those attracted to the seamier side of life, the brutes looking for a taste of forbidden fruit, uncensored looks at anything that a civilized society would normally be denied, whether it's penetration shots of a famous but talent-challenged TV actress and her rock star boyfriend, or the beheading of a Middle Eastern hostage. The world is bloodthirsty, voracious in its appetite for the unappetizing, its collective stomach rumbling whenever scandal and viscera are about to be served. In a world where life is cheap and sanctity and decorum no longer existed, I was a self-appointed curator of the world zoo... and it was feeding time.

After clicking through my local Yellow Pages, I emerged from the destitute darkness of my humble San Fernando Valley abode into the scorching, relentless sun, which shrank my underdeveloped pupils into pinholes. Sol's glare was so white-hot that it took several minutes before my brain could process my surroundings. When the world around me had irised back into visibility, I climbed into the Beemer to do some shopping.

One benefit from being out of work: mid-day traffic was light as I made my way over Coldwater Canyon from the Valley to the Basin. Pico Boulevard was filling with the kosher lunch crowd at its numerous delis, which punctuated the car repair lots, the used- book stores, the faded fabric shops, and the medical supply houses. I parked and pumped the meter with all the change I could round up and found that it wasn't the medical supply houses that offered what I was looking for, but *surgical* supplies I sought. I suppose Home Depot would have served my needs as well as what I was looking for here, but as a movie guy (okay, fine, television guy), the visual mattered to me. Well, normally the surgical supply houses were limited to those only within the medical profession, but after a couple hours and a half-dozen triple soy latte espressos trolling the boulevard, I stepped into a dark, dusty, cobwebbed little den that proffered all I had hoped for and more.

Though the surroundings within the tiny Silver Elite Surgical Supply store were grimy and ill-attended at best, the displays of gleaming, hungry scalpels, cutters, and other flesh-rending devices were immaculate. They stopped the heart; these challenged the gorgeous, horrific creations of the Mantle Twins in *Dead Ringers*. As I stood alone in the shadowy, seemingly abandoned little shop, I felt the theatrical stillness rent by a ripple in the air and the shuffling of old leather on the weathered wood floor.

"May I help you?" wheezed through the tiny shop, barely more voice than breath.

I looked up, then down to find the proprietor, a grizzled, hunched little man of indeterminate ancientness. His eyes, under the melting brow, were a pale ice blue beneath the milk of cataract, and peered out over the luggage of drooping lower lids. His liver-spotted scalp was studded with a few coarse white bristles pretending to be hairs, shellacked and pomaded across the cranium. He was bent over, a frail Quasimodo in the form of a permanent four-and-a-half-foot question mark. His surprising, solicitous smile was toothless.

"I need some surgical instruments," I told him.

"Hence your presence in a surgical supply shop." But his sarcastic reply was delivered with such an ingratiating grin that I did not feel insulted. "Are you a member of the profession?"

"Well, I hope to be."

"Ah. A student."

"Exactly. A student." I stood over the display case, taking in the instruments that gleamed in theatrical light. "These are beautiful."

"Thank you. I've made them all since we opened, back in 1948."

"Wait; you mean you actually craft these instruments yourself?"

He smiled again, and if there were blood coursing through his Paleolithic veins, he'd have blushed.

"The finest in the world, if you'll forgive me the sin of Pride." He looked at me, though I doubted he could recognize me a second time. "What do you need?"

"I need a couple of scalpels and a nice pair of cutters."

"Ribcage or smaller?"

"Um... digital? You know, fingers, toes?"

"It seems you have a very specific *speciality*." Yes, he said the five-syllable version.

I didn't answer, and he went to the glass case and removed two gorgeous, gleaming scalpels and a pair of cutters that fit perfectly into the hand. Really beautiful craftsmanship-- and I told him so.

"You'll swell my head," he replied. "So, these will do?"

"Perfectly. What do I owe you?"

"Let's see, that's, oh, $2,850."

"Yikes! I had no idea they were so expensive!"

He looked at me with some curiosity. "These are not surgical steel, young man.

They are bladed in solid silver. Cleanest cut in the industry. Quality has its price. I'm not making much of a profit on this, you know." I didn't know what to say, so I kept my mouth shut. He peered at me in a face-rumpling squint. "Well, you *are* a student. I suppose we could call it twenty-five hundred and everybody goes home happy."

Yeah, well, everybody but me.

"Of course, I could send you to some mail-order shop, where you can get the same instruments used by the *hoi polloi*. Naturally, your student identification and medical cards are up-to-date for the transactions, right?"

Well, money wasn't going to mean much to me soon, anyway, was it? So the dregs of my savings weren't doing any good just sitting in another collapsing bank, were they? Visa could cover it for now, and when the time comes, let the devil collect his due.

"Do you take plastic?"

He sighed. "It's a plastic world now, and it breaks my heart." He took my card, ran it through the manual reader, scrawled the amount and handed it over for me to sign. I scribbled my signature as he gently swaddled his creations in soft, elegant black velvet. It was obvious I was getting my money's worth. Transaction completed, I took the luxuriously bundled instruments under my arm as he shook my hand in his own surprisingly soft one and bid me goodbye.

Ensconced in my meek little Sherman Oaks dorm, I sat in front of the iMac, seeking the sites that would most likely yield the quickest access to the Web's sanguinary sippers. I put together a little ad with a PhotoBooth shot of my feigned innocence under the title *You want a piece of me? I will begin to remove my body parts live on webcam at 10 p.m. PDT Thursday at TylersThirdAct.com. The first one's free!*

After setting up a PayPal account that would be funneled to the home that lodged my demented mother, in the guilt-easing hopes that she could live out her waning and oblivious life in comfort and splendor, I purchased little animated spots on Fangoria, Bloody-Disgusting, Shock Till You Drop, Horror.com, Dread Central, Arrow Through the Head—all the horror sites—as well as the notably tawdry TMZ. This proved to be an auspicious and prescient choice. As soon as they began to run-- *literally* within hours of them being posted-- both Google and Yahoo! picked up the story, linked to my site, and the news went viral. Once CNN picked it up, there was no stopping the inferno that raged. Everyone assumed it was fake, of course; why wouldn't they? But it didn't keep them from checking it out. I did my best to exercise my Constitutional right to privacy, so no one was going to track me down on this, not until I was ready. I was getting hundreds, then thousands of hits on the site... and it was only Saturday!

In five days, I fully intended to begin my own disassembly, my personal contribution to the world's culture, blood of the lamb spattered all over the screens of the lions.

Blood, sweat, and self-sacrifice are the backbone of success in Hollywood, according to all the screenplay books. But I'll bet Syd Field didn't have the guts, the true intestinal fortitude to put his internal self on the screen the way I intended to.

I didn't bother looking into the legality of this. I assume there are laws against suicide... but they must be pretty toothless, since if you succeed, prosecution would prove to be a problem. I was merely taking the modern primitivism of self-mutilation and skin art to my own personal level. It was artistic expression, damn it!

If you went to the site before its premiere on that fateful Thursday, you would have subjected yourself to a little dance of snapshots from my life to date, which gave way to a full screen with my face and hands taking the shape of a clock, ticking down the hours, minutes, and seconds until the first excision was to take place. Beneath my beaming countenance, a calendar clicked away the days. Other than that, nothing else, aside from the same words seen in the ads. In the upper right corner, a button to click to join, a $100 payment payable only through PayPal, refundable only up to the moment of the first shearing. The first removal, as promised, was to be free, but if you wanted to see more, well, open your wallet, pal. Nothing worth anything is free, especially my own Silver Diet. Its webcast would be live only, no video podcasts, no replay recordings available. Though I am sure there were hackers capable of capturing and rebroadcasting the events and posting them elsewhere, I thought there were enough of the famished, ghoulish public out there with enough disposable income to make it pay. It was a one-way site, clean and elegant: no postings or blogging from me and no comments from the Peanut Gallery. I had no interest in what they had to say anyway. It's my life, and I'll do what I want.

Thursday seemed endless, a train never to emerge from its tunnel. My guts were roiling in anticipation, and I was unable to eat a thing. I tried to go to a movie, just to get out of my little abattoir of an apartment and make the day pass before the ultimate curtain would be drawn. But I couldn't concentrate on a thing. The Arclight was buzzing with mid-day customers—mostly the elderly and the Hollywood-unemployed—and as I passed through them, I could feel the occasional burn of recognition. Eyes surreptitiously tracked me out to the parking structure... unless it was opening-day nerves and paranoia I felt on the back of my neck. I was useless out in the real world, as usual, I guess, so it was back into the Beemer and the too-brief ride back to Valleyheart Drive.

The apartment was choking on itself, closed-up and fetid. The air conditioning had broken down—again—so I opened a window, and curdled, beige, air-like San Fernando Valley fumes reached inside to caress me.

I hung a purple velvet curtain behind the Aeron chair that faced the computer, and artfully trained a light against it. I positioned another light directly over the chair, throwing myself into a cone of illumination. For further creative effect, I threw in a sidelight. I didn't want the audience to miss any of the salient details. A crystal bowl, which, at showtime, would be filled with ice, was placed on the desk, right next to the hypodermic needle and attendant bottles of alcohol, anesthetic and antiseptic. At the end of the row of implements, a George Foreman Sandwich Grill was plugged in and heating up. To give me strength and solace, a tall, unopened bottle of Jack Daniel's was placed close by, with a nice, clean glass.

So now, the only thing to do was wait for 10:00, and my first leading performance. I vacuumed the apartment, did the dishes, took out the trash, washed the windows, threw the newly acquired DVDs of the last few weeks into their alphabetical homes, whipped up a smoothie which I couldn't drink, took a shower, shaved, made my bed, turned on CNN, wiped down the 80-inch screen, checked my messages (zero), washed out the blender, took a sip of my smoothie, and watched the clock.

It was not even five.

So, I surfed. I lingered over YouTube, got sick of the amateur-hour spoofs, the mediocre music, the decidedly democratic and creativity-challenged cultural contributions of the unpaid and unwashed, and listened to my stomach howl in protest. I scoured the more obscure sites offering up terrorist videos of physical disengagement, but I couldn't bring myself to watch. My stomach is tender when it comes to the real thing.

Give me foam latex body parts and Karo syrup blood, and it's giggles and grins; show me the real thing, and I've passed out on the floor. So, this was going to be a real event.

I checked the counters: more than half-a-million visitors had gone to my site! So far, I had fifteen hundred paid subscribers—that was $150,000!—and it was sure to go up after tonight's display. I could have quit now and suckered them, but making a profit for my incognizant Mommy—or even myself—was not the point. My meaning in life came in its disassembly.

It was only half an hour or so before the curtain was to be drawn. I changed into my performance attire: a nice suit and a hand-painted Argentinean tie I had acquired on a trip to Buenos Aires. My fingers were uncluttered by jewelry, which would be important tonight. Running my hand through my thinning hair one last time, straightening my tie, I sat before the screen, counting down the seconds before activating the camera.

Finally, Act Two in the life of Tyler Sparrow had faded

to black, and I typed, for the last time, "fade in".

My third act had begun.

By the time the webcam was switched on, there were over 900,000 ravenous denizens waiting online. I hated them for their lust, their tawdry, base instincts, their witless, plotless, pointless lives, their vampiric need for my blood. But I didn't have to like them, or even respect them. I could despise them, pander to them, and still fulfill my own destiny.

I did not speak. I did not perform. My face, hopefully expressionless, dispassionate, uninterested, stared back at me from the iMac as I took the hypodermic needle in hand, filled it with Lidocaine, plunged it into the base of the little finger on my left hand, and depressed the plunger. Shooting holes all around the base of the spastic digit, I emptied the hypo, and jammed my protesting finger into the bowl of ice. As I waited for the anesthetic to take full effect, I looked into the lens of the webcam-- into the greedy eyes of my audience-- without so much as a blink. I cleaned the cutter with alcohol and a soft cloth, and it gleamed a silver grin. My whole left hand was going numb, as dead as my heart, so it was clear the moment was near.

No words, no music. Silent drama in its purest form.

I held up my insensitive left hand, and it shook in nervous anticipation. My mouth went dry, and I couldn't keep from repeatedly clearing the cotton from my throat. I splayed my fingers wide in front of my face and picked up the eager cutters in my right hand, which also betrayed me with nervous tremors. I swallowed, then drew the shining silver implement close and opened its rapacious maw. Perspiration besotted my brow and trickled down into my eyes, making them sting. I ignored it and drew the cutters closer. Now or never; the heat from the Foreman Grill roasted my right side.

I took a deep breath and...

Snip!

In a single cut, the shears clipped through flesh and bone, and my unappreciated left little finger plopped onto the little white satin pillow I had placed on the desk. It sat motionless in a crimson corona of my blood, as the red stuff flowed mightily from the new stump at the end of my left hand.

Shock wrapped me in its shawl; there was no pain, only the dull throb of an accelerated heartbeat. Regardless, after holding it up on display for the voracious audience to prove to them that it was real, I brought it down to George's jolly little Grill and stubbed out the bleeding with a cauterizing sizzle. I screamed reflexively and gagged on the smell of my own burning meat, gulped down a double dose of Jack Daniel's, jammed my hand into the bowl of ice, and shut down the webcam.

I turned off the lights and sat in darkness, unable to stop the palsied shake that overtook my body. My hands shook most of all, and my heart was a rocket to the moon. Mission accomplished... its first chapter, at least. I took deep, ragged breaths, trying to bring down my pulse. Sweat broke out in a sheath over my body, cold and slippery, and I had to lie down on the couch. Still, there was no pain, though I knew it would come.

Even pharmaceutically and alcoholically deadened, the thudding beat of my pulse was strong in my stump, and it felt as if it were trying to expand. So, I swabbed it in antiseptic and wrapped it carefully in gauze and adhesive tape.

I lay staring at the cottage cheese ceiling, breathing deeply, not missing my useless finger, just trying to slow down my body's panic. Calm down, fella; it's over, it's going to be okay, you did it, just breathe, breathe, slower, slower...

It started to work; my eyes began to regain their focus,

my brain turned off the olfactory assault of my burning flesh, and my heart began to give up its sprint for a jog. One more long drink directly from Jack's neck and I was nearing functionality again.

When I was able again to get to my feet, I returned to the beckoning eye of the iMac and woke it from its slumber.

Over 1,600,000 viewers joined me for my little anatomical demonstration... and over two-thousand of them had actually paid for the privilege! Which led to this realization: I had just been paid more to cut off my finger than I'd ever gotten for writing a script. I cogitated on that for a while, trying to put it all into perspective. That, however, proved impossible.

I had to get out of the apartment, which closed in on me, threatening to crush the life out of me. I stumbled to the carport and climbed into the Beemer, bouncing clumsily out onto the street and ultimately up Coldwater Canyon, the night atypically cool and the traffic light. At the intersection of Coldwater and Mulholland Drive, I pulled haphazardly into the Tree People lot and stepped out into the last expanse of nature in the center of Los Angeles. Though the park was closed, I made my way through the valley oaks and piles of dog shit until I reached an open clearing. The San Fernando Valley was laid out before me, a dying harridan choking on her final gasping breaths. The NBC/Universal tower lorded over all it could see, a black obelisk of fortitude; lights twinkled and cars obliviously choked the Cahuenga pass into Hollywood. The city lay open and exposed, an autopsy pinned wide open for me to inspect. I saw the corpse decomposing before me, and its rot was contagious. A piece of me had been removed, and the course of action to follow was laid out. I felt lightened, relieved, excused from gym class. The network piranhas had been taking bloodless bites out of me for years; my destiny was now in my own diminishing hands. The Southern California sky wrapped me in its arms and put me to sleep.

"Roger, no!"

I woke suddenly to a new dawn and a stream of hot wetness. My furry alarm was a Jack Russell terrier relieving himself all over my head, its horrified owner, two-hundred fifty pounds of jogging jiggle stuffed into the finest Lululemon athletic wear that money could buy, screaming to wake the dead.

"No! Roger, bad dog! Get over here!"

I stood, hung over, my face dripping with Roger's pee, and remembered where I was and what got me there.

"Oh, God, I am so sorry!" She pounded across the dirt path and chased the prankster terrier in a circle as he easily evaded her, laughing a maniacal doggie laugh. I stood, weaving, glaring through confused, bloodshot eyes as she handed me a towel from around her neck. *"Roger!"* She shot away in pursuit of her little urinating monster, never to return, and I wiped away its possessive piss, fully humiliated, before vomiting all over the ground.

I climbed into the Beemer and joined the sardines that choked the only artery into the valley. Naturally there was rush hour construction on Coldwater, but again, there was no hurry to get home, was there?

As it turned out, there was.

When I arrived, media trucks surrounded the Valley Vista Apartments. News crews were buzzing on Starbucks and scandal. I parked and was immediately engulfed by a ravenous cadre of cameras and slick, sexless, Barbie and Ken news monkeys, each shoving their phallic microphones into my face for a multi-network blowjob. They shouted at me, rolling tape and demanding my cooperation. I was not up for this impromptu press conference and shoved my way through them and into my apartment, locking the hollow, plywood door behind me. Who had known I'd be so easily found?

This was not what I expected.

Though I had sought the spotlight as an artist, I had grown accustomed to the relative comforts of anonymity and resigned myself to being a meaningless cog in the entertainment wheel. Suddenly, the spotlight glared on me, and I sought the shadows.

This is what it took to get their attention? My blood? Jesus, you guys are *easy*!

The thin door and single-paned windows did little to muffle the roar of the needy tabloidmeisters outside, but I pulled the curtains and threw the chain bolt and retreated to the comforting glow of the iMac. It awoke with a click and showed me a list of dozens of unexpected emails, mostly from unfamiliar addresses, and almost none of them Viagra spam. I guess I was not so difficult to track down: my email address was tylersparrow@ymail.com, after all. My answering machine blinked "full". This lonely little hovel had suddenly overflowed with unexpected popularity. I had been elected King of the Prom! And all it took was the excision of a relatively useless digit (well, useful if you want to type "A" or "Z" or "Q", but otherwise overrated).

The phone kept ringing and the knuckles rapping on my chamber door, but I blocked it all out. I disconnected the telephone, shut down the mobile, and ignored the invaders until they at least quit knocking and shouting for me.

Muzzy-headed, the remnants of Jack seeping out through overactive pores, I hovered over the iMac and scrolled through the messages. Most of them were from the anticipated crazies, a bunch of fundamentalist Christians spewing hateful fire and brimstone, print and website reporters looking for a quote from the Crazy Cutter, a few friends and co-workers from around the various writing tables I'd occupied over the years looking to have coffee and talk. As I had no family beyond my mother in the Home, there were no outpourings of love and concern. Just more people who wanted something from me. Which is why I was where I was in the first place.

I opened my website and found a spike in the visitors. Five thousand people had now PayPalled to see the continuing dismemberment! Tonight's installment was an important second step. It was time to grow the audience, to bring eyeballs and open wallets to the site, to feed the chattering, nattering diners a second course to their virtual feast.

Ding!

The computer alerted me to more email, and I returned to find a message on top of the new pile, with an attachment. The address caught my eye: piecemeal82@gmail.com.

Surely a kindred spirit.

I clicked it open. The attachment was a photo of a young woman, very attractive, but not in the obvious Hollywood manner of TV bimbo: no blond hair, no boob job, and slightly snaggled, imperfect teeth. She had dark bobbed hair, glasses, seemingly flawless skin, and a face and body that offered hidden promises that could be missed on first appraisal. Of course, this was only a still photo, but it looked like it had been snapped privately, certainly never Photoshopped, and had a sense of very personal outreach. Her gold eyes looked directly into the lens, as if defying me to find her irresistible.

The message was simple: *I admire what you're doing. Want to videochat? Sally*

I stared at her picture, which stared back, expressionless. There was a trace of the Mona Lisa about her. Was that hint of a smile conspiratorial, a secret bond between us, or was she mocking me? I couldn't take ridicule right now; I was feeling very vulnerable. What was it exactly that she admired?

I looked back into her inscrutable face.

What the hell? How many attractive young women actually go to the trouble to seek me out? My life was now a deck of cards cast to the wind; there was no structure, no timeline, no appointments (at least nothing before 10:00 tonight), no *anything*. So, I hit Reply and wrote her back:

Sure, let's chat. Where do you live? In LA? When would you like to webcam?

Her response was immediate.

You took my breath away last night. I'm in Ojai, but I feel much closer to you. Are you by your camera now?

My heart started pounding. I reeked; I was shrouded in Jack Russell pee and Jack Daniel's vomit.

Give me half an hour, I typed.

Ignoring the mounting streamliner of emails and the scarlet flash of phone messages that pulsed beseechingly, I lurched into the bathroom, and after an endless strone of relief, submerged myself under the stinging nettles of a hot shower. Revived, if not refreshed, I blew myself dry and climbed into presentable attire before taking my place before the computer. Breathing deeply to slow my heartbeat, I typed in her FaceTime address and activated my own.

Her face filled the screen, looking directly into mine. And she was lovely. "Tyler," she said. "I can't believe it's you!"

Her voice was husky, smoky, seductive. And Jesus... *she* couldn't believe it was *me*! "Yeah, it's me," I answered. "I can't believe it's you."

She smiled, and I was delivered unto her. My heart was imprisoned in her cage from that first grin.

"You're beautiful," she said.

"You must be looking in a mirror," I told her. "Did you watch last night, Sally?"

"I did. You're very brave. It was quite a performance."
She paused and bit her lower lip before she went on. "It...
excited me." It was obvious: she was breathing more heavily,
and her face betrayed a sudden flush of passion. Cutting off
my finger excited her?

What was I getting myself into?

"I don't know what to say to that."

She stared right into the webcam... and my face. "Did it
excite *you*?" she asked.

Hm. To be honest, I had never considered the erotic
possibilities of my own dismemberment. I find no pleasure
in pain, nor have I ever found rendered flesh to be any kind
of sexual stimulation, even in fantasy. My arousals seem to be
much more Catholic than that. Suddenly, I felt square and
prudish and vanilla, but didn't want to appear so to this odd
young woman.

"Um," I began wittily, "not at the time."

She seemed disappointed, which in turn disappointed
me. I didn't want to let her down.

"Oh," was her succinct reply.

There was more pounding on the front door, but I
wasn't home. "Are you alone?" she asked me.

"Oh, yeah."

"Do you live by yourself?"

"I do. How about you?"

"All alone." Another long pause, then, "Are you lonely?"

It took me by surprise. A heavy rotting ball of isolation
started to expand within my chest, and I felt myself sinking
under its weight. My mouth worked, but no words came out.
Embarrassed, I could feel my eyes inexplicably filling with
unspilled sadness.

Lonely? Was I lonely? I hadn't noticed... until now. Her
face, calm in repose, watched me without judgment, and I

shrank in embarrassment under her gaze. She waited patiently for my reply, and it became clear that I could tell her the truth.

"I guess maybe I am." She nodded. "Me, too."

It wasn't possible that this beautiful, soft-spoken young woman could ever be allowed loneliness, and I told her so.

"The world is crowded," she replied, "but I don't walk among them." I knew how she felt, and she did not require an answer.

"Show me your hand," she said. I held it up to the camera.

"Can you take off the bandage?"

"You sure?"

"I'm sure."

Caught in her hungry gaze, suddenly and inexplicably sprouting an erection hiding beneath the desk, I slowly unwrapped my hand, where the wound gaped, red and raw. She gasped.

"Does it hurt?"

"Not so much."

"Hold it closer."

Her breathing went deeper, and so did mine. I could feel my blood coursing hotly through my body, pulsing with an accelerating beat. She leaned closer.

"I wish I could kiss it better."

My throat choked with emotion, and it took a moment before I could reply. "So do I." And I did.

More pounding on the door by my adoring public. "Will you do it again tonight?" she asked.

I nodded. "That's the deal. You wouldn't believe how many people have paid for me to do it."

"Yes, I would."

"Are you one of them?" She nodded and smiled, revealing a slightly crooked canine that made her even sexier... despite her bloodlust.

"I didn't think it was real. But it was worth the gamble."

The doorbell kept ringing and voices kept piercing the thin walls and windows of my Sherman Oaks chalet. Emails and IMs kept filling the background of my computer screen. Even my silent mobile phone kept up a vibratory boogie over on the counter. I was under siege.

"What's all that noise?"

I sighed. "I guess I've become very popular since last night."

"Is there a crowd there?"

"Just turn on your television; I seem to be all over the place." I spotted a video camera peering between a gap in the curtains and rushed over to pull it shut.

"I don't have a television," she told me.

I liked her even more. She was oblivious to the expendable fruits of my labors. She had no idea that I had settled for a grasp that far exceeded my reach.

"Well, it seems to be time for a personal crucifixion. They're all out there begging for it."

She started to speak, then backed off a moment. "What?"

She hesitated again, then continued. "If you want to get away from them, you can always come here."

As the cry for my literal blood ratcheted up in the background, I considered her generous offer.

"Really?"

"Really."

I looked at her peaceful, welcoming visage, and realized I'd never seen anyone with gold eyes before.

I needed to hide.

It didn't take long to ditch the hounds of journalism, and within half an hour I felt free of their slavering jaws as the Beemer sped northward up the Ventura Freeway. Fish-scale clouds domed the browning San Fernando Valley, but they had thinned into a gleaming blue by the time I'd passed through Moorpark. As I cleared the final mountain that announced the citrus farms of the Ojai Valley in a dramatic opening act reveal, I was stunned at how a 90-minute drive could change the world so dramatically.

The car's GPS led me through the tranquil little Old California farming town, now best known for its spas and weekend getaways, even while being hemmed in by endless groves of oranges. I passed through the two blocks of downtown, passed a dry but restful old cemetery, and wended my way around the outdoor ramshackle used stacks of Bart's Books, eventually winding up a dirt road to a tiny little Craftsman bungalow, removed from its neighbors. Giant valley oaks cast a canopy of cool shade, papery leaves rustling a welcome in the breeze. As the tires spat gravel and I coasted to a stop, a silhouette revealed itself behind the shutters.

My heart pounded a military tattoo as I cleared my throat and made my way to the door, not knowing exactly what to expect. I popped the trunk, climbed out of the car, and hefted my iMac to her porch. She met me there, and we stood facing one another through the rusty screen door for a wordless eternity. Her oddly lovely face was unmapped by experience, smooth as a ten-year-old's, a translucence seemingly never kissed by sun.

Her face was framed in a bob of auburn hair, and her astonishing golden eyes were wide in expectation, glinting in the sun. She was tiny, much smaller than I'd expected: barely five feet. She wore jeans and a loose, white cotton blouse under a sort of shawl, as simple and as unadorned as her face. But she was luscious, and her visage soon bloomed into a convivial smile as she held her arms under the shawl to ward off the chill.

"You made good time," she said as she pushed open the screen with a creak.

I stepped into the cool time warp of her home and felt embraced by it. It was furnished mostly in Stickley—or very good copies. The burnished old Mission Oak style suited the house, the setting, and its occupant. It felt untrammeled by the present, save for the modest computer sitting in the corner, out of place on the old desk.

"Where should I put this?" I asked, hugging the iMac.

Limping slightly, she led me to the dining room table and I set it down. There were no lights on inside; the house was illuminated only by the sunlight filtering through the oaks and the open windows. "Do you want something to drink?"

"What have you got?"

I watched her go into the kitchen and open the fridge. "I've got water, um, beer, iced tea, Diet Coke."

Beer sounded good, and she pointed me into the living room while she poured the Michelobs. I glimpsed into the bedroom on the way back, noticing a tidy and comfy lived-in quality as I passed. The bed was made, and there was silent-scream art on the walls of a darker nature than you would expect from that soft, sweet face. I sat on the overstuffed couch and took it all in. The place had a history, a permanence, something that I lacked. I was a loose end, at sea in a riptide.

She walked into the room, the tray of beers on one hand, and I stood to take it from her, settling back on the couch once she sat. I was trying to understand her, loving the breadcrumb clues as she offered them.

"Thanks for letting me come up here," I told her. "Thanks for sharing it with me," she replied.

"Why did you contact me?" As much as I appreciated it, I still didn't understand. "Because you did something bold and brave. And because I thought I recognized someone of a like mind, and I don't see many of those. Was I wrong?"

"I hope not."

With that, I reached tentatively to take her hand, and she let me. But I was greedy; I wanted both. So, I reached with the right hand as well, and her breath caught in her throat. She stared into my eyes, searching, before she wordlessly drew her left arm from under the shawl. It ended halfway between elbow and wrist. I was only beginning to understand the erotic charge coursing through me. Gingerly, I reached out, knowing she wanted me to, and touched the end of her arm, held it gently in my hand. I wanted to kiss it.

My voice broke as I asked, "Did you have an accident?"

"Not exactly," she replied.

"How did it happen?"

She scrutinized me again before deciding to tell.

"I work in a print shop. I was cutting and binding a big job, and as I watched the guillotine hacking off blocks of paper, over and over and over, it sort of cast a spell on me. It was so hypnotic. It kept cutting, chopping as new stacks of paper were fed into it, and it just drew me closer and closer into it." She looked at me, deciding whether or not it was safe to go on. It was. She gripped my hand tighter. "I don't know, I just couldn't keep myself from feeding it. Before I knew it, I'd shoved my hand in, and pulled away what was left of my arm, spurting blood all over the piles of paper. My life was all over that book."

She looked at me for a reaction, and I stared back in bewilderment. "Did it hurt?" I asked her.

"Maybe. But it made me come."

When she said it, I almost did the same. I was raging underneath my jeans. She dropped her single hand into my lap, knowing what was going on down there. I leaned in to kiss her, and she hungrily sucked on my tongue.

I carried her into the tiny bedroom; she barely weighed

anything. She was irresistibly petite, and her erotic appetite was completely at odds with her gentle demeanor. As we kissed, her eyes rolled back in her head, and her cries as her body became drenched in sweat were guttural, uninhibited, downright feral. When I laid her on the bed, she wouldn't let me stand and look at her; she pulled me down into the bed with her, and feverishly unbuttoned my shirt, willing me to do the same to her. I was happy to oblige.

Her skin was as alabaster-new everywhere, practically aglow, as if lit from beneath.

When I removed her blouse, the flesh beneath was almost as white as the fabric. She took my hand in hers, bringing it to her mouth, sucking on each of the fingers before settling on the new, raw wound. The wet heat of her mouth was as soothing as it was exciting.

I unfastened her pants, and she eagerly raised her hips to accommodate their removal.

They caught as I'd drawn them halfway down, and I struggled to pull them all the way off as her breaths came hot and rapid. They had hung up on the straps of her prosthesis. Her leg below the knee was rubber and steel.

When she said "Take it off," I knew what she meant, and removed the artificial limb.

Repelled yet hopelessly drawn to it like a moth to light, I kissed and tasted its fleshy sweetness. When I finally entered her, I did not last long.

I woke to darkness as an old mantel clock chimed eight times; the day had lost me in post-orgasmic slumber. The spot on the bed next to me was empty but still warm.

Moonlight reached in through the window with chilly fingers to touch me, and I felt vulnerable, dressed only in gooseflesh. I looked down the hallway to see Sally sitting in the dining room, illuminated by the cool light of the iMac.

She had set it up while I slept. I slipped out of the bed and into my jeans.

"I didn't want to wake you," she said, and I was grateful for the rest. "I hope you don't mind me setting it up; it was getting late." I thanked her and sat next to her to sign on. She turned away while I entered the appropriate passwords to prepare for tonight's performance. Once that business was attended to, she kissed me, running her tongue under my lips and over my teeth, fully waking me, before watching me prepare for tonight.

There were no more free samples on TylersThirdAct. com. This was now an exclusive club for paid visitors only. Over three thousand of them by now. I could tell that Sally was impressed, but she did not speak as I opened a bag and set up the *accoutrements* of my public dismemberment: the bowl, the hypo, the anesthetic, the Silver tools, the Foreman Grill, the white satin pillow. As they lay out in strict anal- retentive order, my hands began to shake again, and I turned to look up at her over my shoulder.

"Beautiful," she sighed.

"Okay if I take a shower?" I asked, and she nodded.

So, I did, shivering and convulsing as the shower washed the slime of my life down the drain. I vomited a thin, liquid gruel of my sins; that's all that was left inside me. And now it had been cast out like a wicked demon.

When I had completed my *toilette*, I returned to the iMac, Sally, and my future. It was close to nine now: one hour from the next chapter.

"You look beautiful," Sally told me, meaning it.

No. She was the beautiful one; all I could do was stare at her, take her in, worship her. If she thought I was beautiful, that made me happy. But I saw innocent, vulnerable beauty sitting before me, tiny and unprotected, and my heart sprung a leak. I took her face in my hands and kissed her, lovingly and lustlessly, gently pressing my coarse, stubbled cheek against the cream of hers.

"What will you remove tonight?" she asked me. "I—I was thinking of another finger," I stammered. "Aren't you..." She stopped.

"Go ahead," I said. "Aren't I what?"

"Just... aren't you afraid of repetition? I mean, were you planning to just do a finger at a time, then maybe your toes?"

"Um... kinda, yeah." Was there something wrong with that?

"I think your audience wants some, well... *escalation.* You don't want to lose their interest."

Escalation. For a moment, she sounded like a network executive. But I understood immediately that she was right.

"Like an ear?"

She took my hand in hers.

"Like a hand." She kissed it and looked up into my eyes.

"A hand." I swallowed. There was no turning back now. I had set my course of action, had outlined my final act, and committed to its fulfillment. I had made a contract with myself.

It was quarter after nine. The clock on the wall ticked away the seconds ominously, stealthily, and I could swear that the speed accelerated. But that was probably just my heart.

"And after the hand?"

"Let's think about that after," she said. "After the hand."

"You're right," I told her, and she smiled, her golden eyes igniting. She kissed me deeply and at length.

"I don't know if I have the right tools," I said.

Her face still aglow, she said, "I do." I didn't doubt her. She left the room and returned with an oversized paper cutter. She set it gently on the table in front of the iMac, and opened its heavy steel jaws. They gleamed in anticipation. I reached over and slammed the guillotine shut, and the hungry *shing* of stainless steel caressing itself sang me a lullaby.

I looked at the computer screen and saw emails and last-minute subscribers piling up.

I turned to the clock and saw that it was 9:35. "Well, what do you think?" she asked.

My soul and I had filed for divorce. I had sought resignation from the planet, solitary and insignificant, a single card misfiled among the millions. I looked into the eager eyes of another outcast, tiny and getting tinier. My worth came only in my diminution and eventual demise. So far, my audience had spent close to half a million dollars to watch my self-destruction, to witness an immolating soul cease to be. I found company, romance and solace in the act of dismemberment, elements that had eluded me in life, but burgeoned in the compressed time left.

"I think 'yes.'"

I saw her eyes fill with joyful tears and welcomed her approval as she hugged me tight. I began to tremble again, utterly exposed and at her mercy. She pulled away and looked at me, holding a question behind her eyes as I quaked.

"What is it?" I asked.

"Do you want me to make the cut?" I could tell that it's what she wanted; maybe it was what I wanted as well. When I nodded, the spasm within my body settled and calmed. I was truly in her hands.

"We'd better get ready," she said. The clock's synchronous symphony continued.

As practiced as a nurse, she injected the Lidocaine all around my wrist. I could feel the tingle as it began to take effect. She put away the needle and massaged my arm, and I absorbed her heat.

"You got any Jack Daniel's?" She had some Maker's Mark, and I made do. As its burn was absorbed by my veins, I calmed even more. The seconds on the clock pounded ferociously by, a telltale heart counting down. Just minutes until showtime. She sat me in a chair right in front of the iMac and took her place on a chair just out of the camera's range. Just before ten, she slipped on a simple, black Halloween mask.

"You ready?" she asked. I was.

I turned on the webcam and faced the camera. Another three hundred paid subscribers had come online in the last few minutes, and their number kept ticking up right up until ten.

I held my hands up to the camera, like a magician about to do a trick. Sally swabbed around my wrist with alcohol. I lay my sleeping arm on top of the paper cutter, and she helped me get it into position. The gleaming blade sparkled in wait. I tilted the screen of the computer so that the camera held my arm in a perfect frame. Then Sally took hold of the blade's handle and, before I had a chance to object, slammed it down, and my hand dropped to the satin pillow like a slaughtered starfish.

I jammed the stump of my wrist into the Foreman Grill and passed out.

It's a hoary writer's device to have the lead character lose consciousness and awaken to a new plot development with the passage of time. It's cheap but effective, and I confess to adopting it numerous times, even within this account.

Including now.

As I had no idea of all the events that transpired during my disconnection from consciousness, all I can convey is my awakening, and the overwhelming aroma that accompanied it. It was the heady, meaty scent of cooking flesh.

My body was bent in an awkward, uncomfortable

position, lying on a blanket that covered a hard metal surface. I opened my eyes and waited for them to focus, forgetting momentarily where I was. It was immediately apparent that I was not in my Sherman Oaks apartment. I was in Sally's house, of course, but in a rusting metal enclosure. It was a cage of thick iron bars, barely four feet square. My head was muzzy and clouded, my vision tentative, my body in varying levels of discomfort. Then I realized that my mouth felt dead and swollen inside; there was merely a stump where my tongue used to lie.

I lifted my head toward the kitchen, where a pot sputtered on the stove, delivering its beckoning bouquet. There were voices. I turned to see that Sally had company. Half a dozen visitors were seated around her dining table, each behind an elaborate Martha Stewart place setting. Though they were of varying physical types—corpulent, slender, tall, diminutive, and of varying shades and ethnicity—they shared this trait: each was lacking in various body parts. Their flesh houses had been hacked away.

When Sally entered the room, carrying a steaming platter of meat on her single hand, she looked in surprise and delight to see that I was awake. When she said "Good morning," all eyes were on me, and backed me into a corner of my cage. It was then that I recognized some of them: One was Daniel Power, VP of Dramatic Programming at NBC; another was Carolyn Pfenster from Turner; a third was some low-level Development guy from Universal, his name long forgotten after a failed pitch meeting last year. The others were unfamiliar to me.

Then I looked down to see that, aside from sitting naked before them, I was missing more than a hand. An entire leg had been removed as I slept, making my shrunken, dangling privates merely my second leg.

My stomach growled.

"Are you hungry?" Sally asked me. Everyone at the table answered in the affirmative, not realizing the question was not meant for them. I shook my head, denying the starvation that ravished me. I could not cry out for help.

The repast on the table before the gathered group was complete now. There may have been vegetables on the table, but I didn't see them. All I could see was Filet of Sparrow laid out in mouth-watering fashion, and the group of diners tucked into their delectable meal with relish. This show was no longer my own, I realized; the series I had created of my own demise had been taken over; I'd been replaced as the showrunner.

Tyler's Third Act now ran on a new network, co-opted by the new owners and relegated to their own website.

Sally got up from the table with a dish and kneeled before me, just inches from the other side of the bars. Through an opening at the bottom of the cage, she slid in a small plate. My disembodied hand lay there like a pink tarantula, tender meat barely clinging to the bones. "Go ahead," Sally urged me. "It's really good." Yeah, I thought. And so good *for* me.

I couldn't eat it.

That was then. Now, needless to say, I have developed a taste for human flesh, or I would not be here today. Well, what's left of me, anyway. My limbs are gone, and just about everything else. Nothing else could be removed without it being the end of my life; I look like home plate.

They say that it's not how you die that matters, but how you live. I beg to differ. As someone whose life was lived in anonymous mediocrity, my impending death was all that was unique about me. Tonight will be my final dinner party at Sally's. The only pain is in my heart, not my body. Existence is highly overrated. I will not miss it. And if your subscription is paid up, you will join me in my bon voyage party. Sally has gently bathed and groomed me for the wrap-up of my third act, and the webcam is about to be activated. I hope you'll join me for this very special episode before I fade to black and the commercials run.

SNOW SHADOWS

Winter fell softly but relentlessly outside the rippled old glass of the windows, frosting the edges with snowflake crystals. Sheer curtains hung like whispers, half closed, as the fireplace radiated copper heat against the dappled grey sky outdoors. Counterpoint, thought Nicholas. That's what life seems to be: up versus down, cheer versus anger, warmth versus chill. The stops in between were not worth noting.

He stood in front of the scarred, heavy old oak wardrobe, trying to choose which of the starched white shirts he would put on for class today-- not that it would matter to eighteen quiet, supernaturally well-behaved prepubescent students. He would do his best to inspire them, but couldn't tell if he was doing any good. They were so damned reserved. Could ten-year-olds truly appreciate art, the creative muse, the subtlety of a brushstroke as opposed to the fingertip slide across a capacitive screen? Maybe some of them, *surely* some of them, but he'd yet to meet one.

Fresh young faces crossed the schoolyard outside the window of his apartment, their risen- cream skin painted with chilly pink winter cheeks. Back home in Phoenix, the quad would be filled with raucous cries and roughhousing, but here in Twombley-on-Ravensbrooke, one of those alarmingly charming, all-stone medieval little towns you might stumble across on the motorway en route to your Lake District holiday, the children were quiet, serious, even inscrutable. Not that they were humorless, mind you. He'd seen them laughing with one another, but rarely in his class, despite his attempts to lighten the mood. In Phoenix, he was the funny, eccentric art teacher who was generous with an easy A. At the Ravensbrooke Youth Academy for the Arts, he was at sea. He wanted to feel clever and charming and make the kids like him but had not yet found his way. Maybe it was the difference between teaching public high school students in the U.S. and teaching ten-year-old supposedly gifted kids at a private academy in the U.K., but it was starting to get to him.

Even though the light outside was dim, the light in the apartment was dimmer; he was invisible to the children making their way to their first morning classes. Nicholas was still not used to the jacket-and-tie requirements for instructors at Ravensbrooke, and pulled his shirt out of the wardrobe and over his shoulders.

The sudden, gentle touch of a warm hand at the base of his bare back startled him, made him jump a little. But when it began to slide slowly over the curve of his rump and its mate started at his stomach and slowly worked its way up into the curls of the hair on his chest, he relaxed into the arms that surrounded him. He felt the light, moist kiss at the base of his neck, and was surprised, though not disappointed, at the warmth that held him.

It was a rare event when Rose initiated intimacy, even more so in the morning before classes. The decision to come and work at Ravensbrooke had been a mutual one, but he knew it had been harder on his wife than it had been on Nicholas. He knew that she agreed to it for him, not for her... nor even for *them*. Her moods had been all over the place, but mostly hovered at the lower end of the emotional spectrum. And for her to come to him with an embrace, to turn him toward her and kiss him so deeply before pulling away with the wickedest of smiles was, well, unheard of since they had come here. Hell, it had been pretty much unheard of in Arizona, too.

She slipped her hands under his unbuttoned shirt and slid it off of him, letting it drop to the floor. When he bent to pick it up, she kicked it away and shook her head.

Well, this was different.

He glanced over his shoulder to see the children still scurrying about the yard, clouds of misty breath huffing, still completely oblivious to what was going on on the other side of the distorted glass.

"They can't see anything," Rose said. "What if they can?"

Her smile was atypically salacious. "Well, they're here for an education, aren't they?"

She wrapped her arms around Nicholas and backed him to the sturdy old bed of massive mahogany posts and lumpy, marshmallow mattress, then eased him onto the rumpled sheets.

Nicholas wasn't sure how long it had been since last they had made love. Or even fucked. Two weeks? Three? She had been dark, quiet, detached for months. Though she tried to hide them behind the bathroom door, he knew that her crying jags were frequent, would wrack her body with violent sobbing. So... though he knew that he might be late to his first-period class, which was a pretty high-falutin' offense at Ravensbrooke, he was not about to push Rose away. She was a beautiful woman when she let herself be so, and most men would find her hard to resist when she was approachable. Her hormones had been his best friend and his worst enemy, with way more of the latter of late; he was not about to discourage this sudden burst of passion.

So when she had him on his back and tasted his neck, his eyes couldn't help but close. And when her hands began to unfasten his newly-belted pants, how could he object? He reached up, gripped her head in both his hands, and pulled her to him, kissing her deeply. He pulled away to look into her slate-grey eyes, which drilled into him. She was taking control here. When he started to speak, she put her hand over his mouth to shut him up. She slowly lowered his pants and shrugged out of her silk robe.

A knot in one of the fireplace logs suddenly exploded with a bang, tossing a cinder onto the bed, just missing them. It burned out immediately, but not before breaking the moment.

"It's okay," Rose told him. "It's out. But I'm not."

Neither was Nicholas. But he was facing the window, and there was activity outside. He wondered what it was, but knew the fragility of the moment was not worth risking. Rose, though, saw the flash in his eyes.

"What is it?"

He shook his head, but peered out the glass from the bed. It seemed that the students were all headed in a single direction, which was odd. Something was going on out there. Now naked, he moved from the bed to the window, curiosity overwhelming lust. He stood at the edge of the wispy curtain to see the children move across the now-white lawn, thick clusters of snow drifting in slow motion around them. They were all looking up. Across the quad was the highest structure in the village, a 400-year-old spire that reached high into the sky, its masonry long gone black and mossy. It had a giant, golden clock-face, a clock that still was as accurate as any chronometer; but that is not what held the gathering young crowd in its thrall.

Rose stayed put on the bed. He was certain she was getting angry. When she put her robe back on, he took that as proof. It would be a long day.

The imperfections of the glass made it difficult to see clearly all the way across the schoolyard, but he could see there was a figure all the way up at the top of the clock tower spire: almost certainly a woman. He knew immediately who it must be.

Rose came up behind him, holding her robe tightly around her.

"What's going on?"

* * *

The Ravensbrooke Academy was sturdy, ancient, had withstood battles and burnings, having served many lives before its current incarnation as a training ground for artistic but otherwise socially incompatible youngsters. It had only been designated thus for just over the last century: barely a tick of the clock in Twombley-on-Ravensbrooke terms. Its grounds were expansive, breathtakingly beautiful, and, despite the heavy drifting snowfall and chilly grey stone walls, was surprisingly welcoming. In spring the trees were lush and full, but now their skeletons held up armloads of thick snow, which offered its own amount of picturesque appeal. The annual fees were dear, though there were scholarships for children of extraordinary talent and promise.

David Sutcliffe was one of those extraordinary children. He was the Odd Boy, even by Ravensbrooke's standards, which is odd, indeed. Always quiet, seemingly friendless by choice, David's command of the English language was masterful but rarely exercised. When he did deign to speak, his utterances were brief but almost always complex, even confusing, not just to his nine-year-old peers, but particularly to his elders. His gaze, when he bothered to look you in the eye, was piercing, as if he were measuring you, judging you, figuring you out. Though he was quiet and strange, he was not unkind. His manners were impeccable and old-fashioned. His lineage was uncertain: as a baby, he'd been abandoned on the steps of the constabulary, his little eyes blacked, his left arm broken, and it never did set properly. It looked like his arm had two elbows, though only one of them bent. He'd been adopted by a working-class couple on the east end of London and had proven a bit of a handful. He seemed born with a frightening intelligence, speaking sentences not long after he was a year old, and arguing about the merits of the Classicists vs. the Impressionists by the time he was eight. The Sutcliffes knew David was special, and loved him with all of their hearts, but also knew that he was not like them, which made them nervous. When his school principal came to them with news of a possible scholarship opening up at such a prestigious institution as Ravensbrooke, they did all they could to deliver such an opportunity unto their quiet, gifted, strange young son.

David trudged through the morning snowfall, greeting the drifting clumps around him as if they each had a name. He felt strong, released as he walked through the wide-open schoolyard, breathing deep the gathering gloom. He liked the dimness of the sky when it snowed; bright light hurt his eyes. He was used to living on a narrow little street in a narrow little house with narrow little neighbors who all looked and sounded alike. The massiveness of Ravensbrooke was a revelation to him, and he breathed it in as if it would leave him if he dared let it out of his lungs.

He didn't notice the cold; he was composing a piano duet in his head, and the parts were caught up in a fight. He didn't hear the gasps around him at first, nor did he see the other students shove past him to the base of the school's clock tower, as the left hand in his brain was battling the right for supremacy, *forte* pounding the *pianissimo* into submission.

Then, one of the larger students, a beefy girl called Penelope, bounced off of him and knocked him to the ground, his fall leavened by the heavy pelt of snow beneath him. As she bounded off, not having even realized what she'd done, David stood and brushed snow from his crimson-tipped porcelain face. As all the other children were looking up, David did the same; his eyes, the deep, clear blue of a frozen lake, turned grey as they reflected the snowy sky.

"Miss Featherstone..." he breathed aloud, her name appearing in a cloud.

His theatre arts teacher, a tiny bundle of nervous energy who seemed always to think she was on the verge of being chastened, stood like a cuckoo bird at six in front of the giant clock face on the tower that loomed over the campus. Her shiver seemed more from nervous anxiety than from the cold, though she was dressed only in a navy blue skirt and matching unbuttoned sweater over a crisp white blouse. Her eyes, deep brown and wide, almost always showed the whites around her irises, but they were wider now, and unblinking. She plucked at the snowflakes as they dropped to her shoulders, as if it mattered, and her entire body was quaking. Tears were freezing on her cheeks and her long, straight black hair was being gnarled by the breeze way up above the crowd forming below. She seemed to be trapped in some kind of hysteria, her cries seeming more like laughs much of the time. She seemed to be talking to herself in mutters that were carried away by the wind, and then shouted:

"Laugh at me now!"

David didn't want to laugh at her. He didn't want to cry, either, but he certainly didn't want to laugh. She seemed so sad, so pitiful, so kind of, well, crazy.

Some of the kids were laughing at her, though, which made David uneasy. He didn't understand how other people seemed to think, if they thought at all. He didn't want to understand them.

* * *

Nicholas charged out of the teacher's apartment and

into the snow, pulling on his overcoat and wrapping a scarf around his neck. Oh, Jesus, he thought. Has it come to this?

Gemma Featherstone stood quaking atop the clock tower, the toes of her simple black shoes curving over the edge of the masonry. Nicholas charged his way through the young crowd of students as they stared up to see their drama instructor precariously balanced on the clock's lip. It was not the cold that froze him into place at the base of the spire.

Gemma locked eyes with Nicholas, then pointed to him, fury mixed with pain.

"Laugh at me now!" she cried out again. "Laugh at me now, Nicholas!"

He didn't want to laugh at her and wondered why she so commanded him. He didn't remember ever laughing at her. She wasn't really very funny.

Her timing, though, was impeccable. As the accusation left her lips, Rose entered from stage left, wrapping a coat with a faux fur hood around her, rushing up behind her husband.

"Get back inside!" Nicholas shouted at Gemma.

That just made the tiny woman above them shake her head like a petulant child. "Go ahead, laugh at me now!"

"No one is laughing at you!" Well, nobody other than the mean kids clustered on the east end of the quad.

"What is she doing?" Rose asked as she rushed up behind her husband, laying her hand on his back.

"Laugh at me now, Nicholas!" Gemma cried again.

Rose lifted her hand from Nicholas's back, and looked at him, a shadow crossing her face.

Nicholas didn't dare look at her... or away from Miss Featherstone. "Don't do this!" he shouted, but that only made her willful.

Her eyes clenched shut, she leapt, her petite figure adrift

in the wind and snow as the clock struck the quarter-hour.

* * *

David watched in mesmerized fascination as Miss Featherstone took to the air, a navy blue angel, as time slowed to a crawl. She was held aloft as the clock stopped ticking and nobody blinked or breathed. As much as it was possible for a nine-year-old, David fell in love with Gemma Featherstone at that very moment. As the wind teased her hair and rustled her skirt, she seemed to look right into his eyes, and David could tell that she loved him as much as he loved her. Which meant: *forever*.

And then, because only he could see in slow motion, he observed something lift from the pocket of her sweater. It was small and white, a slender envelope that lifted into the sky, tumbling through the air like a wounded bird, drifting, falling.

He saw her lips move, and would swear forever more that she spoke to him: three simple words, words that no boy wants to hear until he's a man, and even then only when he's lost his mind to passion. But these were special words to a special boy like David, and they stole his heart.

She said, "I love you."

The clock's second hand clicked over and time returned to its whiplash pace in the blink of an eye. Miss Featherstone's body raced to the granite walk and shattered, breaking her neck and taking her life as the crowd gasped as one and rushed back to keep from getting hit.

David, though, didn't move. The slender white envelope tumbled, falling on its end into the snow before him, slicing into it and disappearing beneath its soft cloud. Looking around to make sure that no one else had seen, he reached in and pulled out his personal little mail delivery and slowly backed away from the ensuing bustle of activity.

* * *

Gemma Featherstone stared up from the broken pile of her body through wide, freezing eyes. As her life quickly retreated from the body that had held it for the last thirty-two years, she saw the face of the only man she'd ever loved loom over her to look deeply into her. But once glimpsed, he—and everything around him—faded from view forever.

* * *

Nicholas stood at a distance as Gemma Featherstone's delicate, battered body was scooped up by the ambulance team, covered with a sheet, and trundled into the vehicle before disappearing behind the solid slam of metal doors. The cooling corpse, its head lolling horribly, was so tiny that she seemed like a doll: an exquisite, fragile imported doll meant to be protected under glass, but now hopelessly and irretrievably broken. All the king's horses and all the king's men. Mr. Wedge, the corpulent and testy schoolmaster, was at a loss, trying to herd an unruly gaggle of privileged and talented youngsters into the buildings. Ms. Tarragon, in charge of counseling the girls, tried to assist, but kept choking on her own tears. Other teachers stood horrified and unbelieving at the proceedings and were unable to speak, though that would change quickly. The teachers' lounge would *not* be quiet this morning.

Rose had already retreated to the apartment, standing at the window and holding the curtain, which half covered her face, in her hand. Her morning's joy had long been extinguished.

Nicholas glanced over his shoulder, but before he could lock eyes with his wife, she pulled away, back into the darkness. He would have to deal with that later. For now, he watched, still stunned, as the ambulance pulled away, its swirling red light disappearing into a deepening drapery of blinding snow.

Nicholas had known that Gemma was unstable—what artist wasn't?—but he never thought she was capable of this. He had no idea how much she was hurting, but knew that he was the reason for all that pain. From the moment he saw her he found her intriguing, if not particularly attractive. She couldn't have been five feet tall—no bigger'n a minute, his Nana would have called her—with wide, seemingly frightened eyes that rarely blinked. When she smiled, it seemed like a performance that she drew from some kind of Stanislavskian memory course to dredge up joy and happiness and charity, rather than her own experience and emotion. When she spoke, and when you could hear her, which was rare, as she had so little confidence that she spoke in whispers and mutters, she was surprisingly witty, if not exactly funny, but anything but seductive. She certainly was not his type, if he had one. Gemma's frame was slender to the point of skinny, a head that was almost too large for the body that supported it, with a build that bordered on boyish. Rose, whom he'd married only three years before, was more voluptuous than anything, and a good half-foot taller. Gemma's hair was glossy and soft, long and wavy; Rose's was thick and black and cut to a stump at her jawline. In the beginning, though, it was Rose's smile that enchanted, engaged, drew him in. It was luminous, lit up her entire face... and *his*, though that was a while ago. All that seemed to remain of that smile were the creases that it left in its wake. He missed that most of all, though once in a while, as it had that very morning before Gemma killed herself, Rose's face would light up again and the world would be reborn.

Gemma's smile, when it dared emerge—the *real* smile, not the one she tried on for the public— was shy, sad, and, in hindsight, endearing.

Gemma was the last of the instructors that Nicholas had met when he came to the Academy. As Rose attended to her administrative duties behind a massive, centuries-old desk, Nicholas and his Art History class had volunteered to paint the sets for the junior division's performance of *Romeo and Juliet*, a story certain to resonate with ten-year-old star-crossed lovers everywhere. He found Gemma to be quite wonderfully encouraging with the kids under her tutelage, but when he'd tried to strike up a conversation as they painted Juliet's balcony, she became even more diminutive, and couldn't even look him in the eye.

He developed a fascination with her after that. She seemed a bit like a little mouse, frightened of her own shadow when around adults, but sweet and commanding when alone with her students, all of whom seemed to adore her.

Nicholas tried to draw her out, and would always greet her with a big, American "hello" and a grin, which seemed to embarrass the hell out of her. But more than once, he caught her giving him a quick, interested look. He certainly never sensed the approach of danger or flirtation or even infatuation, but it happened.

He had needed a volunteer for his Life Drawing class, which, of course, when conducted for prepubescents, did not involve nude models. Rose was going to sit for his class, but at the last minute, the Wedgehog decided he could not do without her actuarial expertise in the office and held her captive there for the rest of the afternoon. He'd seen Gemma running lightly on tiptoe down the hall outside the open classroom door and went out to stop her.

"Do you need to be somewhere?" he asked her. She

looked down at her feet, never at his face.

"I never need to be anywhere," she muttered below her breath. That made him smile. His smile made her flush.

"Could you sit for my Life Drawing class? It would just be for an hour or so."

Her face went bright red, even though the trace of a smile sneaked out. "Oh, no," she said, "I couldn't do that."

"Sure you could," he encouraged her. "You'd be a lovely model."

That made her look up at him, but without lifting her head. "No. Really." He could tell she wanted to be convinced, and he felt like convincing her.

"Oh, come on. It will be simple; just sit on a stool for an hour and let the kids sketch you.

The kids will love to draw such a pretty woman." That lifted her head.

"I've modeled before..." she whispered, but when he asked her to repeat it, she just shook her head. Her shyness was captivating, brought out a beauty that Nicholas had missed in her before. This hint of a past, something beyond the walls of the school, was somehow a bit provocative to him on top of the frightened little woodland creature that she seemed to be, and he felt the first little tug at his heart.

"Then you'll help me out?"

She pondered it for a moment, then nodded. "Yes," she said, "I'll help you out."

"That's great, thanks. I owe you one."

"And I plan to collect," she mumbled, hoping Nicholas didn't hear her. Of course, she just meant it as a little joke. Of course.

* * *

Needless to say, classes were cancelled for the day, which was a Friday, anyway, and led to a welcome holiday for students and staff alike. The students—Junior and Senior levels both— gathered in the dining hall for an orderly luncheon and took to their rooms to get out of the cold and into their forbidden electronics that so many of them had sneaked into the academy.

Instructors and staff tended to look the other way when the youngsters battled one another on their iPads and PSPs-- as long as they didn't make too big a deal of it-- and kept them out of the classrooms.

But David, the Odd Boy, was not so electronically inclined. Besides, he had a secret, and wanted to be alone. So, while the other students decided to take this opportunity to slaughter a few more brain cells in honor of their dear, departed drama teacher, David made the long walk to the music building, which was dark and empty, and whisper-scuffed to one of the little piano studio chambers at the end of the hall. Normally the hallway was filled with a civil war of battling instruments and melodies from behind the not-quite-soundproofed doors of the studios. But on this day, it was eerily silent, empty, abandoned. Which, of course, was exactly why David was there. He opened the unlocked, padded door of room 32, flicked on the lights, which stuttered into dull illumination, closed the door behind him, and took a seat on the padded piano bench.

Once he was seated and alone, he realized how hot it was in here. He was sweating, his palms slick. He wiped them on his pants before he dug into the pocket of his sweater and held out the letter from the world's most beautiful teacher. His hands shook as they held the little ivory envelope; it was blank, save for a tiny heart drawn in red ink on the upper right corner where a stamp would be, addressed to no one.

But it had been delivered unto David. He touched the little heart with the tip of his finger, tracing it as she had drawn it, and felt the heat of her as he did so. He could smell her, and held the envelope close to his face and breathed the scent of her perfume deeply: rose, subtle and distant, but rose. He could even smell its redness. He touched the little heart to the tip of his lips and kissed it. He was sure it kissed him back.

He slid his finger under the flap, slowly and carefully easing it open without tearing the parchment. It was still damp with her saliva, he realized, as he slowly teased it open. Once the flap was free, he ran the tip of his tongue across the gum, tasting the mint of the sticky envelope on top of another, more organic flavor. He tasted her kiss.

He pulled the envelope away, knowing what he was doing was wrong, weird, perhaps even naughty. He held it carefully in both his hands, as far from his body as he could, staring at it, feeling guilty. But he could not keep from her message to him for much longer; he needed to know what she had needed to tell him. His heart pounding, he opened the envelope and drew out the single scented piece of thick paper within. He carefully laid the envelope onto the piano's keyboard, unfolding the letter, which was creased in half.

"I love you," the letter told him. "I don't want anyone else."

Then, a faint lip print of subtle pink, and what appeared to be a small spatter of dry blood.

She loves me, David thought. *I knew it!*

For he loved her, too, always had, only didn't know it until now. Now that she was dead.

He ran his fingers over the lip print, his hands kissing her lips before he dared to touch it to his face. But he could not resist her kiss for long; he touched the paper gently to his mouth and felt the lipstick stick lightly to him. He drew it away from his face and stared at it; the lips spoke to him, told him again, "I love you, David."

He placed the letter on the music holder on the piano and stared at it, his hands suddenly inspired, and he began to improvise a gentle composition that invented itself as it went along.

* * *

The sun began its early evening winter descent, though it was barely four o'clock; the police had come and gone and the staff had clustered together to cluck and coo and conjecture about what had driven Gemma Featherstone to take her life. Theories abounded—these were teachers, after all, and teachers of the arts given to flights of imagination—but theories is all they were.

Miss Featherstone (and she was always Miss, never Ms.) was quiet, shy beyond the point of painful around adults, and very private. She worked in the theatre, then trundled off to her apartment, her evenings always spent alone, never really joining in. They had never trusted this queer duck, this tiny, quiet creature who would always look like an aging girl, never truly a woman. She may have been in her early thirties, but if you didn't look closely, she could have been twelve. Not really part of the Ravensbrooke family, but she did a good job, and the theatrical presentations that she produced were always impressive, and often won awards.

When the last of the loitering onlookers had given in to the chill that followed the setting of the sun, Nicholas knew he could no longer avoid his home and his wife. The blackout curtains were drawn inside his apartment, and he dreaded what lie in wait for him behind them. He felt hollow, detached, emotionless, though he knew this was only temporary. Still, he could not feel a goddamn thing.

So, he turned and took a final look at the clock tower that threw its dimming shadow over him before he walked back to the teachers' quarters and into his home.

Nicholas walked into the apartment to the scent of a simmering stew. He peeked into the kitchen to catch a glimpse of Rose's back, standing in front of the stove, stirring the pot. She did not turn to acknowledge his entrance. He peeled the scarf from around his neck, hung his coat on the hook by the door, and stood in the middle of the living room, not sure what was coming next. He had no appetite for beef stew tonight.

When he could no longer stand silently in the living room, he entered the kitchen, approached Rose from behind, and wrapped an exploratory arm around her waist. She let him, but did not reciprocate. She didn't even turn to him. She just ladled out two bowls of the stew and stepped out of his arm to set them on the heavy wormwood table. Nicholas, his arms empty, had no choice but to take a seat. They sat at opposite ends of the table, neither of them hungry, staring into their stew as it cooled before them.

Finally, Rose looked up at him, and he could see she was quaking, tamping down the explosion she really wanted to release. Her jaw flexed as she clenched her teeth.

"What was that all about?" she finally asked. Their eyes met and froze.

"I haven't a clue," he replied. "Who knows why anyone takes their own life?" He knew that's not what she meant.

"She was one big secret," he offered. "It's sad."

It was sad, but not the reason that unspilled tears began to well in her eyes. "She was talking to *you*," Rose said. "Why was she talking to *you*?"

"I swear to you, I don't know," he lied, his stomach roiling. "Were you fucking her?"

"Jesus, Rose!"

"Were you having an affair?"

"Of course not!"

"Then why was she shouting at you when she jumped? Why did she do it?"

"I don't know."

"Did you love her?"

"Goddamn it, Rose, no! I love you!"

She went silent, accepting the answer for the moment, staring down into her stew. Nicholas watched her, hoping things would calm down now, when she suddenly picked up her heavy ceramic bowl and threw it at him with all her might. Nicholas ducked, and the bowl shattered against the wall, spattering it with meat and gravy.

* * *

It was dark out, and Theatre class had long been over. Gemma and Nicholas were dappled with paint from their overhaul of the ambitious *Romeo and Juliet* set, but the chore had been finished. The stage stank of linseed oil and tempera and whitewash, and it clung to them like a blithe spirit. Nicholas loved the smell, had been away from it for far too long. His own painting efforts had practically vanished once he started teaching. And here at Ravensbrooke, with all the problems adapting to life in small-town England with a wife given to dark rounds of depression, inspiration had fled him, and only blank canvasses sat waiting in his closet for his attention. So even though it was only slathering sets and cycloramas with paint, it felt good to wield a brush again.

They toiled in silence after the last of the students had left, so when Gemma asked Nicholas to tea, he was taken by surprise by her invitation.

"That would be nice," he said, warming to her smile when he accepted.

Gemma's apartment on the campus was on the other side of the Academy from his own, on the fourth floor of the Music and Drama building. It was set up pretty much the same as his, though the rooms were a bit smaller. However, the walls were filled with framed showbills from ancient pantomimes, West End productions, and even some obscure motion pictures. It was a collection: some of them seemed quite valuable. There were a couple of awards that he did not recognize sitting on the old upright piano in the corner, as well as an assortment of photos chronicling the life of an actress named Gemma Featherstone, all in heavy antique frames.

Nicholas roamed the tiny parlor, taking it all in as Gemma brought the water to a boil, admiring the theatrical artwork and, finally, the photos.

"Are all of these you?" Nicholas asked, just before the teapot began to scream.

"All of which?" she asked, entering the room with a mug of steaming chamomile in each hand.

He looked up from the photographs and beheld her face as she entered the lemon-warm light of the parlor. He hadn't realized before quite how lovely she was, how delicate her features, how deep the soul in her eyes.

"Oh, those..." She blushed charmingly.

"Don't 'oh, those' me. They're quite beautiful." She wanted to say *stop it*, but instead thanked him.

"You said you had modeled before," Nicholas said. "Photographic or paintings?"

"Both," she said, shyly. "And that sculpture, too." She pointed at a small bronze nude statue under the glow of an old lamp on a wooden side table. It was, well, provocative, and a freshly fascinated Nicholas began to see her in a new light.

"It's just a sketch; the actual piece is life- size, in a museum in Leipzig."

"I'm impressed!" he told her. And he was. He looked closer at the photos: some were obviously from stage productions, but a couple of them looked like publicity photos from films.

"Did you give up acting to teach?"

"Did you give up painting to teach?" she shot back.

"Touché." There was a large photo album sitting on the side table next to the sculpture.

Nicholas was dying to give it a look. "Did you do any films?" he asked her.

"A couple," she answered evasively. "A dozen years ago."

"Anything I might have heard of?"

"I hope not. Nothing I'm particularly proud of. Which is why I sort of gave it up."

"I'd like to see them," he said, meaning it. He wasn't just being polite. "What were they called?"

She just shook her head, her face rosy with embarrassment, only piquing his interest further. He walked over to the table and picked up the photo album. "Do you mind if I take a look?"

"Drink your tea," she replied, and he sipped, burning his lip. She watched him wince, and he watched her watch him.

"Really," he said, "Can I take a look?"

She sipped at hers like one of those little toy birds that bob in and out of a glass of water. "If you must."

"I must," Nicholas said, as he sat on the piano bench and hefted the album onto his lap. He patted the seat next to him, and she sat down, their thighs touching. Perhaps it was intentional.

He opened the book, which groaned from a lack of use,

flipping through the heavy pages, taking note of the yellowed newspaper clippings and reviews, lovely photographs of this shy little drama teacher in an entirely new light. She was pretty here, with a touch of makeup, her hair tousled artfully, dressed to impress—maybe even beautiful in some of the shots—and even, dare it be said, *sexy*.

"They're beautiful, Gemma, really lovely."

"Thank you."

He kept turning the thick black pages, taking in the pleasing images of this newly alluring creature whose thigh was melting heat into his. He hit a couple of blank pages, but that didn't stop him. She sat silently in anticipation as he turned another page to discover a small gallery of tasteful, artistic nudes. Nicholas dared not look up at her yet... though he could feel that her eyes were fixed upon him.

Another turn of the page, and there was an 8X10 from a press kit for a smutty British trifle from the Nineties called *Confessions of a Chimney Sweep*. Topless, saved by the bottom half of a maid's costume, her hands up and her mouth agape in the classic, startled *whoops-m'dear* pose that could only be found in a British sex comedy, Gemma was barely recognizable in this playful, farcical, artless frame blow-up.

"That's enough," she said, folding the dusty old book closed, but leaving it sitting on Nicholas's lap. He looked up at her, not knowing exactly what to say, and she did not evade his gaze this time. She stared boldly back at him, waiting to hear what he had to say, now that he had seen her two-dimensional form naked.

"No," he said. "It's not."

They faced one another, the place where their legs met catching fire. Her face, lit by the mellow tone of the lamp, turned into a Renaissance portrait, her deep, brown-and-green, wide eyes hooded now, reflecting the light in her wide-open pupils. You could hear the heavy, gothic clock in the bronze-sculpted form of Pan on the mantel tick away the seconds as they were caught in one another's hearts. Without looking away from him, Gemma reached down and lightly touched his hand with her fingertips, then lifted it to her cheek, and he let it form around her face. She closed her eyes and cradled her face in his hand, letting her lips delicately kiss the skin of his palm. He brought his other hand up to hold her head close to his, then dared to bring his mouth to hers, and lost himself in the taste of her kiss. He tasted each of her lips before exploring her more deeply, unlocking the tactile, sensuous, needy woman that had been hiding within the mousy little drama teacher. She was as voracious as he, and showed not a trace of shyness when he opened her blouse and dropped it to the floor. She opened his shirt, running her hands up and down his chest, bringing her face to it and burying it in the curls of his hair, kissing and tasting him.

Her face flushed, she stood up, slid out of her skirt, and stood shamelessly naked before him.

Her pale body was hairless, smooth as an ivory sculpture, and gleaming with a sheen of perspiration. Her tiny breasts, the taut sinews of her slender arms and legs, and the mess of her hair now sticking to her sweaty flesh, filled Nicholas with a desire he had not felt in years.

Breathing heavily through her mouth, she stared at him, needing him, and turned and walked into the bedroom.

Nicholas had no choice but to follow, and when finally the inevitable coupling occurred, it was an unleashed, acrobatic exorcism of heretofore-unknown passion and lust. It lasted for a couple of hours before it drained them of heat, fluids, and new ideas, and left them panting, waiting for their hearts to slow and their wind to return to normal. That would take another half hour or so.

"I love you," Gemma told him as they lay on the damp sheets.

That made Nichols smile, even let out a silent little laugh with the sweet absurdity of her words after mating with him but once. She turned away from him, suddenly going cold, and he realized in hindsight that this might have been a fatal error. He went still, his mind not yet returned from the cave it had run off to during the course of their fevered lovemaking. He answered her with a sweet, gentle, decidedly un-carnal kiss on the lips, and she snuggled into his armpit and pulled the sheet over them, not daring to look him in the eyes again.

"You okay?" he asked her.

"Shhh," she said, placing her fingers over his lips as she clicked off the lamp and thrust them into darkness, then settled into him as if for the night.

Nicholas glanced at the alarm clock that glowed blue numerals from the nightstand: it was after seven.

"Oh, Jesus," he said. "I've got to go."

He climbed out of her bed, but she clung to his hand. "No. Don't."

"I have to, Gemma."

It may have been awkward for him, but it was devastating for her.

* * *

The school had been somewhat somber after Miss Featherstone's death. Chatter was softer, the mood darkened; even the sky stayed grey, with a shroud of snowfall piling high on the leafless trees and hedges. The fabled laughter of schoolchildren was muted and hesitant.

David was the youngest pupil in his Composition class, but easily the most talented. Though his reach was less than an octave, his hands were active, adventurous, agile. His playing skills were impressive, especially for a nine-year-old, but it was his writing that was his most prodigious talent. He created music that twisted and turned on itself, muscular exercises that stretched the boundaries of the musical scale, that had mathematical logic, but sought and found beauty in the most unimagined places. The melodies he produced were fragile, delicate, and wrapped in cadences that came from someplace otherworldly. It was the rare creature like David that spawned the idea of divine inspiration. Surely a child, a protected, unworldly, shy child like this could not draw from a lifetime in the arts to create such original, imaginative work. But David, who hated God for letting Miss Featherstone die at his feet, had no room for divinity; his music was his own, borne of his own brand of rapture.

So, as he performed this new piece for the class, for Mr. Potter, and for Miss Featherstone, he lost himself in his music, grunted and hummed in blissful oblivion as he laid his grace at the feet of the woman he loved. When he finished, the room was momentarily silent, and David had been transported elsewhere, to a void, a deep and distant blackness where he floated as he played. But the sudden outburst of enthusiastic applause from the other students—most of them teenagers and unlikely to enjoy the creations of a mere nine-year-old—along with Mr. Potter's own cheers of "Bravo!" brought David back to our planet, where he gave a simple nod to acknowledge his gratitude.

But he was not really playing for any of them; he was playing for his beloved, in the hopes that his devotional might bring her back from the dead.

Class over, David sought solitude as he walked alone down the hallway and out of the building. It was afternoon, and in winter, afternoon was practically night. Shadows were vanishing like ghosts in the waning light, and David was alone with his thoughts as he watched the other students head anxiously to their dormitories. David sat at the feet of an old stone lion, sketching notes on a staff as he notated changes in his new creation. It would be his greatest composition yet. Snow settled on him like ash as he worked until it was too dark to read and write.

He closed his notebook and looked across the schoolyard to the dormitory, where warm light filled the windows, then up at the heavens, where the moon had yet to reveal itself. The Music and Drama building towered and glowered over him, the lights of the classrooms blinking out for the night, one by one. The rooms he knew had been occupied by Miss Featherstone until only days ago were dark. David was cold; David was lonely; David was in love.

He stepped back into the Music and Drama building and into the empty ground floor corridor. It was quiet, peaceful, inert. He stood and listened, but there was no movement, no footsteps, not even a breeze leaking through the double doors. He stepped quietly to the stairwell and climbed: one, two, three floors above.

The fourth floor was carpeted, lined on either side by two apartments for the instructors. The rooms were silent, unoccupied so early in the evening. David made his way to the end of the hallway, to the rooms he knew had been the home of his beloved, and stopped, staring wide-eyed at the door. He looked at the distorted reflection of his face on the shiny brass doorknob, which was obliterated by the growing image of his hand as he slowly reached out to wrap his fingers around it. The door, of course, was locked, as he knew it would be. But this was an old building with old doors and old locks, and David could easily trick such a lock with the awl in his Swiss Army pocketknife. So, he did.

The door opened unto him, and he entered Miss Featherstone's warren, pulling the door shut carefully behind him. He dared not turn on any lights, but didn't really need to; the dim, emerging moonlight offered sufficient illumination for him to inspect her shrine. He stood in its center, transfixed by her magic, at the heart of her mystery, enveloped by her home. The scent of rose tickled his nostrils, and he walked to the piano to look at all of the framed pictures of the most beautiful woman in the world. He couldn't help but touch them, and as he did, they came to life, movies that portrayed snippets from her life: a laugh, a tear, a somersault, a dance in the rain. They were but moments, pieces of time, but each of them was enchanting, each of them made him smile, each of them proclaimed more loudly his love for her. She could not be dead if she lived in these frames. He walked to the little sculpture by the lamp, tracing its naked-lady form with the tip of his finger. If it had a tail, it would have been a mermaid; as it was, it seemed to swim in the cool, grey moonlight.

He picked up the photo album, which was heavy with her history. He opened it, flipped through it with fascination, seeing the stages of her lives from girlhood—a picture of her from a school production when she couldn't have been any older than him, where she wore painted-on freckles and a red and white checked Raggedy Ann dress—to angelic adulthood. When finally he reached the chapter of her story that featured an appearance in *Confessions of a Chimney Sweep*, he breathed a shocked gasp at her so inelegantly revealed body and closed the book with a bang. He felt his face go red and hot, felt a surge down below that he'd only felt at night in his dreams. He looked around to see that none of the pictures were looking at him. Somehow, they were not.

He passed through into the bedroom, that most private chamber of his Gemma's life. The bed was neatly made, but the furnishings all seemed of another era—as she did—and all of exquisite femininity. A place for everything, and everything in its place. Cut roses were drying up in a vase on the nightstand, but their smell was undiminished. It was her smell, the scent he would always equate with her, and with love.

The bed looked soft, inviting, even beckoning. He sat tentatively on its edge before he dared to lie upon it, nestling his face into the Featherstone scent of her pillow, where he promptly fell into sleep and dreamed of her sweet, chaste kiss on his cheek.

He jolted awake only minutes later, his sweet dream overpowered by a black-feathered, ivory-clawed beast with six-inch fangs ripping his angel to wet, meaty pieces. His heart battering his ribcage, David sat up, breathing heavily. He looked around the room, and it took a moment for him to remember where he was. He didn't like to dream; dreams always woke him up. But this was the worst one yet.

He heard a distant, muffled door slam in the apartment next door, the sound of heavy footsteps going deep into the chamber. A telly was flicked on, and he heard voices rumbling through the walls, with the attendant laughter of a silly comedy. It had to be Mr. Potter, who loved *The League of Gentlemen*, and was always trying to imitate them. Potter, who was famously hard of hearing, had the volume up high, but the walls were thick enough that David could not make out the words. He sat up in Gemma Featherstone's bed and let his legs dangle over the edge, staring at the open door that led into the bathroom. In the dimness, he could make out her silk robe hanging from a peg just inside the door and slid to his feet to go and touch it.

Even in the darkness, he could tell it was pink—or rose—and of a satiny sheen that slid sensuously through his fingers. There were lady products aplenty atop the toilet and sink, each of them a fascinating mystery to David, who still felt warmth and pressure between his legs. He took the robe from its peg and rubbed it gently against his cheek. The heat increased, and he ran it across his body, wondering why it felt so good. It crackled, sparking tingles of static electricity against his arm, and he dropped it to the tile floor in shock. It seemed momentarily alive. But it wasn't. It lay there on the floor, somnolent, empty, missing its mistress.

David looked at the bathtub, a grand old gargoyle with lion's claws and a foggy plastic curtain. The ceramic on the old tub was chipped and rusted in places, but was shiny clean. He imagined his ladylove immersed in the water of this bath, and the temperature got even hotter. He stepped over to it, felt the smooth gloss of its surface, smelled the perfume of her bubble bath, which filled an open, ornate, cut-glass jar. He stuffed the rubber stopper into the drain, then turned on the water. He dumped bubble bath into the steaming water, and watched the tub fill as ghosts of steam rose to the ceiling, and the scent of rose became overpowering.

As the room filled with Miss Featherstone's sensory memories, David stepped out of his clothes and into the luxurious bath. Miss Featherstone's bath. The place that she lay naked and submerged in this very bubbly foam. The intimacy of his soak flushed him, made him feel dizzy and funny and confused, but most of all, it excited him, excited him in ways he had not been excited before. It wasn't merely sexual arousal, though that surely played a hand. It was knowing he was doing something wrong, but doing it in the name of a compulsion called "love."

Shyly, he pulled the shower curtain in place and lay back, resting his head at the end of the tub, rocking slowly and amphibiously in the bath, easing his eyes closed to fully experience the sounds, the scents, the heat of the water, the slipperiness of the porcelain. His breathing slowed, and the only sound was the *plip, plip, plip* of the gently leaking faucet. All was still, all was calm, all was dark.

And then...

A sound: the shower curtain rings rattled and squealed gently as they moved across the chromium rod, a musical, metallic ringing sound.

David's eyes snapped open, but the room was dim. The curtain was not moving... but hadn't he pulled it tight to the end? Surely he wouldn't have pulled it shut and then left it open a meter or so. Would he? The faucet continued to *plip*, and the curtain hung limp and still, its tail held in place by the sudsy water.

"Hello?" David whispered to the night.

A cloud cleared the moon, and as the light blossomed blue in the bathroom, he could see an indistinct form silhouetted on the curtain opposite him. It reached its expanding hand-shadow toward him, gripped the plastic drape, and pulled. The curtain rings rang a goose-pimpling *scree* as the shower curtain pulled open, as if on opening night's first act. Horrified, David felt his boy-parts shrivel under the hot bathwater, and pulled away, the spigot stabbing him sharply in the back and making him jump. The curtain opened fully now, he recognized the shadow basking in the dim luminescence: it wore a navy blue sweater over a crisp white blouse, with matching navy blue skirt. Miss Featherstone sat down on the edge of the tub and smiled at David, who cowered shyly beneath the bath foam.

"Miss Featherstone..." David breathed, his teeth starting to chatter. She scooted closer to him and gently laid a hand on the top of his scalp.

"Hello, David, my love." David's heart beat even faster. He didn't know that she even knew his name.

* * *

The stink of paint reeked as Nicholas threw on his black overcoat and made his way out of the apartment, as Gemma remained silent in her bed. Snow fell in clumps now, a feathery flurry illuminated from behind by the night-lights of the campus, the aftermath of some sort of celestial pillow fight. *I'm such a fool!* Nicholas thought to himself. He knew he had made a huge mistake. It was the only time he'd transgressed the sanctity of his marriage, and now, in the crisp, cold night air, he realized how much he had put at risk. Yes, he'd found himself in the arms of an indefatigable lover, and spent himself within her, and their mutual exchange of ecstasy was, well, ecstatic. But there was no afterglow; instead, she proclaimed her love, which was something entirely different, and something he surely did not seek. He had all the love he needed, even though it was shrouded in darkness so much of the time. His heart was taken. The physical act that he didn't realize he'd sought had drained him but had not unlocked his heart.

So now he carried two loads of guilt: one for subverting his marriage, and another for intimacy shared without his heart. Gemma thought she loved him—which was insane; they'd hardly spoken a dozen words before that night, and yes, the lovemaking was good, but still—and now here they were, instructors at the same Academy, living on the same grounds, and he with a wife who worked in Administration. How could he be so stupid?

Nicholas knew that Gemma was a little bit eccentric, even odd, but this proclamation of hers seemed to teeter at the edge of reason, didn't it? Or maybe it was her way, her post-coital release of pent-up emotion, just words. Surely that was it. Christ, she barely knew him.

As with all things, this would work out. It had to.

So Nicholas returned to his apartment, which was warm and cozy against the chill of the blizzard picking up strength outside. There was, however, another kind of chill when he hung his coat and Rose was waiting for him in the glow of the television news. Place settings sat on the dining table, but the plates were empty and waiting.

"Jesus, Nicholas, you smell horrible! Where have you been?"

"I told you I was going to help Miss Featherstone paint sets for *Romeo and Juliet*."

Paint dappled his face and hands, ruined his shirt and trousers; there was no lie here. Still, Rose was skeptical.

"No, you never told me any such thing," she said, wrinkling her nose. "I did."

Rose sighed, then gave in, her scold giving way to a tired smile.

"Okay, my little absent-minded professor. Throw those clothes outside and get in the shower while I heat up the supper that's been waiting over an hour."

Disaster averted, Nicholas did as he was told.

In the shower, red paint circled the drain like the blood from Lady Macbeth's hands.

It was the one and only time that Nicholas and Gemma had conjoined; when they passed one another on the campus after, he was always ready with a smile and an empty, distantly cordial greeting. She, however, could only avert her eyes, her chin tucked in to her chest. This continued for two weeks or so, as the winter turned historically cold.

* * *

Snow continued to fall, making Miss Featherstone's

funeral even more somber. Sound was dampened by the drifts that had overtaken the five-hundred-year-old graveyard outside the even older C of E chapel on the bank of the frozen Ravensbrooke River on the east edge of Twombley. No members of her family were in attendance, if she even had living relatives aware of her presence. Staff from the Academy, as well as its students, both Junior and Senior level, stood shivering around the grave. It was all very sad and reminded Nicholas of "Eleanor Rigby"; Rose had chosen not to attend.

So, the minister ministered, a cloying string of platitudes that would fill the generic services of anyone he had not known personally: calming, anonymous bloviations no one would remember the next day, and which brought no one to tears.

Young David Sutcliffe, however, was the exception. He stood at the edge of the grave, trying to hide the little diamond drops that leaked from the corners of his eyes. He touched the envelope in the pocket of his black overcoat as the minister wrapped up with a sonorous recitation of Bible verses and threw a handful of dirt onto the simple wooden casket before it was lowered theatrically into the frozen earth beneath it. As if class had suddenly been dismissed, the shivering crowd dispersed, eager to leave the melancholy chill of the old cemetery and the interment of their eccentric young instructor behind.

David stayed, though, letting the snowflakes settle like little angels on his hair and shoulders.

He watched the crowd go, the crowd that didn't notice that they'd left him behind. David was used to that; nobody ever took much notice of him, unless he was sitting behind the keyboard of the school's Steinway grand on the Recital Hall stage. Once the crowd had made their way to the cobbled road that led to the Academy, the minister, who had a round belly, a thick mane of white hair, and a rubbery, misshapen nose that was covered in a roadmap of thin red veins, put his big, rough hand on David's head and tousled his hair.

"She's in a better place, son. She's with the angels now." He took a deep drink from a silver flask to ward off the winter, then left David to his thoughts, which were plentiful. He wished that he had been able to kiss the casket; more than that, he wished he had been able to kiss Miss Featherstone goodbye. But once the crowd and the Man of the Cloth had left, the two burly gravediggers, one of them Indian and the other African, rolled the mechanical pedestal out of the way, pulled the green carpet of artificial grass from the mountain of freshly-dug soil, and started to shovel it in, filling the hole. David sat on one of the chairs and watched them cover his lady love with dirt, but his mind was not on the body moldering in its new grave; rather, it traveled back to the scene of the crime, the place and the moment when he fell in love, the love that had been dashed at the moment of its birth, shattered at his feet and no longer breathing. However, that is not what the eyes deep in his head were seeing; no, David saw her flying from the clock tower toward him, sprouting wings before she hit the brick walk, hovering magically in the air, and settling gently on the ground next to him, before wrapping her wings around him in an angelic embrace of devotion.

That's how it should have been, David thought. *That's how it was supposed to be*. "Should've would've could've," said the soft voice from the seat next to him. "What was is; what wasn't isn't. No use crying over spilt milk."

"Miss Featherstone!" David exclaimed. She stood next to him, dressed demurely in black, her dark eyes hidden under a lace veil.

"Hello, my little love," she said. "Thank you for staying behind, making sure I was bug snug under the ground."

"I missed you," he told her, and truer words were never spoken.

"And I you, my angel," she replied. It made David smile; *she* was the angel, not he. He stood before her approving smile.

"Are you cold?" she asked.

"Not anymore," he answered. And it was true.

She reached for his hand, and he gladly took it; though he was only nine, and small for his age, their hands were almost the same size. "Shall we walk?" she asked as she led him through the thick carpet of snow that lay atop the graveyard like foam. He nodded, and let her lead him through the towering monuments, leaving two sets of footprints in their wake. They wove their way through the stones until they were alone in the middle of the oldest section of the cemetery, a place where the monuments were bigger than life, with gothic sculptures of seraphim, forest creatures, towering gods and monsters that commemorated lives that had otherwise been forgotten. The stonework may have been crumbling, but still they stood lo these last few centuries.

Away from the living, Miss Featherstone stopped David, and knelt in front of him. "You love me, don't you, David?" she asked.

"Of course I do," he replied.

"And you know that I love you, don't you?"

He reached into his pocket and pulled out the letter that fell into his possession when she had plummeted to her death, the letter proclaiming her love. "I do. I have your note to me."

She smiled, and to David, that smile melted all of the snow that surrounded them, melted the snowflakes before they could ever touch him.

"You are the sweetest boy."

He smiled as big as he could, and didn't understand why tears were filling his eyes. He certainly didn't feel sad.

"I would do anything for you, Miss Featherstone."

"Would you, David? Would you really?"

"Of course! You know I would!"

"What would you do for me, David?"

"Anything! Anything at all, I promise! Anything you ask!"

She stood and looked down at him, though she was only a few inches taller than he.

"Anything?"

* * *

The last place Nicholas wanted to go after the funeral was home, but there was no other destination. He never felt welcome in the pub. The locals obviously weren't fond of the Yanks, and he got sick of the jokes at his expense, as well as the indoor smoking. What he wanted was to just drive, to be alone with his thoughts, but small chance of that with the roads all blocked with snow. It might be weeks before Twombley-on-Ravensbrooke would be dug out.

So he walked the road to the Academy, surrounded by students and staff, but feeling all alone, snow collecting on the shoulders of his black wool coat. Though not all that distant, it was a long, solemn hike. Voices were stilled by the cold and the sad little ceremony. Even the children were quiet.

Nicholas straggled, not wanting to be a part of the slow-moving herd. He let them go on ahead, marveling at the beauty of the ancient homes and shops of the little town. It could only be England, for better or for worse. He felt as if he had taken a step out of time.

He could not help but ponder the mystery of Gemma

Featherstone. Why was she hiding here at this Academy? She could be lovely, almost beautiful, even, when she cared to be. Instead, she chose anonymity, seclusion, spinsterhood. What was she afraid of? Everything, it seemed: even human interaction... up to a point. Her ability to plunge so deeply and ferociously into physical intimacy was shocking-- and exciting, Nicholas had to admit to himself. His face flushed with shame for having taken advantage of her obvious loneliness, though he had never planned such a thing. And he never really expected to end up in her bed... did he? And now this. She lay in a lonely, solitary grave in a little English town, missed only by the students she taught and the people who worked with her, who would soon forget her. Red-faced with guilt at the thought, he hoped he would forget her soon, too.

He dragged his feet in the snow, leaving long trails behind him.

Once home, darkness fell quickly. Nicholas took off his coat and scarf, hung them up, and took his chair in front of the fire: a warm spot in a very cold apartment.

Rose was in the bedroom, and the door was shut. He could hear the quiet clattering of the keys of her laptop. A diary entry? Emails? Nicholas wondered what had his wife so engaged... but was grateful for it. Life at home had not been pleasant of late. Not that there were explosions and battles erupting between them, though in some ways, he thought, that might have been preferable to the icy silence they endured. They shared a bed but faced opposite walls when they went to sleep at night, when sleep finally decided to descend. The gulf between them was narrow but freezing cold.

Nicholas had still not admitted to the single tear in the fabric of their marriage, but Rose did not believe him. He never would, and neither would she.

So Nicholas sat in front of the fire, too enervated to turn on the television. All he could do was stare into the fire, and see the ghost of Gemma Featherstone taking shape in the flames. He closed his eyes, held the heels of his hands against them, aching, life drained from him. The logs crackled and Nicholas got up to stoke the blaze, watching tiny sparks flee up the chimney like little demons.

Nicholas listened: Rose's typing had stopped for the moment. The fire grew, throwing Nicholas's giant shadow against the wall. He listened to the snapping of the burning logs, the howl of the wind from the chimney up above, the ticking of the mantel clock. It was the definition of melancholy. A hole opened up in the clouds that covered the moon, and suddenly the room was filled with shadows of the falling snow dancing about. Nicholas felt like he was living in a snow globe. He looked out the window, realized that the curtains were wide open, leaving him exposed on a night that needed to be private. He went to the windows and reached up to pull the drapes shut and froze.

Out in the middle of the schoolyard, alone in a vast acre of thick, white snow that was burying a battalion of footprints, a small figure stood alone. It was a child, couldn't have been more than eight or nine years old, a little boy, and he was staring right into Nicholas's apartment... no, right into Nicholas's *eyes*. Nicholas stared back at him, but the boy never moved. He would not be intimidated.

Unnerved, Nicholas pulled the curtains shut and stood in the middle of the room, all alone.

This did not feel like home.

* * *

David lay in his bed, his tiny radio under his pillow,

playing Rachmaninoff. His fingers fluttered along with the recording, living the music, feeling it without even being aware of it. As the music filled his body, Miss Featherstone filled his heart. Her note lay atop his stomach, and he had embroidered it with scrawled valentines of hearts in purple ink. His roommate, a ten- year-old artist named Simon, slept so soundly that he snored, though David never noticed. His mind was otherwise occupied.

A shadow fluttered outside his window, but David was enraptured with Rachmaninoff, and didn't notice at first. But as the shadow grew, stretching wings up and finally blotting out the opposite wall with darkness, David sat up in bed. He looked at the window and saw Miss Featherstone hovering outside, her white, feathered wings flexing gently behind her, holding her aloft in the blowing snow. He went to the window, his face blooming into a welcoming smile.

"You're here!" he whispered, so as not to wake Simon.

Miss Featherstone nodded back and placed a moist kiss on the glass in front of David's face. "Go to bed," she whispered to him, and even though thick glass was between them, he had no trouble hearing her words. "Dream."

"Take me with you!" he whispered eagerly.

"No, not now," she answered him. "Go to sleep. Dream of me."

Yes, he thought. *Dream of her. That would be best.*

So, sleep overtook the boy and opened his mind to dreamland. He dreamed of angels; he dreamed of love; he dreamed of blood.

* * *

Even when the snowplows reached the village, the snow continued to fall and fill in the roads leading in and out. It was becoming claustrophobic, maddening, even miserable. The boys and girls at the Academy were running out of games, of chatter, of joy, and the adults were at wit's end; and no place showed the strain of the hellish winter more than Nicholas's apartment. He spent as much time between classes as he could in front of an easel at the back of his classroom, trying to rediscover what had driven him to pick up a brush in the first place. Despite the years of teaching, his own skills had rusted shut; the confidence of his brushstrokes had gone into hiding, and the work he attempted now was dreary and lifeless, as fallow as he felt himself.

Still-lifes were too still, portraits too stuffy and bland, faces without lives. He had never achieved stature as a true artist; and now, he wouldn't even qualify as an illustrator. The excitement he'd felt painting in his youth had shriveled up. He had become a teacher—worse, a teacher of children. He looked forward with dread to the remains of his life surrounded by moppets and cartoon characters and videogames. Gone were the galleries and the thrill of discovering a talent with a new way of seeing and showing; gone was the high brought on by a fresh palette dabbed with blooms of paint and the open window of a newly stretched canvas.

But still, it was better than sitting in front of the television with Rose at the far end of the couch, yawning through *Coronation Street* because the alternative was to confront the withering of their marriage by conversation. Silence beat confrontation.

So here he sat, daubing mauve oil paint to yet another series of stylized tombstones, last stop on the great ride of life, melancholy covering him like a funeral shroud. He was alone with his thoughts, which was a dangerous place to be.

The painting, like the last half-dozen he had begun and abandoned, was a failure, self- conscious and dreary. He surveyed his work in disgust, then turned his brush around and stabbed the canvas through its heart, ripping through it until it turned to wet, sloppy tatters. His heart pounded, and he made a decision. It was time to clear the air about his single dalliance with Gemma Featherstone. He would go to Rose, tell her the truth, and hope for her forgiveness. If she could forgive him, they could go on, rebuild their union, and perhaps even reignite the joy he got from her, from life, from art. It would be a fresh new beginning. Rocky at first, of course.

But they would get past it, as they had gotten past so many hardships. Isn't that what "for better and for worse" was all about?

He boxed up his paints and sent the destroyed canvas flying onto a heap of its brethren. The janitor would take it to the trash tip in the morning. In a new mood of resolve, Nicholas cleared out his personal space to make way for tomorrow's classes.

As he stowed his easel in the cabinet, he paused. Behind the constant grind and click of the classroom clock over his desk, there was another sound coming from outside the door: footsteps. Little, cautious steps that tried not to echo through the hallway. Singular steps were a rarity in this building at this time of night. He latched the easel in its closet, then made his way through the rows of desks, and opened the classroom door to the corridor beyond.

A boy came to a stop in the middle of the hallway, startled by Nicholas's sudden presence. He had seen this boy before, staring at him from the snowy fleece of the schoolyard through his apartment window.

David Sutcliffe's heart pounded wildly against his ribcage. He had come merely to get a closer look at the American teacher, but now, as the tall, raw-boned instructor walked up to him, he wanted to be anywhere else. He could not move, planted into place as Nicholas's shadow approached him and wrapped him up.

"You lost, son?" Nicholas asked the child quivering in the hallway. The boy looked up at him with an expression of such terror that it made Nicholas take a step back. After a long silence, David just slowly shook his head.

"Were you looking for somebody?" he asked, trying to calm the child with encouragement.

Snow pattered softly against the hall windows, its shadows peppering the walls. David took a deep breath, staring past Nicholas into the night. The boy's heart slowed and his breathing relaxed a bit. Snow shadows fluttering across his eyes, David turned again to Nicholas, and his green eyes glowed with a golden ring around the iris.

After a long silence, the boy answered in a soft little voice, sounding surprisingly sophisticated with its perfect British diction. "Actually, Mr. Stephens, I was looking for you."

"For me?" Nicholas responded. Suddenly, he recognized the boy: this was the piano prodigy he had heard so much about, this year's Beethoven. The boy had generated quite a bit of conversation in the teachers' lounge. He had seen the child perform his new polonaise at the Fall Recital. A gifted boy, but... *strange.*

"Yes, sir," the boy said.

David looked up at Nicholas, craning his neck. *He's not so handsome,* the boy thought, looking closely at the art teacher's pale face. *His eyes are different sizes, and his nose is far too big. Why, he looks like a cartoon.*

"What can I do for you?" The boy would not be intimidated by Nicholas's size, and stared right into the teacher's eyes without fear.

"You smell like paint," David said, and Nicholas smiled.

"That's because I've been painting." David did not return the smile. He cocked his head like a little, tow-headed judge trying to decide a particularly difficult case.

"What have you been painting?" David asked. "Nothing much," Nicholas answered. "A landscape."

"May I see it?"

Nicholas wondered why this boy, this stranger, was interested. "Not tonight. It didn't turn out very well."

"Still, I'd like to see."

"It's late. Hadn't you ought to be in your room?"

The boy looked out the windows over Nicholas's shoulder, and Nicholas turned to see what he was looking at. All he saw was snow blowing across the moon.

"Let me see your painting and I'll go to my room."

Nicholas knelt to look David in the eye. "Are you bargaining with me?" David looked him right back: "I suppose I am."

"I thought your interests were in music."

"I have many interests," the boy said. "Don't you?" Nicholas cocked his head; why did that sound sinister?

David walked to the door of Nicholas's classroom, then, without asking permission, entered.

Thrown off-guard for the moment, Nicholas just watched him, then hurried into the classroom behind him. By the time he entered the room, David had already made his way to the pile of art carcasses, and lifted the slashed canvas up to lean against the wall.

"Excuse me, but I didn't give you permission to..."

David looked up at him. "Is this the one you were working on?"

The landscape-- what you could see of it between the tatters-- was still wet, and depicted rows of snow-covered gravestones, with one simple marker in the very middle, a sad, lonely monument without a name.

"Is that Miss Featherstone's grave?" David asked.

Nicholas was taken aback. Who was this child? Why was he here?

"Okay, young man, you've had your peek. Time for you to get to your room now."

David looked up at him, then back at the picture, studying it. As Nicholas stood over him, blanketing him with his shadow, the boy turned back and looked up at him. "It isn't very good, is it?"

"That's enough. Get on to your room now." Nicholas was getting a bit unnerved with this little oddball.

David nodded, then turned and made his way to the door as Nicholas watched him. When the boy reached the door, he turned back to Nicholas.

"Did you love her?" David asked.

Nicholas's heart started to pound. But before he could say anything, as if anything needed to be said, David turned and disappeared into the darkened corridor outside the doorway. Nicholas and his beating heart stood alone in the dark classroom.

* * *

David was fast asleep in his room, oblivious to Simon's asthmatic snores. A beatific smile lay atop his face as he dreamt not of sugarplums, but of melodies and dark brown eyes.

On the nightstand next to him, a little brass sculpture of a nude woman bathed in blue moonlight.

* * *

The snow continued to fall, even a week after Miss

Featherstone's untimely demise.

Snowplows had made their way to Twombley-on-Ravensbrooke, allowing shipments in and out of the little township, but within another day or two, the roads were impassible again. Cabin fever was rife and tempers were frayed. But still, life at the Academy had to continue; young minds had to be nourished and life had to go on, even in the chill of the region's cruelest winter.

A new day bloomed as feathery snowfall continued to embrace the region. The sun, barely a bright spot in the sky of even grey cloud, cast its glow half-heartedly.

It had been another night of spotty sleep for Nicholas, whose activated mind would not allow him the luxury of slumber. The lids over his eyes grew heavy, and the whites were pinked with tiny red veins. His brain throbbed with ache as he resigned himself to another day. He sat up, the lack of rest putting him in an ill humor. He looked over his shoulder to see that Rose was still sleeping soundly, and resented her for it. He ran his hand through his matted hair and tried to shake himself out of his doldrums. He got up and made his way into the bathroom and turned on the shower, letting the chilly room fill with clouds of steam.

His stomach was curdled and protested with a long, gurgling growl as he relieved his bladder. He flushed and entered the shower, the stinging needles of hot water jolting him further into consciousness. He wondered if today was the day he would tell Rose about the night with Gemma Featherstone. No. Not when he was feeling like this. Not today. He wondered now if that day would ever come. He lathered his face and body, but his heart pounded throbs of leaden pain through his head. The headache was making him nauseous. He closed his eyes, let the water rinse him, hoping the pain would follow the lather down the drain. As he rinsed, he felt the caress of a cold hand run down his back and around his bottom. It startled him and gave him goosebumps. When he lurched in surprise, the hand pulled quickly away. He opened his eyes, the bathroom now a steam room, billowing with clouds.

Nicholas was confused. Had his wife actually lifted the shroud of solitude enough to touch him, to caress him gently in the shower? Was she opening the door a crack?

"Rose?"

He turned off the shower and stepped out onto the cold tile, grabbing a towel and roughly rubbing himself dry before stepping into the doorway.

Rose still lay on the far side of the bed, facing away from him. "Sweetheart?"

She pulled the blankets up over her head, giving Nicholas all the reply that he needed. He shaved, got dressed, and headed off to his first class of the morning. He'd be early, but he didn't mind that.

Nicholas crossed the quad, which was barely waking up. Edmund, the elderly groundskeeper, nodded "hello" as he battled vainly to groom endlessly mounting snow from the pathway with a noisy blower. Nicholas waved, then ran his hand through his hair, which had frozen in ice the moment he stepped out of the building. Even the kids had not yet ventured out; he couldn't blame them for wanting to wait until the last minute in this weather.

So, once again a solitary man, he made his way to the Arts building, which was still empty and locked when he arrived. He took out his key, unlocked the door, and flicked the wall switches on to illuminate the building, but for some reason, the lights did not go on. He flipped them down and up and down and up again, but to no avail. That was the curse of such aged buildings; they were beautiful, but were subject to persistent failure when it came to such modern luxuries as electricity and good plumbing. Oh, well, he'd let somebody else worry about it.

He found the stairway in the dim winter light, and made his way up to his classroom domain. Waiting for him at the top of the flight, barely a silhouette in the dark at the top of the stairs, was a familiar figure: young David Sutcliffe sat, elbows on knees, chin in hands, watching him ascend.

It startled Nicholas, who was not expecting company this early in the morning.

"What are you doing here?" he asked the boy.

The boy no longer seemed the shy, diffident child he had first encountered. He stood right up as Nicholas reached the top of the stairs. David didn't bother to answer Nicholas's question. He just looked at him.

"Shouldn't you be in the Music Building?" he asked David. "It's early," David answered.

They stood looking at one another for a moment before Nicholas turned and continued down the corridor toward his classroom. He was not surprised when he heard little footsteps following him down the hallway, but still, it made the hairs at the back of his neck prickle. He suddenly turned, hoping to scare and intimidate the boy, but David stopped, stood calmly as Nicholas faced him.

"What do you want?" Nicholas tried not to seethe. "Nothing," David said.

"Where are you going?"

"Nowhere."

The darkness was not letting go. The sun was not coming out of hiding anytime soon, and the hall was filled with shadow.

Nicholas turned from the boy and toward his classroom, doing his best to ignore him. He unlocked the door and entered, reaching for the lights and flipping them on. But they did not illuminate. The room remained dim, and the walls filled with the animation of drifting snow shadows.

He went to his desk and draped his overcoat and scarf over the back of his chair. He looked to the back of the room to see that the janitor had not cleared away the junked canvasses that he'd left stacked there the night before. With a sigh, he walked to the back of the room and put the canvasses up on end, stacking them neatly against the wall, his head still throbbing, his heart made of lead.

When he turned to go back to his desk, he saw that David was standing in the doorway, his cherubic face an expressionless mask. Nicholas struggled to fight off the anger growing at the pit of his stomach.

"What are you doing here?" he demanded.

David would not be intimidated. His eyes didn't leave Nicholas's face. It seemed that he didn't even blink.

"Did you love her?" the boy asked him.

"Who?" Nicholas said, his irritation growing. "Did I love who?"

"You know who," David answered. And then the boy entered the room, walking along the far wall to approach the cupboards filled with art supplies. He ran his fingers across the rows of charcoals, of curdled tubes of oil paint, over the camelhair bristles of paintbrushes.

"I love her," David said, sounding not like a little boy, but like one gentleman challenging another to a duel. Nicholas felt gooseflesh creeping up his back.

"I think you'd better go on to your classroom," Nicholas said.

David's hand settled on a palette knife, still crusted with a residue of blue paint. "You hurt her," David said, wrapping his little fingers around its wooden hilt.

This had to stop. Nicholas went up to the boy, doing his best to tower over him, which was not difficult. "Go on, son, get to class."

David turned to face him, gripping the blunt-ended palette knife tight in his white little hand. Nicholas opened his hand. "Come on, give that to me."

David did, but not in the way Nicholas anticipated. The boy slashed it down with all his might, slicing a new lifeline across Nicholas's palm. Nicholas stared in horror at the new mouth in his hand as it gushed blood that spattered on the floor. David continued to slash away at Nicholas, but the flat blade of the knife mostly just bent and bounced off of him. Even with the power of both his hands, David was, after all, a nine-year-old boy, and a nine-year-old boy's strength was no match for an adult male, even an adult male art teacher. Recovering from the shock of the sudden attack, Nicholas grabbed the boy's wrist, but not before he brought the edge of the blade against Nicholas's cheek, slashing through it and slamming against his upper teeth with a metallic *clack*.

Enraged, Nicholas lost his control and grabbed the boy in both hands and threw him to the floor, where he rolled and crashed against the wall. David screamed and tears began to flow as he crashed against his double-elbowed arm, breaking it anew. Guilt and rage battled within Nicholas's pounding skull, blood leaking from his face and hand with each pulse.

He looked at the boy, now huddled in the corner, crying and holding onto his fractured arm. The anger evaporated. This was a child, and Nicholas-- an adult who should know better-- had hurt him. Holding bleeding palm against bleeding cheek, Nicholas approached the boy, who, seeing him coming, scuttled furiously away like a beetle on its back, pushing his little feet wildly against the linoleum floor, covering it in a flurry of black shoe-scuffs.

"Stop it," Nicholas said, reaching for the boy. "I'm not going to hurt you."

"You already did!" David screamed back at him, a little boy again. A wounded, frightened little boy. "And you hurt *her*!"

"Just settle down, you hear me?"

David would just not settle down. He scrambled to his feet and ran across the room, holding his shattered arm against his chest. Nicholas took off after him, stumbling over a desk and falling to the floor, giving David the moment he needed to escape.

The boy ran out of the room and into the hallway as Nicholas got up off the floor and took off after him.

"Stop it, son," Nicholas called after the boy. "I'm not going to hurt you!"

He ran out into the corridor in time to see David running down the stairs in tears, frantic, scrabbling furiously away. Nicholas was as confused as he was angry, as confounded as he was frightened. He ran out of the classroom after the boy, grabbing for the post at the top of the stairs, his hand slick with blood. It slipped from his hand and his heel skidded in his own blood, causing him to tumble painfully down the steps, slamming against them, bashing and gashing his forehead just as the lights decided to flutter on.

David ran out of the building before Nicholas could even get to his feet.

Students and faculty were just beginning to filter into the schoolyard and the clouds had chosen that moment to part and let the sun take a look. Snow continued to fall, though more lightly now.

David, his red face wet with tears, ran across the yard from the Art Building. Nicholas emerged into the blossoming daylight, dizzy, weak, feeling his pulse throb throughout his body. He surveyed the grounds for the boy as he stood, wavering, ignoring the looks of the students who were horrified by the blood that flowed down his face. The others gave him wide berth when he caught sight of David and ran after the boy.

* * *

David crossed the schoolyard, his eyes on the heavens. He suddenly felt empty, scared. He searched the skies, hurting on the outside, but even more on the inside. He looked up at the chapel ahead, the shadow of the cross at the peak of its spire falling across his face. Blackbirds circled and bellowed, calling him, but it was another winged creature he sought. He felt lonely and abandoned, and needed to be told what to do. His arm hurt him terribly; he needed to be kissed and made better. He had never felt so young, so alone.

The chapel's door stood open, a welcoming maw, begging him to enter, to give him solace. He was as confused as he was frightened, and the tears would not stop. He needed his angel. Surely this is the place he would find her. But the chapel was empty, its pews cold, the vestry abandoned. This very special boy was denied his divinity, just as he had always expected.

David wandered through the pews, then came to a halt in front of the lectern, never so alone as he was now. Music began to form in his head, a dirge, a droning left hand pounding the low end of the scale, slowing with the beat of his heart. It was all tone, no melody, a lost chord, seeking and not finding a rhythm. Then, at the far end of the chapel, a light flickered from within an open door that led to a narrow stairway. He wasn't sure, but he thought he glimpsed a shadow fleeing up its worn stone steps. The bare light bulb that hung behind the door continued to flicker, as if a Morse code siren, and its draw on the boy was magnetic. He sensed that he was *supposed* to go up the stairs, that it was his *destiny*. The slow sonata that was forming inside him encouraged him to follow the stuttering light, to take his stairway to heaven.

He didn't notice that his arm didn't even hurt anymore. He followed his music out of the quiet chapel and into the skinny little stairwell.

* * *

Nicholas saw the boy run cater-corner across the snow-covered lawn, leaving tiny footprints in the otherwise unblemished whiteness. Lack of sleep and blood dizzied him, and his eyes were finding it difficult to focus. But he knew he had to catch up to the child, to stop him, to get him help. To get *both* of them help. He followed the little footprints into the chapel and out of the cruelly burgeoning sunlight.

Little shoe-shaped puddles of melting snow led Nicholas through the chapel's tiny lobby and into the center of worship itself. He felt the weight of the centuries within, a weathered Christ bleeding on a tarnished cross, worn smooth by worshipping hands. Hymnals lay on the empty benches, waiting patiently for Sunday services. But the room was otherwise empty, hollow of spirits. Nicholas followed the little footprints through the chapel and into the claustrophobic stone stairwell that led only one way: up. As he stepped into the dank, chilly little passageway, the bare light bulb that was flickering finally gave up and died. Long, narrow stained glass windows that followed the curves of the winding steps offered the only light.

* * *

David was sweating now, running as fast as he could up the stairs, his feet wet and slipping against the smooth stone. He just kept going up and up and up. The stairwell was a coil, curving around itself as it reached to the top of the ancient building. And there at the top, way up above him, a door opened out to the world beyond, a doorway that was filled with bright morning light that beckoned to him, begged for his presence. High musical notes played in a two-handed flurry, calling him as if by name, a crescendo orchestrating itself beyond David's control.

He followed it blindly, his breath ragged as he continued to run up and up and up. The bright light was getting closer, and the symphony in his head was joined by a choir, and the choir was calling his name.

* * *

Nicholas could see the boy high on the steps above him, scrambling higher and higher. "Stop!" he called out to him. "You're going to get hurt!"

The boy either couldn't hear him or ignored him. Nicholas charged up the stairs two at a time, trying desperately to catch up. He pushed against the walls as he made his way up the steps, leaving crimson handprints on the rough, ancient stone, his brain starting to go squishy. Focus was becoming harder to maintain. But still he pulled himself up the worn, stone steps, one at a time now, weakening, his breath becoming labored.

David, however, felt no such ravages; he was driven to take the steps, and continued to bound his way up with as much energy as when he started his climb. The steps finally ended at the little room at the top, a claustrophobic, hunchbacked little chamber mostly filled with the works of the giant clock. Oversized gears and pulleys and ratchets and chains and counterweights all performed brilliantly in a concerto that was masterful even without a conductor. The mechanics, coated with a grime of grease and age, maintained a beat of mathematical perfection, and David stopped to stare at it, his mouth open in awe. And then, in a grand flourish of crescendo, the clock struck the hour, and the movement ended in a chorus of pealing bells. The sound was overpowering, but David did not even flinch. He loved when his body and soul, if there were such a thing, were filled with music, and he could feel its vibration coursing throughout him.

But Nicholas, still a hundred feet or more lower in the steep tunnel of stone steps, pressed his hands against his ears to try to stop the overpowering pain. He ceased his climb, trying to reclaim his breath. The stairwell was growing ever dimmer as he left a trail of patters of blood in his wake.

When the chimes came at last to rest, David, energized by the music, stepped past the bells and machinery and out into the new morning.

* * *

As he stepped out onto the ledge at the base of the enormous clock face, the overwhelming new brightness the sun had denied the Academy for weeks seared David's eyes. He had to shield them with his hands until they gradually adjusted. It seemed as if he could see the whole world from his perch, even though it hurt to look. His feet at the very precipice of the ledge as the giant second-hand clicked loudly behind him, David felt tiny to the point of insignificance. He wavered there, the earth's vastness overwhelming him.

Click. Click. Click.

The clock spoke to him, urged him on. He sought the

skies, startled when a flock of pigeons shot out of the belfry behind him to circle this curious boy among them. He grabbed onto the hour hand, which had only just struck Golden Lucky Seven, for balance. David looked down to see tiny people gathering on the snow-choked schoolyard way down below him. They looked like toys, like cartoons, little bug-things scurrying, like ants in an ant farm.

Click. Click. Click.

Then a new sound brought his eyes up from the pointing fingers on the play people down below: a strong whooshing noise, the sound of giant, powerful wings. He felt their power blowing the hair back from his face. And there before him, more beautiful than ever, her fully extended, white-feathered wings grandly flapping to hold her aloft, was Miss Featherstone, her brown eyes filled with love, her lips turned up in a welcoming smile.

"I knew you'd be here," David told her.

"I've come to be with you, David," she said, gently. She held her arms out to the boy, whose face was swiftly cleansed of hurt and pain. His own smile was as bright as the new sun, and filled with just as much joy.

"Come to me, David," Miss Featherstone coaxed, lovingly. "I'm afraid I'll fall," David said.

"How can you fall," she asked, "when you have wings?"

He thought it a curious thing to say until he shrugged his shoulders and felt new muscles flexing themselves. He turned his head to see brilliant, white-feathered wings being born from his own flesh.

Miss Featherstone smiled and nodded gently.

"Come to me, David," she repeated. "Jump. I'll catch you."

So David jumped, aloft in slow motion, the world once again holding its breath as he and Miss Featherstone were alone in a cloud of stillness and silence. Tiny hand reached out for tiny hand, finally meeting in a loving grasp as she pulled the boy into her arms. She folded him into a kiss as their wings moved grandly through the air, and David was happier than he'd ever been. Music swirled about them, melodious and cacophonous at the same time, urging them ever higher into the heavens. And then, with a swoop of their wings in glorious unity, they lifted off ever higher, disappearing behind the clouds.

* * *

"No!" Nicholas cried as he emerged from the clock tower and onto the stone ledge. But it was too late. The boy had leapt, way beyond Nicholas's reach.

The clock at the top of the chapel tower clicked relentlessly with each second, as it did in sunshine and rain, war and peace, and the sunshine glinted off its golden surfaces as it ignored the lives it marked. The growing crowd below, teachers and students alike, watched in horror to see the tiny body above launch itself into the heavens, seeming to hover for just a moment before it plummeted down and horribly down to a sudden, shattering halt on the freshly plowed stone walk.

David the Odd Boy lay half on the path and half in the snow, broken and battered. His eyes filled with tears that soon were tinted crimson by blood, and his limbs were splayed in all the wrong directions, jointed in ways never intended by nature. The crowd slowly gathered around him as his final breath came out in a cloud that dissipated almost immediately. All were surprised by the smile he wore at the end of his life.

It took Nicholas several minutes to make his way down the endlessly long stairwell to the schoolyard below, oblivious to the rawness of his own opened flesh, which throbbed with each pounding heartbeat. He had to push his way through the curious children and horrified adults to kneel at David's side. The boy was already gone, the authorities already called when he took his hand and felt it going cold, colder, coldest. Pale blue eyes, now rimmed with an emerging ring of green and gold, darkened as life had fled, and they seemed to deepen into a rich, chocolate brown before death breathed its fog over them and turned them milky. Nicholas, trapped in their lifeless stare, blood stiffening on his lacerated face and once-white shirt and navy jacket, could not remain in their gaze, and reached to close them with the tips of his fingers. His hands started to vibrate uncontrollably, quivering like spastic puppets.

When Rose came up behind him, he was still folded over the child, his grief overwhelming. She haltingly laid her hand on his shoulder, then pulled away in horror when she saw the dead broken child splayed in such horrific angles at his feet. Her eyes clenched tightly shut, but it could not remove the horrific image of the dead boy lying crumpled on the ground. Choking back a sob, she turned and ran back to the apartment, leaving her husband behind.

Nicholas never even realized she was there. He gripped his hands into fists, pounding on the boy's chest, trying to beat life back into it. He reached down and, despite the mask of his blood, pressed his lips against the boy's, hoping his kiss could bring life back to him. But it was too late for breath. Nicholas would not be redeemed. Two lives had ended here, and he felt complicit in both. He slowly stood, reeling in dizziness as the crowd around him gaped at him and backed away. It was not just the blood freezing on his face and hands that so horrified them; it was the look of madness in his eyes.

He turned and recognized the solitary figure of his wife as she ran to the shelter of the old building that contained their apartment. He closed his eyes, feeling terribly alone. When he opened them again, the boy was still a corpse leaking blood into the snow. It was not just an awful dream.

Two lives had ended here at the bottom of the tower, a litter of broken bones and freed blood that sought the snow, seeping into it and reddening it with their memory. He looked up at the tower, at the cross at the very top, and felt its shadow, a new shadow in the harsh new light of the winter sun, wrap around his face and body. A wind grew, whispering its way around the clock tower until it grew into a howl, a howl that seemed to call his name. The clock struck the quarter hour, and the declining notes rang out in a hollow melody, joining the singing wind in a tiny concerto that spoke only to him: a blood symphony of lives lost and loves rent asunder. The shadow of the spire was short, but long enough to caress him as the coagulating blood on his face slowly turned to red ice.

* * *

Night fell in silence on the campus, a snowbound stillness that held its breath. Nicholas sat alone in front of the fire, watching the flames hungrily devour the logs. Rose had left two days before, and Nicholas was alone with his memories. He could feel the stitches in his cheek and palm throb in a nearly military cadence, so those memories would not be leaving him anytime soon. All he could do was wait for classes to begin on Monday, to be surrounded by fresh young faces to blot out those that haunted him.

Off in the distance, the clock at the top of the steeple chimed a lonely midnight bell, a low, forlorn toll that rang out as if calling him by name. He looked out the window to see the tower standing tall against a bright, full moon. Nicholas went to the window as the bell rang out its dozen mournful calls, watching the seconds tick away.

Click. Click. Click.

The seconds called him by name:

Nick. O. Las. Nick. O. Las.

Mesmerized, he watched the second hand circle the golden face of the clock, illuminated by the nearly full face of the moon above it. Then a shadow crossed the snowy schoolyard that stood between him and the clock tower, too quick to make out.

Curious, Nicholas took his coat and scarf from the peg by the door, slipped into them, and went out into the hungry night.

He stepped out into the middle of the smooth, unmarked snow of the quad, watching the second hand idly click away time, bathed in blue moonlight.

A wisp of cloud cleared the face of the moon, which, now naked, shone more brightly than ever. The night lay in a hush as Nicholas bathed in it, staring at the clock, then looking to the moon, just as some kind of giant bird flew across its face in a dramatic silhouette.

No. Too big for a bird. Winged, yes, but not a bird. Something more momentous, more balletic.

Still the clock sang his name.

The flying thing, the winged creature, hovered over the trees, finally swooping to a rest on the ledge in front of the clock, flexing its wings one last time before retracting them behind its body.

Nicholas, the wind whispered, joining the call of the clock. *Nicholas*.

Nicholas crossed the schoolyard, needing to get a closer look at this creature that sat perched at the top of the tower. Even in the distance, he could see that it was watching his every move. He recognized this creature, knew it. It beckoned to him. *She* beckoned to him.

"Come to me, Nicholas," she whispered.

She was perched so high, it was almost a perch on the way to Heaven.

He walked to the base of the building, never taking his eyes off of the landing that towered above him. Something was dripping from there, pattering lightly at his feet. Tears? No, too dark for that. Surely it was blood.

Her voice gently called him again, the clock and the wind joining the chorus that urged him ever upward.

With nothing to lose, Nicholas answered her call.

SALOME

A NOVEL

ONE

I thought I hated my wife. Until she was murdered.

I thought I knew her, too. Better than anyone. I still do, if it means anything.

But now the world has seen her from the inside out; the photos and video that flooded the eye of public consumption were not for the squeamish, but everybody took a peek anyway. By now, her viscera are as familiar to the great unwashed as her ephemera were to me. She was beautiful, I'll grant her that. Few would disagree. But her physical charms were forever voided by a very sharp knife.

I'd first met Chase at the Emmys, where she presented the Best Comedy Teleplay a decade or so ago. Her greatest fame, of course, came at the age of 14, when she played the preternaturally pneumatic 12-year-old Ellie Frazee, one of a dozen mixed-race adoptees on the timeless comedy, *The Crazy Frazees*. She had driven a nation of men into a frenzy of guilt with her just-this-side-of-naughty double *entrendres* and poolside bikini scenes that kept the wretched show going for three years. The scandal that broke when she was impregnated by the show's married, 52-year-old Executive Producer ended his career, but only enhanced her appeal to the tabs, if not to potential employers. Pictures from the resulting abortion in Pacoima made the rounds of some of the seamier tabloids, and are easy enough to find if you just Google "Chase Willoughby and botched abortion". They still stand as a gruesome precursor to the end of her own life.

It was a lean year for quality in television, even more so than most, if you can believe it. I wasn't nominated, of course. Comedy isn't what I do, and they don't hand out awards to the kind of television that I write. I had just broken up with a nominated writer on *Cherry Pie*, who was in the hospital recovering from a suicide attempt, and she asked me to be there to accept the award, just in case, as intelligence indicated her chances were high. Her shrink was out of town, and she had no one else to turn to. I'd love to think that she tried to kill herself *because* of our breakup, but our relationship was neither so Shakespearean nor so romantic. This woman was a speed-talker who was always on, always funny, always brilliant, and always swallowing whatever she could find in the medicine cabinet. Hers or anyone else's. A guilt-ridden, nonobservant Jew, her life was all about output; nothing entered her realm of self. But the sex was phenomenal. She was as physically creative as she was mentally dexterous: a fatal combination. She finally succeeded in taking her life last Christmas, in front of a video camera, running it live on her blog. People thought it was a joke. Again, easy enough to find on YouTube, if you haven't seen it enough already.

Sorry, when I'm not working in a three-act structure, I tend to run off-topic now and then. But life's more about the tributaries than the Great Lakes, isn't it? Mine is, at least. Especially for the last year or two.

We were talking about Chase, and how I met her, and how I grew to hate her, and how she died:

So my ex won the Emmy that night, her second, and I was tuxed up in the best monkey suit I could afford to rent at the time, and went up to accept the award for Susan. Though it had been a while since Chase had been on a series, now that she was all grown up and more gorgeous than ever, ABC was gambling on stunt casting her as a conscientious doctor having to make the decision whether or not to perform an abortion on a raped lesbian activist in a coma. It was an episode arc on *Frankel's People*, and her appearance on the Emmys was to promote the show's premiere the following month.

When Chase handed me the Emmy itself, which is a lot heavier than you might expect, there was a spark of static electricity that jolted us both, and we dropped the award to the floor, where it shattered and made a horrible dent in the stage floor. The inebriated members of the Television Academy gasped as one, and everything passed in slow motion for the next few minutes. As they whisked another statuette out from backstage, handing it to Chase to hand it to me, I held it tight this time. She leaned in to give me a congratulatory kiss on the cheek—for an award that I had not won—and I could smell the lightest waft of curry on her breath. She took my hand and looked directly into my eyes with an expression that gleamed, eyes that twinkled and sparkled and changed colors under the stage lights. She held onto my hand just a little bit longer than she needed to, and I, like everyone else who was watching and had harbored the guilt of a private lust over her passing childhood, was smitten. There was nothing childish about her this night. She was sheathed in a simple black creation, slit so high up one side that underwear were not allowed. The back dipped so low that just the dimple at the top of the crack of her perfect peach of an ass was revealed. The slashed sides of the dress allowed a teasing peek at the delectable plumpness of her breasts, leading you to believe that if you stood *just so*, or if she just leaned *just this way*, you might get to see the nipples that topped them... the nipples that teased you as they proudly announced themselves from under the simple sheath of black silk.

I had been marked on the cheek by the lipstick print of her lush and sensuous mouth, and when she held my hand and led me off the stage, my heart was pounding a hip-hop anthem.

When they lead you off the stage, you are shepherded into an area where all the photographers and TV people converge to document your momentous genius. Well, it was obvious it was not *my* genius being celebrated that night, and that nobody wanted to photograph or interview me. I was standing there with somebody else's award, after all, and hell, none of these people had ever seen the show I wrote and created, or if they had, they certainly wouldn't admit to it. So I wandered the gauntlet of flashbulbs and tabloid correspondents with an admitted bitterness that I couldn't hide. Not that ET, TMZ, or GMA would ever notice, or give a shit.

Chase, however, my beautiful Chase was chum in the water, devoured by the media sharks, each one taking a bigger bite. She had not been on the air for nearly ten years, but nobody who looked like this could avoid the spotlight for long, especially with her ignominious and salacious past. *Frankel's People* was just assumed to be a massive hit.

But for some reason, after making her way through the march of shame, she saw me tippling the complimentary champagne and nibbling the cunning miniature shrimp all by my lonesome, swept up next to me and slipped her arm through mine.

"I hate this shit," she whispered in my ear, close enough that her lips touched me. The heat of her breath left me instantly aroused. "But I love *Slaughter*." That's the name of my claim to fame: a grim hourly manifesto of madness and grotesquerie that runs on a premium channel that *isn't* HBO or Showtime in the late night hours, up against the pun-titled porn for overweight virgins, way up in the high channel numbers.

Her hair was disheveled, and there was a sheen of perspiration across her face, beading on her upper lip. I wanted to taste it.

"Thank you," was all I could think to say.

"I'm not complimenting you. I like it. I like dark shit. *Smart* dark shit."

"You'll swell my head," I told her.

"Which one?" she asked. And I was hooked. We got to know each other biblically that very night, in the marble stall of a backstage men's room at the Shrine Auditorium on Jefferson Boulevard—nobody's idea of Hollywood glamour—coupling desperately until we both combusted, collapsing breathless and giggling on top of the lid of the toilet, our rapture echoing throughout the room. Inelegant, yes, but accessible to the needy as well as the handicapped.

Yes, ours was a relationship founded in Eros and finalized in Thanatos. But the physical part was passionate, a ripe plum constantly devoured by the both of us, equipped perfectly to mate... except when it came to that part after the orgasm; or, in the early days, orgasms. It started with the occasional sniping that seems inevitable to some as a marriage matures. The little things that began as annoyances—sleep schedules, to procreate or not to procreate, atheism vs. a belief in God, Bravo vs. IFC, Bill O'Reilly vs. Chris Matthews—soon grew into battles *royale*. Her sleep was skittish at best, light and uneasy, and she rose with the sun. On the other hand, I couldn't sleep until deep into the night, and did not rise until the clock struck double digits, as the imaginary Lord intended.

Within two years of our wedding, we lived in separate bedrooms, on separate floors, our televisions broadcasting opposite ends of the cultural spectrum. The sweetness of that naughty little teenage wet dream was corroding, and I had no doubt that it was mostly my fault. Our lives were cleaving apart, our interactions receding. Her new series turned out to be shockingly unsuccessful and the reviews were unkind at best. Chase Willoughby was inarguably breathtaking, but the charm of the fourteen-year-old Lolita did not make up for the lack of depth and acting chops when she danced well into her twenties.

After the miscarriage, any semblance of a marriage jumped off a cliff, and we never tried again to create a little human from our combined DNA. We both realized later that that was probably a good thing, for us as well as for the child, and even the planet, but at the time it was devastating.

My own writing grew darker, and *Slaughter* soon dropped from the radar of the disaffected as I endeavored to go into the independent feature world with stories even more sanguinary and hopeless than the midnight hauntings of the local Landmark Cinema. Well, there is no longer an independent film world, at least not in the professional sense. Movies today have to cost over a hundred million dollars or under a hundred thousand. And that leaves me out. No free-of-charge YouTube postings for me, thank you very much.

So we failed together and alone, and the blood of happiness drained from our marriage. Hate sex left weekly bruises, and, though I didn't think there was any extramarital fooling around—I know there wasn't on my part—we were only a couple publicly. Failure took hold like a mold, blanketing our marriage in a festering penicillin that did not heal. Her value was only to the tabloids; mine... well, I had none.

Sometimes I would look up and see her caught in the sunlight, her mind a million miles away, her face deep in repose, and see a radiance that had been the Chase that I married, the woman I'd fallen in love with, the sun backlighting her unkempt hair just so, and my heart would skip a beat. And then, as if feeling my eyes upon her, she would turn to me and her eyes would darken with such venom and resentment that I had to leave the room.

I couldn't write. She couldn't act.

We lived together apart in a shrinking south-of-the-boulevard Woodland Hills bungalow, and all we could do was hate.

I'd come home from a screening at the TV Academy of a friend's pilot; it was silly and just like all the other pilots you've ever seen before, but the food was good, and it was a respite from being at home in our little emotional Frigidaire. I chatted with my producer friend, if a producer could ever truly be a friend, putting off the trip home as long as possible. The crowd thinned as asses had been kissed and everyone saluted everybody else's genius, and it was time to leave.

Resigned, I trudged to the parking structure and fell into the long, slow departure lane and the lonely drive to Woodland Hills.

The house was dark when I drove up. Chase had no doubt gone to bed by now, but that didn't explain the total darkness that enveloped our home. Night had fallen like a purple curtain. The porchlight, the living room, everything was wrapped in gloom. She must have been pissed at me. Again. That's all right; I was pissed at her, too. For something. Give me a minute and I'll think of a reason.

I unlocked the door and entered the still and forlorn little house. A shiver passed through me as I saw what it once was:

a little showbiz love cottage, a place where two Hollywood professionals with hope and ambition and a new start in life made passionate love and laughter. And now, all that remained was darkness and shadow. And memories, good and bad. The good ones were getting harder to recall.

I started to head upstairs, but for some reason decided to check on Chase. I tiptoed to her room on the ground floor. Her door was ajar, so I crept forward and peeked inside. Her still- unmade bed was empty.

"Bitch," I said to myself as I turned and made my way upstairs to shower off the cloak of Hollywood self-congratulatory goo.

I was pissed off when I went to bed, and just kept reading the same paragraph in the latest Carl Hiassen, which didn't make me laugh. Cradled in champagne and Floridian foul play, the house trapped in a stillness that approached tranquility, I fell into a sleep that would not last.

It seemed like my eyes had just closed when the phone rang. As usual, the startling sound had worked its way into the dream that wove in my slumbering brain: a woman—Chase? But with wings that were shedding their feathers—was screaming at me, shrill and horrific, as blood poured from her mouth. I opened my eyes in the darkness and stared at my iPhone as it danced next to the Ambien bottle, not quite understanding what it was trying to say to me. As the shroud of sleep slipped off of me, I realized what it is that a telephone does, but did not recognize the number proclaimed in big white digits. It was close to three in the a.m., and I was in no mood to talk to an Unknown Caller. But thinking that it might be Chase, who might be calling because she was in trouble, I forgot that I hated her and answered the call.

It was not Chase, however, but yes, she was in trouble: trouble I could not fix.

"Mr. Turrentine?" said the officious voice on the phone, and I knew this could not be good news.

I croaked a three o'clock response.

"This is Deputy Sheriff Hardy with the La Paz County Sheriff's Department in Arizona." No good news ever starts with "this is Deputy Sheriff Hardy with the La Paz County Sheriff's Department in Arizona."

Chase had been found murdered in a tiny, ramshackle motel on Highway 60, not far across the California/Arizona border in a flyspeck town called Salome.

I was stunned, unable to speak.

"Did you hear me, Mr. Turrentine?"

"I'll be right there." They told me that it wasn't a good idea for me to come all the way out there, but I got the information and clicked off the phone, perspiration suddenly seeping out of me, a Gordian knot of nausea welling up from within. I vomited until only empty retching remained, but even those dry heaves took a long time to recede.

It was only when I was retrieving the Beemer from the garage that I realized that Chase's Prius was missing, had been when I came home, too, but I just didn't bother to notice. My mind was a vacuum as I wound down the narrow road until I reached Topanga Canyon, during the rare three hours of quiet that settles there every night. I sat and waited at Ventura Blvd. for the light to change; silly, as there was no cross traffic. The 24-hour people who feathered in and out of the all-night Ralphs supermarket at the corner were bleary-eyed, anonymous; they looked like insects to me. Impatient, and knowing that under the New Economy there would be no police to notice, I ran through the red light and blasted onto the freeway heading east.

Chase was dead, messily and verily deceased. It was hard to accept, or even fathom. At three in the morning, she seemed practically a stranger to me. I could easily recall the Chase Willoughby I had wooed and married, but the wife, my partner in matrimony just lived in the same house as me. The woman with whom I'd shared so many laughs, movies, martinis, waltzes, orgasms, award shows, film festivals, toasts, tears, fights, screams, and threats was drawing flies in a dumpy little James M. Cain motel in Arizona. That Chase, the dead Chase, the one who turned away rather than lock eyes with me, the woman who'd lost so much respect for me that her disgust radiated every time she was in my presence... I didn't know her. I lived with her, assumed the worst, and forgot to remember the best. Until she was dead.

I had a good five hours or so to remember her as the Beemer shot across the 210, past Pasadena, bisecting San Bernardino before I hooked up with Interstate 10, beyond the faded concrete giant dinosaurs in Cabazon, past the hundreds of lazily spinning massive windmills that skirted the outlet mall and casinos, rocketing past Palm Springs, where we had run away and become husband and wife. Even at 4:45 in the morning, the heat radiated over the desert highway, creating a mirage that resembled real life. The sun's rosy glow began to nip at the horizon now that I was leaving civilization, and I set the cruise control to 85. California has topography of every kind: verdant mountains, beaches, hill and dale, but the desert, the flat, stinking characterless desert was just a cruddy expanse of the occasional Indian casino and Denny's. The freeway was straight and monotonous, and with only an hour or so of sleep under my belt, the 740i thrumming a lulling one-note symphony, only the picture in my mind of my slaughtered wife kept me awake. In my hurry, it seemed to take days, not hours, to make my way to the scene of the crime. Even still, I couldn't bear to turn on the radio; I needed the quiet.

The scrub, ugly and gnarled at the best of times, was even more grotesque in the summertime, when it was dry, brown, and hungry. And this was not a desert of sands and dune: no, it was dirt and rock and lizards painted across the highway, the occasional greedy service station called Love's hoping you'll run out of gas and pay their exorbitant prices.

As the sun cleared the horizon, it shone directly into my eyes for the next two hours before I could get it to hide behind the visor. Blythe was the last California town before the border, and I was glad to leave that nasty little desert harridan in my exhaust. Arizona announced itself with the sudden presence of saguaro cactus standing tall and waving welcome with their thick, spiny arms. The gas gauge was ticking on empty, the fuel light flashing, its belly rumbling. I stopped in Quartzite to fuel up, and it was crowded with early morning rock hounds setting up stalls for an outdoor event. Lines of RVs driven by hunched and wizened agate collectors curled around the gas stations, keeping me from Chase; they were cranky and slow, honking their horns as they jammed in front of me in line. My engine died just as I pulled up to the pump. Kill me before I get old, okay? Oh, shit, I felt guilty once the thought flitted across my mind.

The tank was full and I sipped on a bottle of water, horned my way through the clotted arteries of Winnebagos, and shot back onto the freeway. Not far beyond lovely Quartzite, my GPS found the turnoff to Highway 60, and I was on my way.

Salome is an elegant, evocative name for an Arizona town, but not a particularly appropriate one for this dog turd of a burg. Much less than a town, straddling a two-lane artery along the western border of Arizona, it was the sun-baked bastard offspring of Oliver Stone and Jim Thompson. It didn't just radiate the brutal August heat in alcoholic ripples, it *festered*. There was an ancient cowboy bar and taco parlor across a parking lot of dirt and crushed gravel, with dull grey rocks that kept you from parking against the wall. A couple of decomposing motels sat under sagging faded signs begging for your business. The most inconvenient of convenience stores sat at its one intersection, with a couple of furious, emaciated dogs tearing noisily at one another's ears. A couple of Mexican men shaded by dirty, once-white vaquero hats were laying down dollar bills on the dirt as the battle continued and blood was spilled. The place smelled like rotten eggs, even with the Beemer's vents closed. There was no residential area that I could see: not even so much as a post office.

The sign for Salome reads "where she danced." Frankly, I could not imagine such a dance taking place here, with or without the veils, though I could easily work up the image of John the Baptist's decapitated head being served up on a tray.

But most of the activity in Salome now was centered at Sheffler's Motel, a dilapidated shithole announced by a long-peeling sign and anchored by rusting pickup trucks on blocks and billboards proudly proclaiming ice cold beer and special family rates. The only family I could imagine taking a room here was Manson's.

Three Sheriff's cars and an ambulance were parked haphazardly in the wide dirt lot when I pulled in. I set the emergency brake, took a deep breath to batten down the sudden pounding of my heart, and stepped out into a blast of 120-degree heat, just as the EMTs carried my wife's sheet-bound corpse out of one of the little rooms on a stretcher. The linen wrapped around her was soaked with her crimson blood.

As I stood from my car, Salome did indeed dance around me, as I was instantly dizzy, caught in the climate change from air-conditioned BMW to Arizona blast furnace. My first breath of the scorched air was enough to dry my windpipe and lungs and make me hack.

Fighting vertigo, I rushed from the car to stand in the way of the gurney to keep it from being loaded up into the ambulance.

"Wait!" I cried. They looked up with grumpy, work-to-do faces. "That's my wife."

They stopped and stood there, casting a look at the motel room. A crowd, well, maybe a dozen people, but surely a crowd by Salome standards, stood sweating in the heat of the parking lot behind the crime scene tape, sipping from bottles of water and beer, one of them popping pictures with his drugstore disposable Instamatic; none of them had mobile phones. This was the event of the season here in the desert. Most were men, grizzled and craggy, mainly but not exclusively Latino. They had lived hard lives. The few women were either massively overweight and heavy-breasted or emaciated, puffing on brown cigarettes. There were two or three dirty, barefoot kids of about five or six, one of them holding an iguana to her chest.

One of the EMTs behind the gurney, a tall, gawky, alarmingly white-skinned kid with pink eyes and white eyelashes, told me to talk to the Patrolmen. As he spoke, two deeply tanned men emerged from Room 4, putting their mirrored sunglasses on as they stepped into the searing light of day, just like in the movies. The larger, more muscular of the two looked up at me.

"Mr. Turrentine?"

There was no question who I was. Beemers don't stop in Salome; they pass through as quick as they can.

"Sheriff Hardy."

He nodded curtly, and his beefier, shorter *compadre* was happy to leave the business to his partner.

"Thanks for waiting." As if they'd been hanging around

waiting for me to show up.

"We're just wrapping up the scene, Mr. Turrentine." He looked a little upset that I'd arrived before he had gone back home to Phoenix. "There really was no need for you to come here, sir."

"She's my wife. I assumed you'd want me to identify the body."

"There's no doubt about the identity of the victim, Mr. Turrentine." A silence as hot and dry as the gust that kicked up passed between us. "I... I'd like to see her."

Hardy looked at his partner, who looked away. "You sure about this?"

"If it was your wife, what would you do?" Hardy sighed. "It's not a pretty sight."

"I don't expect it to be."

I could only see my own face reflected in his movie-cop sunglasses as he stared me down, but I could see the crinkles form around his eyes as he squinted at me. The EMTs were watching him expectantly. Knowing better than to argue, or maybe just not having the energy, Hardy took a deep breath, blew it out like a bull through his capacious nose, and nodded to the gurney handlers.

Now I wasn't so sure I wanted to see Chase this way, and stood frozen for several seconds. "You sure?" Hardy asked again.

Girding my courage, I nodded and stepped over to the head of the gurney, the bloody sheet going brown and dry as it hit the broiling sunlight. I looked up at the rangy, pimply albino med tech, and he looked away from me, taking the edge of the sheet and slowly, respectfully, lowered it to reveal her face, as the simmering crowd of Salomean onlookers eased forward as one.

I closed my eyes, breathed, and looked down at the face

of the woman I had once loved.

My heart stopped. Despite Hardy's warning, I had no idea it would be this upsetting, this horrific. Her face had been deeply slashed from forehead to windpipe, her nose hacked off and her once wide, elegant blue-green eyes punctured, leaving red-black holes in their wake. This monstrous corruption of human beauty was more than I could take, and I must have lost consciousness.

The next thing I knew, Hardy, whose touch was surprisingly gentle and respectful, was helping me to my feet. The EMTs were loading the gurney through the open vehicle doors, and I snatched a final glance of Chase's covered body— its center thick and wet with drying blood—as it was devoured by back of the ambulance, its mouth slammed shut in finality.

"I warned you."

He had. But I thought I could take it.

It was an image I cannot shake to this day, one that defies understanding. I have hated in my life, had even hated this very being that was on its way to a morgue somewhere, but I could not possibly fathom the depth of the savagery that had been unleashed against my wife. Is a respect for life what makes us different from animals? Here was savagery more vile than any perpetrated by any of nature's beasts against another: intentionally wicked, bloodthirsty, this had nothing to do with self-preservation. This heinous brutality had been unleashed in a fury of passion. Whoever sliced up this ethereal goddess had obviously enjoyed the act. Even at the highest peak of my mountains of madness, I could not imagine a brutal fury capable of such an act. It reminded me of nothing more than poor Catherine Eddowes, Jack the Ripper's next-to- last known victim, whose mutilations had been carved in a seemingly similar frenzy.

"When did this happen?" I asked Hardy. "We think

sometime after midnight."

"Do you know who did this?"

"Not yet. But I promise you we will."

"I want to believe you."

He shrugged.

"You want some coffee?" he asked. I nodded, still woozy in the Arizona sun. I suddenly realized that the adrenaline had quickly fled my body; the heat was surging, and my desiccated larynx started to wheeze.

"I would," I told him. And he led me across the street. "You okay?"

"No," I said. "Definitely not okay."

He grunted, then led me to the edge of the road, as a cluster of three recreational vehicles lumbered past, trailed by dervishes of red dirt. Once the behemoths had trundled past, he led me across the blacktop.

Two

The spouse is always the first suspect. You feel guilt regardless of how far you are from the scene of the crime. As I had been sledgehammered by the potent cinematic reveal of my dead wife's slashed-open face, I could not help but feel complicit, that our mutual and growing hatred had somehow taken root and led to this. I knew it wasn't true in a legal sense, but I felt dirty with responsibility regardless.

Of course, the slaughter in Room 4 had taken place at a time when it was impossible that I could have been anywhere nearby. It was a five-hour drive from Los Angeles, I'd been seen by hundreds of witnesses at the TV Academy Theater, I'd been called at home and wakened around three in the morning. Still, my stomach roiled.

There is no police station in Salome; hell, there's not even a Starbucks. Christina's Restaurant and its adjoining Cactus Bar stand as the pulmonary center of town. A faded, classic Southwestern adobe desert outpost, it has withstood scorching heat and wind for nearly a century. A 10-year-old Kia sat on mismatched tires in the parking lot, next to a 1962

Rambler station wagon, completely stripped of its factory paint job, but also, somehow, clean of rust. A twenty-year-old Harley leaned against the wall. Cute, vintage weathered wooden signs offering terse knee-slappers like "laughing gas, a smile with every gallon", and "Arizona roads are like Arizona people: good, bad and worse" were nailed up around inept and peeling desert landscape paintings on the walls. The Cactus Bar was not open for business, but the door was wide as the floor was being hosed off in a torrent of vomit and cheap beer, and the peek within was a glimpse into somebody's nightmare of the past. The bar itself was ancient, wooden, spectacular, and the modern neon beer signs were at odds with the kitschy cowboy clutter and worn, upholstered Naugahyde. It was gloomy and dense with knickknacks, and decades of tobacco smoke covered the wall in a gummy grey lacquer.

Hardy led me next door into the restaurant side, which at least was sunny. Though not large (what could be in this miniscule apology for a town?), it was spacious, with a large U-shaped counter surrounding the grill. The place had just opened for business, and a couple of old-timers sat slurping at thick, chipped ceramic mugs of coffee, sucking on cancer sticks. You can still smoke in restaurants in the great state of Arizona, where time and civilization stand still. The stench of bacon and eggs was enough to choke on... and I did.

All eyes were on me as we walked into the bright yellow room. We took two of the upholstered red vinyl stools at the counter; the duct tape patches were curling and sticky, and the stools rocked precipitously, so I sat with caution. The waitress, stuck in the 1940s, had bright red lipstick that crept into the smoker's crevasses that radiated around her mouth, and hair that had been dyed a jet black, piled up in a bluff over her furrowed brow. Osteoporosis curled her back, but she proudly displayed her ample bosom in a push-up bra that acted as titty bowls, offering up her quivering, age-spotted, stretch-marked breasts in proud display. If she was working her assets for tips, it would be a while before she made the rent. Her smile was amateur artifice, broadcasting capped teeth with grey ridges, yellowed by her Tareytons. She gingerly laid a menu in front of me and greeted Officer Hardy.

"Mornin', Billy, hon. Scrambled, bacon crisp, pumpernickel dry?"

"Just coffee for me, Jackie. Mr. Turrentine?"

The smell of eggs curdled an already off-kilter stomach. "Just coffee, thanks. Black."

"Got us a new blueberry pie Jimmy just brought down from the Costco. Looks mighty nice.

Talk you into a slice?"

"Sounds good. Mr. Turrentine?"

"Just coffee."

My energy had collapsed. Having seen Chase's ravaged body had left me feeling like the corpse. My hands had been cramped and shaky since letting go of the steering wheel after five hours, but they were settling now. I could feel exhaustion creeping me over like a predatory cat. I felt heavy, sunken, deflated.

The two cowboys at the table by the window kept throwing glances my way, but nobody spoke. They knew who I was and why I was here. Jackie turned on the radio to fight the oppressive, stuttery silence, but if I were scoring this scene, I wouldn't have chosen "Tie a Yellow Ribbon", even for ironic counterpoint. Jackie served up the promised diner coffee, and it was better, darker, stronger and more potent than it had any right to be.

I stared at Hardy's hands, and they seemed remarkably soft and young. His job must not require much physical activity, despite the fitness of his body.

"Do you know how it happened?" I asked him. He took a deep breath and stared into his coffee.

"We've dusted, photographed, spatter-patterned, and blood analyzed the whole scene. All of those tests will be conducted in Phoenix, quickly and carefully, by a very competent staff."

"I don't doubt your competence; I just want to know what happened to my wife."

"So far as we know, she was in the room when her life was taken. It was a brutal killing with at least one very sharp blade."

"I saw her face. But it seems the sheets were hiding a lot more." Hardy sipped his coffee and nodded.

"What else?" I asked him.

He really didn't want to talk about this with me. And he was right. It was horrid. "Whether I can take it or not," I told him, "I need to know. I'll find out anyway."

"I'd opt for later if it was me."

"I don't want to hear about it on CNN."

Hardy took off the mirrored shades and turned to me. His eyes were alarmingly small and deep-set, and of a blue so icy they were almost clear. But though they were tiny, they radiated an intelligence he was loath to proffer. I knew better than to pick a fight with him. He locked eyes with me, apparently trying to peer into my soul to see what I could handle. I'd already passed out in front of him, and I'm sure he didn't want to have to keep picking me up off the floor.

I just stared at him, fear and repulsion eating away at my stomach lining, but needing to know anyway.

He blinked.

"She was eviscerated, her body opened up and the organs displayed. Her breasts were slashed open, and her face was disfigured in a frenzy. The walls and the bed were covered in her blood. The room was not booked; in fact, there were no customers staying at Sheffler's, so the manager had gone home at about ten. Apparently whoever killed your wife broke into Room 4 and, and... had her way with her behind closed doors."

It was like being hammered by Ali, one blow after another to the head and gut. I couldn't look at Hardy, and by now he couldn't look at me. It didn't stop Jackie, who hovered as close as she could as she served up the hunk of pie to hear all the gory details, staring cataract-clouded holes through me.

I could hear my heavy, thudding, rushing pulse pounding through my ears. "You made me tell you..." I waved him quiet.

"Was she... was she raped?"

"There was no seminal evidence of such an event. We'll know more after the tests are completed."

"And nobody saw anything, what kind of car they arrived in, heard noise from the room?"

"We're doing our job, Mr. Turrentine. No witnesses have come forward yet, but it's early.

We'll find him. I can promise you that."

It was an empty promise. Too little too late. And nobody should ever make promises they can't keep.

"Go home, Mr. Turrentine. There's nothing more you can do here."

He was right, I guess. But I couldn't just drive out here for five hours, see the hacked and slashed body of the woman I once loved, then drive home. Aside from the exhaustion, my wife's blood kept me here. Our pulses had once beat in synchronicity, our fevers had risen together. I could not abandon the life that she'd spilled so copiously after a mere glimpse of its empty vessel.

"I've got your mobile, right? If there's any news at all, I will give you a call right away."

I—and the dozen or two humanoid vultures that crowded around the crime scene tape— watched as the three marked County Sheriff's cars pulled out of the gravel lot, evaporating in the morning sun. Room 4 had been evacuated, left hollowed but newly painted in Chase's blood.

As the cop cars eased up Highway 60, out of Salome toward Phoenix, I looked down to see that I cast no shadow.

Once the law had left, the townspeople had nothing to look at but me, and I became the monkey in this zoo. They kept their distance, but could not keep their eyes off of me. It was uncomfortable for me, the writer, to suddenly be the center of attention, and I withered under their inconsiderate stares. Exhaustion had caught up with me and made me its mate. The hour or so of sleep had not made a dent in the inertia that suddenly took me over. I stared at my car, which was still ticking as it rested in the middle of Sheffler's parking lot.

"Go home," Hardy had told me. Driving another five hours across the monotonous blacktop was the last thing I was capable of doing now. I looked up at the hungry sun, down the deserted highway, across the sea of faces seeking distraction from their tedium, and felt nailed into place. Before I could allow the sun to melt me, I made my way to Sheffler's office.

The manager, maybe Sheffler himself, I don't know, had rheumy eyes magnified by thick glasses wound with adhesive tape, and a bald, shining skull with some kind of lump or tumor on its crown. Tufts of tight, curly grey hair nestled in the caverns of his ears, and he wore a Hawaiian shirt bedecked with Route 66 signs all over it. His limbs were long and bone-thin, though his stomach was round, distended, voluminous. The stench of his breath hinted of late- stage cancer.

"I'd like a room, please," I told him. It was as if I'd shot him.

"It was my wife who was killed here, this is the last place I'd want to stay, I was you." He just kept shaking his head, like I'd asked him to take a bite of my shit.

"You know, we was closed. Denny had already gone home. They must've busted in or something. We can't do nothin' about somebody breaks in when we're not even here." Maybe he left out words because he didn't want to waste what time was left for him.

"I'm not blaming you," I told him again. "I just need to rest. I've been up all night."

He kept shaking his head as he got me the key. "Me, I think you're nuts, but it's your picnic, ain't it? How 'bout Room 1? Furthest place from the scene of the crime. You mind moving your car to one of the designated spaces?"

Room 1 was a toilet. It had last been decorated around the time we won the war... and you know how long it's been since we won a war. There were dusty framed "paintings" of horses and flowers nailed to the walls, and the anemic single bed sagged like an aging nag about to be put out of its misery. The tattered curtains wouldn't discourage the dim light of a bad idea, and the door wouldn't even close all the way. When I finally just collapsed on the bed, a cloud of dust settled over me as the bedsprings howled in protest.

It felt better to be horizontal, though my head swam in fatigue. I closed my swollen eyes, and my head throbbed with an ache I hadn't noticed until now. I knew that Room 1 was fateful in Hitchcock's *Psycho*, but for me, it was respite from the sun, a bed to crash in, a rest stop between interstate journeys. Sheffler's was thankfully devoid of taxidermy, unless you counted the sawdust and sand that had replaced my brain.

As I lay there waiting to drown in sleep, all I could see was the corruption of Chase's beauty, its lovely features and her very femininity that had been so violently violated, destroying an inarguable, God-given beauty and sending it to hell. The lushness of her very womanhood had been purloined. As I lay there in a near-dream state, feeling like the bed was spinning and about to be sucked down a drain, I started to forget why I'd hated my wife. I remembered her smile, so rare of late; her teases; her tender kiss goodbye the first time she had to leave for a location shoot in New Mexico; our first night in our brand new Woodland Hills homestead; the California king-sized bed that became our own personal DMZ in those early days. The fights, though their memories would return, often but more distant, fell away, and I wept in sorrow.

But sleep... sleep would not befriend me this day. It teased me occasionally, but just as I was about to fall into its abyss, it pulled away from me, left me with open eyes and pounding heart. It knew I wanted it badly, and was just being an asshole. Nerves vibrating and my brain overloaded, I went into the bathroom and took a shower instead. The water alternated between scalding and room temperature before it gave out entirely, leaving rusty soapsuds swirling down the tub's fetid drain. I could imagine Janet Leigh's unblinking eye glaring back at me.

I toweled off in a strange state of disassociation, removed from my surroundings but somehow moving through them. As I dressed, I saw Sheffler, if there was indeed a Sheffler here, heading across the street to Christina's. Knowing that sleep was hopeless, I waited behind the peeling door until he entered the diner, then opened it and stepped back out into the baking Salome sun.

The gawking crowd had dissipated when the Highway Patrol took their leave, so I was alone as I trod the gravel of the parking lot. An unhealthy curiosity drew me to Room 4, which was draped in yellow crime scene tape. The crime had been committed and documented, so I felt no compunction about taking a look. Trepidation, certainly, and the heartsick nausea that hung from me like a shroud, and the need to see how and where Chase had spent the last moments of her life drew me inexorably to reach for the doorknob and give it a turn.

It wasn't locked, which could have been why the killer had chosen it. The door opened with a raw creak.

I lifted the tape and stepped under it and into the room with the curious sunlight, knowing I shouldn't.

Once in the room, I froze. As the rusty, rotting smell of spilled blood simmering in a closed, stifling box of a motel room reeked around me, my eyes adjusted to the lack of light, but only let in more darkness.

There was a double bed in the middle of the room, which was slightly larger than my own. Blood, lots and lots of blood, seemingly gallons of it, surely more than one petite woman could hold, had seeped into the mattress. The browning substance had spattered two of the walls in hideous dark art. Without warning, the contents of my stomach suddenly lurched up and I vomited on the floor, despoiling whatever active crime scene might remain here.

I was done with Salome and the veiled secrets she held. I left the sticky battleground of Room 4, reeling in heat, exhaustion, and nauseous sorrow, and climbed back into my Beemer.

I must have fallen asleep behind the wheel in the parking lot. Dreams had pinched and taunted me with screaming faces and rivers of blood. I came conscious with a jerk to the sounds of tires on gravel on either side of me. Two television remote trucks had pulled into Sheffler's, and they disgorged competing Barbie and Ken dolls, each wielding phallic microphones my way, demanding sound bite blowjobs.

"Mr. Willoughby! Mr. Willoughby!" the generic blonde news bimbo shouted at me. "Do you have a statement about your wife's murder?" I guess I had always been Mr. Chase Willoughby, but this was the first time it had been shouted at me, as her cameraman shoved his lens right up against my windshield. The half-witted jock in a J.C. Penney's suit and tie came around the other side with *his* cameraman, fighting for my attention. Oh, to have been pursued this way by producers...

I fired up the engine and peeled out of the lot. With any luck, I knocked them all to the ground.

They did not pursue me.

Back on the road, Chase's murder grew more real, its mystery more baffling. Chase Willoughby could be maddening, petulant, intractable, and self-centered, but I could not think of a reason for anyone to kill her. Divorce her, yes, leave the room rather than face her ire, maybe. But to rip her up and destroy this creature seemed unfathomable to me, the one who hated her most.

But as I drove, the malevolent Arizona sun now at my back, all that animosity melted away.

Maybe I never really hated my wife. Maybe she just drove me mad.

Maybe I would miss her.

THREE

I rolled over and looked at the clock. 3:32 a.m. Fuck!

I could tell that my sleep was over for the night. It had been so evasive of late, and I missed it. I knew I was growing grey circles under my eyes; just what I needed: another reason not to be cast.

He was watching television downstairs again. When the hell would he just give up and go to bed? It was the typical soundtrack: screams and screeching electronic strings, murder, violence and mayhem. Jesus, if you're going to be up at 3:30, then why don't you just fucking *write*?

I tried not to get angry, but it was getting impossible. This house, once so cozy and embracing, had become my prison, and James my warden.Sure, I could leave whenever I wanted, but whenever I came back, he'd still be here.

I remember that night at the Emmys like it

was somebody else's dream. A friend—well, a guy who would not take no for an answer, so kept pushing my buttons—had given me the box set of *Slaughter*, and I'd watched them all on a rainy L.A. weekend. It was sick and twisted, but there was an ironic intelligence behind it. It tried hard to be transgressive, and it was, but it was funny, too, in its sick and twisted way. Lots of blood, lots of viscera, but in a way that didn't piss you off. Well, it didn't piss *me* off, anyway.

And there he was that night, dressed in a tux and really quite handsome. He seemed removed from this horde of ass-kissing Hollywood automatons, a true outsider—especially having just watched the complete *Slaughter*—and the fact that he seemed like he'd rather be anywhere else was kind of a turn-on.

The *Frankel's People* costume designer had really done me up for the show, and I felt exposed, naked. I was sick of having fifth-rate, sixth-billed series bit players offering the world as they spoke to my chest. The transparent bullshit of money- grubbing, lowest-common-denominator entertainers had left me enervated. It was getting impossible to paste on that shit- eating grin and make it through another event honoring a bunch of people I've never heard of flogging shows I'd never even consider watching.

And here I was again, one of them. How do you spell self- loathing?

I knew I looked good; I'm not stupid. But that didn't mean I was offering myself up for sale. And I wasn't Ellie Frazee anymore, no matter how hard they wanted me to be. I'd grown up in body and mind, but they all wanted the former. I felt like I was a dirty joke, the girl from Nantucket. I'd had my fingers burned more than once on the Hollywood stove, but a girl has to make a living; you make your best choices from what is offered to you. My savings from *Crazy Frazees* was long gone, and the traffic accident that claimed both my parents, my rare, loving, devoted parents, left nothing but deep pockets of debt and an end to romance. I knew I wasn't going to make a living off my painting, and *Frankel's People* looked like it might actually be kinda good. So here I stood, painted and plumed and perched upon 6-inch Manolo Blahniks, presenting some kind of award to someone I didn't know, and certainly didn't care about.

The winner wasn't there to accept, and in her place was somebody, well, *interesting*. Yes, he was handsome, but not in that interchangeable pumped-up Equinox-sculpted, Red Bull- swilling, Hollywood Boulevard tabloid-courting, capped-and- sabre-toothed, ego radiating, Special Guest Star, vacuous, insufferable intellectual midget that continued to throw himself at me and anyone else with breasts and a few credits kind of way. No, he looked like he was unshaven because it wasn't important to him, not because it would look good and arty. He was uncomfortable in his tux, and it looked it. And the look we exchanged on our way to hand off the statuette seemed to signal that we'd both rather be anywhere else. When we touched for the first time and there was a *literal* burst of electricity, I felt that it actually might have meant something. Or I wished that it did.

Besides, he was a *writer*, a *good-looking* writer, if that's not an oxymoron. And I had just been introduced to his oeuvre, and it impressed me. It wasn't about the same old same old, it was smart and weird and different, and rarely led to a happy ending. Did I love it? No. But it intrigued me, and that night, so did he. I was in the mood for intrigue, which is in rare supply at events like the Emmys.

Yes, I'm embarrassed by how we got to know one another biblically that night; I'd certainly never done anything like *that* before, but I didn't regret it, either.

That took a while.

I loved Jimmy, and I respected him… which is one of the reasons *why* I loved him. It thrilled me when I'd curl up in his arms in that big bed and he would read me the pages he'd just written. It was sweet and sexy and intimate in ways I'd never known before. The sex was good for a while, but that didn't matter so much to me. I'd had more than my share from the time I was fourteen. And the abortion affected my plumbing in ways I never wanted to discuss with anyone.

It hurt when *Frankel's People* was such a disaster. Not because they stopped booking me on Leno and the magazines and blogs quit photographing me, but because I was no longer busy, surrounded by funny, talented people trying to make something special in a wasteland where mediocrity is something to aspire to. I didn't *need* to be on TV, but it was fun and fulfilling to have a home. It was kind of old-fashioned and silly, I guess, but I was glad to have a husband to go home to. I wore my wedding band as golden shield.

Soon it was back to humiliating myself at audition after audition. I know I'm not a great actress, but I work hard at it. With classes and coaching, I'm hoping that I can be good enough to snag a role with some meat on it.

But as I continued to swim my way upstream, things seemed to change around the time *Slaughter* was cancelled. Here we were, now matching Hollywood clichés: the out of work actress who'd really rather be a painter, and the brooding, handsome Hollywood writer whose seldom-seen series had been cancelled, tossed aside to make room for more clutter from the cookie cutter. You'd have thought it would have brought us together. It was painful how far it threw us apart.

It's like James had just given up. Here was a ferocious talent that was sexier than any steroid-enhanced Muscle Beach bum, an intellect that was powered by a dark imagination that liked what it found when it peeked under the rocks. What I wouldn't have given to be so perceptive and verbally dexterous and complex.

My blessing had also been a curse. I've been told I'm beautiful for as long as I can remember, certainly since early childhood. And that's great, of course, to be thought of that way, whether it's true or not, and it's been a part of my life for so long that maybe it is. You get treated special, and I can't argue that it's an advantage. But it has also come to imply that vacuousness is a part of the package, that with an appealing appearance is the expectation that you're spoiled, shallow, more concerned about designer goods and cosmetics than intellectual achievement and acuity. Being admired for the shape of the breasts that just happened to grow that way, a face that was formed in a way that humans find attractive, left me feeling that my external self was all I had to offer. The preening gym rats with shaved chests and plucked eyebrows and waxed pubes with their penis-replacement Maseratis and room temperature IQs had no books on their shelves, only multiple copies of their promotion reels on DVD. When your favorite work of art is the mirror, it's time for me to call for the check.

I paint because it's something I can do

on my own, and it gives me pleasure… even if I know I'm not very good at it. But I pursue it in the hopes that I'll get better.

James, however, was born with a true gift, and rather than feed it and nourish it and build it into what it could *really* be, he let Hollywood tell him that he didn't know what he was doing. When his series finally crashed and burned, he took it personally, and just couldn't motivate himself. He let the industry tell him he was shit, and he believed them.

I did everything I could to encourage him, to tell him how brilliant he is, to try to be the muse that he had called me in the early days of our relationship, but he turned away, watching movies rather than writing them, gaining weight and growing his hair, shaving a couple times a week, usually when he was being interviewed by some fat, pimply 20-year-old kid for some website or magazine you've never heard of.

I thought he was beautiful in the beginning, but his beauty faded when he abandoned what he was. I thought he was so special, so deep, so caring.But when he quit writing, I think he quit loving, too.

It seemed as if he were reduced to playing the part of the high-minded *artiste* outsider, the Man in Black, a caricature of a cynical, loft-living LA genius. It was hard to hide my disdain for what he had become, my lack of respect for him as he spent his days reading and watching movies on the 60-inch plasma. His inertia and growing slovenliness made him so much less attractive that our lovemaking grew less frequent, and much less satisfying. I submitted when I had to, and resented him for my weakness.

After I lost the baby, I never wanted to have sex again, not just with James, but with anyone. I reverted within, and happiness and I had lost our friendship.

Sleep has been difficult for me as long as I've been an adult: when it snatches at me, all it takes is a single thought to pull it away. My mind races when I'm in bed, and if I dare try to think about going to sleep, my cause is lost for the night. I will wake at the crack of dawn, no matter how tightly the curtains are closed, so I do my best to get to bed early.

Unfortunately, James is a night-owl, a writer trained to do what he does after the sun goes down, a vampire of letters, when he would bother to compose. So even from the beginning, sharing a bed was less than ideal. But in the beginning our newfound love and its exhilarating and overwhelming acrobatic romance cured all ills. Sex, which had been so curdled by the abortion after Peter Garrity had knocked me up and killed my career, was fun and extemporaneous and exciting again. But only for a while.

When I lost my respect for Jimmy, I lost my desire for him as well.

And so there we were in our mutual

misery, living not only in separate rooms, but separate floors, each occupying a solitary bed, our dreams stripped of eroticism and replaced by regret.

I had never been so lonely.

James asked me if I wanted to go to the screening at the TV Academy in North Hollywood, but I just couldn't bear the thought of painting on my Hollywood face and trading chit chat with the Botox brigade again. Yes, it might have been good for my career—and Jimmy's—to hold hands and hobnob with the network brass, the producers, and all those potential employers who would no doubt be in attendance, but I just couldn't think of a worse way to spend the first night of my period. So James slammed the door, peeled away in his repulsive giant Gila monster of a car, and I threw back four Ibuprofen and went into my studio, where I started pencil sketches of two faces tearing apart from the same body, before I realized that I was doing another primal scream. I couldn't bear to repeat myself like this, so I assembled a bunch of knickknacks from around the house and started a still life, instead.

But it was shit. It was all shit.

This house, which I had so loved, was a prison. My marriage, which had so filled me with happiness and eager hopes for a fantastic new future, had become a deadening present, a life stuck on a treadmill that needed oil. More than anything, I wished that if I couldn't have a baby, at least I had a dog.

I put on my running togs and jogging shoes and left the bungalow that harbored so much pain.

It was a rare summer sky framed by the hills behind the house.

Giant cumulus clouds formed cotton candy animals across its expanse. I jumped into the Prius and headed across the Valley to the hillside park I used to frequent when I had the house in Sherman Oaks, way back in another life. I pulled my hair back in a ponytail and wore those giant, Fearless Fly, Angelina Jolie privacy sunglasses, and felt anonymous in my baggy T-shirt and shorts. It was an atypically cool August evening, and I just wanted to blow off some steam before they shut down the park at dusk. The Fryman trail was nearly deserted, which was fine with me. I liked it when there was no eye contact, anyway. The last thing I wanted to encounter here was an Ellie Frazee fan. There seems to be an inexhaustible supply of them in the Valley.

My thighs burned as I made my way up the steep slope that started the trail, but it was a good burn, a punishment that I felt I deserved. I was working up a sweat already, despite the unseasonably mild temperature. Big, puffy clouds were going pink as the sky purpled, daylight ebbing away. It looked more like fall than August; summer skies in LA were usually cloudless. This sure beat the elliptical machine at home in the bedroom. It was just what I needed, at least for the moment.

My greater needs would have to be attended to later.

Having made the two-and-a-half mile loop, I returned to the parking lot energized, practically reborn despite my exhaustion.

As I climbed into my car, I heard a voice calling my name. It happens a lot, and I've found it's best to ignore it. It's never anyone I know, anyway.

But this time it was.

Toni McLoughlin came trotting over to the car, her eyes bright, and she seemed genuinely happy to see me. The glow of her late afternoon workout looked good on her, despite her inability to tan. She gave me a big hug and asked how I was doing. I couldn't answer her. How I was doing was badly, but I wasn't about to tell her that. Words stopped in my throat before they could find a way out. I couldn't say anything, not even the mindless, meaningless chatter that passes for conversation in LA.

She could see that something was bothering me, and the smile slipped from her face. At her expression of concern, my eyes filled with tears. She took my hands in hers.

"What is it, Chase?"

I just shook my head. What it was was me. My life. Another skid mark on the bloodied streets of Hollywood. I hadn't seen Toni in a couple of months, but she was as close a friend as I supposed I had. It hit me at that moment that, though I knew a lot of people, I didn't really have any friends. I had a husband I'd grown to despise, a manager, an agent, an attorney, and a couple of neighbors I chatted with once in a while, as well as passing acquaintances, but no one I considered a true friend, no one I could turn to in an emergency, no one to whom I could open my broken heart. James used to be that friend, but it had been a long time ago.

Toni and I had worked together on *Frankel's People*. She'd done my makeup on the show and my wardrobe at the Emmys, and was always the first person I'd see in the morning and the last at night. Part of her job is to get everybody in a good psychological place before they gathered on the set, and she was terrific at it. She was always in good spirits, and it was infectious. She wore her heart on her sleeve, and it was difficult not to reciprocate with her. That and the fact that she made me look my very best, knew how to shade my nose and highlight my eyes in ways I'd never discovered before, made her something more than just a member of the crew.

"Are you okay?" she asked me, though it was obvious I was not. I reached for composure.

"I'm just having my period.Everything's a lot worse when I'm bleeding."

"Tell me about it," she said. "It must be the moon; it's my time, too, and I'm ready to bite the next dog that barks at me."

I smiled, but I knew she saw my lip quivering. I told you I was a shitty actress.

"Are you and James okay?" Jesus, how obvious could I possibly be? More tears came, and I shook my head.

"When's the last time you went out dancing?"

I couldn't remember, and I told her so.

"Well, then, tonight's the night. Let's get you home and showered and all dolled up, and let's make 'em drool over us, what do you say?"

"No," I told her, "I'm really not up to it tonight."

"Sorry, Ms. Willoughby. I don't take no for an answer. We're going out and having a good time tonight. I'll take you home, help you look even more beautiful, and then we'll go out and break some hearts. We'll come back for your car later. Okay?"

What could I tell her, especially if she wouldn't take no for an answer?

FOUR

The drive West was even worse than the drive East had been, Interstate 10 a dismal blacktop inferno bisecting the bowel end of California. Traffic, seemingly mostly made up of giant trucks that trundled along at half the speed limit, blocked that bowel like a deep-dish pizza, and for some reason, vehicular accidents bloomed in season.

On this trip, however, I was not alone. It might have been foolish to turn on the radio, but I could not take the solitary loneliness of the road any longer. CNN and MSNBC kept me company all across the desert; thanks to a Sirius subscription, I did not have to jump from local station to local station, and I could steer clear of idiot blowhards like Rush Limbaugh and Michael Savage, who seem to have laid claim to all stations across the AM dial. But the news was not cheery; the death of my wife had crept out into the media's bloodstream, growing more thunderous as the day wore on. My iPhone, cradled in its cup holder, buzzed and danced, begging for conversation from unrecognized numbers. The morning bloviators wept crocodile tears over the violent death not only of my wife, but of a nation's childhood. The innocence of beauty had been torn asunder by a mindless maniac and his bloodlust, leaving the corpse of a crumbling society soaked in its blood.

The News, its antennae vibrating as always to the tones of celebrity slaughter, missing Michael and Farrah and Whitney and their too-soon-deceased like, had grown erect on Chase's death and its cautionary tale. They saw her as the chipper, chittering, pre-teen playmate of America. We'd grown up with her, loved her, shared the pain of her exploitation by her horndog producer and the resultant cast-aside fetus. They spoke of a woman unfamiliar to me, when it should have been me telling them all about who she was.

But no. I could have turned off the radio, or at least tuned it to a music station, but as I felt complicit in the death of my wife, at least psychically, I took the electronic tongue-lashing as my own personal punishment.

Hardy had been honest with me about the slaughter of my wife, but only to a certain point.

The details of her murder were even more horrendous than those related to me. The more personal details of her murder—the missing strips of her skin from her back, the heart pattern shaved into the back of her scalp—were so far removed from the woman I lived with, the woman I had once adored and explored in intimate detail that it was difficult to reconcile them with Chase. The radio was talking about a case on *CSI*, not about the woman with whom I'd shared the last four or five years. This was a tale for the great unwashed, entertainment for the blood lust of the *hoi polloi*. Ratings.

Perhaps the cancellation of *Frankel's People* had been a mite hasty.

My eyes were filled with the grit of sleeplessness, my skull throbbing with voodoo jungle drum pain, my stomach so empty that its digestive juices worked on its own lining. I wanted Chase back. I wanted her sweet and beautiful and loving and sanguinary and voluptuous all over again. I would not scorn her again, I vowed to the skies, knowing I could never be held accountable. I would do what I could to love and support her, and deserve her love in return.

Big fucking deal, right? A lot of good my word ever meant to anyone, least of all to Chase. If there were such a thing as reincarnation, maybe I'd get the chance to do my penance and work my way up the evolutionary ladder. But more likely, I would merely spend the rest of my life in miserable servitude, then take the route from ashes to ashes, dust to dust.

I pulled over at a dusky little Mexican place on the sandy end of Indio right off the freeway. It was a low and squat little white stucco place, far removed from the snooty pavilions that lined the exclusive Country Club Drive a couple miles south. This place was working class; nary a Benz in the lot. My eyes had to adjust when I entered the gloomy little eatery, which was bedecked in sombreros and tiny, twinkling strings of multi-colored Christmas lights. There were WPA-era paintings of saguaro cactus and sleeping vaqueros and gloriously voluptuous wenches and stridently manly bullfighters on the walls, which were otherwise a drab sandstone color, smudged with decades of palm oil on the edges.

Soccer played silently on the TV set that hovered near the low ceiling in the corner. There were no other customers, it being between the assumed breakfast and lunch rush, so the waitress, who I guessed had been very pretty a couple of decades ago, and still moved with the carriage of a beautiful woman, smiled as she told me to sit anywhere I wanted. Her smile was unforced, genuine. I had none to return.

I sat in a corner in the windowless room, which was frigid; the air conditioner was stuck on high. The cold breeze felt good, and I let it caress me before I ordered a Mexican breakfast. The cathode ray magnet drew my eyes to its screen, even though I have neither knowledge nor interest in sports of any kind. Even though the volume was low, the excited Spanish chatter of the play-by-play filled the room.

The waitress, seeing that the game was getting under my skin, picked up the remote and started flipping through the channels until she stopped on Univision *Noticias*, where a lovely newscaster was telling the Latin world all about my wife's demise. There was breathless video of the motel room, with loving close-ups of the blood on the bed and the walls. There were clips, replete with laugh track, of the nymphet who had launched so many nocturnal emissions, being adorable and wise beyond her years. Nobody seemed to understand that this was a character, written by middle-aged men, portrayed by a little girl who found herself moved from a dairy farm outside of Bakersfield to a soundstage in Studio City, another in a long line of precocious innocents growing up under the tutelage of a studio teacher and hungry, predatory Hollywood heavyweights.

I remembered the girl I married. Her guard rarely came down, but when it did, when she exposed the bright, slightly sarcastic and wounded young woman, in those long-distant moments when she trusted me enough to reveal her creamy white filling, she had been sweet. And then, sour.

The television showed a montage of video of moments in Chase's life, including a shot of our wedding in Palm Springs, just down the road from this little Burrito Babylon. I was struck by how genuine our smiles were at that impromptu little ceremony, and by how radiant Chase was in simple white lace and a veil. The waitress, who seemed held in thrall by the news, audibly gasped, and her hand fluttered to her chest like a wounded dove. She looked at me, her eyes now glassy, and pointed at the TV.

"Is that you?"

I just nodded, and she told me over and over how sorry she was. All I could do was breathe.

When she brought my chilaquiles and beans, all I could do was stare at them. I took some sips of the ice water, but that was all I could take in. Christina's powerful coffee had left its memory in my protesting stomach. The waitress was perceptive enough to turn off the TV and go back behind the cash register, pretending to be busy and giving me my privacy. But that just made this empty little café even lonelier. Sitting in the dim glow of twinkling holiday lights, I took a bite of the chilaquiles and tried to keep it down. There wasn't room for anything but regret inside me, so I threw a twenty-dollar bill on the table and took my leave.

The ride home was excruciating once I got past the 15, bumper-to-bumper under a scrim of orange pollution and ninety-five degree heat. All six lanes of the freeway, even the Diamond Lane, were slower than a Russian Oscar contender, jammed to capacity with angry Angelinos. All I wanted was to be home, out of the car, off this fucking endless freeway, and back in my bed, the place where this nightmare had begun. With luck, I'd awaken to a new morning, find that it had all been a dream, and go right down to Chase's room and tell her I'm sorry. But luck and I have never met. Luck is for, well, the lucky. So here I sat, ignoring the belligerent iPhone as it filled with pleading voice messages. I needed not to be driving; I needed to sleep; I needed to beg Chase's forgiveness.

There may be no place like home, but that's not necessarily a good thing. When I arrived, the news trucks surrounded my house like Conestoga wagons. A forest of portable antenna towers reached high, and the little *cul de sac* was a warren of videocameras and directional microphones. My first temptation was to turn right around, but where the fuck was I supposed to go? The tidy lawn was filled with media interlopers and curious bystanding gawkers crowding one another to get a closer look at I don't know what.

Instead, I nudged my car through the audience throng, forcing my way into the driveway.

The ghouls descended, pressing their greasy little paws and faces up against the windows, leaving smeary prints all over the glass. I pushed the button to open the garage, and I was astounded by the *cojones* displayed by the handful that tried to enter the garage with me.

Frazzled and outraged, I shouted at them that this was my property and to get the fuck out, hoping the door would squash them as it came tumbling down. The invaders backed away, and I stood alone in the hot, stuffy garage, reeling and wondering what to do. I opened the kitchen door and entered the house, locking the door behind me.

The first thing I did was to close all the shutters from the prying eyes and camera phones, feeling like I was blocking out the zombies in a George Romero movie. Late afternoon light still peeked in, but the gloom was palpable. Almost immediately, the doorbell rang. I tried to ignore it, but it was incessant. I could hear my name being shouted as if in a curse, and the telephone began wailing as well. Whoever was ringing the doorbell gave up and started pounding on the door, a sharp knock at first, but giving way to a heavy-fisted pounding. The shouts became more insistent. I silently cried uncle, and made my way to the front door and opened it.

Two men in dark, anonymous suits from Sears stood closest, with a famished pack of wolves clawing up from behind them. Microphones tried to reach around and past them, but they stood their ground, looking authoritative and immobile. One was white and the other black, but their size and features were nearly identical. Their faces were bland, and I'd never be able to pick them out in a crowd if I ever saw them a second time.

"We've been trying to reach you, Mr. Turrentine." I felt like I was in trouble with the principal.

"Donald Freemantle and Eric Press, Federal Bureau of Investigation. May we come in?"

I knew I looked as thrashed as I felt, and was clearly not in the mood for visitors, but it wasn't like I had to make them coffee or anything. And I knew I'd have to talk to them sooner or later.

"Of course," I replied, and looked into the ravening hordes beyond them. "Any way you can help me get rid of... *them*?"

"Well, you have every right to order them off of your private property. Or..." He tried not to smile as he continued; "You could turn on the lawn sprinklers."

Naturally, I chose the latter, and my uninvited guests quickly evacuated the front lawn, hovering just beyond the reach of the rainbow water show.

Freemantle and Press entered the house and stood in front of the couch, waiting for me to give them permission to sit. It took me a moment; my social graces were still in hibernation. They sat, and I took the old Stickley chair across from them.

The men were very officious. I'd heard that the FBI recruited primarily from Mormons, and I could imagine each of these guys riding bicycles in their white shirts and ties in their formative teen years, going door to door and peddling the Word.

"First of all, let me offer our deep sympathy for the loss of your wife," Freemantle—or Press—said in a soft, sincere voice. I thanked him.

"Your wife was killed across the state line in Arizona, which makes it a Federal crime, hence our presence."

Well, I've written a couple of lawyer and detective episodes in my day, and I didn't realize that was the case. But my legal education had been conducted entirely at the University of Google, so I had to take their word for it.

"I understand."

"Mind if we record this?"

Did I? Yeah, kinda. But I certainly didn't want to seem defensive. So... "Of course not."

"Thank you." The black one, Press, I think, took out an oversized Samsung slab of electronica from his jacket pocket, tapped it on, and aimed it at me.

"Where were you last night, Mr. Turrentine?" Freemantle asked.

"I was at a screening at the TV Academy, then came home and went to bed. The Sheriff in Arizona called and woke me here to give me the news of my wife's death." My voice cracked, turning the final word into two syllables. It was starting to hurt. I glanced up over their shoulders at the density of objects on display around the living room, and realized that this was Chase's house, not mine. Every bit of its considerable decoration was hers; she had spent the first couple of years filling it with eccentric oddities that somehow worked, turned a simple little domicile into a home that reflected her personality. I just agreed with all of her choices because I didn't really care, though I knew that the house had become something really special. She was an artist, and our home reflected her creative choices, not mine. I just lived here.

"I'm sorry if this is painful for you, Mr. Turrentine, but we promise not to take too much of your time," Freemantle continued.

I just nodded, remembering the trip to New Mexico where she found the old saddle that sat by the fireplace.

"Why didn't your wife go with you?"

I looked back at him, realizing that there was a good chance I was under suspicion after all. I felt defensive.

"It wasn't her kind of thing. This was a pilot that a friend of mine produced, and she really didn't know him or care to see the show."

"Do you know what she planned on doing last night instead?"

"I assumed she was going to stay home and paint or something."

Press's face was as blank and expressionless as an Abercrombie and Fitch model's. The camera he held trained on me was starting to make me uncomfortable.

"Do you have any idea where she might have gone last night? Or how she ended up in Arizona?"

"I do not," I answered honestly. "I wish I did."

"Would you say you and your wife were happily married?"

How the hell do you answer something like that? Honesty seemed not to be the best policy here. Our marriage was only defined as such by a paper at the bottom of a drawer somewhere. *Happy* wasn't a word I'd considered in quite a while, in *any* context. Press kept watching me from the screen of his Note.

"Well, we've had our problems, like any marriage, but I'd say yes." We *were* once, sure. "What kind of problems?"

I started to sweat. I felt the hot breath of Chase's anger huffing against the back of my neck. As the two men stared at me with serene, unblinking, expectant faces, waiting for my answer, my heart rate accelerated.

"Well, you know, we've been going through a little rough spot for a while, and things have been, just, you know, a little, um, edgy, I guess."

The two men glanced at one another, and I swear Freemantle threw the trace of a smile at his partner. My throat went dry, but no matter how much I tried to clear it, the mucus remained stubbornly in place. I was sure now; I could tell that Press was doing his best to hide his joy at my discomfort. But they just silently stared at me, letting me squirm in the scythe of their purview. And that accusatory camera-phone glared at me, daring me to claim my innocence. I refused to fill the guilty silence.

"What do you mean, 'edgy'?"

"You know, the business is in a pretty bad place right now, and it's taken a toll on both of us.

Neither of us is where we want to be in our careers right now. And I guess maybe we kind of took it out on each other." That certainly was true, as far as it went.

"Did you kill your wife, Mr. Turrentine?"

"*Of course not!*" The outrage was genuine, but probably didn't play that way to the camera. "I was here in LA when she was killed! I just got back here from seeing her body in Arizona!"

"Did you have her killed?"

"*Are you crazy?*" I said, probably sounding like William Shatner on the 911 call when he phoned in the death of his wife.

They just looked at me, placidly awaiting an answer. "Did you?"

"No!" I proclaimed.

Something about this didn't seem right. Again, I don't know much about the law, but what the fuck were the FBI doing here on the first day after a murder that took place in Arizona?

They seemed to be enjoying my uneasiness way too much for by-the-book Feds. "Can I see your ID?" I asked them.

"Do you have something to hide, Mr. Turrentine?"

These guys weren't FBI; more likely, they were TMZ. "Let me see your ID!"

Press, or whatever his real name was, kept that damned camera running, extending his arm to get it right up into my face.

"Get out of my fucking house!" I yelled, and they stood, backing away as I shoved them. I grabbed for the phone, but Press anticipated me and yanked it away, keeping it running. I charged them and Press tumbled over Freemantle, and the phone went flying. We dove for it, and I grabbed it away, threw it to the floor, and stomped it like a rhinoceros putting out a fire. Both of them scrambled for it, but by the time they got their filthy mitts on it, it was in pieces.

"Hope you've got a great lawyer," Freemantle snarled as they stood up against me. "You're trespassing on private property! Now get the fuck out!"

"You invited us in, remember?" Yeah, like inviting Count Dracula into your home so he could be free to suck your blood.

"Get out!"

They did. Without their fucking Samsung Note.

The house was often still when I was alone in it, but this was the first time it really felt lonely. Remote news vans, having bled all the footage they were going to get, began to pull away, and the crowd receded with the setting sun. The little house grew quiet within and without, and I felt unimportant, an intruder, useless, undeserving of residence here. All around me were monuments to a beautiful slaughtered woman; I stood alone in a room that she had dressed, a living set that she had created and occupied. My contribution here was a big screen Pioneer plasma display, a couple of Blu-ray players, and cabinets filled with discs filled with somebody else's imagination. She chose the artful antique Mission-style cabinetry that contained them, painted the coral and turquoise walls, festooned the rough-hewn open beams with painted strands of ivy. Her presence was everywhere; mine was subsumed, internal, insignificant. Chase was the light that filled the room; I was the darkness that extinguished that light.

I had dreamed of a time when we could escape the noose of one another, when I could lift myself out of the *ennui* of rotting matrimony, when I could man up and offer her a ticket out of this wrestling cage. I knew that both of us—and thinking about it now, especially Chase—could bloom and take flight once we were free of the chains that bound us to one another.

Why had we not divorced, if things grew so awful? I wish I had an answer. It wasn't as if we fought that often; we mostly just kept out of one another's way. I suppose it just seemed like too much work. Just like *everything* seemed like too much work for the last couple of years.

Getting out of bed was a daily ordeal. The treadmill in my little office out back called to me every day, but the thickening cobwebs of disuse muffled its cry. After my morning chai latte, I would dutifully fire up the iMac, the one with the biggest screen I could order, and go through the emails, scan the trades and resent the seven-figure deals being made by twenty-one-year-old writers on hundred-and-fifty-million-dollar comic book adaptations. My Facebook page needed attention to deal with the friend requests from another couple of fat, virginal *Slaughter* fans, and there were YouTube videos of alligators eating water buffalo and puppies singing "Happy Birthday" that had to be acknowledged. And then, of course, it would be time for lunch.

There just didn't seem to be much time to deal with my marriage. We'd get around to that. We'd either fix it or end it, and the latter seemed far more likely... and far less work. One way or another, we'd take care of it.

But we didn't. Somebody else did it for us.

The gravity of Chase's murder was descending on me now, alone in the cheerful cacophony of design she left in her wake, though her cheer had been kept from me for some time. I wondered if she had smiled with friends when she was away from me. And then I wondered how long it had been since I'd even *had* any real friends. As the framed paintings and posters and the carved wooden lady salvaged from the prow of an old Mexican boat smiled down on me, as the hanging Balinese dolls and German marionettes hung frozen in their happiness, as the kitschy stuffed animals and carnival dolls danced in poses inspired by Chase, I couldn't even cry.

I walked to the counter and the answering machine was blinking the double zeroes of "memory full". I held my finger above the Play button for a full minute before I depressed it, only to unleash a torrent of eager reporters and a handful of acquaintances offering their sorrow. Chase's family had been killed in a car wreck a few years ago, and I'd had nothing to do with mine since I left home at sixteen, so there were no blood relatives on the line. There was a message from Chase's agent, one from mine, and another from our lawyer and business manager. That was about as intimate as it got. I erased them all, unplugged the hard line, and went upstairs to bed. This time, sleep was eager to claim me.

Since I had fallen asleep long before the sun had even set, I woke when it rose. Even so, it was a long night, even without the Ambien. But I had to pee like a racehorse. I relieved myself, staring in the reflection that watched me from the mirror above the toilet. I had to look away.

Then, suddenly overwhelmed by an urgent rush of nausea, I threw up.

Disgusted, I flushed, threw on my morning sweats, and made my way downstairs with a new purpose.

I needed to know who killed my wife, and why.

Morning sun had a completely different effect than the ebbing sun of the afternoon. It did its best to inject cheer, making the place take on an actual glow, as if burnished. But the gloom was doing its best to overcome the light. I tentatively approached Chase's bedroom and eased open the door.

The room wasn't exactly messy, but it looked lived-in. The bed was still not made, and a T- shirt and running shorts were still damp with the musk of her sweat as they lay in a despondent heap on the floor. I picked them up and held them to my face, taking a deep breath, drawing Chase's scent deep into my own body. I sat on the bed and touched the sheets, which had gone cold in the air-conditioning. I picked up the pillow, and her scent mingled with a light perfume of vanilla and rose. It had been a long time since I'd stepped into this room, or even felt welcome here. It felt as though I was being naughty by being here, that I was going to get in trouble. I felt ten years old.

I lay back on her bed and closed my eyes, and could practically feel the gentle breeze of her breath. My skin erupted with gooseflesh as her ghost stroked my face.

My eyes flashed open, and it was just the flap of her pillowcase falling against my cheek. I didn't belong in this room; I didn't deserve to be here. So I left and went to the kitchen.

I put on a kettle and surfed to the *LA Times* website. After the crowd that greeted my arrival home the previous day, it was surprising that the story wasn't even in the first section, but saved for the front of the local news. It had much bigger placement on the *VARIETY* site—"Moppet Topper Stopped by Slasher!"—with the *Hollywood Reporter* joining in the chorus. But it was the lead story on Yahoo!, Google, and all the other search and showbiz sites. Video of my home was linked everywhere, and the number one YouTube video was the final episode of *The Crazy Frazees,* the one with the bikini. Today was a shining beacon of reportage.

I looked over at the telephone sitting silently on the counter. As the teapot began to sing, I went over and, after long moments of indecision, plugged it in. Almost immediately, it began to ring. I looked down at the caller I.D.: *L.A.P.D.* I knew I should answer it.

"Is this James Turrentine?"

"Yes."

"Did your wife drive a 2009 Toyota Prius?"

"2008."

"It's been found in the parking lot at Wilacre Park over at Franklin Canyon."

"Off Laurel Canyon?"

"Exactly."

"I'll be right there."

He started to say something, but I didn't stick around long enough to hear it.

FIVE

It was barely eight o'clock in the morning, but the San Fernando Valley was already starting to crisp in the dry summer heat. A dirty grey scrum obscured the mountains, and the Ventura Freeway was predictably jammed. It took me half an hour just to reach the 405, another twenty minutes to the Laurel Canyon turnoff. From there, I just had to eat shit and exhaust for another fifteen as I was caught in the cluster-fuck of the regularly employed headed over the hill to Hollywood.

When I finally pulled into the lot at Wilacre Park, the police were dusting the car for prints as it sat under the shade of sheltering oaks. I broke through the morning workout crowd that surrounded them, announcing my presence and presenting my spare key. The uniformed officer who took it from me was built like a fireplug: short and squat with a shaved head and an empty hole in his left earlobe. He wasn't fat, exactly, though his dark blue shirt struggled a bit at the buttons, and he had a bit of muffin-top action going on over his holster. I could see just the top of some Japanese characters tattooed to the back of his neck, peeking over the top of his dampening collar. Perspiration was already pooling at his armpits.

"Thanks for this, Mr. Turrentine," he told me as he took the key and unlocked Chase's royal blue Prius. "Looks like the car was left here last night, and was reported here in the morning.

The park closes at dusk, and it's not legal to park here overnight, so when it was called in to us this morning, we ran the plates and found out that it belonged to your, uh, late wife."

I nodded, watching the slim, feminine handprints magically taking shape on the car door and window as they were dusted with carbon powder. There was no question that they belonged to Chase. She had lovely hands with long, tapered fingers, slender to the point of delicacy.

"Sorry. Officer Demetrious." He reached out and shook my hand, even though he wore latex gloves. "Arizona Sheriff's called in, and we're doing them the courtesy of lifting prints for their investigation. I'm very sorry about your loss, sir."

"Thank you."

He stepped over and reached for the car door, then stopped and looked at me. "You mind?"

"Of course not."

He opened the door and it sighed a cool breath into the August heat. I looked inside and was not surprised to find it fastidiously tidy. Aside from a bottle of water and a copy of a book called *The Highly Sensitive Person*, the car was as barren as if it had just left the showroom floor. I noticed the ring of lipstick around the sports cap on the water bottle and realized that it had come from Chase's mouth. I hated to think that it had been her final kiss.

Another officer was dusting the passenger side of the car. The gathering crowd was an interesting mix of grey-haired organic types in sagging tie-dyed T-shirts, perfectly sculpted tight young actors with shaved chests and legs, former soap stars hiding behind giant sunglasses, beautiful but aging women with six-pack abs and robust augmented breasts barely haltered in stretchy sports bras, a school gym class, grotesquely overweight women with their Chihuahuas hell-bent for the *Biggest Loser* tryouts, and the occasional dog walker with her gaggle of golden retrievers, Italian greyhounds, boxers, and Yorkies, each seemingly eager for a taste of human flesh.

I watched in fascination as Demetrious laid thick strips of clear, sticky tape across the carbon powder to lift the prints before he pressed them onto blank white pages in a book. He probed the car for fibers, pulling up a strand or two of long, glossy black hair: obviously Chase's.

"Anything on your side, Tony?" he asked the skinny Latino cop behind the paintbrush full of grey powder.

"It's clean," Tony answered, to nobody's surprise.

Demetrious held out the book of prints to show me. "These appear to be all from the same person. I'm guessing your wife."

"Looks like her hands," I replied.

"We'll run them anyway, just to be sure."

"Great, thank you," was the best I could muster.

"I think we've got everything we need here, sir. Would you like an officer to take your wife's car home?"

"Would you do that?"

"Of course."

"You got a pen? I'll write down the address."

"That's okay; we know where it is."

"Could you just put the key through the mail slot on the door?"

"Glad to, sir."

Everybody was being so nice and California-polite; it

unnerved me. "Thank you," I offered. "That's our motto: to protect and serve." He turned to his partner. "Tony, could you drive the car to Mr. Turrentine's residence?" Tony returned the request with a mock salute, and Demetrious handed over the key to him. And that was it. Tony hopped in the car, threw me a smile, and pulled out of the parking lot in my wife's car.

"You have a nice day, sir," Demetrious said before he hopped into his marked cruiser and made his way out of the lot. I stared after him, incredulous. Have a nice day? I mean, really, the day after my wife's been slaughtered, mutilated, virtually hacked and slashed to pieces: *have a nice day?* If this were a *Law and Order* assignment, I could never have gotten away with such a civil, courteous exchange with the husband of a murdered TV star. And then, interview over. Hell, it had never even taken place.

I stood in the parking lot as the crowd started to disperse, again draped in the cloak of staring eyes. That was it? They found Chase's car, checked it for fingerprints and fibers, and split?

Some investigation.

The shade of the towering oaks was a respite in the blooming morning heat. Even with the choking traffic of Laurel Canyon Boulevard just on the other side of a row of eucalyptus trees, the air smelled different here. I hadn't spent time outdoors in a long time; home was a cave where I slowly became a hermit, a typing misfit with little contact with the world outside. My friendships and associations were mostly virtual or electronic, my outings rare. It felt strange to be under a sky and not a roof, the scent of spruce needles baking in the heat of the sun.

I remembered feeling her dampness on the workout clothes I had found on the floor of her bedroom, and realized that she must have been running here, that this might have been the last place she'd been before her fatal journey to Arizona. I decided to retrace her steps.

The trail has a steep beginning, and I was winded from the time my hike had commenced.

But the summer wildflowers embraced me, encouraged me to keep going. Avoiding the ubiquitous mines of dog shit, I made my way up the hill, wondering if Chase came here often. It's funny how little I knew about her life of late; as I hibernated in my cave, I assumed that she hibernated in hers. But this was a world far removed from her paintbrushes, from her career; this was outside, open, a little bit scary. Maybe it didn't intimidate her, but it was starting to frighten me. I kept climbing up and up, seeking some evidence of her presence, something that revealed her to me. She had been a secret, but over time, as we grew closer, more intimate, I learned the combination to her safe full of mystery. But as we used up our pleasure together, the door slammed tightly shut, and her secrets asserted themselves anew.

I was out of breath when I hit the peak of the trail, the halfway point that overlooks Coldwater Canyon with a breathless view. The San Fernando Valley was spread out before me, and I knew it was offering up its puzzles. If only I spoke its language.

Individual, interchangeable young women of an anonymous beauty jogged past me, and their amplified breasts didn't even bob; they had no relation to the physics of gravity. They all looked alike, as if there'd been a sale on those noses and lip jobs on Rodeo Drive this week. Chase had never been one of those. Once met, Chase was never forgotten. The little swoop of her nose was not a flaw; it made her more uniquely beautiful. One eye was a little bigger than the other, and it gave her an incredibly sexy little squint. No surgeon's blade had ever touched her skin; no color ever tinted her nearly raven hair, which usually just hung long and free and straight, a stranger to rollers and perms. Pretty poison, indeed.

I was winded, sweat drying in the arid breeze that kicked up dirt on the trail. A dust devil swirled toward me, then twisted around me, throwing me into the eye of this miniature hurricane. Grit filled my eyes and a brown cloud blinded me. Then, suddenly, it passed, a dervish that ran ferociously down the hill I had just traversed. I turned around and went back down in its wake, dust settling just before I trod in its path. There was nothing for me here, nothing but a decision. Since I drove her away, probably to her very death, I would avenge her murder. I would seek out its source, try to make things right. The clock would be turned back to a time when she needed me as much as I needed her right now. Chase, I swore to the whispering wind as it withered to a dusty breeze, I will honor your memory. I will be redeemed.

I thought I heard her voice laugh in the sky above.

We were homebodies, Chase and I, cave-dwelling artists who dimmed in the light of social intercourse. It was so even before our infatuation with one another had turned to enmity, but grew worse when we retired to our individual warrens. Chase went out more than I did; were there haunts that she frequented? I didn't even know. I had lost track of her life, and knew little of her time away from the house. So for now, at least, the only place I could think to go was home. So home I went.

The blue Prius sat in the driveway, safely and carefully delivered. The media, having already sucked whatever visual life it could from the home of the murdered television child star, had not returned to lick the bowl. A handful of civilians littered the sidewalk in front of the house, but as I pulled up, they maintained a respectful distance. I pulled around the

Prius and into the garage, and entered directly into the kitchen and an empty, silent house.

This time, the archaic answering machine registered few calls. They were deletable, either reporters or strangers leaving weird and creepy messages, and I threw them all away, putting the machine back to zero. I picked up the phone and went back through screen after screen of caller I.D., just wondering if any of the names or numbers might provide a clue. All it provided was a headache. All I wanted were the calls that came in between the time I'd last seen my wife on Wednesday morning and the midnight hour of her death that night. But there were no calls at all at that time. What I really needed to see was her mobile phone, a more direct line to her life. I wondered where it was.

I went into her studio, and the walls were lined with her Primal Scream series of sketches and paintings. The rage and fury they expressed had never been so overt, so extreme as now, in the wake of her death. Faces howled in animal anguish as bodies split apart between devil-vs.-angel dualism. The wounds grew deeper on each canvas. They grew more colorful, too; the stack of canvases started with charcoal, monochromatic sketches, but she turned to oils, and the color palette grew more crimson with each attempt. The paint grew thicker, too, more three- dimensional, as if the art was created from the body's own offal. But there, off to the side, hidden behind the gathered objects of a projected still life, a simple painting lay against the wall. It was obviously a self-portrait, just a few minimalist strokes in blue paint: hair, wide, sad eyes, a hint of a nose, and no mouth at all. Its mute peace stood in bold contrast to the ferocious howls of the faces in all of the other works, and made it all the more disturbing.

I snapped out of a trance, finding myself standing in the middle of the living room for God knows how long. The house mocked me with Chase's presence. Seconds ticked past, leisurely and inevitable. The box of light from the living room window crept slowly across the floor, threatening to burn my feet.

What happened to you, Chase? Where did you go?

Who did this to you?

And why?

I looked over to her bedroom and the open door that begged me to enter, and answered its call.

The room was filled with daylight, striking the hanging crystals and making a kaleidoscope of colors dance on the walls. Her workout clothes were still in a heap on the floor where I'd left them, but when I picked them up they were dry. There was a faint, salty crust outlining the armpits, but that was the only trace left of her now. I held them to my face and breathed deeply; the hint of her perspiration's tang was temporal, and dissipating quickly. I shook out the T-shirt and shorts, folded them, and draped them over the foot of the bed.

I slowly ran my hand over the rumpled bed, feeling the slight dip of where her body had lain, alone, night after night. I don't know why, but I decided to make her bed.

I pulled back the covers and fluffed the pillows, discovering myself caressing them as I carefully lay them in place. The pillowcase was very slightly discolored in the middle from the oil of her skin. I tried to smell her there, but none of her scent remained.

I began to smooth the bottom sheet... and something caught my eye.

It was tiny and barely noticeable as it lay against the off-white bamboo fiber sheet. But it was right there in the middle of the bed, coiled like a delicate copper spring: a red, curled pubic hair.

Chase's hair was a brown so dark it was nearly black. And besides that, she did the near- Brazilian thing; the only hair between her legs was a short little landing strip that pointed at her clitoris. As I stared at the nasty little curl, my mouth gaping in wonder, the late morning sun hit it and made it gleam.

My heart started to pound and my stomach curdled. Who was the red-haired scumbag who'd been fucking my wife?

And did the red-haired scumbag who'd been fucking my wife kill her, too?

I bent down and picked up the nasty little hair, holding it close to my face. It was surprisingly delicate, fine, almost fragile. I pulled a Kleenex from the box on the nightstand, gently folded it around the hair, and put it in my pocket.

Who did she know with red hair? For that matter, who did *I* know with red hair?

At that moment, the shock that my wife had taken a lover was almost as devastating as her murder. I was thunderstruck, flabbergasted, dumbfounded, all of those words that don't quite reach the level of nauseous astonishment that had me reeling.

I stormed out of her bedroom and into her studio, where her laptop stood open but sleeping next to a messy stack of papers on its antique Art Deco metal desk. With a brisk swipe of my finger across the trackpad, it woke to a cheery desktop photo of Chase holding a pair of snakes at the mouth of a cave at a Thai temple from a vacation we took on our first anniversary. I was notably absent in the shot.

Her address book opened with a simple click. It was a long list of names, mostly familiar, many not. They appeared to be primarily business-oriented: lots of network and studio names and numbers. Not a lot of personal ones, much like my own contact list. Those that I did not recognize meant nothing to me.

I bit my lower lip as I stared at her Mailbox. Even though she was no longer alive, it felt wrong to delve into her email correspondence. Her privacy, however, was no longer an issue. It was the only place that I could turn for clues to her murder, so I clicked, and it all opened up to me.

All of that nothing. EBay receipts, a couple of scripts from her agents, an ongoing chat with a gallery on La Cienega that was doing a show with art by celebrities. Nothing at all of a personal nature. Her Inbox was even more devoid of life than my own.

I opened her iPhoto files. Most of the pictures were from vacations we had taken, a big group of wedding pictures when we both wore smiles, on-set photos from *Frankel's People*, some gallery shoots, even a handful of arty nudes that I had shot right after we came back from Thailand. There were a few shots of Chase smiling with some groups of friends, but as the dates drew more recent, those shots were less frequent and filled with fewer faces.

Nary a redheaded stranger among them. I closed the laptop, completely at sea.

The stack of papers beckoned me next, atypically slovenly for my somewhat anal-retentive bride. There were bills and scribbled notes and receipts on top of a lined yellow legal pad.

Edges of a pencil sketch peeked out from under the detritus, so I pushed it aside. The drawing was mournful: a woman's face seeming to melt to the edge of the paper below her. It was sad, heartbreaking even; but when you looked closer, it was even worse. The lines that formed the drawing were letters, and they spelled out a single word:

Lonely.

From that moment on, the Hate tank registered empty.

There was a knock on the door, gentle, tentative, but I

was glad for the distraction. I left Chase's fortress of solitude and opened the door to two familiar figures: my agent and hers. Their faces were pale, sympathetic, but not in a phony, Hollywood way. They stood in genuine sorrow as they asked if it was okay to come in.

Jerry Atherton represented me, though we hadn't had much to do for the last couple of years. But he was still doing what he could for a client stuck in neutral. He stood close to six-foot-five, but was thin and uncoordinated. The tailored suit tried to make up for his ungainliness, and almost succeeded; it surely cost multiple thousands, but the Swatch on his wrist kind of ruined the effect. Though not much over thirty, his hair was thinning rapidly. Theresa Black had been Chase's agent since the *Frazee* days. Her real name was Schwarzwald, but she'd simplified it when she'd had her nose bobbed and the lipo. She was sixtyish, her hair blonde frosted over black, neither hue with roots in reality. Her face was tight and her forehead shiny and immobile. Her hairline hadn't met her ears in a decade. If she measured five feet tall, she had to be in heels.

"We tried to call, but I'm sure the phone's been crazy for you," Theresa said in her *faux* British accent, taking a seat on the couch.

"This is terrible, Jimmy," Jerry said, laying a hand on my shoulder. "A real tragedy. We're so, so, sorry." Theresa nodded and her eyes started to tear. She took a handkerchief out of her purse and dabbed at her nose, sniffling. I had never seen her express an emotion before, other than greed.

Jerry opened a white paper bag and pulled out a big Starbucks cup. "I brought you a chai latte."

I thanked him and sat on the Stickley across from them. It moaned from the weight I'd put on since *Slaughter* was cancelled.

"Thanks for coming by," I said, my voice a croak. I hadn't

been using it much of late.

"It's the least we could do, honestly," he said, and Theresa nodded in concurrence. "Are you okay? Is there anything we can do for you?"

"I'm shitty, but thanks for asking."

They looked at one another, maybe sorry they'd come after all. I regretted it right away. "Sorry," I apologized, "but this has been a total shock. I went out to Arizona and saw her body, and... and..."

"You have nothing to apologize for, James. This is horrible, horrible..."

"Horrible," agreed Jerry. "Listen, I can have Janet take care of all of the funeral plans, if you want. You shouldn't have to worry about shit like that."

Funeral plans? I hadn't even thought about a funeral. I suddenly felt thirty pounds heavier. "Thanks, Jerry."

"Really, no problem. Anything you need, you just let me know, okay?"

"Thanks."

"Or me," Theresa added, ever the competitor. "Great. I will."

There was a long, awkward silence before Jerry spoke up again. "Do they have any idea who did it?"

I shook my head. "Not that I know of. They said they'd call with any information."

"Horrible," Theresa added. "Just horrible."

Salome danced in my head again, and Chase's butchered face stared at me in angry accusation.

"He... he cut her up," I said, not to them or to anybody, I guess. "Bad."

"You shouldn't have seen that," Theresa admonished. "They should never have let you look at her that way. That's no way for a husband to remember his wife."

I shook my head. "I had to."

"Horrible," said Jerry. And then, more awkward silence.

"I'm going to find him," I said to myself. "I swear to God, I'm going to find him."

"Good for you, James," Jerry said.

They looked at one another, mystic knights of the Spectacular Artists Agency, bound in a secret handshake. They surely had more to discuss, but neither of them wanted to begin the conversation.

"Thanks for coming by," I said. "I really appreciate it."

"Sure, sure," Jerry said. "The least we could do."

"The very least," Theresa chimed it. But neither of them rose from the couch. "You look good, Jimmy," said Jerry, "considering."

"I look like shit and feel like shit. But thanks, Jerry. I appreciate your concern." I stood up, hoping to encourage their departure.

"Anything you need, Jimmy, you hear me? Anything."

"Thanks, Jerry. Theresa."

They still wouldn't get up off the couch.

"All right, I'll take it," Theresa spat, shaking her head in disgust at Jerry. "There's one other thing. I know this is a terrible time to discuss business, but this is something that's just come up, and it's something we have to talk to you about now."

The phone started to ring; it was from the La Paz Sheriff's Department.

"Excuse me a second," I told them, then answered the phone. It was Hardy. I held up my hand.

"Mr. Turrentine?" Blah, blah, blah. Niceties. Cut to the chase, okay? I'm busy with my misery.

"I just wanted to check in with you, bring you up to date a little. We haven't recovered any evidence that might lead us to a suspect yet; no weapon, no fingerprints, no witnesses, no unaccounted for excretions or fluids." He was very matter-of-fact, but more gentle than officious. Human, even.

"Thanks, Sheriff. I appreciate your keeping me informed."

"Listen," he continued. "We're coming to L.A. tomorrow to continue the investigation, and we'd like to spend a little time with you, if that's okay."

"If that's okay?"

He chuckled. "Well, whether it's okay or not. Busted."

"It's okay," I told him. "I'll be here."

"We can probably be there around lunchtime. Not a big deal, just the usual questions, check your wife's belongings, things like that."

Murder investigations were much more polite than I'd imagined. "Fine."

"Great. See you then." He hung up, and I was back with the Terrors of Tinseltown. They looked at me expectantly, so I fulfilled their expectations. "That was the Sheriff in charge of the investigation in Arizona."

"Any news?" Jerry asked. "Nothing."

"Just horrible," Theresa said.

This was getting tiresome. "So you were saying?" Or *not* saying... "Right." Theresa gave her nose another wipe.

"Bravo has come to us with a proposal. They want to document the investigation into your wife's murder, ride-alongs, forensics labs, witness interviews, the whole magilla. They've got Anthony Pellicano and his team on board, and they'll guarantee thirteen episodes, with an option for another thirteen, should the continuing investigation merit it. John Walsh has given a tentative yes to hosting, and you'll get E.P. credit, twenty grand an episode, doubling the total if the murderer is caught as the result of our investigation, triple if he's caught while cameras are rolling."

I just stared at them, my mouth in a Neanderthal gape, my eyes unblinking.

"I know, I know, it's absolutely tasteless. Disgusting." Theresa's face took on a disgusted sneer, as if this was all of a sudden way too tawdry to even discuss. "But as your representatives, it's our duty to convey this to you."

"It's a pretty sweet deal, really, Jim," Jerry said. "I know times have been tough for you lately, and it's a way to put that behind you."

"And it's a way to get the full weight of one of the finest private security companies in the world in on the investigation," Theresa added eagerly. "Do you really think some hick Arizona sheriff is going to solve this? These are some of the top criminal minds working!"

Now Jerry started to get excited. "The working title is *CUT TO THE CHASE: Avenging the Childstar Angel*. But if you don't like it, you come up with your own. You're the creative one, and you have full title approval."

"The Bravo brass are very high on this. And they feel it's got huge international potential, and that's a whole other pot." Theresa was practically licking her fingers. "And I think I can get them up to twenty-five per."

"And it's Bravo! *Housewives* is starting to sag, and they think this can be their next big show!"

They sat there panting like eager contestants on The Dating Game. I just stared at them, incredulous, for long, silent moments.

"What do you think, Jim?" Jerry asked. What did I think?

Yes, my marriage to Chase had withered into disaster. We couldn't be in each other's presence without a war of words, or, worse, a journey to the silent ice planet. But I had seen her beauty hacked away by a madman's knife, her blood spattered against the walls, the rusty scent of her death permanently etched in my nose.

I stood up above them, and they looked up with eager, expectant smiles. "What do I think?"

"That's what we're here for," Jerry answered. "I think *fuck you!*"

I yanked them up out of the couch and shoved them violently to the door.

"I think you are the slimiest, greediest, ugliest fucking scumbags I've ever seen! Chase's death is not for sale! Get the fuck out of my house, you fucking insects, you talentless, parasitic, bloodsucking, money-grubbing, planet-spoiling, lame fucking excuses for humans!" As a writer, I wish I'd been more eloquent, my invective more annihilating, but it was the best I could come up with at the time.

I shoved them hard against the wall, and Theresa tumbled over her Loeffler Randalls. The look she aimed at me was pure hatred.

"You fucking hypocrite! I know what was going on with you and Chase. You didn't even *like* her! And she felt the same about you! It wouldn't surprise me if *you're* the one who killed her!"

I threw open the door.

"I said get the fuck out of my house!" I shoved them out.

"*Chase's* house!" Theresa spat as I slammed the door in their wake. I stood with my back against the door for a long time, begging Chase's forgiveness.

Joni Mitchell was right: you don't know what you've got 'til it's gone.

I walked to the picture window and watched them leave. They drove off together in Theresa's Mercedes. She slammed into the mailbox on the way out of the driveway, knocking it to the ground before she peeled away in embarrassment... if an agent is capable of being embarrassed.

Chase's Prius sat alone in the driveway; it was time to put it away. I saw the key, still on the floor in front of the front door, where the L.A. cop had dropped it through the mail slot, picked it up and went outside. As I strode the rock path under the canopy of roses, the postman came walking to the end of the *cul de sac*, his heavy bag of mail over his shoulder. He was in his summer togs, long legs with bony knees trailing from his Government Issue grey shorts, sweltering under his U.S.P.S. safari helmet. He stared at the collapsed mailbox, then at the stack of mail in his hands.

I went over to him. "I'll take it," I offered, and he looked up, and jumped with a start. "Thanks," he stuttered, not quite sure what to say. I hadn't seen him before on this route, but Chase was the one who always picked up the mail, so I wasn't sure if he was new or not. I took the stack of correspondence from him, and he was sweating profusely in the Woodland Hills summer heat.

"I... I'm sorry for your loss, Mr. Turrentine," he offered from beneath his sunglasses. "Thank you," I answered. He stood there, not knowing the proper etiquette. I guess he was waiting to be dismissed. "I appreciate it," I hinted.

He lifted the helmet and wiped his brow with the back of his arm, then ran his fingers through his long, thick, wet, wavy red hair that fell around his face in angelic ringlets.

"Okay, then," he said. "Guess I'd better get going." I must have gaped, as he squirmed under my stare. All I could see was the hair, the red hair, the crimson halo, the copper mane. It flared like a dying flame in the sunlight. The rest of the frame around him had been erased.

"What's your name?" I asked him. "Wesley. Wesley Malone."

"A good Irish name."

"I guess so."

"They call you Red?"

"There's some I let call me Red. But not without an invitation."

"Did my wife call you Red?"

"Sorry?"

"Chase. Did she call you Red? Did she get your invitation?"

"I don't understand." Yeah, I'll bet he didn't.

"Yes you do. You understand perfectly, don't you?" I pulled his hat away and threw it across the lawn.

"What did you do that for?"

"I asked you a question!"

He walked across the lawn toward the hat, but I kicked it away from him, grabbed it and held it to my chest, like a nine-year-old playing keep-away. His pale, almost opalescent skin was pinking on its way to match his fiery locks.

"What's the matter with you?"

Suddenly furious, I sent the hat sailing with all my might, a jungle Frisbee taking flight like an Ed Wood UFO.

I ran up to him and grabbed his shirt in both hands, yanking him face-to-quavering-face like I was channeling Jason Fucking Bourne or something. Jesus, I would never have written a scene like this. But I was out of control, practically rabid; I could feel projectile saliva being flung with each crazy word.

"Did you fuck my wife?"

"What?"

I pulled him even closer. He'd had a hot dog with sauerkraut already today. "You heard me!

I said, *did you fuck my wife?*"

The disbelief and consternation that overtook his

expression brought it suddenly to a close. "You're fucking crazy, man. I've never fucked anybody's wife."

The obvious innocence of this gawky, fresh-faced kid with the cherry Jesus crown put out my fire, and it was time for my face to flush, with a shame I could not hide. The tough guy I wore fell away, and I was once again a failed TV writer, creeping painfully past thirty with a softening middle and a dead wife that everybody wanted a piece of.

I let go of his shirt, and wrapped my arms around him in a hug, which understandably made him squirm.

"I'm sorry, man," I said into his shoulder. "Chase is dead, and I'm going a little crazy."

He gently peeled out of my embrace, and I was glad he hadn't chosen to put the dog repellent to use.

"I get it, dude, it's okay. I'm really sorry." He was being more of a mensch than I would have under the same circumstances. "We all go a little crazy sometimes."

Shit, even the mailmen spoke in Hitchcock references in L.A.

"I'm gonna go now," he said as he slowly, cautiously backed away from me, "okay?"

I nodded, apologetically raised my hands, letting him know everything was cool. His image rippled in the water pooling in my eyes.

"I'm really sorry," I repeated, because I really was. A quick look around the *cul de sac* showed faces watching from behind the neighborhood windows, and closing blinds and curtains as our eyes met. I quickly made my way to Chase's car and climbed inside. The garage door opened at the push of a button, and I coasted in on silent electric power, closing the door behind me.

I sat in the gloom of the silent garage, thinking about what an asshole I was.

Six

It always comes down to sex, doesn't it?

I'm not a Freudian or anything, but it does seem to be the primary motivator for all human interaction, right? We begin our lives with an orgasm—hopefully two—from happy zygote to a trip down Mama's birth canal. From the suckling of the teat to mating for life, if such a thing is possible, we live our lives orally, carnally, physically. Yeah, maybe a kiss is just a kiss, but for me, it used to mean something.

I was an only child, and though I felt love from my parents, it seemed delivered at a distance, politely, without much physical expression. I think my parents were uncomfortable with such intimacy, even between themselves. To this day, I still remember a time when I couldn't have been more than five or six, sitting on my father's lap as he watched cartoons with me. I don't know why, but I just felt overwhelmed with feeling for him, and hugged him and gave him a big kiss, right on the mouth. Rather than return the kiss, he seemed to get angry with me. I felt a hardness forming in his lap, and he quickly lifted me up and sat me on the floor. He looked like he wanted to spank me, and I wondered what I had done wrong. I just felt that swelling of love that a daughter had for her daddy, and it got me in trouble. I withheld those feelings after that; I thought that they were bad.

It was not a huggy, kissy, feely kind of a family; my parents showed their love in other ways. They indulged me, but I'd like to think they didn't spoil me. We didn't have a lot of money, and Bakersfield wasn't the kind of place where you dream about Prada and Mercedes, but I got most of what I needed, if not everything that I wanted. And that was good enough. I didn't really want all that much, anyway.

It was a funny feeling, right around the time I started middle school, when people started to treat me differently, let me move to the front of the line, gave me their deserts at lunchtime, wanted to be my friend. Boys would either punch me or kiss me; I never knew which to expect. But I grew to learn that they both meant the same thing.

So when my mother drove me down to Hollywood for an open casting call for *The Crazy Frazees*, it was a shock to be ushered into a waiting room filled with pretty little girls who were just like me. But most of them had makeup on, and sexy clothes, and acted like they'd been here and done that a hundred times before. And none of them would talk to me… or each other, for that matter.They all seemed *mean*.

Maybe that's why I got the part; I hadn't learned to be mean yet. Well, that and my early development. I'm sure the tits on a tweener had a lot to do with it. Like I said, it's always sex. But this was my first ever audition, and I got the role. I had no idea how rare that was.

It's easy to see why actors can become raging egomaniacs. You get special treatment all the time, people want to be photographed with you, be around you, hope that some of what's special about you will rub off on them. They give you things, they call you beautiful, they don't let you do any of the physical work; there are people to do that for you. And later on, if you really care about acting, you have to be sensitive enough to portray the broadest range of emotions and insensitive enough to be judged and rejected almost every time you step into a casting office.

But the *Frazees* experience was like being in a new family together. And when Peter, a handsome, dashing man with swept- back hair that was silver on the sides, always dressed in a suit and tie, with teeth and a tan too perfect for nature, when he paid special attention to me, when he hugged me after a good take and left his hand lingering on my shoulder, I curled into its warmth. He told me how special I was, but it was private; he didn't want the other cast members to see that I was his favorite. He treated me like a grownup, and I blossomed as I began to feel like one. At fourteen.

And when the ultimate hymen-busting ritual finally took place— at night, in his office, after everyone had gone home—it started with dryness and pain, and ended in a shocking physical sensation I'd never felt before. Amid tears and wet spots, I fell in love with him, and knew that he loved me, too; he told me so on all of our subsequent secret nights together.

Then the periods stopped, and so did his attention. When I told him I thought I was pregnant, he sneaked me off to a friend of a friend, who performed the abortion in a Beverly Hills home theater, the better to keep this from the press. It hurt, and I bled and bled, and Peter's special affection ceased. And I never wanted to make love again.

I did, of course. Sometimes it even felt good.

But I didn't combust again until Jimmy, and even that eventually curdled. The fire burned brightly, leaving embers glowing in memory, if not in fact.

I knew what it was to be desired, but what I needed was to be wanted, to be loved.

It was like that at first with James, but after the raging inferno or our first year or two, desires were slaked, the real world crept in, and the fire was put out.

Honestly, I didn't miss the sex all that much, and I don't think Jimmy did, either. What hurt was the loss of all of that feeling we'd shared after the walls came down. I returned to my lockbox, and hid the key under the mat.

So I said yes to Toni, in the pine-scented heat of the Wilacre Park parking lot. I resisted at first, feeling cloistered, introverted, solitary. But she was very convincing. Her smile and her enthusiasm and her very lightness charmed me, brought out a grin of my own that had lain fallow for way too long. You know what? I could stand having a night out surrounded by people and music and fun again.She laughed, clapped hurray, and gave me a big hug, then pulled me like a teenager over to her little convertible Mini, and pulled us out onto Laurel Canyon, blasting the Poppees on her car stereo. I felt a weight lift off my shoulders, and actually started to sing along, even though I didn't know the words.

I was surprised to see that James's behemoth Beemer was not at home when we pulled up. He was rarely away from the house. I felt better going inside without him there to harsh the new- found buzz. The sun was warming with breaths of hot wind and the little house welcoming, like a little slice of lemon pie begging to be eaten.

By the time we entered the house we were giggling like teenage girlfriends. I always love the reactions of people when they enter my home. It's been my project, my passion, to make a place that really welcomes you, makes you feel at home. It's cluttered with eclectic stuff: you know, dolls, antique little baby carriages, ancient Thai headdresses, elderly puppets and toys, turn-of-the-century stuffed animals, Art Deco copper ballerinas, old costume skirts spread onto the walls like tapestries, even a couple of my paintings hiding in the corners.

When Toni entered for the first time, she actually gasped, laughed and clapped her hands. People either loved the place or were silent when they first saw it, and Toni's delight made my day.

"Oh, Chase, what a beautiful place! Did you do this yourself?"

I probably blushed under the weight of her enthusiasm and told her yes.

"It's like out of a movie, some kind of fairy tale or something! I've never been anyplace like this!"

"You sure know how to say all the right things, don't you?"

She gave me a hug, like an excited little girl. I felt a little awkward, I mean, I didn't really know her all that well, but I hugged back.

"You want some iced tea or something?" I asked her as she inspected our little cottage.

"After you give me the grand tour," she said, taking my hand to be led from room to room. The house isn't exactly Disneyland or anything, but it held her in its thrall nonetheless. The

tour didn't take long, as it really is a pretty tiny little place with not many rooms, but she loved it, and it really raised my spirits.

We ended up in the kitchen, and I poured us some iced green pomegranate tea. It tasted great after our summer hike, and I closed my eyes as I held the icy glass to my forehead.

"This is great!" Toni said. "Did you make this?"

"Trader Joe's," I answered. "Listen, make yourself comfortable. I've got to take a shower. I must smell like a football player."

"You smell great," she said. But I knew that wasn't true.

I gulped down the rest of the tea, rinsed my glass and put it in the sink.

"You didn't show me the bathroom."

She was right; I hadn't. "Come on."

I led her down the hall and opened the door. I knew she would love it. It was one of my favorite things about the house. The ground floor bathroom, *my* bathroom, was one of my pet projects.

The sink, tub, and toilet were all Art Deco, sea-foam green ceramics. I'd done the floors and lower walls in black and maroon period tiles, and all of the fixtures were period chrome. I'd painted the walls with undersea scenes inspired by the murals in the Casino Theater on Catalina Island.

"Oh, my God," she breathed. "It looks like Catalina!"

"I can't believe you recognized it!"

"Are you kidding? It's gorgeous! Who did you get to paint it?"

Time for me to blush again. "I did it."

"Chase! Are you shitting me? It's awesome!" I thanked her.

"God, I had no idea you were so talented!"

I was starting to drown in her praise. It was more than enough.

"I'm going to take a shower now; I don't think I can take any more compliments."

"I'm sorry, but you know I mean it, don't you?"

"Thanks, Toni. I'll just be a minute. Make yourself at home."

"Sure. Thanks."

She headed back into the living room, and I stepped into the bedroom and out of my stinky trail clothes. They were sopping wet.

The tiles were cool as I padded across the bathroom floor to the tub. It felt nice after the day's heat. I had to admit that my spirits had been raised.From the dead. Toni had really cheered me up, and as I looked around at the bathroom, I felt the sin of pride well up a bit.

A ripple of gooseflesh ran the length of my body as the air conditioning blew on me. I liked my shower lukewarm, but blasted the water at full force. I stepped under the 1920s waterfall showerhead, and tensions were washed away with the layers of sweat. I lathered up with the French verbena soap and closed my eyes. I actually started to feel like going dancing again. I hadn't done that in a couple of years, and frankly, had never really understood the attraction. I don't know; I guess I've got the music in me, after all. That was a surprise.

As I luxuriated, I heard Toni turn on the stereo. It must have been my New Age Pandora station, gentle, light, not really "music", but it put me at ease. I thought she'd change it to something more her style, but she just left it there and turned it up a little. Andes pipes or something. It was nice.

Anyway, I was smiling, and looking forward to our little outing tonight.

I was lathering my hair and got a little shampoo in my eyes.

I rinsed it out, and reached out of the shower curtain to dab my eyes with a towel. When I looked up, Toni was standing still, silhouetted in the doorway, watching me from a distance.

"I'll just be a minute."

Then she stepped into the bathroom and out of the shadows, and I saw that she was naked. I was a little confused… and a little embarrassed. She crossed into a slash of golden sunlight, and it was as if she'd stepped into a spotlight on stage. She was tiny, and her skin was a creamy alabaster, spattered with soft orange freckles from head to toe. She wasn't shy about her nakedness in the least. Her tiny breasts were mostly nipple, but those were large and extended. Her body was mostly hairless, except for the light, almost transparent patch of her pubic hair that didn't hide a prominent clitoris. Her mane of red hair was striking, even clumped and sweaty. I could not help but stare at her, and not in a sexual way, not really. I could appreciate the beauty of the female form, but it was not sexually attractive to me. Toni was quite unique-looking, undraped and presented almost as a sculpture or painting.

Standing starkers as she was in that shaft of sunlight, she was almost a museum installation. She wouldn't normally stand out in a crowd, this little red-haired Irish pixie, but undraped and so dramatically lit, it was hard to look away.

She crossed the tile floor toward me, and, I don't know, call me stupid, but I wasn't sure what she was doing. She came right up to the tub, gently peeled aside the shower curtain, and asked, "Okay if I join you?"

I was surprised and embarrassed and even a little disappointed, and I'm sure I blushed from head to toe.

"I… I don't think that's a good idea," I stammered like a 10- year-old.

"I won't hurt you." Her look was sweet, undemanding, not lascivious in any way. Still, I was disappointed that sex was rearing its ugly head again. It could lead to no good.

"Toni. No."

She just stood outside the tub, the shower curtain in her hand, looking into my eyes. Not staring at my naked body, not being lewd.

"I know you're lonely," she said. And that's when I started to cry.

She stepped into the tub with me, wrapped her arms around me, and kissed me, sweetly, gently, with her mouth closed. When I did not push her away, the tip of her tongue slipped between my lips for a taste.

Here it was again, the sweet devil of desire. I could usually fend for myself pretty well, but sometimes I just let things happen because it was easier than putting up a fight. It was too embarrassing or confusing to push someone away, someone who was merely expressing an attraction to you. I know, I know, I live in Hollywood, and I've been around the block, but this was a first for me. Of course I'd had women come on to me before, but I was good at playing dumb, oblivious, and had never had the classic college-dorm experience with another woman. It just wasn't in my playbook.

But Toni was gentle, sincere, and I discovered how empty and needy I felt. Man or woman, at that moment in my life if they'd handled me so tenderly and sweetly, it would have been hard to resist. It wasn't a *woman* who was wrapping around me in the soapy shower; it was someone who cared.

She kissed the tears from my eyes, running her fingers through the shampoo in my hair, and I allowed it, though the tears flowed even harder. She took my face in her hands, and made me look into her eyes. I tried to look away.

"Hey," she said, and I looked back at her. Her eyes were pale green, and seemed to look right inside me. Then she closed her eyes and kissed me again, and the tears stopped.

Somehow we ended up on my bed, and the softness of her feminine touch was startling, a little scary, but explosively erotic. I have to admit that I was the passive one, letting her do all the work, but she didn't seem to mind. On the contrary, she seemed to delight in being the explorer, the leader, the teacher. When she kissed her way down my stomach and nestled between my thighs with the light touch of her lips, then began to probe deeper with her tongue, the resulting orgasm was nearly immediate, shocking, overwhelming… and embarrassing.

I couldn't keep it from happening, but in its afterglow, I

didn't think I wanted to do that again.

I broke out in gooseflesh, despite the

summer heat, and shivered. When she came back up to kiss me, I could taste myself on her lips, and turned away.

Toni eased back and took my hand.

"You okay?" she asked.

I couldn't answer. I didn't know.

SEVEN

I could smell Chase's scent in the Prius. Not just the touch of vanilla and rose that seemed to symbolize her, but the sweet muskiness of her. I sat in the car in the dark garage, and just breathed her in, feeling guilty and repentant. Not that it would do her any good now.

I turned on her radio, realizing that I didn't even know what radio stations she listened to. I went through the presets, and they were predictably eclectic: New Age, Sixties, some really aggressive Hip Hop, Classical, even Metal. But it was all music, no talk. No news, no Oprah, no comedy, no words. I turned it off, and let her silence caress me.

Who was in that bed with you, Chase? How long have you had a lover?

And what took you to that shitty little motel in Arizona?

I looked in the compartment between the seats, but all it held was some loose change, a tin of mints, a little bottle of hand sanitizer, and a microfiber cloth to wipe her sunglasses. It was all so mundane. I pushed the button over the sun visor and the garage door closed.

Settling into darkness, exhaustion and a sudden

enervating *ennui* overwhelmed me. I felt smelted into place, barely able to open the door to go inside. I just stared at the steering wheel, dreading the rest of my life.

And then, I was startled by a brief vibration that made me jerk. It happened again a few moments later before the fog lifted, and I realized it was her phone ringing. I started digging around for it, and discovered it just under the driver's seat at the moment it stopped buzzing. I looked at the screen of her iPhone: I was disappointed to see that it was a text message from AT&T saying her bill was ready.

Thanks for the information.

It did, however, open my eyes to traceable evidence. My skin warmed and I felt the tips of my ears begin to burn. I swiped the screen to unlock it, and went directly to the recent calls.

Right under the AT&T number was a short list of numbers from the last several days. A couple from Theresa, one to Louise's Trattoria, and five calls in a row from a Private Caller whose number I didn't recognize.

Five calls. In a row.

All within an hour or so of one another, and all before midnight the night my wife was killed.

It took a while to realize that I had stopped breathing, that my eager heart was thumping audibly, as if trying to escape. My mouth was dry, papery. I stared blankly at the phone and the list of recent calls, then finally reached out with the tip of my finger and tapped the number.

It seemed to take forever to connect, and then, with a hesitant stutter, it began to ring. My heart beat even louder now, its pulse rushing in my ears. With a click, the ringing stopped and a voice came on the line.

A female voice. Bright and chipper.

"Hi, I'm not here, so you know what—oh, wait! I hear

a car in the driveway, let me see if that's me! Nope, sorry, false alarm. Leave a message!"

Beep.

I didn't leave a message. I didn't know what to say. I just sat in the garage, and the dim overhead light extinguished itself. The glow of the iPhone was my sole illumination, so I stared at it, and could feel my irises widen.

I tapped the Google icon, and recited the number into the phone. After moments of searching, a name and address came up to match the phone number: Antoinette McLoughlin, in Montrose, just above Glendale.

I punched the address into the GPS, pushed the garage door opener, and, despite overwhelming exhaustion, backed out into the real world again.

Oh, Christ; I was on the road again.

The Ventura Freeway, acting as the large intestine to the San Fernando Valley, had not yet become tumored with traffic. I actually sailed across the Valley at something close to the speed limit, until it bottlenecked a bit when it met the Hollywood Freeway. Traffic tangled again as afternoon blossomed when I passed the Santa Ana Freeway, but it was navigable, and eased up as I drove further east. My heart fluttered in my chest, fear and anticipation engaged in a grudge match. Finally, I hopped onto the Glendale Freeway, eventually finding my way to Honolulu Avenue, the anachronistically bucolic town's Main Street.

I'd been to Montrose before. It's a favorite location when you're shooting post-war small- town America. The place has an old-fashioned, Middle American kind of *Leave It to Beaver* quality, though the little mom-and-pop bowling alley has since been shuttered and modernized into shops. Still, it's a diner and soda fountain kind of place, with a big jeweler's clock in the middle of the town's square, with benches and jacaranda trees, pedestrian traffic, and an old ladies' clothing shop that's been there since the 1940s. Lots of pastel.

Gaggles of young families had lately taken the place over, and I had to navigate around hot young mommies pushing their thousand-dollar strollers while their little darlings screamed and barfed on their princess dresses. I slammed on the brakes and left a screech of rubber when one such mommy, jogging in her lululemons as she pushed identical two-year-olds in her Bumbleride double stroller, ran through the red light directly across my path. I burst into a cold sweat as she turned and gave me the finger. Because *she* ran the red light in front of me.

Fucking bitch.

I turned off the main drag as the GPS led me into a modest neighborhood of well-kept little homes with neat yards and relatively low rents. Toys and Hot Wheels and porch flags and SUVs and boxy little Scions were ubiquitous here, but Coventry Street itself was deserted. The GPS, speaking in the voice of John Cleese, directed me to the last house on the left. I parked across the street, and took its temperature.

The house at 1795-97 Coventry was a tiny, single-story Craftsman, built of dark wood and rounded grey stones, and had been converted into a duplex some years ago. The porch overhang shaded two entrances, with a stone and masonry wall dividing them. There was a dusty Mini Cooper parked in the driveway, with a vanity plate that read RT ONE. *Right one? Arty one?*

I'm guessing the latter. It looked like it hadn't been through a car wash in over a year, that's how arty it was; some comedic firebrand had finger-painted *eat me* in the dirt on the back window. There was a rock garden outside, and a couple of environmentally conscious cacti. A litter of pinwheels sat motionless in the summer stillness around a barrel cactus.

An antique wheelbarrow was piled with dirt, out of which a ventriloquist's dummy was poking his head. A Wheel of Fortune, faded from years in the sun, provided a backdrop to the mesquite tree, from which dolls were hanging by the neck from thin, colorful ribbons. Yeah, *arty one* for sure.

I got out of the car, crossed the street, and climbed onto the front porch. Antoinette's address was the unit on the right, so I rang the bell, which chimed like a call to Sunday services, deep and resonant. It died out into silence as I waited. A small dog started barking from the adjoining unit, its voice angry and high-pitched. It scratched madly against the door, and I did my best to ignore it. I rang again, just as a gust of Santa Ana wind, hot and forceful, huffed across the yard, setting the pinwheels into rattly motion. The Wheel of Fortune creaked and grunted as it made a half turn. Still no answer, just the little mutt next door getting more and more pissed at me. I tried to peer through the pebbled glass window at the top of the door, but couldn't make out a thing. Old mahogany blinds in the front window were clenched tight.

I knocked, knowing it wouldn't do any good, and called out to her. "Antoinette!"

Another gust of wind was the only response, shoving sheets of newspaper down the still deserted street.

I went over and knocked on the door to the adjoining unit, and the nasty little mongrel squeaked and ran whimpering to the back of the house. It was easy to call the little fucker's bluff. But no one answered there, either.

I wasn't prepared to give up. I didn't come all the way out to Mayberry just to knock and accept no response. I looked at Antoinette's dense maple door. It wanted me to open it. I looked down the street, which remained empty. I looked at the doorknob, crusted as it was with decades of dark grey hand grime. It was begging for me to use it. There had to be a reason that, when I reached out and gripped it, it turned so easily in my hand. It wasn't even locked. The ancient hardware clicked and clacked, and the heavy door sighed open with nary a creak.

With the lights out and the blinds drawn, the little domicile was surprisingly cool; they really knew how to build a house in the days before air conditioning. It was dark, too, though buttery afternoon light leaked through from the back of the little bungalow, reflecting off the high gloss of the polished bare oak floor. I stepped into the gloom of the tiny living room. A row of antique dolls in lacy dresses sat atop the stone mantel over the rock fireplace. The bust of a Devil sat on the grate in the fireplace, grinning a plastic smile. All of the furnishings were faded and elderly—I'm sorry, *vintage*—and the eclectic lack of style pronounced itself stylishly. There were two racks of clothing in the middle of the room, as well as a row of three dressmaker's dummies, each attired in 1940s couture. There was a stack of costume sketches on top of the low, wide, coffee table that sat on faux elephant's feet. At least, I hope they were faux. An old neon bowling alley clock was on the wall above the fireplace; the second hand labored around its face with a grinding sound, but the time was off by hours. A parrot stared at me from an ornate iron cage. I wondered why it was so silent until I saw sand leaking from its rear end. Bad taxidermy.

I stepped back toward the hallway, and the worn crocheted rug slipped out from under my foot; I had to grab for the wall to keep from hitting the floor. The little dog next door started barking again. I kicked the wall, and heard him run away, yelping as if I'd kicked him in the nuts.

Next came the little kitchen. Its window was uncovered, wide open, and sunlight was eager to make its way inside. The walls were yellow, the appliances varying vintage pastels:

green refrigerator, pink stove, pale blue sink, all self-consciously eclectic, but it seemed to work anyway. Dried flower bouquets were set on the table and windowsill, and abundant fruits and vegetables grew fragrant in the sun. I'll bet they were organic. But the kitchen, charming as it was, provided none of the answers I sought, so I dismissed it.

The little home was only one room deeper, so I stepped back into the narrow hallway to enter it. The smell was my first warning.

Okay, you know what's coming, and if I'd been reading this or watching it on TV, so would I. But it was different living it. I guess in real life we're a little bit dumber than in the movies, or at least we don't quite hew to the three-act formula so slavishly. I did not expect Antoinette McLoughlin's captivating little bedroom to be an abattoir.

I'd experienced the post-cleanup scene at Sheffler's in Salome, but here was the slaughter in all its three-strip Technicolor glory. A tiny, naked redhead lay sprawled across her bed, skin like porcelain and every inch of it dressed in freckles. But the body had been rent asunder, torn open, its innards outward, sliced open from groin to chest. Blood had shot against the walls, soaking the framed photos on the headboard with a darkening glisten. The woman's smile had been enlarged, the edges of her mouth cut from one ear to the other. A knife or something had slashed viciously across the chest, cutting a line across her meager, girlish breasts. Her nakedness was as horrid as the violence done to it, and I had to look away, suddenly dizzy, choking on the heat, returning to the magic land of *déjà vu*. The brutality I'd so laughingly, even mockingly depicted on *Slaughter* was not nearly so amusing in real life. The body was no temple, my oeuvre proclaimed, it was merely meat. At a remove from the prop-shop body parts, that may have been so. But having seen my wife revealed to me in a blanket of her own blood, and now, confronted with a human being splayed mercilessly before me in loving close-up, a once-living-now-dead lovely young woman lying in her own offal without further commercial interruption... I was not amused. I was not entertained. I hated the flesh and blood that comprised me. I wished I were without body: mere thought, mere memory.

Alas, I was not.

No. I was in the Small Town American hamlet of Montrose, mind and body reeling, standing in the middle of the blood-spattered bedroom of a petite, once lovely stranger, a *redheaded* stranger, struggling not to look at her mangled corpse, in a time machine tumbler that took me to a little motel in a little desert town in Arizona, smelling the rotting-copper stench of decaying blood and flesh, confirming my lifelong suspicion that Life is not Beautiful, after all.

Somehow, I had become the sun at the center of a solar system of death. I was melting.

My skin was suddenly drenched in a foul wash of perspiration, and I leaned weakly against the wall. I could feel the blood rush from my face, my legs wobbling, struggling to breathe but choking on the taste of blood in the air.

No more death, I begged the Fates. Would that it were so.

And then, a vibration in my pocket brought me back to earth. It repeated itself, begging for attention. I reached in and pulled out my nagging phone. It was Sherriff Hardy calling. I stared at his name and number as it buzzed in my quaking, sweaty hand. I looked up at the corpse in the bed opposite me, the body of the young woman staring, unblinking, through wide, green, accusatory eyes, deep into my soul. The phone hummed again, allowing me to look away from the slaughtered lamb... but there was no way I was going to answer it. I was drenched in guilt just standing intimately in the bedroom with this naked, mutilated creature. The phone went still, and I left the little house.

I sat in nauseous confusion in Chase's Prius across from the duplex for long, lonely minutes, wondering what to do. The silence was suddenly broken when a half-dozen pubescent boys rounded the corner and whizzed by on their skateboards, shouting and declaiming one another, flipping their boards, tumbling to the street, and climbing back on to continue their play. A couple of them threw looks at me, the stranger sitting alone on their street, but they had no time for me; they had shins and elbows to scrape and scar. The street went quiet again, and I was the only one who knew what lay behind door number two.

I couldn't put this off any longer. I returned Hardy's call.

"Mr. Turrentine, good to hear from you. I just tried to reach you."

"Yes, I know," I phumphered; "I'm returning your call."

"Just wanted to keep in touch, sir," he told me. "Not much new to report, I'm afraid. Only the fact that there was no evidence of sexual assault. I hope that puts your mind at ease at least a little bit."

I closed my eyes. No, my mind was not eased, not even a little bit. "Sherriff..." I choked.

"Yes?"

"I have something to report to *you*..."

The little neighborhood was no longer quiet. Three LAPD patrol cars, an ambulance, god knows how many unmarked official vehicles, and a rodeo of news trucks jammed Coventry Street. Bland, whitewashed blue-eyed blonde news reporters of disposable and forgettable beauty, daydreaming of movie-star careers, did their stand-ups within inches of one another, delighted that the story had broken just in time for their dinnertime broadcasts. The live remotes fit perfectly around the commercial breaks; too bad it wasn't in the middle of May sweeps.

August would have to do.

I sat in the living room of Antoinette McLoughlin's little house, peering through the wooden slats. It was a hungry crowd out there beyond the police tape. I sat on a leather couch opposite a rather enormous local homicide detective who spilled over the edges of what appeared to be an Eames chair. Detective Maldonado was well over six feet tall, with a beetled brow that hooded deep-set brown eyes. His hair was thick and so black that it was almost blue, making me think, for some reason, of Superman. His build, however, was far less heroic. He was gargantuan, and stuffed into an ill-fitting Hugo Boss suit that he probably bought second hand. A roll of fat extruded over his shirt collar, which, despite the oppressive heat, was buttoned tight and knotted with a red tie. His shoes had thick soles, but were well worn at the heels. His hands were meaty; his wedding ring was being swallowed by the flesh that surrounded it. His nails were immaculately manicured.

I'd told him everything about finding the phone number on Chase's phone and tracing it here, to this hipster bungalow in a decidedly non-hipster neighborhood. I'd told him everything about the discovery of the body. But I did not tell him about the little red hair I had found in Chase's bed.

He just stared at me from under that Neanderthal brow, not breaking the silence, waiting for me to divulge something more. My guilt, perhaps. But I had nothing left to say. He tried to wait me out, but I was done. I wanted to go home.

We both turned to watch the EMTs roll the gurney with the covered body down the hallway and out the front door. I peered through the blinds as they emerged into the sunlight, as the press swarmed like lawyers in an emergency room around them.

Maldonado returned his patient gaze to me. Finally, giving in, he broke his own silence.

"So," he sighed. "You didn't know Ms. McLoughlin."

"Never met her."

"Did you know *of* her?"

"I never heard Chase mention her, if that's what you mean."

"But she was a friend of your wife's?"

"Not that I know of. But that doesn't mean she wasn't."

"You don't know your wife's friends?"

"My wife didn't have many friends. But we work in a business with lots of acquaintances. It wouldn't surprise me that she knew her. But it would surprise me if they were close."

Well, that wasn't exactly true. I had a little red hair in a Kleenex in my pocket that hinted at extreme intimacy, but that was my secret. My mind was roiling. Had this girl been in bed with my wife? Had she been having an affair with her? I'd never seen the slightest interest or inclination toward women from Chase, most certainly not when I'd hinted at the possibility; it just didn't seem to make any sense.

But here I sat under the inscrutable, watchful, disturbingly unblinking gaze of LAPD Homicide Detective Raul Maldonado. This guy must have been a crackerjack poker player. I was drenched in sweat, but he, despite the black suit, the tight collar and tie, and his considerable girth, was fruit salad cool.

"Did your wife have enemies?"

Only me, is what I should have said, but I didn't.

"Everybody liked Chase. She was kind and generous, if a bit shy. Again, she really sort of kept to herself."

"And you don't know Ms. McLoughlin."

"No."

"Never met her."

"Not to my recollection."

"But it's possible that you've met her at some time in the past."

"Possible, but not likely."

"Not likely? Why is that?"

"I would probably remember."

"Why is that? Do you find her attractive?"

"I would remember because she was petite, red-haired, unique-looking."

He nodded, not taking his eyes off of me. And not blinking, either; the Bizarro-world version of Hannibal Lecter or something. His stare felt like the glare of a 10K on me.

I tried to wait him out, but he had more patience than me.

"Do you think," I asked, "that she was killed by the same person who murdered my wife?" He blinked, but never released me from his gaze.

"I'd be astonished if she weren't," he answered coolly. His look indicted me, threatened me, but he just sat there, a malevolent Santa in an Eames chair, waiting for me to tell him what I wanted for Christmas.

"The husband of the victim is always the first suspect, isn't he," I said. He nodded. "Yep. And he's usually guilty."

"And you think I murdered my wife. And this woman."

"The thought hadn't crossed my mind, frankly. Why, should I?"

"Of course not!"

He let a trace of a smile sneak onto his face. "You don't seem like the type."

It sounded like an insult. "*Did* you kill your wife?"

"No."

He stood up and slapped imaginary dust from his palms on his thighs.

"Good enough for me," he said. "I think we've got everything we need here, Mr. Turrentine. You're free to go."

"Really?"

He raised his Cro-Magnon brow. "Unless there's something else you'd like to tell me." I just shook my head and he lifted his hand, guiding me to the hall.

I never stopped, never looked back as I stormed the gauntlet of the media; as they swarmed around me, I just flipped an elegant middle finger, slid into Chase's car, and pulled through them, not giving a shit whether I hit one of them or not.

By now, the drive back to Woodland Hills was back to its normal afternoon clot. I sat behind an immense truck with Baja California plates, idling and spewing thick black smoke from its rusted emission pipes. Deadlocked in a sea of single-passenger vehicles, I was shrouded in insignificance. I was the Invisible Man, too unworthy to even garner suspicion in the death of my wife. In my profession, I toiled in obscurity until that plug had been pulled. I lived on my wife's savings and tiny residual checks for work I had done years ago, each of them losing weight as the time since their original broadcast had passed.

There's not a soul on the planet that would give a shit if some alien transport hovered overhead and sucked me aboard to whisk me away to the planet Oblivion. If my heart stopped and left me dead behind the wheel, it would only piss people off because I was blocking traffic. Someone would no doubt have to pay the Times for my obituary to be listed; I wonder if my agent would bother. Not that I deserved better. I was the master of my domain, but that domain didn't extend beyond my little office at the back of the house. My world had shrunk, my hairline receded, my waistline expanded. And here I was, in the wake of Chase's horrific death, feeling sorry for myself.

What an asshole.

Redemption, remember? I had a cause, an excuse to take up space on the planet. I had loved Chase more than I had loved anyone else, and it was getting easier to bring those memories back. It was the hate that had faded, if not been erased. If I had any purpose whatsoever, it was to avenge her, to touch once again the spirit I had so mercilessly abused and ignored.

Whereas I was at first resigned to being stuck here at the nexus of the Hollywood and Ventura Freeways, now I was getting pissed. Get me the fuck out of here! Not that it helped, of course; the traffic was at a standstill for another fifteen minutes before it started to budge. It was another forty-five minutes before I reached the Topanga turnoff, and another twenty before I reached the house.

I pulled into the garage, turned on the sprinklers, and entered the kitchen through the garage door.

I went directly to Chase's bedroom, which had once been *our* bedroom. She'd always insisted on sleeping on the left side, closest to the bathroom. It didn't matter to me. We'd played in that bed, she'd cried in that bed, I'd held her in that bed and actually made her feel better. It might have been a long time ago and a galaxy far, far away, but this bed maintained its secrets, held the joy and its decay deep inside. I saw us from the mirrored closets, tussling and laughing, naked and rapturous. I saw myself banned from the room in a storm of recrimination. But mostly, I saw silence, a closed box of Chase Willoughby, dying like the unattended marigolds on the windowsill.

What have I missed? What didn't I see? What had I

closed my eyes to? What did I make her turn to?

I couldn't take her bedroom anymore, and went downstairs and into her studio.

The paintings, all in rage and pain, glared at me, pissed at me. I knew the Primal Scream series, and felt responsible that her art had taken such a dark turn during our marriage. But there was memorabilia of the life that had passed before on those walls, as well. Framed photos of her and her parents. The *TV Guide* cover from *The Crazy Frazees*. A cast and crew photo, with the face of the slimeball producer who impregnated her and tossed her career over a cliff blacked out in felt marker. Some guest star photos from failed pilots: one with a very young George Clooney, another with a very old Tony Curtis. And finally, the last stop on the wall of fame, a framed color shot of the cast and crew on the last day of shooting *Frankel's People*.

Chase looked luminous at the center of the frame, hugging Dermot Mulroney and Eddie Izzard. Her smile could not have been more open and sincere, expressing a joy I'd successfully extinguished over the years. I scanned the happy faces; this was obviously a warm set. I'd seen them before. *Slaughter* was definitely not one of those.

Then, I saw it, peeking out at me: an elfin little redhead, perhaps the happiest of the bunch, at the center of a cluster who lifted her high so she could be as tall as the rest of them, looking different not covered in blood, her smile narrower than the murderer's blade had left it.

Antoinette McLoughlin.

So there was a link. But I didn't know what to make of it.

Chase Willoughby and Antoinette McLoughlin occupied the same frame.

EIGHT

Hollywood Forever has to be the most embarrassing name for a cemetery in the history of buried bodies. Located smack in the center of the fading, industrial, primarily Latino east end of Hollywood, right over the backyard fence of Paramount Studios, it was the resting ground for luminaries from Rudolph Valentino to Peter Lorre to Jane Mansfield to Tyrone Power to a couple of the Ramones. Buses filled with Japanese tourists made daily pilgrimages there, and during the summer they'd host outside screenings of horror movies against the crypt walls.

Classy joint.

I could not believe the size of the crowd that overflowed the charming little Old World chapel that morning for Chase's memorial. The anticipated news trucks and their collective spires of antennae huddled in the circular drive just inside the graveyard's gates, and veins of asphalt that meandered throughout the park-like grounds were filled with cars. I'd gotten there early, not wanting to be photographed arriving, but the media had staked their stalking grounds long before I ever arrived.

There was no family there, at least not of a biological nature; but the rainbow coalition of the actors who made up *The Crazy Frazees* were all in attendance. The female former moppets from the show, none of whom had been employed since then, were startlingly grown-up. Each of them was troweled with makeup so thick that it left their features immobilized, despite their tender years, with yeasty, expanded lips that were covered in wet, red lip gloss. The youngest, Darlene Harvey, who was only six years old at the time of the show, had already been inflated with pneumatic breast implants that must have given her back muscles an extreme workout.

Each of them was making the most of the exposure they'd get on the evening news. The boys were there, too, sullen-faced with a week's growth of beard. One of them wore a black hoodie out of respect. The other three had ties on over their colorful shirts, with jeans that hung low to reveal gym-sculpted abs and a waxed pubis. Peter Garrity, the evil producer with the potent spermatozoa, tried to slink in unnoticed under dark glasses and a slicked-back mane of now- stark-white hair, but Channel 7 recognized him, and ran close to track him into the chapel.

Jerry Atherton, dressed in Armani and shod with ridiculous Italian shoes with incredibly long-barreled toes that looked like they belonged in Oz, was there with his twenty-year-old date, who looked sixteen, despite her tasteful Cavali dress, which was at least *mostly* black. Theresa Black, squat and resplendent in sturdy boots and belted black chamois that had to be worth more than the ten percent she was giving up with Chase's demise, was surrounded by a coterie of fellow agents from SAA, all male, and all in matching black European suits, identifiable only by their ties, which were a mix of red, blue, and green.

Among the throng of fans in their thirties and forties was an assortment of washed-up middle-aged and older stars of long-gone, unremembered series. Each of them had flared brightly in a single vehicle, then left at the off-ramp of their series' cancellation, never to be heard from again. But here they were as if it were an autograph weekend at the Beverly Garland Holiday Inn in Universal City, faces surgically tightened into ever-present, impossibly white smiles, brows incapable of human expression, their hair frosted and dyed into colors not found in nature. And this was the same for the men *and* the women. There were no A-listers in attendance.

I recognized one group from the Bravo network; I guess they had not yet given up hope for the series. Maldonado was there, too, in the same black suit he'd worn at the little house in Montrose. I almost didn't recognize Hardy, as I'd only seen him in uniform. He nodded to me respectfully, clearly uncomfortable in jacket and tie.

Most obtrusive, of course, was the army of doughy, greasy-haired, perspiring paparazzi: these cave-dwelling parasites with giant telephoto lenses searched the crowd mercilessly for tears, facelifts, and embarrassing expressions. These bottom-feeding salamanders of the press breathed foul air heavily through their open mouths as they tried in vain to get crotch shots of the female celebrities as they exited their limos or took their seats.

I was the only one sitting in the section reserved for family, the only occupant in a section comprised of two rows of a half-dozen chairs each. It felt right to be alone.

The overtaxed air conditioning had failed as the chapel filled with silent observers, in the thick of one of LA's hottest summers. Fans on high stands were quickly whipped into position, but all they did was move the stuffy, overly perfumed air around. The onlookers fanned their gleaming faces with their memorial programs, and organ music began as everyone took their seats.

At the head of the Chapel lay the closed casket with Chase's corrupted body preserved within. Ornate sprays of flora filled the open space with bright colors that seemed to be an insult to the solemnity of the proceedings. I could only stare at the burnished black oak coffin and imagine what was within, how she'd been stitched and spackled together in a drastic attempt to restore some semblance of her unique beauty. That the coffin was closed made my dark imagination run free, and the nausea that had been eating holes in my stomach lining since that first call from Sherriff Hardy was getting noisy.

Religion had played no part in our lives, and certainly had provided no salvation to Chase. Still, this testament to her life demanded someone to minister to the world her valedictory, and the roughly handsome, Nordic-looking six-foot Methodist seemed cast by Lynn Kressel. His voice was mellifluous and calm, respectful and gentle. He spoke as if he knew her, but it was clear that they'd never met. I could not pay attention to the tired bloviations his job required; I could only stare at the coffin and feel my throat constrict. I caught the occasional phrase— "Chase wouldn't want to see the tears spilling from her friends' eyes"—but it was just so much verbiage. I'd been there for Chase's tears, as well as her laughter, and I'd seen both end in a vat of resignation.

It took me a while to realize silence had fallen. I looked up from Chase's casket to see the good Reverend looking to me with a beatific smile, his hand outstretched in welcome. It took a moment for the webs to clear and realize that I was the first one who was supposed to speak my memories of my late, beloved spouse. Whispers and shuffled feet filled the silent gap as I came to my senses. I had notes I'd made on a couple of folded sheets of damp blue paper that I was worrying with my moist, shaking hands; when I stood, my legs buckled in nervousness as I made my way to the front of the chapel. The minister moved aside as I lay my pages down to sleep on the lectern, my hands shaking uncontrollably. At least I could hide them here.

I looked up, and a sea of wide-eyed, eager faces were focused on me, hundreds of them, waiting to hear what I had to say about this beautiful woman who meant something to them. I was their fantasy; I slept with this goddess every night, we had conjugated, shared an intimacy that they had no hope of ever experiencing. I was their surrogate, their direct link to life with the glamorous Chase Willoughby.

I couldn't look at them; their faces were too hungry, too eager, too prying. Some of them had tears in their eyes, sniffling and wiping away their sorrow with Kleenex. I looked down at the crumpled pages I'd printed out, and the words lost focus. I just couldn't read them.

I looked up again and opened my mouth. But at the sight of the sadness that was being fanned through the whitewashed chapel with the raw, exposed, dark wood beams, I felt my mouth pulled back, my throat shutting down. I clenched my eyes shut to stave off the rush of sudden, unexpected tears. No words would come. I could not speak. Trying to control my breathing, I returned to my seat, broken.

The crowd was embarrassed, maybe for me, maybe for making a shambles of the event. It was too much for me to take.

NINE

It was done. I didn't regret it, I guess, so much as I just wanted to put the sex behind me. It couldn't be undone, but I could move on, and I was ready to do so.

"You still want to go dancing tonight, don't you?"

"I don't know, Toni. I think I just want to stay home."

"Unacceptable answer. You've just-stayed-home for far too

long." She sat up, covering herself with the sheet. She could tell I was discomfited, maybe filled with regret, and tried to push it aside and return me to a happier place.

"I will accept no change in plan. We're getting dressed up for a night on the town. I'll take charge of wardrobe, and we will dance and party until the clubs close down."

It sounded like work to me.

"No," I sighed. "I was never a party girl,

and I don't think I want to start now."

"Fine. Then we go dancing, put all the bullshit behind us, and have a good time until you're ready to go back to your lonely little Duxiana bed. Okay? Okay." And with that, she leapt out of bed, unembarrassed by her nakedness, and strode on tiptoe across the parquet floor.

I huddled under the blankets, shy and embarrassed, as Toni went through my closet. She was much tinier than me, but I was guessing that she could find something that would fit. Once she disappeared into the walk-in closet, I emerged from the bedclothes, strode quickly across to the antique Irish wardrobe, and quickly climbed into my underwear, feeling unwholesomely exposed. I threw my silk Chinese robe on over my green La Perla dainties, feeling foolish and girly as Toni emerged in a tight little red jersey dress that clung tight to her skin. She rolled up the hem, which was the only place it was too long for her, and when she shook out her copper hair, all traces of tomboy evaporated.

"What do you think?" she asked.

"It looks great on you!" I told her, truthfully.

"Should I wear a bra?" Her nipples were proudly evident. "Only if you don't want everyone staring at your tits."

"Maybe I do!" And she started laughing. Her face blossomed into a joyous, simple elation so sunny that it was hard not to be infected by it. I laughed, too, and the awkwardness of what had just transpired began to fall away. I think she was being careful not to acknowledge it.

"Now," she said. "What are we going to do with you?"

She started going through the dresses, pulling out the slinkiest, most revealing ones she could find. She held up a loose, clingy Versace I'd worn to the Heal the Bay benefit last summer at the Santa Monica pier.

"This is the one for you tonight!" she proclaimed.

"Too sexy!"

"There's no such thing!" She giggled again. "Just let me be your costume designer for the night, okay? You've got the perfect body for dresses like this. So don't deny the world the experience."

I felt silly, I felt self-conscious, but I also felt ready to emerge from my cocoon, at least for the evening. She extended the dress toward me, urging me to take it and put it on. My smile dam broke, and I laughed at her insistence. It made us both feel good.

"Okay, *fine*! You win!"

"No, *you* win."

I stepped into the pale green raw silk dress, which crackled with static electricity against my skin. I felt caressed by it, it fell into place so perfectly. It had been a while since I felt so much like a girl.

"Lose the bra," Toni said.

"No!" I objected.

"Look, with a body like yours under a dress like that, it's like artillery or something, like you're wearing a chastity belt. You were born sexy, so *be* sexy."

Sexy: everything good and everything bad in my life came from that cursed blessing.

"I like the bra," I said. "It's La Perla."

"Well, for God's sake, at least let it show." She reached over and adjusted the neckline so that the silky brassiere could be seen cradling my breasts. "You know, I think that's even better. Good choice."

We stood and regarded ourselves in the full-length mirror.

"You know, we're a couple of pretty hot chicks, aren't we?" It was as if our little conjugation had never happened, that we had never been intimate in my bed, even though it had just transpired. Toni was more perceptive than I'd given her credit for. And she made me laugh again.

And, as a matter of fact, we *were* a couple of pretty hot chicks.

"You want me to do your makeup?" she asked.

We were starving, so we got a quick bite at Kate Mantilini's on Ventura. It was early for the dinner crowd, so we got a seat right away. Warren Beatty was with Annette Bening and their kids in a corner booth away from the *hoi polloi*. Kim Basinger was alone at a table not far away, picking at a salad, the paparazzi having already forgotten her. I hoped I would age as well as she.

We went unrecognized, which was a relief, seated right in the middle of the restaurant. It was dark now, and I was ravenous. I hadn't had bread in ages, and when they brought a basket of

rolls still steaming from the oven, I tore one apart and submerged it in olive oil and gobbled it down as if it were the last supper.I looked up and Toni was smiling at me.

"What?"

"It's nice to see you enjoy your food. I'll bet you've been eating like a girl for a long time. Looks like you've lost a little weight."

"I can't remember having been this hungry. I think I'll even eat some *meat!*"

"Oh, you naughty little carnivore!"

The waiter took our order and nodded approvingly when I ordered a rare steak and sweet potato fries. "I like a girl who eats like a man!" he said. He was thin, even a bit wispy, and his manner exaggeratedly effeminate. He obviously had worn big plugs in his ears when they were fashionable, as the holes remained, making his lobes long and limp.

"I'll bet he prefers a man who eats like a man," Toni whispered to me once his back was turned. We both broke out into peals of mean-girl laughter, and he turned back to us with a giant smile on his face.

"Tell me! I want a laugh, too!"

That made us laugh all over again.

"Oh, no," Toni told him, "it's at your expense!"

"You are so *bad*," he said. Then he leaned down to my ear and whispered confidentially, "You know, I still have a poster of Ellie Frazee on my bedroom wall!" then rushed our order back to the kitchen.

"Somebody's got a fan," Toni said. "Maybe we'll get a free dessert!"

We did.

Unbelievably, I'd devoured most of the slab of cow that had overhung my oversized plate, as well as the preceding salad and the gratis crème brulee after. I was having a protein rush, a surge of superpowers hitherto unknown. I'd lived on garden clippings and bean curd for so long that I forgot what it was like to dine like a flyover American. I wouldn't want to do it often, but rather than making me logy, if anything, it made me a little hyper, eager to be out, even looking forward to some loud music and a good time.

"Where would you like to go?" Toni asked.

"Just someplace that nobody knows me." I just wanted to be one of the crowd, not a tabloid princess whose claim to fame was a shitty sitcom and a fucked-up pregnancy.

"Well, that isn't LA," Toni said. "Your fame and infamy is a beacon here. But I've got an idea."

"Tell me."

"Let's go to the desert!"

"Jesus, Toni, it's ninety-seven degrees in Woodland Hills and you want to go to the desert?"

"Absolutely! It's early; we've got the time and the air conditioning. Let's get out of Dodge!"

It was nice not to be making the decisions for a change.

Jimmy had become so passive that he would never take command. Anything was okay with him. I was sick of having to be the responsible one, the one who gave a shit about anything, and it was nice to let Toni take control.

"You're the driver," I said, and she whipped out of the parking lot in a rubber-burning U-turn, and flew onto the freeway and headed east.

Once we got past the San Gabriel Valley and the blinding lights of Los Angeles County, the deepening sky presented itself in awesome focus. Constellations shimmered against a black velvet background, surrounded by the spilled jewelry of the heavens' royalty. It was kind of magnificent, really, this view that was hidden from city dwellers. The air was hot, dry, and unscented here in the less-developed expanse of Southern California, and I opened my window, letting the hot wind whip my hair into a tangled mess. The Sixties music that she'd loaded onto her iPod was the perfect soundtrack for a night like this as we zipped from lane to lane at 80 miles per hour in her nimble little Mini Cooper.

By the time we pulled off onto Highway 111, melting into Palm Canyon Drive, the main drag was bustling with tan, leathery, lizard-skinned locals, middle-aged gay bears trotting from Starbucks to TCBY in flip-flops and beige cargo shorts, European tourist families with weird sunglasses and bright pink fanny packs, and students looking to raise a little hell. We zipped around the corner and into an uncrowded public parking lot. I gasped when we stepped out of the car and into the Palm Springs broiler. It must have been at least 110 degrees. A dry heat, yeah, but Jesus! Toni linked my arm in hers, and we walked in jolly step, like Dorothy and the Cowardly Lion, around the corner onto North Palm Canyon.

Las Casuelas seemed to be the town's heartbeat, serving up giant margaritas with chips and salsa to already-toasted, red, sweaty-faced imbibers on the patio, as a graying band of classic rockers pounded out "My Sharona" in a perfect, soulless replication of the Knack record. The smoking crowd on the sidewalk luxuriated under the misters that sprayed overhead, the mist evaporating in the night's blast furnace before it hit the ground. This wasn't my idea of a night on the town.

"Um… this isn't exactly what I had in mind, Toni."

She laughed. God, she was always laughing.

"Just stick with me, kid!" and she kept hold of my arm in a kind of high-school-best-girlfriend kind of way. "We're just starting."

She dragged me into a place called Zeldaz on the corner just past the Mexican place. House music blared, and the pounding bass made the floor-to-ceiling windows vibrate to the beat, trying to disguise the fact that it was really too early for any kind of crowd. There might have been a dozen people inside at most, and the massive room suddenly was really depressing. Each of them looked at us hungrily, as if they were hunters seeking edible prey. No one was on the dancefloor, despite the desperately ear-shattering electronics. Ten of the dozen patrons were men, blow-dried and hairy-chested, and their capped teeth and dyed hair made them look older, rather than providing the hoped-for disguise of youth and fitness. They literally roamed the boards, drinks in hand, when we walked in, as if staking their claims. Two women sat at the bar, dressed like twins, though one of them was Asian and the other some kind of self-styled princess. They both had long nails, tube tops over surgically enhanced bustlines, and healthy muffin tops sprouting over their low, wispy skirts. For some reason, the barracudas writhing across the dancefloor toward us had kept their distance from the competition at the bar. Perhaps they'd been rebuffed.

We blew our kisses and were out the door within two minutes, the militant bass beat still throbbing in my medulla oblongata. We headed south and grabbed a couple of iced lattes at the Coffee Bean & Tea Leaf across the street. Most of the desert action had moved to Indian Wells and Rancho Mirage, but that's not the kind of night either of us was looking for. Just some music and fun and dancing where maybe *we* were the only ones dressed to impress.

The next stop was a place called Gumbo Joe's, and there was already a crowd forming outside. We downed the dregs of our lattes and went inside. The playlist had at least gotten as far as the Black Eyed Peas, which was an improvement. And though I wasn't exactly seeking a *fashionista* haunt, we could have done better than the T-shirts and cargo shorts this crowd had chosen as their uniform. It was fine for our first way station on this night of freedom, but I wasn't ready for drinks yet, and the dancefloor was still abandoned. I certainly was not going to be the girl to christen it. We were way overdressed for Gumbo Joe and his family.

"Strike two," Toni called out over the music. "Let's blow this hot dog stand."

And we did.

Fracas was just down the block over a Ben & Jerry's, so I didn't have high hopes about its entertainment value, but once we went in, we found a place that was already in swing, kind of cozy, youngish enough, with music that wasn't something you'd find on the radio forty times a day. The dancefloor was on the small side, but couples were bopping and grinding and generally enjoying themselves already. It seemed a welcoming and friendly place, and we felt comfortable. There seemed a pretty even mix of men and women, and a low percentage of amphibious trawlers.

Toni turned to me for my approval, and I nodded.

"What do you want to drink?" she asked me.

"A merlot.But let me get it."

"Not a chance in hell. Be right back."

I knew I drew looks when I crossed the room; it happens all the time, it's a fact of life. Not bragging; it's given me more grief than pleasure. I've learned to just ignore it and not make eye contact. But I was very aware of how Toni had dressed me, and how exaggerated my femininity might have been. I was high enough on estrogen, but I know the effect was enhanced on this night. I hoped my pheromones were keeping to themselves, but I knew I threw off a womanly scent I could not control.

I found a tiny empty table in a corner and took a seat, making sure Toni saw where I was going. She waited in a cluster at the bar for our drinks, and the room throbbed to the Arctic Monkeys. I could feel eyes on me, could practically feel their caress, and it made me want to back away. Maybe this wasn't such a good idea, after all. Maybe I should be back in Woodland Hills working on my art. Yeah, maybe I should be hiding in my studio so that I don't run into my husband and hear him blasting brutal Japanese horror movies in the home theater instead of writing, hoping that we don't meet in the kitchen and start yelling at one another. Maybe I should be in that little house, dreaming of escape, huddled in a blanket of self-loathing, hiding from the world outside so they don't see how much I've fucked up a promising life. Maybe I didn't want to smile anymore, or have any friends, or dream any dreams that didn't wake me up screaming or in tears.

Considering the alternative, collecting stares from strangers in a bar in Palm Springs wasn't so bad.

I looked back at Toni, who had worked her way halfway through the line. And then, that sinking feeling as my eyes locked with a guy who was staring at me, waiting for me to return his gaze. I knew he considered himself handsome, and though he was probably about my age, he was far from my type. He had the torso and the hair, but he was just too fucking confident for me, like he could have me if he wanted me. Well, think again, Mister. He wasn't bad-looking, in fact, I'll bet most women would have been attracted to him, but he was just too aware of his appearance—maybe a bit too metrosexual—for my tastes. Any man who puts that much time and energy into his look kind of turns me off.

I looked away as quickly as I could, but it was too late. I'd been caught in his bright blue high beams, and he started to cross the room toward me. I started shuffling through my purse, just to have somewhere else to look. That wouldn't last long.

He pulled up the chair opposite mine and grinned a bright, white, but slightly snaggled smile. I kind of liked that his teeth weren't perfect.

"Mind if I join you?"

"I'm waiting for my friend over there. She's getting our drinks."

"She?"

Oh, shit. I might as well as handed him an engraved invitation.

"My friend."

"I'll keep you company until she gets here. Looks like the bartender is kind of overwhelmed." He looked at me with unsubtle desire. "And so am I, to tell you the truth."

Ugh. I hate lines. Why not just say hi and ask me my sign, for God's sake?

He held out his hand to me as he swept into the seat right next to me. "I'm Jaxon," he said. "With an X."

I needed a publicist to protect me from social intercourse. But here I was, alone against Jaxon with an X. I wished Toni would hurry the fuck up. I was being forced into introducing myself; I could see no way around it. But I kept my hand to myself.

"Chase."

"I know."

Oh, shit. Outed again.

"You know?"

"Oh, yeah. I used to pleasure myself to your picture on my *Crazy Frazees* lunchbox when I was thirteen."

Sudden nausea coursed through me as I stood and pulled away from him. "Okay, that's it. Not nice to meet you, Jaxon with an X. Go fuck yourself."

"Hey," he said, mystified by my angry response, "I meant it as a compliment." I flipped him off and headed to the bar. Toni was just placing her order when I grabbed her by the shoulder and turned her to me.

"I was just ordering!"

"Not here."

"Somebody bother you?"

"You could say that."

So we left the air-conditioned comfort of Fracas and headed back into the blast furnace of Palm Canyon Drive. I could escape Jaxon with an X, but I couldn't escape Ellie Frazee, that bitch.

"I've got an idea," Toni said, her face lighting up. She hailed a cab and we hopped in. "Take us to the Riviera," she told the cabbie, who whisked us away. We were there in a couple of minutes; it couldn't have been a mile away. Feeling guilty, I over-tipped him.

So we pulled up into a 1950s retro,

oversized Googie-style hotel, luxuriating in its vintage trendiness, huge murals of Rat Packers and Rat Pack Fuckers on the walls. Frank was singing "Come Fly With Me" over the speakers throughout the compound, and the lobby was filled with California casual young adults.

It's the kind of pop-kitsch thing that refuses to die, but it all seems to make sense in the desert, whether it's Vegas or the Springs. And tonight, it felt like fun.

We breezed through the lobby, past the little black guy who sat riffing on the giant white piano, and made our way out to the pool area, where three men, dressed as Frank, Sammy, and Dino, sang with a nine-piece band, surrounded by couples smoking and sipping wine, Jack Daniels and pricey champagne in the open- air blue-stripe cabanas. Sinatra's doppelganger threw a gesture to the band, and a brassy intro led into "This Town," which felt a bit mean-spirited, self-flagellating, and somehow extraordinarily appropriate for this crowd, which was mostly skimpily attired in their naughtiest beachwear… unless they were in evening dresses and jackets with ties. The severe desert heat was mellowing, but only slightly, so the pools were filling with amorous bathers as they climbed atop the big canvas-covered blue floats and made waves as they got frisky.

"What do you want to drink?" Toni asked.

"How about a real girl drink, like a Brandy

Alexander?"

"Ooh, Old School! I like it!" She turned to the bartender, cutting in front of a long line of patrons waiting their turn at the bar. "Two Brandy Alexanders, please!" The bartender, young and blonde and wearing a black T-shirt and board shorts, was happy to serve us, the interlopers, despite the complaints from the people waiting in line behind us. Toni held the drinks high as we squeezed through the dancers, then handed me mine as she sipped at hers.

"Oh, hell, fuck being dainty," she said as she slammed the drink and tossed the plastic cup over her head. I chose to sip mine, but it didn't take long for it to disappear.

The beat was as sultry as the night air, and supple bodies in bikinis and board shorts were shiny with perspiration as they danced in rhythm.Dancers surrounded the pools, and the scent of sex was beside the point. Toni dragged me into the throbbing crowd and started to dance with her typical girlish abandon. I felt awkward and out of place here, embarrassed and clumsy.

"Come *on*, Chase! Dance!"

"I feel stupid," I curmudgeoned.

"Me, too!" she answered. "Isn't it great?"

She grabbed both my hands and she started to swing me. It didn't take long before I started to feel the cocktail ignited by the music, and I started to swing and sway on my own. Once I was grabbed by the rhythm,

Toni swung away from me and started dancing with the guy behind her, which by this time was fine with me. The music was swingy and great and had taken hold of me, and I had no problem dancing on my own. Toni had been consumed by the crowd of dancers by now, deep in the belly of the beast, but I was happy to be out here on the sidelines, right near the band, feeling the blast of the horn section lighting up the night. Guys would come up to me and start dancing in front of me, but I was happy to be on my own, with my eyes closed, my drink long gone, and "Fly Me to the Moon" stringing me along.

When next I opened my eyes, I found them fixed on Little Sinatra, who was staring right at me. There was nothing subtle about his gaze, and I resented it at first: yeah, the singer in the band choosing his playmate for the night. But to be honest, he really had a great voice, and his look, though it strove for seduction, was really a little bit shy… at least, it seemed so to me. It was like he was expected to use that come-hither look with the ladies, but a little embarrassed to exercise it. He was slender and a little too tall for Frank, I realized, and when he took off the stupid hat, he really looked nice. His eyes were Sinatra-blue, as well, and I could tell they weren't contacts. There were pools of sweat ringing his armpits under the blue Sy Devore jacket, and he was selling that song for all it was worth. For me. It was really sort of cute.

I hadn't felt that little pulse of attraction in a long time. Yes, there was that one time on *Frankel's People*, and I blush to even think about it. Thank God it was just a guest star and not a regular, but I can't believe I let myself give in to it.

Jimmy and I had been having our "problems" for about a year by then, and I guess I was just vulnerable. I'd never gone for the Pretty Boys, even back in high school, but I was lonely and hurting and when someone that good-looking and that gentle and that sweet gives you so much time and energy, and when we ran lines together at his apartment on Barrington on the other end of town, well, it now seems so obvious and inevitable that I cringe when I remember it. The lines were memorized by eight, but they'd be rewritten before the next morning. In series television, you can never count on the text you're studying; there's a roomful of writers and producers who have to work their egos into every episode.

We knew the text wasn't important; we knew, as well, why we really were together that night at his place. I allowed myself to be seduced, knowing that I was just another in a long line of conquests for this Hollywood Bowflex Commando. I was a married woman, but I hadn't felt married for a long time. At the end of the night, my ass in a cooling puddle of dysfunctional, unsatisfying coupling, I regretted it all. I was glad when the episode ended, and we moved on to the next guest star. That was the one and only time I stepped out of my miserable marriage and into another man's bed, and in hindsight, it was worse than the miserable marriage. I haven't heard from him since, though he was nominated for an Emmy last year on *CSI: Miami*. He lost.

So here I danced, feeling heat in my loins for the first time in I can't remember how long, sharing a trance with a Sinatra impersonator. It felt tawdry, to say the least, but my level of self-respect was at an all-time low. If this were 1956, and the real Frank Sinatra were making ring-a-ding eyes at me, singing like the song was written for me, surely I would have wilted in his embrace. Or would I? But this young, athletic-looking version of Frank Through the Looking Glass and I were sharing hormonal desire that could only lead in one direction. Well, the band reached the moon, and Pseudo-Dean Martin grabbed the mike from Frank, and started belting out "Everybody Loves Somebody." It was goofy and cornball and played for all its camp value, but the crowd started slow-dancing together anyway. It was as good an excuse as any.

Without even so much as a look back at his band, Frank left the bandstand, and came right for me. "May I have this dance?" he asked me, with 1950s politeness. I wanted to resist, but the Brandy Alexander didn't. I guess when you're unhappy, it doesn't take much. So I let him take my hand and put his arms around me.

He was a pretty good dancer: a hell of a lot better than me.

I was happy to let him lead. His hands lay gently on my shoulders, and as our bodies pressed together, warmer even than the Palm Springs night, I let them caress my bare back. It felt good to be in a man's arms again. Though his dancing was smooth, his seduction was tentative. His hands never dropped lower than the middle of my back, and, without thinking, I allowed my head to rest at the base of his neck. I could smell his sweat overwhelming the antiperspirant, but it was a masculine, welcome musk. I fit pretty nicely against him. This was so unlike me. Physical intimacy has to work its way through a padlocked barricade for me, and takes lots of time and patience. I don't normally like to be touched, but this sweltering night found me somehow needy, emptier than usual, and this good-looking, talented singer dancing me gently across the concrete lip of the Riviera's swimming pool, under the approving influence of a couple of cocktails and the seductive music of another era, was melting me.

The crowd had quieted as the music had slowed, and it was easy for me to be mesmerized. I opened my eyes to look up at the wash of stars through the palm fronds as a gentle breeze kissed me. I felt relaxed in a way I hadn't in a couple years. I looked out at the sea of dancers, all of them held in thrall by a journey into the past, dancing together, some of them kissing, most of them smiling. But one dark face stood out, and my heart thumped me out of my reverie. Halfway across the concrete dancefloor, Jaxon-with-an-X was glaring at me.

"What's the matter?" Frank asked me.

"Nothing. I'm okay."

"You sure?"

Of course I wasn't, but I said I was. I looked back into the crowd, but my lunchbox fan was nowhere to be seen.

The song ended to quiet applause, and it was time for the band to take a break. I looked through the crowd, wondering what had happened to Toni. I couldn't see her anywhere. I had lost track of Jaxon, as well.

"Can I buy you a drink?" Frank asked.

I couldn't think of a reason to decline, so I didn't.

"A Brandy Alexander for the lady," he told the bartender, not having to wait in line.

TEN

When I got home from the funeral, the house felt as empty as I did. I threw my black jacket onto the back of the couch and walked into the kitchen. I opened the refrigerator and just stared at its contents, forgetting what I was doing there. My stomach soured as I looked at the heat- and-eat packages from Whole Foods. I wasn't hungry, I wasn't thirsty, I was psychically evacuated. I looked around the kitchen; all of the flowers that had cheered the room before were browning and shriveled. In my head, I imagined the same thing happening to Chase inside that closed coffin. I left the kitchen and made my way to my office, the one place not occupied by the ghost of Chase Willoughby.

I turned on the iMac and headed to JustSpotted. com, the celebrity-tracking site, and searched Chase's name. Fortunately, the site tracked even the most minor celebrities, most of them a mystery to me, so it didn't take long to find that Chase had been pegged by some camera-phone stalking fan at Kate Mantilini's in the Valley earlier the night of the murder. The house was closing in on me, stifling me; I could barely breathe. At the funeral, all I wanted was to get home.

Once I got there, all I wanted was to get away. So I drove out to Kate Mantilini's for lunch.

It was a quiet afternoon, well, barely even afternoon, so it was early for the lunch crowd. I went to the bar and ordered a JD rocks. I used to drink it a lot in my single days, but when my marriage started going sour, I found that it just made me more melancholy. I figured I couldn't get more melancholy than I was now, so I ordered the next one without the rocks.

It was plain that the raven-haired bartender with the enormous brown eyes knew who I was by the way she avoided my gaze. It was obvious that she was a hopeful actress by her looks, of course, but also by her outgoing manner with all the other customers. She kept her charm at a remove from me, knowing she had nothing to gain here. But a trace of sympathy made its way through her officiousness; I had lost my wife, after all, even if I was an asshole.

She kept herself busy polishing the opposite end of the bar, hoping that Shawn Ryan or Ryan Murphy or some other more important Ryan might pull up a stool and settle in.

"Excuse me," I called down the length of the bar. She looked up, but kept her distance. "You sure you want a refill?"

I held up my current drink, still half-full, to show her I was content in the drink department. "Were you here when Chase Willoughby came in for dinner the other night?"

A shiver seemed to run up her spine, and she shook her head, going slightly pale. "I work days."

"Do you know who waited on her?"

"That was Danny. He already talked to the big detective."

"I'm not a cop," I told her.

"I know who you are," she told me back. "I'm sorry for your loss. Your wife was beautiful.

She used to come in a lot."

"Yeah, sometimes with me."

Our conversation stalled for a moment. "Is Danny working here today?"

"He works nights. Though he hasn't been in since... well... since that night. He was pretty upset when he heard about it on the news. We all were. We really liked her."

As opposed to you was left unsaid, but I knew how to fill in the blanks. "Is there a way I could get Danny's number?"

"No, I don't think I can do that."

I grabbed a napkin and a pen, and scribbled my number on it.

"Here, give him my number and ask him to call me. It's important. I need to know what happened to my wife."

"And you don't trust the police?"

"Would you?"

She didn't answer, but she did take my number and put it in her pocket.

Opening a "Who Killed Chase Willoughby" Facebook page was either the best or the worst idea I'd ever had, but I was at a literal dead end. Lacking any kind of evidence to work from, other than a corpse, her presumed pubic hair, and her unanswered calls to my wife's mobile phone, I didn't know where to turn next. The police, in LA and Arizona, would conduct their investigations at their own speed, alongside hundreds of other cases that demanded their attention as well. I might as well get the Great Unwashed involved to do some of that legwork for me. So I opened the account and offered $100,000 to any information leading to the capture and conviction of whoever the fuck killed my wife. Obviously, I didn't have that kind of money in the bank, but I'd find a way to get it, even if it had to be from SAG insurance. It didn't take long before the site attracted traffic; obviously, people were searching Chase Willoughby and ending up here. "Fans" and "likes" started racking up immediately, in startling numbers, along with private messages from every crackpot admirer and dreamer, every amateur Sherlock Holmes and loose cannon would-be psychiatrist.

Still, I had to look at every message, hoping beyond hope that a clue would come from the outside, anonymous world. The messages came flying in, but most of them were obvious creeps, typing messages from Mommy's basement in deplorable grammar, everything from love notes to "she got what she deserved." It was assumed that if you were a celebrity, then the public owned you, claimed purchase to your life rights in perpetuity. They deserved to control your life, you were there to please them, and if you crossed them, they would reject you, ostracize you, hate you to the point that you deserved to die. Here was a woman known for being a precocious and beautiful young teenager, and she drew such invective from outraged Christians for having been impregnated by an Older Man that she deserved to be immolated in the deepest chambers of Hell. Lots of notes on how beautiful and charming she was, but practically as many about what a shitty actress she was. Human beings are fickle, self-centered, detestable creatures sometimes.

There was communication from within the Hollywood community, as well. More reality show producers tried to make contact here, the real low-end bottom-feeders from channels I'd never heard of. Or the Hollywood hopefuls who just knew they had the right take to attach their leechy, fanged sucker-mouths to Chase Willoughby and ride her cadaver to fame and fortune.

But as for meaningful clues? Maybe later, certainly not now.

My eyes were red and burning; I hadn't looked away from the screen in hours. When I did look up, I saw that the August sun was setting, shrouding itself in pink and purple clouds. My head was throbbing, and I pressed my palms against my eyes, suddenly aware of the dull, thudding ache. Then, the phone in my pocket began to ring. I pulled it out to check the caller ID, but it just read "blocked". I answered anyway.

"Mr. Willoughby?"

I guess that's who I'll be until the day I die. "Close enough," I answered.

"This is Danny Reed, the waiter from Kate Mantilini? Delores told me you wanted me to call you?"

"Danny, hi!" I couldn't believe it. His voice was lilty, like some sort of gay caricature on *South Park* or something. "Thank you for calling me back. Listen, I'd love to talk to you about the night my wife was there."

"Delores told you I'd already spoken with the police, didn't she?"

"She did. But this has nothing to do with the police. I just need to know what happened to Chase. Maybe you can help. Where do you live? I can come to you…"

"No, not my place. Do you know Aroma, on Tujunga in Studio City?"

"I know it. Meet you there in an hour or so?"

There was a long hesitation. "Okay. At about nine, right?"

"Good. I'll see you then."

I didn't know what would come of this, but at least it seemed like some sort of progress.

Aroma is a cute outdoor coffee house and café on one short, charming block of Studio City, sort of halfway between the CBS Studios and Universal City. The coffee and tea drinks were good, and the desserts elaborate and expansively caloric. Almost all of the seating was outside in a jumble of mismatched tables and chairs, under a canopy of oaks and elm. Its sweetness, however, meant that there was always an endless line for service that snaked out the door and down the street. It was a popular hangout for out-of-work actors and writers and TV weathermen. It was a rare table that didn't sport a pile of trade papers and a clattering MacBook Air, and the atmosphere was always charged with chatter about The Industry. The place was particularly photogenic at night, when the strings of little white lights wrapped around the trees were ablaze. It was probably ninety degrees or so on this night, and the crowd was dressed accordingly, sipping iced lattes and scooping the last melting remains of Italian ice cream from the tiny cups they'd gotten from the gelato place a few doors down. At least a couple dozen of the patrons had their fashionable dogs with them, which acted as magnets for the opposite sex.

I had no idea what young Mr. Reed looked like, but I figured he'd know me, so I just sat on the bench out in front and waited for him to arrive. Soon I felt the sensation of eyes on me. It seemed like any time I looked up, someone was just looking away. Call it paranoia if you like, but I know that I was being recognized in the only way I would ever achieve any sort of fame: as the husband of the slaughtered TV star. Before long, the people around me didn't even bother to hide their glances. I felt I was living in a scene directed by Roman Polanski.

I was relieved when the thin, frosted-haired young man with the pierced, drooping earlobes in the white tennis shorts and matching immaculately pressed short-sleeved shirt and pink Crocs walked nervously up to me. He was holding a shivering little Italian Greyhound cradled in one arm: shivering despite the ninety-degree heat. It looked as nervous as its owner.

"Mr. Willoughby, sorry I'm late." He reached out with a trembling hand to shake. "It's Turrentine, actually, but just call me James. Can I call you Danny?"

"Of course. I'm sorry. I'm so embarrassed."

"Don't worry about it; it's not the first time anybody made that mistake. What can I get you?"

"Iced soy chai latte?" he ventured.

"Great. Pick us a table, and I'll find you."

The spot he snagged happened to be tiny, and right next to a long table filled with young thespians. Acting class must have just gotten out, as the entire group was engaged in theoretical approaches to representing the human condition. From the Russian stage to three-camera sitcom technique, from Stanislavsky to Roy London, from improvisation to the Method, they argued amongst themselves as if it really mattered how they played the third Terrorist from the right or the guy in the Fruit of the Loom grape costume. It just made me tired.

I handed Danny his chai latte, and settled into the uncomfortable wrought-iron chair that seemed to have daggers pointed at the center of my back.

"Thank you, Mr. Turrentine," said the polite young Danny.

"James, please. Thank you for meeting me, Danny. So far as I can tell, you're the last one to see my wife before she... before she, you know..."

His eyes were filling with tears, and the little Iggy he held so close was licking at his face, its long legs looped over his arm.

"She was a beautiful woman," he practically sobbed. I nodded in agreement, hating the use of the past tense.

"Was she alone that night?"

"Oh, no! She was with the little redhead, like I told the policeman. The other one who was, um, killed. Didn't they tell you that?"

As a matter of fact, they didn't. "Of course. Besides her," I said.

"No, just the two of them. It was a ladies' night out, they said."

"So they seemed happy?"

"Very happy! Like girlfriends out for a night on the town. Your wife even had the porterhouse!"

I'd never seen Chase eat a mammal, as long as I've known her. "I gave her a crème brulee, but don't tell the manager."

"So they were cheerful, then."

"Absolutely, that's the exact word. Very cheerful."

"Did they talk about where they were going?"

"Just that they were going out, a night on the town, I think, is exactly what they said."

"But they didn't mention a place?"

He really wanted to have an answer for me, but he didn't. His eyes were glassy with unspilled tears. He just shook his head.

"I feel just terrible about this, Mr.—James. I want so much to help. I just don't know anything else." He pulled a lace handkerchief out of his pocket, like something my grandmother might have given for Christmas, and blew his neatly shaved nose. "I haven't been able to go back to work since... since that night."

I watched him suffer, wondering how he could feel so deeply about someone he'd only served one night in a restaurant, amazed by the power of television and celebrity.

"And they just took off after dinner? No mention of any destination, a club or anything?

Nothing you might have overheard, even if they weren't talking to you?"

He was quiet for a moment, as if wondering whether he should divulge a secret between the girls.

"The only thing I heard Chase say was that she wanted to go someplace nobody knew her.

But I don't know if that helps." I nodded.

"Neither do I." We sat in silence, as the beautiful, hopeful young people at the table next to us with bright eyes, perfect skin, and high hopes chattered incessantly about their future stardom. I didn't want to be the one to tell them the truth; I'd ruined enough lives by now. Danny looked ready to leave, and I could see there was nothing more to learn here, about Chase's death or about life in general.

"And there's nothing at all you can think of that you might have overheard? It's not rude or disloyal, you know. It might be helpful."

He actually squirmed, but that could have been due to the wrought-iron seating as much as any inner turmoil.

"Anything at all..."

"I passed by them quickly when I left her a crème brulee. I thought I heard the redhead say something about the desert, though it might have been dessert."

The desert! The fucking desert! It reared its ugly, sandy head again.

When I got up, the metal legs of the chair made a horrendous squeal across the rough concrete floor, bringing the thespianic chatter at the next table to an abrupt, annoyed halt. "Thanks, Danny. I really appreciate it."

I gulped down the dregs of my mocha caramel latte, and left him with his alien little bug- eyed dog, which he let drink chai from his cup.

When I pulled up in my driveway at about ten o'clock, two vehicles were waiting for me: a navy blue Crown Victoria and an Arizona Highway Patrol cruiser. Sitting in the bentwood rockers on my porch, facing one another, were Detective Maldonado and Sherriff Hardy. I feared for the future of Maldonado's chosen seat, as it groaned under his massiveness. There must have been a sale on that suit, either that or it was the only one he had. But it was sharp, and helped define his indefinably squishy girth. It felt as if he could not exist without the suit, that if you opened it up, he would spill out into a giant puddle of Maldonado at your feet. In it, he had power, shape, function. Hardy, on the other hand, was invincibly defined, exercised and physical, despite the smoldering Lucky Strike in his mouth. His summer uniform shirt fit him tightly, exposing imposing biceps. And yet, given a choice between whom I'd rather go up against, I'd choose Hardy any day. I got the feeling that Maldonado, despite his beefiness and quiet manner, could be ruthless, even deadly.

They stood as I came up the walk from the driveway.

I waved away the smoke from Hardy's cigarette. "I'd appreciate it if you didn't smoke right in front of my house."

Hardy dropped the cigarette and ground it out with his foot... on my doorstep.

"That's what I told him," Maldonado said. "Those fucking things will kill you. Killed my dad, killed his dad, too. Just started growing fat around his heart, slowing it down; kept killing Pop for about eight years before he finally passed." He took a sip off his Jamba Juice smoothie, as Hardy put out his fire with something from Starbucks. Hardy threw a glare at the LA detective. Seemed like some sort of competition was going on here.

"Can this wait until morning?" I asked. "I'm really tired."

"That makes three of us," Maldonado offered. "Yeah, it can wait until morning, but I'd rather it didn't."

"I have to get back to Phoenix as soon as I can," said Hardy.

Maldonado smiled at me, but there was no joy in his grin. "We hear you've been playing cop."

I was in no mood to be put on the defensive. I could see

faces peering from peek-a-boo curtains across the street.

"Maybe we should take this inside," Hardy said.

"Excellent idea," Maldonado agreed. So I unlocked the door and let them in.

Maldonado took in the whole place as he entered, though Hardy's attention was just on myself.

"Cute place," Maldonado said with enthusiasm. "Not big, but cozy. Artsy. I was expecting one of those big, modern places with no personality, you know, one of those cavernous Bauhaus things they have all over the hills, all architecture, no humanity. This place feels lived-in, inhabited."

"I'm glad you approve," I said.

Maldonado frowned. "No need to be sarcastic. I was giving you a compliment."

"Sorry," I said, but I wasn't. "Thank you."

"It is a very nice place," Hardy said, not wanting to feel left out.

"Mind if we sit?" Maldonado asked, as he settled onto the blue velvet sofa like Jabba the Hut. "I'm carrying a bit of a load."

"Please." Hardy remained on his feet. "Sherriff?"

"I'll stand, thanks."

"Suit yourself."

"I'm not usually this big; I've been on cortisone treatments, and it's blown me up like a balloon. You wouldn't believe how little I eat."

I didn't know what to say to that: I'm sorry? So I took a seat in the Stickley opposite the officers of the law.

Maldonado nodded to Hardy, making it clear who was in the power seat here. "Why don't you start, Tom?"

I thought I saw Hardy's jaw tighten in resentment.

"Thanks." Hardy turned to me and away from the big guy. "Mr. Turrentine, did you know Antoinette McLoughlin?"

I turned to see Maldonado huff, and his body shuffled on the couch. "We've been over this with Mr. Turrentine, Tom. I had you copied on our report."

"Thanks, Paul, but I'd like to handle my investigation in my own way." Maldonado lifted his hand magisterially, turning away. "Sorry."

"Could you answer the question, Mr. Turrentine?"

"No," I told him. "I didn't know her. But I found out that she worked on Chase's last series, *Frankel's People*. I saw her in the cast-and-crew photo." Maldonado nodded, like he already knew this.

"But you don't know if they were friends?"

"No."

"Close friends?"

"I'm not sure what you mean." Oh, yes I was.

"Were they lovers?" Hardy's face was expressionless, all business, but Maldonado was smiling.

"No. Chase didn't go that way."

"To your knowledge."

"To my knowledge and beyond. We've been very open about our sexual pasts with one another, Sherriff. Chase had real problems with intimacy with anyone. She had a lot of... of... issues; it took a lot to get through to her, to get close to her. The likelihood that she had a female lover is just, well, it's just unimaginable to me." I'm such a liar. I can imagine it all too well.

My heart was pounding against my ribcage, trying to get out.

"Can you imagine any reason someone might have to kill your wife?"

"Honestly? No. Everybody liked my wife."

"Except you, we hear." Maldonado couldn't keep from contributing to the interrogation. I slowly turned to him.

"What are you saying?" I asked him.

"You told me yourself that you were going through a tough patch in your marriage, right?"

"Yes. But it doesn't mean I killed her."

"Nobody said you killed her."

"Then what are you here for?"

"An education," Maldonado said, sucking the last of his smoothie through the straw with an annoying sputter.

"So you think I killed her."

"Personally?" Maldonado looked wide-eyed and innocent. "No. Like I told you, you don't have it in you. Look, this is an obvious crime of passion, and passion is something I don't think you have much of. But beyond that... I've done this shit for a lot of years, and people are murdered in many ways by many types. I mean, I could be wrong, but you are not one of those types. My friend here from Arizona? He thinks maybe you had something to do with it, like maybe you hired someone to make the hit, but me, I think he's going through the moves, I don't think he really, *truly* believes that, do you Tom?"

Hardy looked like he wanted to kill Maldonado. And I didn't blame him.

"Because I know in my heart of hearts that you didn't. Could I be wrong? Yeah, it's happened before. But I've got a great sense of smell, even with the cortisone treatments, and I don't smell her death on you."

I couldn't tell if this was some kind of tactic, that he was making it seem like an insult to me that I was such a weenie that I was incapable of killing my wife. It was like he was saying *'fraid not!* so that I would say *'fraid so!*

Meanwhile, Hardy was blushing. His investigation had just been scuttled by an overbearing, overweight hot-shot LAPD detective, and now he had to try to justify his existence here. It was a huge tactical mistake for him to have attached his inquiry to Maldonado's. The LA detective just wanted to humiliate the backwater Arizona rube in front of his Hollywood friends.

Hardy was trying unsuccessfully to keep his cool. "You know what? I'm done here. Paul, it's your turn, okay? Thanks for your cooperation, Mr. Turrentine." And he left in the proverbial huff. Maldonado watched him go, then turned to me with a smile. No words, just a smile. In a moment, there was a timid knock on the door. I crossed the room to answer it, and a red-faced Hardy stood there. He looked past me to Maldonado.

"You're blocking my car," he said, and Maldonado took his sweet time rising from the couch and making his way out the door.

Vehicles moved and Hardy's cruiser rumbling away, Maldonado returned, his step more sprightly, and stood appraisingly in the middle of the living room.

"This really is a beautiful little place you've got here."

"Thanks. It's really Chase's taste. She did it all."

"Oh, it's obviously the woman's touch. Still, sweet."

He just looked at it, took it all in. I kept waiting for him to get to the point. "Is there anything else I can do for you, Detective?"

He turned to me, as if startled out of his reverie.

"Sorry? Oh, no, I just wanted to get a look around, get a sense of who this Wonder Woman was. I have yet to hear a negative word about her. I don't think I've ever met anyone who was so well-loved; shit, I didn't know they existed. Unless you have contradictory testimony you'd like to present?"

Was he goading me or teasing me?

"No," I told him. "Even when we didn't get along, it wasn't her fault." I knew that was true.

I knew that I wore the black hat. "She was a genuinely good human being."

"So I hear." He started to walk across the room, his back to me. "Mind if I just look around?"

Did it matter? "Help yourself," I said. And he did.

I followed him as he wandered down the hallway, peeking into the kitchen, and finally into Chase's bedroom. Ornate costumes hung from clothing trees that surrounded the old wooden wardrobe, and he lifted each one, checking them out, nodding approval. He looked at the pictures on the walls and on the dresser.

"No pictures of the two of you together," he noted. I stayed silent. "I'm guessing you have separate rooms? Sorry, 'had'." I nodded, and he just started humming a little song. He smelled her pillow, smiled, then left the bedroom, heading back down the hall. I felt like a puppy as I followed in his wake.

He stepped into Chase's studio and turned on the light.

"I'd heard she was an artist," he said, squinting at her works. "Hm. She was very talented, wasn't she?"

"Yes. She was."

"Big fan of Edvard Munch, wasn't she?"

"I guess so."

"Creepy stuff. Gets under your skin, doesn't it? Get the feeling she wasn't very happy." He turned and looked directly at me for that last bit. All I could do was shrug.

"Mind if I take a look at your bedroom?"

"Be my guest."

"You can say no if you want. I don't have a search warrant or anything."

"I've got nothing to hide."

"I know," he grinned. "I'm just fucking with you." He led me out of Chase's studio, and I led him up the stairs and into my room.

He entered, still nodding, as if this was just what he expected. "Yep, pretty Spartan. Not much of a woman's touch in here, is there?" I assumed the question was rhetorical. So after a cursory glance or two, he turned, forgetting he was a fat man, and tripped gingerly down the stairs and into the living room.

"Thanks, Jim," he said, as if he had gathered a ton of damning evidence. "I appreciate your cooperation. I think that's all I need for now. I'll call you. And you've got my card, right? Just in case you need to reach me directly?"

"I do."

"Good. Sweet dreams." And then he was gone.

I watched through the window as he pulled away, and the house settled into unbroken quietude, leaving me to wonder what the fuck that was all about.

I went right to my office, and awakened the iMac. I went directly to the new Facebook page, and there were already close to a hundred new messages since last I looked. I pored over them, and it was just more bullshit, fawning or raving or loving or hating, anonymous blather about a beautiful girl that the world thought they knew because they had shared her on their TVs. One misspelled message after another, deaf, dumb and blind, each trying to connect itself with the doused flame of celebrity. I was just about to shut it down and go to bed when one message heading jumped out and wrapped its fingers around my neck:

I saw her in the desert.

It was from somebody who called himself Jumbo Jax.

My hands started to shake as I opened his message, knowing it would take me back to heat and sand and mesquite and cactus and blood and death.

I saw her, the message said, *out in the desert. If you're telling the truth about the reward, contact me privately.*

I sent him a message that very moment, and sat waiting for a couple hours before I gave up and went to bed.

ELEVEN

I didn't even like Brandy Alexanders, to tell you the truth. I didn't much care for alcohol at all. But on this night, they tasted like a milkshake, and I felt warm inside and out. My Imitation Sinatra felt like the real thing, and he was so sweet and solicitous and engagingly shy that I felt surprisingly comfortable in his presence. Before long, I was at least as comfortable in his arms.

I'd caught a glimpse of Toni at the far side of the crowd; she hopped up and down to wave at me, throwing me the okay sign when she saw me dancing with Frank. But I'd forgotten about her by now. The band was done for the moment, replaced by a girl trio, and Frank, who had his own band and wrote his own songs, had shed Old Blue Eyes for the night. His real name was Riley, and they were listening to his new demo at Universal right now, and his hopes were high. He loved the

Sinatra gig because it gave him a swagger he didn't really possess. When he was Frank, he told me, he was all those things he couldn't be in his own body: confident, funny, sexy, popular. Beneath the costume, he was shy, a mind hopelessly trapped in a body, an artist. His first kiss was tentative, exploratory, and I felt that I needed to take the lead: me, the married woman, the tower of ice, the lady locked behind the gate. So I kissed him, held his head in my hands, stroked his cheek, tasted his breath.

This couldn't be a good idea.

But that didn't stop me, and neither did Riley. Or Frank.

When we ended up in his room, lying on his bed, clothes lying pathetically on the too-authentic red shag hotel carpeting, I came to my senses. There was no way I should be here. Yes, it felt good to be held, to be kissed, to be desired, but it opened wounds that had hidden behind the desert air and the alcohol.

The chilly breeze from the rattling window-box air conditioner woke me up, and—dressed in nothing but gooseflesh, pressed against his taut young body—I pulled away.

"What is it?" he asked.

"I am so fucked up," I said, pulling the sheet over me. To his credit, he didn't try to pull me back.

"No," he said. "You're beautiful."

His gaze was so appreciative that it was

almost loving, not lascivious, despite the flush of color across his cheeks.I held the sheet in front of me, and he didn't try to take it away. He didn't try to do anything. He had no idea who I was, and that made it harder. I could have been Kathy or Vanessa or Jayne or Linda, and it wouldn't have made any difference to him. But I was Chase. The name of a bank. That's all he knew.

"I don't feel beautiful," I told him.

"Well then, I know better than you do. So your opinion is thrown out of court."

"I shouldn't be here."

"Yes, you should."

I stood in the middle of the tawdry little room, the mirrored sliding closet doors reflecting me into repetitious oblivion in the mirror above the dresser. There were no lights; there was no camera; there would be no action.

"It's not right."

"It felt pretty right a couple minutes ago."

I looked at him and nodded.It did. So what was I beating myself up over? My marriage? Was it being unfaithful if your marriage was a prison? All of the passion and lust that had been fueled by the drinks and the shy, pretty, talented young singer who only came to life in the costume of another came crashing down on me in a sudden revelation: I did not exist. I was a character in a play, whose happiness was shoved back into a dark and hidden chamber between performances. Life and happiness and family and fulfillment were only truly available to me when I played a part. Those real-life moments in between imploded into a denial of existence, a hollowness that tried to scream itself to life on mediocre canvases in my studio.So here I was again, live onstage at the Riviera, Chase Willoughby, with thrilling co-star Frank Sinatra, in *Palm Springs Romance*!

I felt the curtain come crashing down, and my desire leaked out, puddling beneath me at my feet. I had eaten another soul and spit it out.

Tears formed in my eyes and Frank—*Riley*—walked over to me, still naked, shameless, and wrapped his arms around me.

"You don't have to stay here if you don't want to," he whispered in my ear. "I want you here—I *really* want you here— but I'm not going to make you stay."

The tears came harder. I knew I wouldn't be crying if it weren't for the drinks; hell, I wouldn't be in this fucking boho hotel room if it hadn't been for the drinks. But here I was, and here I was crying in the arms of a stranger. He kissed me softly on the cheek.

I sniffed and wiped the back of my arm across my flooded eyes, knowing I had to look like some kind of raccoon by now. I gently peeled myself out of his arms and started climbing back into my clothes.

"I'm sorry," I told him over and over.

"I'm so sorry."

"Me, too," Riley said, sitting on the corner of his bed and

watching me dress. He looked it.

After I stepped back into my dress and my shoes, he asked if I needed him to zip me up… but I was done. There was no zipper.

My back was bare.

I didn't want to have to say that if this were a different time and a different place, things might have been different, that he seemed sweet and funny and desirable to me. But then I'd have to tell him all the other stuff, that my life was a train wreck, that I was incapable of love and marriage, that I snuffed out all life around me. I don't think he'd have liked that at all. And neither would I.

So I just kept apologizing and thanking him for being so understanding. And then, leaving him sitting naked on his hotel bed, I left.

The party was still in swing when I came back out into the night. I had forgotten about the heat until I stepped back into it and it robbed me of my breath. The music was sprightly and the crowd loopy and inebriated; the scent of lust and date palms baked and simmered. My little clutch purse in hand, I roamed the dancefloor, seeking but not finding Toni. Men grabbed at me, tried to pull me into their mating dance, but I was on a mission, and this missionary was not interested in social intercourse. I had to find my ride and get home before curfew.

But Toni, the chipper little leprechaun life of the party, was nowhere to be found. Perhaps she had found solace and romance in one of those very rooms into which I had been granted a peek. Perhaps she was making the beast with two backs under the mirrors to the hushed, panting musings of "Fever", soaking the percales with sweat and perfume. I wondered if she were bedded down with man or woman. Or maybe she had just not been able to find me, and left the Riviera to find her sad-sack friend.

I didn't want to interrupt her pleasure, but needed to make sure that my ride was still around. I needed to call her. I reached into my purse for my phone, but it was gone. Shit! I never forget my phone! But this night, somehow my lifeline had gone missing. I didn't even have Toni's number, but certainly I could look it up. If I had a phone with me, that is. And I didn't. I just kept looking for her, but the options were running out. Finally, having covered every searchable inch of the Riviera's public nightlife, I took a cab back to Palm Canyon Drive, hoping that her bright red hair would call out to me.

The street was filled with summer foot traffic, the night still sultry and inviting. I walked through the walking dead, not knowing where the hell to look next. If nothing else,

I could go to the parking lot and just wait at her car. Surely before long she would find me missing and know where we should meet. Perhaps she was looking for me even now.

So I went to the garage in the high hopes of finding tiny Toni waiting there for me, but I could not have been more wrong. Her little Mini was gone.

Now what?

I stood in the empty parking slot in the sweltering, three- story concrete structure, wondering what I should do. Surely Toni was driving around searching for me, right? There weren't that many places to hide here in the Springs; there was Palm Canyon Drive and… what else? If I kept walking the main drag, surely she would spot me and we'd compare notes and laugh and make fun of ourselves and tootle back to Los Angeles and greet the sunrise over smoothies at The Jumpcut Cafe.

But what if her car was stolen?What if something happened to her?

And why would she have taken her car away in the first place?

I went back around the corner and onto Palm Canyon.The wind kicked up a bit harder, and some dry, brittle fronds from the high palms lining the street crashed at my feet, making me jump. Dates pelted me. A pink Corvette convertible screeched around the corner, one of its hubcaps choosing that moment to break free, bouncing noisily up onto the sidewalk and across my feet, rattling as it tumbled to a stop against a big green trashcan.

No one else seemed to notice, but my nerves were on edge. The night and its attendant demons were turning on me. Beelzebub stood with pitchfork in hand, waiting for me around every corner.

Okay, I'm dramatic. I'm an actress, right?

I was feeling suddenly alone, alone in ways that I was used to at home, but not on this night. This was a night meant to put a Band-Aid over all that loneliness, to remind me how to smile.

Instead, I was starting to get scared.

I stumbled past Las Casuelas, where the night had begun. The aging, pot-bellied, balding classic rockers were putting heart and soul into some horrible, strangled Doobie Brothers song, and a red-faced woman, pinched into toreador pants that were a couple sizes too small for her, lurched up her night's ration of margaritas all over her bloodshot, Hawaiian-shirted date. Their dream dance had come to an end.

Somehow the bright, colorful lights of the night seemed to be getting brighter, an iris opening as if to another dimension.

Whites got whiter, hotter, searing, and I could see deeper into the shadows. I knew what this signaled, and I fought against the onslaught of the pain I knew I would have to endure.If the migraines found me here, I would be at their mercy. I tried to build a wall around my brain.

I watched the slow-motion cluster-fuck of vehicles make their way down the one-way avenue, no place to go, really, but needing to be out in the night air, anyway. No sign of the Mini, of Toni, of my rescuer. I stumbled past the Follies Theater, where geriatric singers and dancers who once had careers that only people older than them remember pulled on their tights and silk tuxedos and performed boogie-woogie hits from the good old days that weren't really all that good. The first show was letting out, and the sidewalk was blocked with wheelchairs, walkers, and oxygen tanks. I felt like Kevin McCarthy, dying to shout out to them, "They're here! They're already here!" But I kept my silence and squeezed passed the wheezing minions.

Dust devils whirled around me and threw sand in my eyes. I stumbled past the library and crossed the street, colliding into two pudgy gay men with matching diamond ear studs, spilling their massive Bloody Marys from Pinocchio's all over us. Funny how *they* kept apologizing to *me* and offering to buy me a drink. I was happy to let them accept responsibility, but I declined the libation. I stood on the corner as the creatures of the night swarmed around me in clusters. My chest drenched with the sticky red beverage, I looked as if a knife had been plunged deep into my heart and I was covered in my own blood.

Calm down, I urged myself. *It's no big*

deal. Toni will pull up any second now and you'll climb in her car and she'll tell you about the amazing guy or girl she hooked up with and how she just left him to get back to you and take you home.

Suddenly, the wind died like a lurching beast that had been shot through the head. I just closed my eyes and breathed, and I felt my heartbeat slow down. I wasn't used to feeling like a damsel in distress. When I started to calm, I opened my eyes, and the world around me seemed to slow down. I sat at a bench in front of the Coffee Bean and wiped the sweat from my brow with the back of my hand. It dried instantly in the dry heat.

The headache was tearing down the wall of Jericho, and I felt it grow like a burning tumor behind my eyes. I pressed my palms against my eyes and felt an inch of relief, but I knew it signaled a pain that would grow and not abate anytime soon.

Fear of the migraine was almost as bad as the migraine itself.

Lub dub, my heart told me. *Lub. Dub.*

Slowing, calming, not pounding my brain so hard. Deep breaths, no fear, this too shall pass. And it actually started to. However, my relief proved to be only momentary.

I let my hands drop from my eyes, easing them open and letting in the lights of the boulevard. It no longer stung; I could see normally, without the painful intensity that the headaches brought with them. Not all of the faces that revealed themselves were staring at me, which was a relief. The children of the desert night were oblivious, maybe even disdainful to me, the crazy disheveled woman with the sticky red goo making her green silk Versace stick to her skin. Fine. I was ready for their backs.

And then:

I saw him seeing me. Jaxon-with-an-X, his unblinking glare fixed on me, stood under the streetlight across the road, casting a long shadow, a slash of light across his face illuminating cerulean eyes that tried to stab me. I gasped as he held me snared in his gaze, frozen, immobilized. When he started to cross the street, ignoring the red light and dancing through the sludgy cross traffic, I bolted like a gazelle stalked by the king of the jungle. He picked up his pace and I ran like hell, pushing pedestrians out of my way as I tumbled through them. He never got faster than a quick walk; I never slowed from a full-on run.

I was not dressed for a chase scene; I ran wobbling on my Ferragamos, and knew it was only a matter of time before a broken heel betrayed me. But I ran for all I was worth, down Tahquitz Canyon Way, foolishly away from the safety of the surrounding—if intoxicated—crowd. I threw a look over my shoulder, and Jaxon was the tortoise, slow and steady, taking his time, knowing how easily he could vanquish a mere woman. I ran like a man, and twisted around onto Indian Canyon drive, seeking a place to hide. The frozen yogurt place disgorged a party of local teenagers just as I passed the open doorway, acting as a blind for me. I lost sight of him then, knowing better than to look back but doing it anyway. I crossed East Andreas, getting further still from the populated center of town, drenched in sweat and the rasp of a parched, dry windpipe. It was the next sudden turn onto East Amado that led to the first broken heel, twisting my ankle with a sudden agonizing tear. I lost my footing and tumbled headfirst against the concrete wall with enough power to make my brain flash. I sat on the sidewalk, hugging the shadows, the arid desert scorching my lungs. My ankle was tender; I tried to stand on it, but it gave out on me, and I fell back to the cement. I tried to control my breathing, will my heart to slow down, but my body had been overtaxed, overpowered by survival mode.

A car passed, headlights wrapping around me and letting me go, returning me to shadow. Only blocks from the bleating, beating heart of the city, Palm Springs revealed itself as the small town it really was. The streets here were nearly deserted. The Mexican restaurant at the corner was already closed. The corner streetlight flickered twice, and then lapsed into darkness. A garden of sparkling quartz gravel lost its glint as it was plunged into night.

I dared to look down Indian Canyon, which was bereft of life, and allowed myself the luxury of breathing. I had escaped. I rested my back against the wall, feeling tears welling in my eyes. I fought them back, refusing to let them spill.

It only took a few short blocks to leave the commercial section of the Springs, and this part of town was alarmingly bleak and silent after the curtain of night had fallen. The appliance repair shop next to the Mexican restaurant had a *For Lease* sign in the window. The mom and pop video store across the street had long been shuttered. Sitting on the still-hot sidewalk, I took off my shoes and shoved them—or what was left of them—into my purse. Long, low sweat stains painted my dress below my arms, and the spilled Bloody Mary was going stiff as it dried and hardened. Using the wall, I eased myself up into a one-legged stand, testing my swollen ankle. It could almost take my weight, I thought.

Then I heard the only sound since the passing car: a gentle, distant *clip, clip, clip* of shoes: *men's* shoes. I held my breath and dared another peek. Sound carries in the desert, particularly at night, so at first I wasn't sure where it came from. I squinted, as if that would give me the X-ray vision I would need to see into the darkness. As it turned out, it was more than a block away: a man's figure, hands in pockets, its endless shadow shrinking as it drew further from the streetlight behind it was taking its time as it approached. It was Jaxon, and he was coming my way.

I looked in every direction, seeking someplace to hide. Down at the next corner, surrounded by businesses that had given up the ghost long ago and lay fallow and reverently dark, light leaked out of an open door. The simple blue neon letters above the entrance were a beacon: *The Clamshell.* I hobbled across the street and down the block, entering the place just as Jaxon rounded the corner. There was no way he didn't see me. I pulled the door shut behind me.

The Clamshell was a tavern, dark to the point of gloomy.K.D. Laing sang a country ballad on the jukebox, and the place was nearly empty. A handful of couples huddled in the corners of the place, and this place was all corners. It was festooned with blowfish and rope nets, cowboy saddles and interstate license plates perforated with bullet holes. The tiny dancefloor had but one brave pair swooning in time to the music, mouths pressed against each other's necks.

The man behind the bar was polishing glasses, dressed in a crisp, white, short-sleeved shirt rolled up to the shoulders, hair slicked back, a gold stud in his right ear, a broken heart tattooed on his swollen bicep, with the word *Jody* broken between its syllables in the rip. I took a seat at the dark end of the bar, the only one occupying a stool, the only one not folded into a clandestine embrace in the nether regions of the tavern.

It was only when the bartender stepped into the red glow of the neon Budweiser sign that I saw that, despite the rough stubble at the base of the chin, he was a she.

"What can I get you, pretty lady?" she asked, her voice surprisingly high and feminine from so masculine a countenance.

"Just a Pellegrino or something," I answered, still out of breath. Another look made me realize that all of the patrons of The Clamshell were women. This night seemed somehow dedicated to Sappho.

"Club soda okay?"

"Fine, thanks."

"Want some extra for the dress?"I looked down to see what a mess I had become. I tried to smile, but it twisted itself into tears instead. Her rough but friendly grin dropped away and grew concerned.

"Somebody's following me…"

At that moment, the door opened, and Jaxon's six-foot silhouette stood tall against the black night. He looked into the place, saw what it was more quickly than I had, and smiled at me.

"You're it," he said.

"Get the fuck outta here," the bartender snarled, her voice dropping a full two octaves.

"Do you know who she is?" Jaxon asked the room, as heads in the shadowy corners turned to me, tiny eyes sparkling from the shaded recesses of the bar.

"I know who she *isn't*, and that's a friend of *yours*. I said get the fuck out." She could have taken him in a dogfight any day.

"Fine." Jaxon flipped her his middle finger, then walked away, letting the door slowly ease shut in his wake.

K.D. wrapped up her sweet, heartbroken song as if on cue, and the little bar went silent.All eyes were on me, but no one spoke. The bartender looked at me, studying me in intimidating silence. I sat awkwardly, pinned under her stare for what seemed like minutes as she searched behind my eyes for something.

"Can I use your phone?" I asked her, and she cocked her head as she stared back at me, studying me as if I were her final exam.

"Who you need to call?"

"A friend."

"Friends are good," she said.

Suddenly, she turned and made her way to the far end of the bar, filled a glass with ice and bubbling water behind her back, squeezed a lime into it, and set it in front of me as a tall, thin blonde with shoulder length hair and a too-prominent nose, wearing faded Lee jeans with deep cuffs and a Dinah Shore Golf Classic T-shirt, crossed the room and dropped a quarter into the vintage Wurlitzer jukebox. Julie London sang "Cry Me a River" and the bartender pulled up a stool across from me, just watching me as I took a sip.

"You okay?" she asked.

"I will be, thanks," I answered.

She picked up an old Princess phone and slammed it onto the bar, just out of my reach, almost as if daring me to use it.

"Frank," she volunteered, extending her hand for me to shake.

I reached out hesitantly, and she wrapped her hand tightly around mine. Her palm was calloused, rough, a worker's hand, and her grip was almost painful. I felt weak, soft, vulnerable. She knew it, too, and it made her smile.

"Thank you, Frank," I answered, hoping she didn't notice that I didn't introduce myself in kind.

"It's okay, pretty lady. I know who you are." Not that that gave me comfort. She wouldn't take her eyes off of me, and I squirmed in her appraisal and took another sip. It was bitter, and I guess I made a face.

"What's the matter?" she asked.

"Bitter," I said.

"Must be the lime."

I was getting confused, and the room started to sway, and not just from Julie London. I reached for the phone, but missed.

"You sure this isn't quinine water?" That's what I meant to ask, but it came out thick and mushy. I started to feel like I felt when I was a little girl, alone in bed, about to fall into a dream when the bed starts spinning, and voices started to laugh at me from every direction. My ears started to ring and I could see every minute, sun-damaged crinkle around Frank's eyes.

When she smiled, she revealed teeth that were tobacco-stained and filled with cracks and crazes.

Then my face met the floor.

TWELVE

I woke at about six, as the sun reached into my bedroom window and wrapped its invasive tentacles around me. I'd forgotten to shut the blackout curtains. As I rolled over, my stomach howled in protest; I had also forgotten to eat anything for dinner. My eyes felt gritty and swollen, bloodshot from hours at the computer. I threw off the sheet, which was soaked with my perspiration, and climbed into a pair of boxers and a T-shirt. I didn't much care for this dawn shit, but now that I was awake, there wasn't much I could do about it.

I trudged down the hall to my office and, grabbing a Power Bar from my desk drawer, woke the sleeping iMac and went directly to the Facebook page. I scrolled through a couple of pages of fan art, Photoshopped images of Chase's face on angels' bodies, messages of love and loss, hearts and flowers, and noted how most of the haters seemed to have gotten Chase out of their systems by now, and had moved on to other celebrities more deserving of their scorn.

Just when I was about to give up on my new hopeful contact, ready to consign him to the heap of phonies and assholes, Jumbo Jax had posted again, ironically only minutes after I had gone to bed.

Call me at 10 a.m., the message said. Other than the telephone number, which was in the 760 area code, that was it.

Great. I had four hours to waste.

The first thing I did was try to reverse-information the phone number, but it came up blank. I couldn't find an address on any of the search sites. Not that it would have made a bit of difference.

I went into the shower and scrubbed myself clean. I shaved. I pulled on a pair of jeans and a *Slaughtered* T-shirt before I realized the horrible symbolism of it. When I saw myself in the full-length mirror on the back of my bedroom door, I flushed with guilt and exchanged it for a plain black American Apparel T-shirt without a logo.

Okay, that was good for half an hour. I still had three and a half hours to wait before I could call Jumbo Jax and find out if he was for real.

I went down to the Boulevard and pulled in to Bobby's for an old school breakfast, heavy on fat and carbs and nitrites. The omelet was enormous, the bacon dripping with grease, and the breakfast potatoes sprinkled with melted orange cheese. It came with a steaming bagel that leaked butter all over the bread plate, looking like a last meal on Death Row. My belly squealed as the first bites struck home, but quieted as I continued to feast. I read the paper on my iPad, trying to take my time, but not able comprehend a word. I flipped through the Calendar section to the weekend box-office report, angry to see that the top grossing films were all sequels and remakes. I wanted to be able to gloat that the ticket-buying public had gotten fed up with all that shit, but they hadn't. America was lapping it up and asking for more.

I was in the wrong business; I just wouldn't listen.

I looked up at the wall clock as the second-hand ground around its face in slow motion. It was almost eight o'clock: two more hours before I could call my new best friend. The butter and grease and unborn chickens and box-office mojo suddenly broke out in a fistfight in my stomach, and I ran into the men's room, dropping my drawers just in time to expel them in a sick, flatulent, watery stream. That was good for another ten minutes.

Physically and psychically evacuated, my body felt wrung out, empty, spindly and useless. In a sudden lurch, I vomited all that had not yet been digested into the sink in big yellow and brown chunks. Someone started knocking on the locked restroom door, and I washed the sweat off my face, and the puke off my chin. I flushed a couple of times, and ran the sink as much as I could, but the stench was foul and omnipresent. I ran my wet fingers through my hair, unlocked the door, and rushed past the business-suited, grey-haired geezer at the door, but not before I heard him exclaim, "Jesus!" and rush back into the restaurant. A rank cloud followed me back to my table, where I paid the bill with cash and left a healthy tip to make up for the stink I left in my wake.

Quivering, I climbed into the Beemer and made my way back up the hill to the house, running through the sprinklers, which had come on in my absence. I went back into my office and pored through the Facebook messages that had accrued since I'd left, but there was nothing new there worth my time. Tick. Tick. Tick. The digital clock on the iMac taunted me. I turned on the television and flipped through the channels of daytime broadcast TV, and it made me want to shoot myself. Every other channel had a courtroom show on, with white trailer trash and angry black folks screaming at one another in furious, self-righteous indignation, threatening and squawking with belligerent hands on massive hips: slender, shaven-headed dudes who stole cars and money from their triple-sized ex-girlfriends; an ex-con sleeping with the sister of his live-in girlfriend, knocking her up, and denying all responsibility; an eighteen-year-old surfer boy claiming he'd awakened at a sleepover at his best friend's house, only to find the friend's naked, obese mother riding him like a pony; he was asking for five thousand dollars for emotional distress. My, how time doesn't fly when you're not having fun.

Somehow the eternity of two hours passed, and I picked up the hard-line phone and placed my call. The guy picked up on the second ring.

"Hi," I said. "This is James Turrentine. Chase Willoughby's husband."

"I figured," the voice on the other end of the line said.

"You said you saw my wife the night before she was killed?"

"That's right. And you said you've got a hundred-thousand-dollar reward?"

"I did."

"How do I go about getting this hundred-thousand-dollar reward?"

"By giving me any information that will lead to the capture of her murderer." There was a long silence on his end, and I heard traffic around him. The connection was too clear to be mobile; I was guessing that this was a pay phone. I looked again to see if the fourth digit was a nine, and it was. That's a pretty good clue.

"So it's not something you'd pay for in cash today."

"I'm not an idiot. Do you have information for me?" Another silence, and then: "What will you pay today?"

"It depends on what you have to tell me."

"I don't want to talk over the phone."

"I'll come to you if you want," I offered.

"Well I'm sure as shit not coming to you." He huffed a mirthless laugh, and I could hear his mind ticking. "How quick can you get to Palm Springs?" he asked me.

Palm Springs. The desert. The cocksucking, motherfucking desert. "Two, two and a half hours."

"Meet me at the Starbucks at Palm Canyon Drive and Tahquitz Way at noon."

"Will you be the guy in the white carnation?"

"I'll recognize you."

Then he hung up. I ran out the door and into the BMW, squealing out of the driveway, away from Woodland Hills and back to the goddamned desert.

I hated the monotony of the road, the listless, sunburned, featureless sprawl of the grey California desert in particular. The sky wasn't even blue, just a bleached, sweltering white. No color, no flavor, no life. I couldn't bear to even listen to the radio, so it was a quiet, almost insufferably dull drive: two hours of heat and blacktop and a stomach that wouldn't settle. Jesus, how I hated the desert, and hoped never to have to go there again. The desert is where you go to die.

I passed the faded concrete dinosaurs, which had been almost completely obscured by fast food restaurants, and knew I was close; once I was on Route 111, all that was left was a sour stomach and anticipation. In all probability, this guy was just an opportunistic asshole. But there was a chance that he could provide information, that I could cut the line between Chase's death and the law enforcement agencies who had no personal commitment to her story. Perhaps Jumbo Jax could help me justify my place on the planet, unlikely as it seemed.

It was about five minutes past noon when I found a parking place right on the street, cater- corner from the Starbucks at Palm Canyon Drive and Tahquitz Way. Finding an energy I thought had left me forever, I bounded from the car and ran through traffic to the opposite corner, where a dozen or so patrons sat comfortably in chairs in front of the coffeehouse. An old woman hiding behind a new facelift and enormous Donna Karan sunglasses sipped her vanilla macchiato as her enormously overweight black Chihuahua snored at her feet. A May-December gay couple tried to keep their voices down as they fought about their financial arrangement, the younger one telling him to take his goddamn car back as he held ice to a swollen eye and bleeding nose. A massively obese black man with one leg sat in a wheelchair with a "Pleeze Help God Blees You" sign planted in a coffee can in his lap. A couple of bearded, liver-spotted old men played chess in total silence, and a table full of MILFs and their attendant spoiled, squalling, begging offspring drew dirty looks. None of them seemed like they might bear the moniker of Jumbo Jax.

I stepped inside and prickled into gooseflesh in the blast of conditioned air. I stepped right up to the counter and ordered a giant iced tea. As I waited for my drink, movement from the corner caught my eye. A guy in sunglasses, a long-sleeved black shirt, black jeans, and worn, buckled, calf-high black boots, maybe twenty-two, twenty-three years old, flicked his hand to draw my attention. If I'd been casting Jumbo Jax for an episode of *Slaughtered*, I'd have passed on this guy for being too on-the-nose. I grabbed my tea and joined him at the tiny corner table. As I started to sit, he spoke, arresting my movement into the chair:

"I'll have a Venti Java Chip Frappuccino. And a blueberry muffin." I nodded, went back to the counter and ordered, then returned and took a seat opposite him.

"Jumbo Jax?" I asked, not really needing an answer, but wondering what the fuck I should call him.

"Jaxon." Nobody extended a hand for shaking, which was fine by me. I didn't really want to touch this guy.

"James," I said. "I know."

His glasses were tinted so dark that I couldn't see his eyes. I wished he couldn't see mine. "So," I began, waiting for him to pick up the conversation. When he proved unwilling, I continued. "You saw my wife on the night she died?"

The barista called out "James!" and rather than answer, Jaxon nodded to her. I went to the counter, collected his breakfast, and returned to the table, laying it out for him.

He took a long suck, draining a good third of his drink.

"You saw my wife on the night she died," I repeated.

"Several times," he answered, trying to be all tough and mysterious. He was no tougher than the whipped cream that topped his Frappuccino.

"Here in Palm Springs?"

"Did you bring your wallet?"

"Do you want to do this here?" I asked him. "Why not?"

I could think of reasons, but if this cocky little asshole couldn't, that was fine with me. He took a big bite of muffin, and crumbs stuck to his three days of beard as he chewed. I pointed to the corners of my mouth, and he wiped his with the back of his arm, smearing blueberry residue up the length of his sleeve.

I blocked the view from the other customers with my back, reached into my pocket, and laid out a pile of cash on the table in front of him.

"How much is that?" he asked. "A thousand bucks," I answered.

"Where's the other ninety-nine thousand?"

God, this desert hipster was an idiot. It was obvious that he thought he was pretty hot shit, but if he were in LA, he'd never get a callback.

"The reward thing works like this," I told him. "You give me information that leads to the arrest and conviction of

Chase's killer, and then you collect, upon his conviction."

"That could be years!"

"It could."

"Fuck that." He stood up and reached for the money. I grabbed his hand.

"Uh uh," I said. "That's a down payment. But you haven't told me shit." I took the money and started to stuff it back in my pocket.

"Wait a minute!"

I sat back down, and he did the same.

He looked at me, looked at my bulging pocket. "A thousand bucks?" he asked. "That's it?"

"To start with," I replied. "But I'll pay more if the information is worth it."

"It's worth it."

"Prove it." I put the money back on the table, my hand laid atop the pile of bills. "Did you see Chase here in Palm Springs that night?" It certainly jibed with what Danny, the waiter at Kate Mantilini, had told me: girls' night out in the desert.

"Yes."

I lifted my hand, and he grabbed the money, jamming it into his own pocket. "Where?" I asked.

"Couple a' places," he answered. "Like, for instance?"

"Like, for how much?"

"You don't know much about civic duty, do you?"

"No. I'm not so good with abstract concepts."

Wiseass. I took a moment to think, to consider. I had taken a plunge, had chosen to believe that he was telling the truth. It was time to throw in all the marbles.

"Is there a Citibank in town?"

"Yeah. Down the street on East Palm Canyon."

"Great. Come with me, and I'll give you another four

thousand dollars to tell me everything you know about Chase's final night. That's five thousand total," I added, just in case he couldn't wasn't good at math.

"That's not as much as I was hoping."

"It's five percent of a hundred thousand. And it's up front. No waiting." The machinery in his brain worked slowly. "Or I could just go to the cops. I know they'd be happy to talk to you, and they wouldn't pay you a fucking cent."

"You got a car?" he asked.

"No, we'll take my wings." He looked confused. "I'm in the Beemer right across the street."

"Cool. By the way, I really dig *Slaughtered*. It's really sick."

Great. My audience. My fan base. I'll have a grande double-shot Rat Poison, please.

We ditched Starbucks, went to the bank, and I took out the cash, which he was all grabby for. "Information first, right?"

He stared at the money, lusting for it. It gave me a sense of power; I was usually the one with my hand out.

"I'm hungry," he non-sequitured. "How about you?"

I didn't think I'd ever be hungry again, but I was eager to get out of the baking Palm Springs sun. "Where do you want to eat?"

"You been to Rick's?"

Rick's was just a diner, nothing more, nothing less, a place that only served breakfast and lunch. All of the gay male clientele was seated in front; the hetero crowd and any party with a female had all been shunted to the rear of the place. I didn't know what to think when the host put us right in the front window.

I just had an Arnold Palmer, but Jaxon ordered a steak.

"Where did you see my wife?" I asked him again. He thrummed his fingers on the table. I didn't want to fuck with this shit any more, so I pulled out the cash and laid it on the table in front of him. A greedy grin washed over his face as he took the money and tucked it away.

"A couple of places."

"And those places were…" I led him.

"A club called Alternate Route, first. I recognized her there. I told her I used to watch *The Crazy Frazees* when I was a kid, and that seemed to piss her off."

I doubted that Chase was pissed off because he liked her show when he was a boy. Surely there was something this dunderhead wasn't saying.

"Was she alone?"

"No," he answered. "She was with this hot little redhead."

Antoinette McLoughlin. It was all tying together, I just didn't know how. But this guy, this Jaxon in Black, was telling the truth. I didn't waste my five thousand dollars, even though I couldn't afford it.

"She left pretty quick after that. Like she was on the rag or something."

I can't say I blamed her. This guy needed to work on his first impressions, and all the ones that followed.

"Did you follow her?"

"I wouldn't call it 'following' her, not really."

"But you watched where she went and then you went there, too."

"Exactly. She made me curious. I was a big fan when I was a kid. And, you know, your wife was really hot." He smiled at me, and I wanted to shove that steak knife in his throat.

I quelled my repulsion and kept my outward calm. "Where did she go next?" I queried.

"To the Riviera Hotel. She seemed to get pretty cozy

with the singer in the band, the Sinatra guy."

"How do you mean, 'cozy'?"

"You know, slow-dancing-with-him cozy."

"Kissing cozy?"

"Yeah, kissing cozy. I think he took her to his room."

This didn't sound like Chase to me, and I could feel my face going warm and red. I hadn't really known Chase in a long time, I guess. I tried to just ask the questions, not feel the scorn, the disregard for our marriage, as pointless and hollow as it had become.

Fighting down my gorge, I asked him, "What happened next?"

"That was the last I saw of her there. I assumed she and the Sinatra dude hooked up, and I just booked. There was no reason to hang around any longer. I thought she kinda liked me, that maybe I had a shot, but once the singer got her, well, that's like game over, isn't it? Chicks love singers."

I could feel my throat constrict. I did my best to keep my voice level, unengaged. "And that was the last you saw of her?"

"That was the last I saw of her at the Riviera." He obviously had more to say, so I waited for it. I wasn't going to do him the pleasure of asking him to continue. He couldn't keep his mouth shut, anyway.

"I went back up to Palm Canyon to see if anything was happening. I sure didn't expect to see her there, and so quick. I guess the thing with the singer didn't work out, after all." He was smiling as he related this to me, the dead woman's cuckolded husband.

"Where did you see her?"

"On the street. Walking. Maybe she was looking for her friend, because she was by herself."

"Where did she go?"

"It didn't seem like she was going anyplace in particular,

she was just walking around town." A shadow flashed across his face at this point, like he was glossing over something incriminating.

"Just walking around town," I repeated. "Pretty much."

"And that was it?"

"Not exactly," he said. "There's a punchline."

"Okay," I told him. "Make me laugh."

"She ended up in a carpet-munchers bar." The smug look on the little bastard's face made me want to cut it off and feed it to a cat. "The Clamshell."

"And that's the last place you saw her?"

"Yes. And as I'm not especially welcome in a dyke-bar kind of establishment, I made a hasty exit. I went back to the Riviera and got lucky with this German tourist chick with a shaved head and lots of tattoos and piercings. Kind of hot, but the metal made a lot of noise."

He took the money back out of his pocket and counted it as I watched him, seething. "The last place you saw Chase was at a lesbian bar called The Clamshell."

"That's right."

"Take me there," I said. He was a bit taken aback.

"I doubt they're going to be open in the middle of the day."

"I don't care. Take me there. You got something else to do?"

He sopped up the last drippings of the steak with a wad of bread, gulped it down with a couple glugs of his Coke, and belched proudly before following me out to the car.

Jaxon directed me to the Clamshell, which was only a few blocks away. The street seemed sandblasted in the harsh mid-day sunlight, surrounded by empty storefronts and sandy, vacant lots. Jaxon seemed a little nervous when I pulled up in front of the place, caffeine jitters animating him like a stop-motion puppet. It was a big change from the mellow, couldn't-give-a- shit hipster I'd been talking to for the last hour or so. I set the parking brake and he ran his fingers through his purposeful dishevelment.

"Well, if you don't need me anymore..."

I didn't. Frankly, I was glad to be rid of the little prick. He smelled like cigarettes, and the leather upholstery was absorbing his reek. I guess he expected me to stop him, because he paused and looked at me when he opened the passenger door, but as far as I was concerned, he was already gone. He slammed the door and left me alone. In my natural state.

I looked at The Clamshell, wondering what pearly secrets it held for me. Unsteady in nervous anticipation, I got out of the car, locked it up, crossed the sidewalk, and grabbed the handle of The Clamshell's door. I pushed, but it didn't give. But when I pulled, it opened wide.

The place was dark and empty, tomb-like. The wedge of sunlight that stretched from the doorway in front of me was like an invasion, curdling the cool, wicked darkness with disinfecting brightness. I entered and let the door fall shut behind me, and my eyes had to adjust to the resumption of dim.

"Hello," I called out, wincing as the word left my mouth. Too loud: this room was meant for whispers. There was no reply, and I stepped deeper within The Clamshell, which was lit only with neon signs advertising beer, mostly for brands I'd never heard of. Since I'd quit drinking four years ago, I don't pay much attention to the brews of the moment, micro or macro. I walked to the bar, and noticed a cigarette burning in a Molson's ashtray, smoke coiling like a charmed cobra all the way to the ceiling. Just smoke, no smoker. I took a seat at the bar and tapped on the old, dented mahogany with my knuckle. "Hello?" Still nothing. It was as if all life had been zapped away by overflying alien life forms.

Suddenly, a door opened on the opposite side of the room behind me, and with the click of the light switch, the tavern was flooded with harsh, nasty fluorescent light. It was immediately apparent that I didn't want to see a nighttime place in the middle of the day: the corners were crusted with grime and beer residue and God-knows-what-else. I whirled on my barstool and locked eyes with the most masculine woman I've seen this side of the Olympics, wheeling a dolly loaded down with cases of beer. She looked leathery, not old but crumpled by constant desert sun. She dropped her load with a grunt and was about to pick up the three cases from the top of the stack when she locked eyes with me. The cases fell with a crash, throwing shards of brown glass and plumes of imported beer across the floor in foamy waves.

"Sorry," I apologized.

"What the fuck are you doing here?"

I didn't yet have an answer to that; I was still stunned by the blast of light and the bulging, sinewy, over-testosteroned arms on this creature. But in a moment, I saw a response to me in her eyes with which I was becoming increasingly familiar: recognition. Nothing like the celebrity of being married to somebody who was a little bit famous and had been messily killed. Oh, to be obliviously unknown again.

"First of all," she told me, narrowing her eyes in an attempt to intimidate me, which she did, "we don't open until four. And second, this is a club for women. In case you didn't know. And I'm guessing you've got a dick."

I tried to squint back in my best Clint Eastwood impression, but it felt silly. It made her smile.

"I'm just looking for information," I said.

"We're all outta that. But we've got it on backorder."

I don't know if she wanted me to laugh, but I didn't.

And neither did she.

"I'm Chase Willoughby's husband," I said. It's all I ever was and all I ever will be, I suppose.

"I know. I recognize you from the TV."

Her grey eyes never blinked, content just to penetrate me, pin me to the bar like a butterfly against velvet.

"I was told that she was seen here the night that she was... "—it was still hard for me to say it—"killed."

That word hung like a poison cloud in the silence that followed. Giving it time to evaporate, she looked down at the lake of beer that covered the floor, then back up to me, letting me know that this was all my fault.

"Your wife? In a dyke bar?" She looked unconvincingly credulous. "That sounds strange."

"To me, too." I could play dense, as well. "Were you working here that night? Did you see her?"

"Chase Willoughby? The TV star? Here at The Clamshell?" I could see that this lady hadn't shaved in a couple of days. And that tattoo on her arm looked like she got it in San Diego when the fleet came in.

"Yes. Was she here? Did you see her?"

"We don't get many TV stars at The Clamshell."

"I don't doubt it," I said. "But just that one is all I'm interested in."

"Who told you they saw her here?"

"A little birdie," I snarked.

"Your little birdie is full of shit."

That might have been true, but I could tell she was lying.

THIRTEEN

What the fuck happened to my head?

I felt weighed down, logy, as if I were wearing a lead fat suit. My head throbbed with a searing, sharp pain like I'd never felt before. My mouth felt thick and dry, as if stuffed with gauze, which it turned out it was. My eyelids were so heavy that I couldn't lift them; I felt like I was waking up from a hundred-years sleep. My neck could not support the weight of my newly macrocephalic skull, and it rocked from side to side. My body was vibrating, jostled, in motion. I could tell I was in a vehicle, but I just couldn't pry my eyes open to prove it.

My stomach was hollow, empty and protesting, but I still wanted to vomit. The gauze scraped against the back of my tongue, igniting my retch reflex, but nothing came up but the groans. I gagged, and the gauze—or whatever the hell it was—was ejected from my mouth and onto my lap with a sick, wet plop.

I kept struggling to open my eyes, but they just kept rolling back in my head, each heartbeat inflating them with merciless agony. We hit a bump, and I thought I was made of glass, because I shattered. Dull numbness had given way to acute sensitivity, and every cell of my being exploded with hurt. I lifted my head from its leeward tilt and finally got my lids to lift. I was surrounded by darkness. Wherever we were, it was not on the planet Civilization. Aside from the tall light poles that whipped past every so often, the expanse beyond the passing asphalt was dark, arid, nonexistent. I tried to squeeze my hands into fists, and they filled with the sparkles of disappearing anesthetic.

"Morning, Sunshine," said a voice from my left, and I turned to look, but it took a while to focus. This was my brain on drugs. Certainly not morning. Black as pitch. Dark as my dreams.

My head lolled as I tried to make my brain function, to remember that eyes see, ears hear, and mouths speak. It dawned on me that I spoke English, but I was afraid to try it out. My eyes rolled again, independent of one another, and then settled into place and found unified peace that allowed them to focus.

The thing at the wheel was watching me, with an occasional glance at the road. I had seen this person before, I just couldn't remember where.

"How ya feeling? Head hurt?"

The army of my brain was starting to build a functioning battalion. I knew this face. This was a woman, and her name was Frank. "Frank?" I said, but it came out "Fwuh?"

There was a sort of smile on her face, but it lacked joy or humor.

"It'll go away soon, Pretty Lady." She looked at me, from my eyes to my feet, and all stops in between. A car rushed by from the opposite direction, and she threw a glance and righted her navigation, but then her eyes returned to me. The veil of unconsciousness was slowly lifting.

"You okay?"

I shook my head, but it hurt. I definitely was not okay. I looked down to see that my hands and ankles were bound with sleeves torn from the same red plaid shirt.

"You are a pretty one, aren't you?" She said it like an accusation. "Is that what you're all about? You're all about pretty, aren't you?"

I was not equipped to answer that.

She reached over and rubbed a thick, dry thumb across my mouth, scraping my lips like sandpaper, and pulling it away with a smear of lipstick. She put it in her mouth to taste it, then spat on the floor of the vehicle. She turned to glare at me with undisguised hatred, and I wondered what I did to earn her obvious ire.

"You look like a little doll," she said as she stared me down.

It was not said with affection. "You don't even look human." She turned back to the road, and I watched as stretches of midnight desert flew past the windshield. I could see that we were in a pickup truck, shining and well maintained despite its obvious age, reflecting the freeway lights as we raced beneath them. Her face seethed with anger, and she gripped the steering wheel in fists that were white with fury. In a sudden burst of rage, her hand shot out, slamming her fist painfully down on my thigh, then pulling it away just as quickly.

"Ow!" I screamed.

She threw a glance my way, then back to the road. It seemed like a Dr. Strangelove kind of thing, a sudden lack of control. She put her left hand over her right and clenched the wheel tight, muttering something to herself that I couldn't understand.

I looked away from her, out onto the deserted highway as it hurtled past us, still reeling, still groggy. I saw two glittering spots in the darkness ahead, which grew rapidly into a shape, furry, four-legged, trapped in the headlights. A coyote stared at us as it straddled the double yellow line, a frightened statue, until Frank narrowed her eyes and gunned the engine and plowed over it at eighty-five miles an hour. The impact threw me against the window and my head exploded in a white blast of light that quickly faded to black.

I roused for a moment as the truck slowed and the gears downshifted noisily. I felt a thorny hand push my head down against the seat, keeping a tight hold on my mouth. I opened my eyes and could only see up, just in time to see the California- Arizona border roll past. We entered the Grand Canyon State without stopping, and a whirlpool of unconsciousness sucked me back under.

I woke again as the truck pulled off onto gravel, slowing to a crawl as Frank turned the wheel with a weird little knob that let her control it one-handed. I lifted a hand to the sore spot on my forehead, forgetting it was tied to its mate. Both hands rose to press against the goose egg above my brow, and when I pulled it away, it was painted with my blood. I didn't need to see that; I was woozy enough already. The pickup slowly ground across the rough, pebbled parking lot, and her face was illuminated by the sickly green neon lights that spelled *MOTEL*. I couldn't make out the name of the motel; it was too long and confusing, and the blue neon wouldn't come into focus anyway.

She eased the truck around the back of the low row of seedy- looking cabins, hiding it in their illicit shadows. There were no other vehicles parked there; I don't even know if the place was open for business. As she ground to a halt, I reached for the door with my bound hands, but there was no handle on the inside. She noticed my move and silently shook her head. As my consciousness returned, I wished myself unsuccessfully back to oblivion.

"Where are we?" I asked, astounded that the words actually came out the way they were intended.

Frank looked at me, and let out a long breath through her nostrils. Without saying a word, she yanked the parking brake, opened her door, then reached in and scooped me up in her muscular, manly arms. I tried to struggle, but I had no strength, so she carried me effortlessly across the gravel, blue moonlight shadow puppets of us following close behind, to the front of the empty, quiet cabins, and kneed open the door to room number four.

Once inside, she closed the door behind her, then dropped me onto the forlorn double bed, raising a cloud of dust and a screech of bedsprings. She stared at me as I lay there, terrified.

"What are we doing here?"

Her face crinkled into a bitter smile. "I'm admiring you," she said. She stood at the end of the bed looking down on me, not tall but powerfully built, her hands on her hips, breathing raggedly through her mouth. She shook her head again. When she reached down for me, I tried to kick her away with my feet, but she just batted at them, and my body tumbled backwards over my head. She slapped me, and I started to cry. She grabbed the bodice of my dress and yanked it violently open, revealing the silk bra underneath. She slid her finger under the strap and snapped it painfully against my tender skin.

"How much did that cost?"

I don't know why it made her angry, so I lied. "I don't know.

It was a gift."

"I'll bet it was." She snorted, scowled and shook her head.

She ran her hand through my hair, then gave it a good yank before she pulled it away. "Are you a woman?" I was confused; I had no idea what she meant. She reached for my face, then pulled her hand away before she made contact. Then she kicked the bed.

"*I said, are you a woman?*" She raised a fist over my face as I cowered.

"Yes!" I answered. "Yes! Of course I'm a woman!"

She reached for me again, then pulled her hand away, fighting some kind of urge to touch me with an equal desire to hold herself back.

"Are you a woman or are you a toy? Are you a woman or are you a fantasy? Are you a woman or are you a love doll?" When I didn't respond, she lifted the bottom of the bed and dropped it heavily to the floor.

"I'm a woman!"

She went to the door and pounded against it with both fists, then stormed back to hover over me on the bed.

"No you're not," she whispered, drawing right up to my face and spreading her hot, wet words all over me. "You're not even real!" I tried to pull my head back away from hers, but she grabbed it and held it tightly in place, looking at my eyes, my hair, my mouth. Suddenly, she pressed her hard, dry, cracked lips against mine, darted her tongue against them, then pulled away in seeming disgust.

"You're just Hollywood, aren't you? Pure temptation!"

I started to cry, horrified at this furious creature that hated me for no reason I could understand.

"What are you doing to me?" I managed to sob.

She leaned down over me, brought her face close to mine, and breathed deeply through her flaring nostrils.

"You smell like a fucking whorehouse," she said with contempt.

I cowered, but she wouldn't let me, holding me by the neck against the bed. I choked, and she eased back a little, but kept me pinned to the bed.

I was terrified. "My friend will be looking for me…" I said.

"Who, the little redheaded pixie? I've already seen her. She gave me her card. Told me to call if I spotted you."

Her grey eyes were wild; despite the darkness, her pupils remained tiny, mad pinpoints of black surrounded by monochromatic, clenched irises.She looked like she was fighting demons, but the demons were winning.

"Do you know how disgusting you are? You're just candy! You let them make you into their toy, their plaything, their little dollycake. Do you know how that hurts us?"

She tore open my dress, pulled on it until I rolled out of it and onto the floor, wearing only my bra, cowering behind my hands. She picked me up with a rough yank and threw me back down onto the bed on my stomach. She yanked the bra apart, then rolled me onto my back, straddling me in her rough Lee jeans and pinning my arms to the bed. When I tried to fight her off, she backhanded me across the face. I started to get hysterical, but it only made her madder.

She stared down at my naked body, her face doing battle with lust and disgust.She reached down with both her hands and squeezed my breasts, hard, and I squealed in pain.

Immediately, she jumped off of me, turning away from me, seemingly revolted with herself.

"I didn't want to do that!" she said, going to the window, seething, her fists pulsing.

"Then why did you?" I cried.

"Because you fucking made me!" She turned back to me, stormed over to the bed and kicked me hard in the side. "How much did those tits cost you?" she demanded. I couldn't answer, paralyzed by her volatile insanity. She reached down and grabbed one in both hands, squeezing hard.

"*How much did they cost you?*" she demanded again.

I was bound by hysteria, confusion, still fighting off the drugs. I just didn't understand what was going on, why I was so awful to her, why she hated me so much.

"They're mine!" I shouted.

"Bullshit!" she shouted back.

I just shook my head and she bent down and took the breast she was holding in her mouth and bit it hard. She jumped off of me again, went to the wall and pounded it with her fists, slammed her forehead against it over and over, fighting this horrible compulsion, and losing. There was only one way this could end.

She turned back to me, holding herself with her back against the wall. "Do you know how much I hate you?" she said, almost in a whisper. I didn't dare reply. "You were made for TV, you're not even real. You're just artificial sex and temptation, a cartoon, the invention of horny men to satisfy their selfish carnal cravings, an affront to women. Makeup and plastic surgery and hair dye and sexy underwear, just to make us want you but we can't have you. You make us all ugly. You make us all unsatisfied, because we can't have the beautiful doll, the empty fucking Barbie doll that only exists on TV. Well, *I* don't want you! You hear me? I don't even want you, I fucking hate you, you ugly bitch!"

She came closer to me, standing over me again, blocking the moonlight that was trying to creep in past the tattered curtains.

"Do you even know what a real woman looks like?" she asked. She reached down and pulled her shirt over her head, towering over me in silhouette, then coming closer for me to look. She was muscled but wrinkled, the definition of her shoulders and biceps and chest creased. Her breasts barely existed over the muscles of her chest, long nipples pointing downward. A line of dark pubic hair climbed up from her jeans to her navel.

"You don't even have any hair on your cunt!" she spat. I turned my legs away, trying to hide my crotch from her, but she yanked them back, slapped her hand around me and shoving dry fingers into me, tearing the fragile flesh. I pulled back in the searing agony.

"Why?" she said. "Why do you want to look like a little girl?

Why did you let them do that to you?"

She seemed to lose control, yanked my face to hers and stuck her revoltingly long tongue into my mouth, making me gag. She pulled away and slapped me, like it was all my fault. Then she pulled up my hands and pressed them against her chest, squeezing, making me feel them.

"That's what a woman is supposed to feel like!" she screamed into my ear.

Then she reached down again and grabbed me. "Not like plastic! Not like fucking balloons!"

"They're real!" I cried. "They're me!"

She let me go and took a step back. That's when I saw that there was some sort of worn leather sheath strapped to her belt. She reached down and unbuckled it with a loud snap. She took out a knife so sharp, so highly polished, that it gleamed, reflected her madness like a mirror.

"Let's just see," she said, and made a fist around its hilt and drew it across her chest. Then, flecks of white foam collecting in the corners of her mouth, she was upon me, the blade flashing across me and splitting me open.

FOURTEEN

I stood across the bar from this steely-eyed, ropy-muscled creature with the slicked-back peppery hair as she glared at me, unblinking, Venus on the Clamshell. The gloom was deadening; it was like I was facing off with a grizzly at the back of its cave. Silence hung between us like a curtain, and I watched the muscles of her jaw working.

"I don't believe you," I told her. "I think Chase was here." I wasn't sure why that made her smile.

"I don't give a fuck what you think, Dick."

"Why are you lying to me?" I really wanted to know. It just didn't make any sense.

All of a sudden, her arm flashed up from below the bar, holding a sawed-off aluminum baseball bat with a leather strap through the hole at the end. She swung it so hard at my head that it whistled, and I instinctively threw up my arms in protection. It smacked against my right forearm with a percussive *crack*. She climbed over the bar, her expression fierce as an aboriginal warrior's. I swung my fist at her as hard as I could, landing a blow across her face that, despite feeling alarmingly creampuff, snapped her head to the side and shocked her. I wasn't very good at face-to-face confrontation, even verbally, but when it came to hand-to-hand combat, I was a writer not a fighter, hopelessly inexperienced and outmatched. Raising the bat high over her head, she charged me. I kicked up as hard as I could, catching her in the crotch, sorry she didn't have family jewels to shatter. It had little effect other than to put off her attack for a few more seconds. She slammed the weapon against my ribcage and kicked me in the stomach, knocking the wind out of me and throwing me into the middle of the room where there was nothing to grab. I felt the beer on the floor seeping through my shoes as I stood, trying not to quake in them.

She glared at me with fierce black-and-white hatred, breathing hard through her nose like a cartoon bull. She was silent, overflowing with hatred as she stood there, hunched, her hands flexing before her. Then she charged me, and I crossed my hands in front of my face. She swung again, but so did I, kicking laterally at her legs, knocking them out from under her and making her slip on the wet floor and crash onto her face and belly. She screamed, and when she pulled herself up, I knew why: a huge shard of brown bottle-glass was embedded in her cheek, lacerating open an additional mouth, which bled profusely. There were other slices in her shirt, new wounds oozing freely. She yanked the glass out of her face, saw it covered with her blood, and threw it at me, missing. But that was the end of my luck; with an animalistic snarl, she stomped toward me, her slips on the beer-soaked floor not slowing her down, swinging the bat as hard as she could, slamming it against my head from the left, then from the right, then from the left again, each collision raising a universe of stars before I was overcome and slipped from consciousness.

All I knew was that I was on my back, and that there were

sharp rocks underneath me. My olfactory senses were ignited before my eyes opened. The acrid, pungent stench of fire woke me up, and when I tried to pry my eyes open, only one of them worked, and that one just barely. My head throbbed, felt lumpy and pulpy. My eyelashes peeled apart, sticky from my own congealing blood. I looked up into the towering, heavily bearded palm trees, clustered around a stream in some kind of desert oasis, no doubt one of the Indian canyons on the cusp of the city of Palm Springs. The pink sun played hide-and-seek just over the colorless, rocky crest of the San Jacinto Mountains behind them, but orange flames roared up and obscured my view.

A work boot kicked me in the head, and I turned to catch the rough, determined smile of the madwoman from the Clamshell glaring at me from overhead in my cyclopean view.

"What the fuck, lady?" I managed to get out.

She just kicked me in the ribs, which probably cracked, I don't know. I already hurt everywhere, and it was all unbearable. When I tried to pull away, I discovered I was bound by a rough hemp rope, which held me immobile. I squirmed like a caterpillar, kicking and struggling, but she just kicked me again, pushing me toward the raging bonfire she had built.

The desert surrounding us was vast and desolate, formations of dull tan rock defying gravity, pockets of oasis palms tucked into the mountain crevasses here and there. The creek was at its summertime trickle, and I wondered why I gave a shit.

She kicked me again, and I rolled, one full circle closer to the fire, feeling the heat sear my tender, swollen, bleeding face. I was destined to burn to ash, to a dust scattered by blazing Santa Ana winds, erased from the planet without a trace. I forced myself to roll back, away from the inferno, but she just planted her heel in my side, and shoved me back. Then did it again, and I was just feet from the flames.

"Why are you doing this?"

That just pissed her off, and she kicked me in the head again. "Why did you kill Chase?"

All that got me was another kick, rolling me yet closer to the fire, which felt like it was cooking me from just a foot or two away. I was covered in sweat, could feel myself baking.

The rage that flooded her face told me she was through teasing. She planted her heel against my shoulder, and shoved with all her considerable might. I screamed as I rolled into the fire, impossibly hot burning desert branches, sizzling as my flesh rolled over them. Using all the strength I could summon, I kept rolling, across the fire and out the other side. I could smell burning hair, see the flames charring my clothes, and kept rolling across the sand until I had put it all out. I hacked on the grit in my mouth, barely able to breathe. Oily smoke welled from the fire, and I could smell me-meat scorching. The burns were agonizing.

Infuriated, she ran through the fire and stomped on me. She put her arms under my body and shoved, rolling me back into the burning branches. Once again, I was able to keep rolling to the other side, acquiring new fires to put out in the sand, new wounds that blistered and popped instantly, the hair on my head ablaze. I rolled, I extinguished the flames, and I laughed, not because it was funny but because it was so ridiculous, and it pissed her off so much. With a simian roar, she strode back through the flames like one of Satan's minions, reached down, and picked me up in her arms. She lifted my objecting, wriggling body high, allowing me the opportunity to ram my battered face into the nape of her neck, where I bit as hard as I could, tearing at her, ripping out a huge chunk of her creased, suntanned flesh, and unleashing a spurting fountain of her own blood to spatter my face.

She screamed, dropped me in a heap, and slapped both hands to her gouting neck. I kicked her legs and she dropped face first onto the fire. I rolled on top of her as she screamed into the scarlet branches, using my weight to pin her there as flames shot up around us. Her blood was still shooting from the hole in her neck, hissing as it hit the burning branches. I could feel the fire burning past her, the flames licking at me and tasting me, but not feeding on me like they fed on her. She choked on fire and smoke, her lungs quickly scorched, her screams drying up and dying out. Her skin bubbled and seared and I rolled off of her before it could consume me as well.

She went still as the voracious fire devoured her, and I watched from a few feet away. The nauseating stench of human barbecue filled the desert air, and as the blaze reached high into the sky, the sun began its final descent behind the mountains, turning the sky, the clouds, and the desert itself a dramatic shade of pink before it settled into a purple that signaled the end of another day.

The skin on my left arm was scorched and festering. The right had been fractured by this crazy woman's bat. Half of the hair had been burned off my scalp, and there was a spot on my ass where my pants had melted into it. It was excruciating to fight against my bonds, but the fire had eaten at the rope as well, and once my force met the weakness of a single burned spot, it finally fell away, and I was able to escape its grasp.

I was able to stand, able to watch the cremation of Chase's murderer as the flesh melted away from the bones, which were turning black as the flames chewed on them, eventually sure to leave them unrecognizable as dust. The fire wouldn't die out anytime soon, and I liked that. It seemed to flare brighter as the sky blackened and the stars awoke. A full moon was in place, but its blue glow was weak against the fire.

Ashes to ashes and all that shit.

I would never know why this woman, this monster, this bastardization of humanity had taken Chase's life. But whatever the reason, there's no way it could ever make sense to me.

I was burned and battered and a complete mess, but I was alive. I didn't deserve it, but I was alive and Chase was dead. I stood here under a cruel desert sky, the smell of death ever-present, a body burning at my feet, and I was alive. I had taken the life of Chase's murderer, but I felt no satisfaction. This creature may have taken Chase's life, but I couldn't help but feel that it was me who killed her. I had dreamed of avenging Chase's death, and perhaps I had, at least technically, but it didn't feel like a victory. All I knew was that I had loved Chase a long time ago, and loved her again anew, but it didn't do anybody any fucking good.

I felt no pity for the body that was being consumed by the fire, but I felt no heroism, either. I was alive, I kept telling myself, but I didn't feel like it. And I certainly hadn't earned it.

The bonfire began to wane after a while, and a hot, arid breeze began to rise. The few clouds had cleared the wakening moon, and I looked up to see a pickup truck reflecting it from behind the grove of palm trees. I didn't want anything to do with it. Let someone who mattered find it and solve their own mystery. Mine now had an ending.

I could see the lights of Palm Springs in the distance, glowing like heaven. A hawk circled the fire that roasted and disintegrated the remains of the beast that killed my wife. It squealed, waiting for the flames to die down and allow it a cooked meal. *You can have it*, I thought.

My body burning and aching and my mind numb and vacant, I began the long walk through the desert and back into the Springs to collect my car and go back to the house that I once shared with the wife who belonged there much more than I did.

FIFTEEN

So I sit, home alone in Woodland Hills. Sometimes a tour bus will circle the cul-de-sac, titillating the Midwestern tourists on board with cautionary tales about Hollywood and the curse of stardom, how even the rich and beautiful are not beyond the reach of madness and murder.

The death of my wife fell out of the headlines to join the pile of corpses stacked high with the likes of Jean Harlow, Marilyn Monroe, Jayne Mansfield, Sharon Tate, and the equally unfortunate victims of celebrity. Pretty high-falutin' company for the little girl with the boobs in *The Crazy Frazees*.

My hair is starting to grow back over much of my scalp, but my arm and my face are sculpted in scar tissue, a scarlet letter well earned in a life poorly lived. The feminine prettiness of my surroundings is a constant reminder of the beautiful, heartbroken woman who still haunts these walls in her death. Sometimes I sleep—try to sleep—in her bed, the bed that used to be *our* bed, but I know I don't belong there, perhaps I never did. I know that we had been happy there, a long time ago, but knew I did not deserve memories so warm. The fights, the coldness, the bitter words, the loneliness that infested this little cottage had fouled it. This house had a pretty face, but it choked on its memories.

I often sit in Chase's studio, surrounded by the paintings of rage and pain, and wonder what kind of art she would have made if I had been someone else, someone who loved her back as deeply as she deserved. Hers was a beauty in a cage, briefly allowed to escape and flower, only to be darkened and soured by me. They say it takes two, but I know that that just isn't true.

In my office, the iMac only glares at me, daring me to take up the gauntlet and fight the good fight. But I am cowed by it; I sit bathed in its accusatory glow, unable to type, unable to think, unable to create. I just feel tired, empty.

I miss Chase Willoughby, and only wish I had another chance to prove it.